"COMPELLING . . . SUSPENSEFUL."
—Seattle Times

"Provocative, challenging . . . Recalls both Arthur C. Clarke and H. G. Wells, with a dash of Ray Bradbury for good measure."
—The Dallas Morning News

"It is rare to find a book about interplanetary exploration that has this much insight into human nature and foresight into a possible future. With wit and intelligence, Mary Doria Russell's novel *The Sparrow* creates a whole new world that is shocking in its alien and human qualities. . . . Vivid and wild."
—San Antonio Express

"[A] strikingly original debut . . . At once thought-provoking and exciting, offering proof of its author's singular talents—and of the continued vitality of science fiction as a genre of ideas."
—Baltimore City Paper

"Brilliant . . . A startling portrait of an alien culture and of the nature of God . . . Shades of Wells, Ursula K. LeGuin, and Arthur C. Clarke with just a dash of Edgar Rice Burroughs—and yet strikingly original."
—Kirkus Reviews (starred review)

"A smart, sad, and engrossing novel."
—The Cleveland Plain Dealer

"Riveting."
—Booklist (starred review)

THE
SPARROW

Mary Doria Russell

Fawcett Columbine • New York
The Ballantine Publishing Group

A Fawcett Columbine Book
Published by Ballantine Books

http://www.randomhouse.com

Library of Congress Catalog Card Number: 97-90649

ISBN: 0-449-91255-8

This edition published by arrangement with Villard Books, a division of Random House, Inc. Villard Books is a registered trademark of Random House, Inc.

Manufactured in the United States of America

Cover art: Front top and back of jacket, Giotto di Bondone, *Scrovegni Chapel Ceiling* (detail), c. 1340.
Front bottom, Giotto di Bondone, *Saint Francis of Assisi Preaching to the Birds* (detail), San Francisco, Assisi, c. 1305

First Ballantine Books Edition: October 1997

20 19 18 17 16 15 14 13 12

FOR MAURA E. KIRBY

AND

MARY L. DEWING

quarum sine auspicio hic
liber in lucem non esset
editas

THE SPARROW

PROLOGUE

IT WAS PREDICTABLE, in hindsight. Everything about the history of the Society of Jesus bespoke deft and efficient action, exploration and research. During what Europeans were pleased to call the Age of Discovery, Jesuit priests were never more than a year or two behind the men who made initial contact with previously unknown peoples; indeed, Jesuits were often the vanguard of exploration.

The United Nations required years to come to a decision that the Society of Jesus reached in ten days. In New York, diplomats debated long and hard, with many recesses and tablings of the issue, whether and why human resources should be expended in an attempt to contact the world that would become known as Rakhat when there were so many pressing needs on Earth. In Rome, the questions were not whether or why but how soon the mission could be attempted and whom to send.

The Society asked leave of no temporal government. It acted on its own principles, with its own assets, on Papal authority. The mission to Rakhat was undertaken not so much secretly as privately—a fine distinction but one that the Society felt no compulsion to explain or justify when the news broke several years later.

The Jesuit scientists went to learn, not to proselytize. They went so that they might come to know and love God's other children. They went for the reason Jesuits have always gone to the farthest frontiers of human exploration. They went *ad majorem Dei gloriam*: for the greater glory of God.

They meant no harm.

1

ROME:

DECEMBER 2059

On December 7, 2059, Emilio Sandoz was released from the isolation ward of Salvator Mundi Hospital in the middle of the night and transported in a bread van to the Jesuit Residence at Number 5 Borgo Santo Spìrito, a few minutes' walk across St. Peter's Square from the Vatican. The next day, ignoring shouted questions and howls of journalistic outrage as he read, a Jesuit spokesman issued a short statement to the frustrated and angry media mob that had gathered outside Number 5's massive front door.

"To the best of our knowledge, Father Emilio Sandoz is the sole survivor of the Jesuit mission to Rakhat. Once again, we extend our thanks to the U.N., to the Contact Consortium and to the Asteroid Mining Division of Ohbayashi Corporation for making the return of Father Sandoz possible. We have no additional information regarding the fate of the Contact Consortium's crew members; they are in our prayers. Father Sandoz is too ill to question at this time and his recovery is expected to take months. Until then, there can be no further comment on the Jesuit mission or on the Contact Consortium's allegations regarding Father Sandoz's conduct on Rakhat."

This was simply to buy time.

It was true, of course, that Sandoz was ill. The man's whole body was bruised by the blooms of spontaneous hemorrhages where tiny blood vessel walls had breached and spilled their contents under his skin. His gums had stopped bleeding, but it would be a long while before he could eat normally. Eventually, something would have to be done about his hands.

Now, however, the combined effects of scurvy, anemia and exhaustion kept him asleep twenty hours out of the day. When awake, he lay motionless, coiled like a fetus and almost as helpless.

The door to his small room was nearly always left open in those early weeks. One afternoon, thinking to prevent Father Sandoz from being disturbed while the hallway floor was polished, Brother Edward Behr closed it, despite warnings about this from the Salvator Mundi staff. Sandoz happened to wake up and found himself shut in. Brother Edward did not repeat the mistake.

Vincenzo Giuliani, the Father General of the Society of Jesus, went each morning to look in on the man. He had no idea if Sandoz was aware of being observed; it was a familiar feeling. When very young, when the Father General was just plain Vince Giuliani, he had been fascinated by Emilio Sandoz, who was a year ahead of Giuliani during the decade-long process of priestly formation. A strange boy, Sandoz. A puzzling man. Vincenzo Giuliani had made a statesman's career of understanding other men, but he had never understood this one.

Gazing at Emilio, sick now and almost mute, Giuliani knew that Sandoz was unlikely to give up his secrets any time soon. This did not distress him. Vincenzo Giuliani was a patient man. One had to be patient to thrive in Rome, where time is measured not in centuries but in millennia, where patience and the long view have always distinguished political life. The city gave its name to the power of patience—*Romanità. Romanità* excludes emotion, hurry, doubt. *Romanità* waits, sees the moment and moves ruthlessly when the time is right. *Romanità* rests on an absolute conviction of ultimate success and arises from a single principle, *Cunctando regitur mundus:* Waiting, one conquers all.

So, even after sixty years, Vincenzo Giuliani felt no sense of impatience with his inability to understand Emilio Sandoz, only a sense of how satisfying it would be when the wait paid off.

THE FATHER GENERAL'S private secretary contacted Father John Candotti on the Feast of the Holy Innocents, three weeks after

Emilio's arrival at Number 5. "Sandoz is well enough to see you now," Johannes Voelker informed Candotti. "Be here by two."

Be here by two! John thought irritably, marching along toward Vatican City from the retreat house where he'd just been assigned a stuffy little room with a view of Roman walls—the stone only inches from his pointless window. Candotti had dealt with Voelker a couple of times since arriving and had taken a dislike to the Austrian from the start. In fact, John Candotti disliked everything about his present situation.

For one thing, he didn't understand why he'd been brought into this business. Neither a lawyer nor an academic, John Candotti was content to have come out on the less prestigious end of the Jesuit dictum, Publish or parish, and he was hip-deep in preparations for the grammar school Christmas program when his superior contacted him and told him to fly to Rome at the end of the week. "The Father General wishes you to assist Emilio Sandoz." That was the extent of his briefing. John had heard of Sandoz, of course. Everyone had heard of Sandoz. But John had no idea how he could be of any use to the man. When he asked for an explanation, he couldn't seem to pry a straight answer out of anyone. He had no practice at this kind of thing; subtlety and indirection were not indoor sports in Chicago.

And then there was Rome itself. At the impromptu farewell party, everyone was so excited for him. "Rome, Johnny!" All that history, those beautiful churches, the art. He'd been excited too, dumb shit. What did he know?

John Candotti was born to flat land, straight lines, square city blocks; nothing in Chicago had prepared him for the reality of Rome. The worst was when he could actually see the building he wanted to get to but found the street he was on curving away from it, leading him to yet another lovely piazza with yet another beautiful fountain, dumping him into another alley going nowhere. Another hour, trapped and frustrated by the hills, the curves, the rat's nest of streets smelling of cat piss and tomato sauce. He hated being lost, and he was always lost. He hated being late, and he was late all the time. The first five minutes of every conversation was John apologizing for being late and his Roman acquaintances assuring him it was no problem.

He hated it all the same, so he walked faster and faster, trying to get to the Jesuit Residence on time for a change, and collected an escort of small children, noisy with derision and obnoxious with delight at this bony, big-nosed, half-bald man with his flapping soutane and pumping arms.

"I'M SORRY TO keep you waiting." John Candotti had repeated the apology to each person along the way to Sandoz's room and finally to Sandoz himself as Brother Edward Behr ushered him in and left him alone with the man. "The crowd outside is still huge. Do they ever go away? I'm John Candotti. The Father General asked me to help you at the hearings. Happy to meet you." He held out his hand without thinking, withdrawing it awkwardly when he remembered.

Sandoz did not rise from his chair by the window and at first, he either wouldn't or couldn't look in Candotti's direction. John had seen archive images of him, naturally, but Sandoz was a lot smaller than he expected, much thinner; older but not as old as he should have been. What was the calculation? Seventeen years out, almost four years on Rakhat, seventeen years back, but then there were the relativity effects of traveling near light speed. Born a year before the Father General, who was in his late seventies, Sandoz was estimated by the physicists to be about forty-five, give or take a little. Hard years, by the look of him, but not very many of them.

The silence went on a long time. Trying not to stare at the man's hands, John debated whether he should just go. It's way too soon, he thought, Voelker must be crazy. Then, finally, he heard Sandoz ask, "English?"

"American, Father. Brother Edward is English but I'm American."

"No," Sandoz said after a while. "*La lengua*. English."

Startled, John realized that he'd misunderstood. "Yes. I speak a little Spanish, if you'd prefer that."

"It was Italian, *creo. Antes*—before, I mean. In the hospital. *Sipaj—si yo* . . ." He stopped, close to tears, but got ahold of himself and spoke deliberately. "It would help . . . if I could hear . . . just one language for a while. English is okay."

"Sure. No problem. We'll stick to English," John said, shaken. Nobody had told him Sandoz was this far gone. "I'll make this a short visit, Father. I just wanted to introduce myself and see how you're doing. There's no rush about preparing for the hearings. I'm sure they can be postponed until you're well enough to . . ."

"To do what?" Sandoz asked, looking directly at Candotti for the first time. A deeply lined face, Indian ancestry plain in the high-bridged nose, the wide cheekbones, the stoicism. John Candotti could not imagine this man laughing.

To defend yourself, John was going to say, but it seemed mean. "To explain what happened."

The silence inside the Residence was noticeable, especially by the window, where the endless carnival noise of the city could be heard. A woman was scolding a child in Greek. Tourists and reporters milled around, shouting over the constant roar of the usual Vatican crowds and the taxi traffic. Repairs went on incessantly to keep the Eternal City from falling to pieces, the construction workers yelling, machinery grinding.

"I have nothing to say." Sandoz turned away again. "I shall withdraw from the Society."

"Father Sandoz—Father, you can't expect the Society to let you walk away without understanding what happened out there. You may not want to face a hearing but whatever happens in here is nothing compared to what they'll put you through outside, the moment you walk out the door," John told him. "If we understood, we could help you. Make it easier for you, maybe?" There was no reply, only a slight hardening of the face profiled at the window. "Okay, look. I'll come back in a few days. When you're feeling better, right? Is there anything I can bring you? Someone I could contact for you?"

"No." There was no force behind the voice. "Thank you."

John suppressed a sigh and turned toward the door. His eyes swept past a sketch, lying on top of the small plain bureau. On something like paper, drawn in something like ink. A group of VaRakhati. Faces of great dignity and considerable charm. Extraordinary eyes, frilled with lashes to guard against the brilliant sunlight. Funny how you could tell that these were unusually handsome individuals, even when unfamiliar with their standards of beauty. John Candotti lifted the drawing to look at it more closely. Sandoz stood and took two swift steps toward him.

Sandoz was probably half his size and sicker than hell but John Candotti, veteran of Chicago streets, was startled into retreating. Feeling the wall against his back, he covered his embarrassment with a smile and put the drawing back on the bureau. "They're a handsome race, aren't they," he offered, trying to defuse whatever emotion was working on the man in front of him. "The . . . folks in the picture—friends of yours, I guess?"

Sandoz backed away and looked at John for a few moments, as though calculating the other man's response. The daylight behind his hair lit it up, and the contrast hid his expression. If the room had been brighter or if John Candotti had known him better, he might have recognized a freakish solemnity that preceded any statement Sandoz expected to induce hilarity, or outrage. Sandoz hesitated and then found the precise word he wanted.

"Colleagues," he said at last.

JOHANNES VOELKER CLOSED his notescreen at the end of his regular morning meeting with the Father General but did not rise to leave. Instead, he sat and watched Vincenzo Giuliani's face as the old man appeared to concentrate on the work at hand, logging his own notes about the day's events and the decisions they'd just discussed.

Thirty-fourth to hold the office of Father General, Giuliani was an impressive executive. A big man, attractively bald, straight and formidably strong in old age. Historian by profession, politician by nature, Vincenzo Giuliani had brought the Society of Jesus through difficult times, repairing some of the damage Sandoz had caused. Steering men into hydrology and Islamic studies—that had restored some goodwill. Without Jesuits in Iran and Egypt, there'd have been no warning at all before the last attack. Credit where credit is due, Voelker thought, waiting patiently for Giuliani to notice him.

The Father General sighed and looked up at his secretary, an unappealing man in his middle thirties, inclined to fatness, sandy hair lying flat against his skull. Voelker was a silent picture of unfinished business, sitting back in his chair, arms folded across his thickening waist. "All right, out with it. Say what you have to say," Giuliani ordered irritably.

"Sandoz."

"What about him?"

"My point exactly."

Giuliani went back to his notes.

"People were starting to forget," Voelker said. "It might have been better for everyone if Sandoz had been killed along with the rest of them."

"Why, Father Voelker," Giuliani said aridly. "What an unworthy thought."

Voelker made a mouth and looked away.

Giuliani stared out the windows of his office for a few moments, elbows resting on the polished wood of his desk. Voelker was right, of course. Undoubtedly, life would have been simpler had Emilio been safely martyred. Now, in the glare of publicity and hindsight, the Society had to inquire into the reasons for the failure of the mission . . . Giuliani scrubbed his face with his hands and stood. "Emilio and I go back a long time together, Voelker. He's a good man."

"He is a whore," Voelker said with quiet precision. "He killed a child. He should be in chains." Voelker watched Giuliani circle the room, picking things up and putting them down without really looking at anything. "At least he has the decency to want to leave. Let him go— before he does more harm to the Society."

Giuliani stopped pacing and looked at Voelker. "We aren't going to disavow him. Even if that's what he v nts, it's wrong. More to the point, it won't work. He's one of Ours, in the eyes of the world if not in his own eyes." He walked to the windows and stared out at the crowd of reporters and seekers and the merely curious. "And if the media continue to indulge in idle speculation and baseless supposition, we'll simply call it what it is," said the Father General in the light ironic voice that generations of graduate students had learned to dread. He turned to gaze with cool appraisal at his secretary, sitting sullenly all this time. Giuliani's voice didn't change but Voelker was stung by what came. "I am not Emilio's judge, Father Voelker, and neither is the press."

And neither was Johannes Voelker, S.J.

They concluded their meeting with one or two businesslike remarks, but the younger man left knowing he'd overstepped his bounds, politically as well as spiritually. Voelker was efficient and intelligent but, atypically for a Jesuit, he had a polar mind: everything was black or white, sin or virtue, Us versus Them.

Still, Giuliani thought, such people could be useful.

The Father General sat at his desk and fingered a stylus. Reporters thought the world had a right to know. Vincenzo Giuliani felt no need whatsoever to pander to that illusion. On the other hand, there was the question of what to do next, regarding Rakhat. And he did feel a need to bring Emilio to some sort of resolution. This wasn't the first time the Jesuits had encountered an alien culture and it wasn't the first mission to come to grief and Sandoz wasn't the first priest to disgrace himself. The whole business was regrettable but not beyond redemption.

He's salvageable, Giuliani thought stubbornly. It's not as though we have so many priests that we can write one off without an effort. He's one of Ours, dammit. And what right have we to declare the mission a failure? Seeds may have been sown. God knows.

Even so, the allegations against Sandoz and the others were very serious.

Privately, Vincenzo Giuliani was inclined to believe that the mission went wrong at its inception, with the decision to involve the women. A breakdown in discipline from the beginning, he thought. The times were different then.

RUMINATING OVER THE same problem as he walked back to his lightless room on the eastern side of the Rome Ring, John Candotti had his own theory about how things had gone wrong. The mission, he thought, probably failed because of a series of logical, reasonable, carefully considered decisions, each of which seemed like a good idea at the time. Like most colossal disasters.

2

ARECIBO RADIO TELESCOPE, PUERTO RICO:
FEBRUARY 2019

"JIMMY, I JUST heard they assigned you a vulture!" Peggy Soong whispered, and the first step toward the mission to Rakhat was taken. "Are you going to cooperate?"

Jimmy Quinn continued to move down the line of vending machines, selecting arroz con pollo, a container of bean soup and two tuna sandwiches. He was absurdly tall, finally done growing at twenty-six but not really filled out yet, and constantly hungry. He stopped to pick up two packets of milk and a couple of desserts and checked his debit total.

"You cooperate, it's that much harder for the rest of us," Peggy said. "You saw what happened to Jeff."

Jimmy went to a table that had only one open seat and set his tray down. Peggy Soong stood behind him and glared at the woman sitting opposite Quinn. The woman decided she was done with lunch. Peggy moved around the table and sat in the still-warm chair. For a while, she simply watched Jimmy fork in piles of rice and chicken, still amazed by the sheer volume of food he needed. Her grocery bill had gone down by 75 percent since she threw him out. "Jimmy," she said finally, "you can't duck this. If you're not for us, you're against us." She was still whispering but her voice was not gentle. "If nobody cooperates, they can't fire us all."

Jimmy met her eyes, his gaze blue and placid, hers black and challenging. "I don't know, Peggy. I think they could probably replace the whole staff in a couple of weeks. I know a guy from Peru who'd take my job for half what I'm making. Jeff got a good recommendation when he left."

"And he's still out of work! Because he gave the vulture everything he had."

"It won't be my decision, Peggy. You know that."

"Bullshit!" Several people looked up. She leaned toward him from across the table, whispering again. "You are not a puppet. Everybody knows you've helped Jeff since he got sacked. But the whole point here is to stop them from sucking us dry, not to minister to the victims after the fact. How many times do I have to explain it?"

Peggy Soong sat back abruptly and looked away, trying to make sense of people who couldn't see the system reducing them to bits. All Jimmy understood was work hard, don't make trouble. And what would it get him? Screwed is what it would get him. "It will be your decision, to cooperate with the vulture," she said flatly. "They can give you the order but you have to decide whether to follow it." Rising, she gathered her things from the table and stared down at him a moment longer. Then she turned her back on him and walked toward the door.

"Peggy!"

Jimmy got up, came close enough to reach down and touch her lightly on the shoulder. He was not handsome. The nose was too long and no particular shape, the eyes too close together and set deep as a monkey's, the semicircle smile and the red curling hair like scribbles in a child's drawing; for a few months, the aggregate had charmed her senseless.

"Peggy, give me a chance, okay? Let me see if there's a way so everybody wins. Things don't have to be one way or the other."

"Sure, Jimmy," she said. He was a nice kid. Dumber than rice but nice. Peggy looked at his earnest, open, homely face and knew that he would find some plausible, contemptible rationale for being a good boy. "Sure, Jim. You do that."

A LESSER MAN might have been put off his feed by a confrontation with the formidable Peggy Soong. But Jimmy Quinn was used to small, insistent women, and nothing affected his appetite; his mother complained that feeding him in adolescence was like stoking a coal-fired furnace. So he returned to his seat as Peggy stalked out of the cafeteria, and thoughtfully worked his way through the rest of his meal, letting things percolate through his mind.

Jimmy was no fool but he'd been well loved by good parents and well taught by good teachers, and those two facts accounted for the habit of obedience that mystified and enraged Peggy Soong. Over and over in his life, authority had proven correct and the decisions of his parents and teachers and bosses made sense to him eventually. So he wasn't happy about losing his job at Arecibo to an AI program but left to himself, he probably wouldn't have objected. He'd only worked at the telescope site for eight months—not enough time to feel proprietary about a position he'd been dead lucky to get. After all, he hadn't taken degrees in astronomy expecting a hot job market after graduation. The pay was lousy and the competition for work was savage, but that was true of almost anything these days. His mother—a small, insistent woman—had urged him to study something more practical. But Jimmy stuck with astronomy, arguing that if he was going to be unemployed, which was statistically likely, he might as well be unemployed in the field of his choice.

For eight months, he'd had the luxury of feeling vindicated. Now, it looked like Eileen Quinn had been right after all.

He gathered the debris from his lunch, deposited it in the proper bins and made his way back to his cubicle, swerving and ducking, bat-like, to avoid the doorways and low light fixtures and conduits that threatened to knock him cold a hundred times a day. The desk he sat at looked gap-toothed, and for that blessed state of affairs he was indebted to Father Emilio Sandoz, a Puerto Rican Jesuit he'd met through George Edwards. George was a retired engineer who worked as an unpaid, part-time docent at the Arecibo dish, giving tours to schoolchildren and day-trippers. His wife, Anne, was a doctor at the clinic the Jesuits had set up along with a community center in La Perla, a slum just outside Old San Juan. Jimmy liked all three of them and made the trip to San Juan as often as he could tolerate the tedious, traffic-choked forty-mile drive.

At dinner that first night with Emilio at the Edwardses' place, Jimmy kept them laughing with a comic threnody, listing the hazards life held for a regular guy in a world built by and for midgets. When he complained about smashing his knees into his desk every time he sat down, the priest leaned over, the handsome unusual face solemn but the eyes alight, and said quietly in a nearly perfect North Dublin accent, "Take d'

middle drawer outta d' desk, y' fookin' tosser." There was only one reply possible and Jimmy supplied it, blue eyes wide with Irish admiration:
"Fookin' deadly." The exchange convulsed Anne and George, and the
four of them had been friends ever since.

Grinning at the memory, Jimmy opened a line and shot a message to
Emilio's system, offering "Beer at Claudio's, 8 P.M. RSVP by 5," no longer
amazed by the idea of having a drink in a bar with a priest, a notion that
had initially stunned him almost as much as finding out that girls had
pubic hair, too.

Emilio must have been in the J-Center office because the reply came
back almost immediately. "Deadly."

AT SIX THAT evening, Jimmy started down through the karst
hills and forest surrounding the Arecibo telescope site to the coastal city
of the same name, and from there drove eastward along the coast road
to San Juan. It was twenty after eight before he found a parking spot
within sight of El Morro, a huge stone fortress built in the sixteenth century, reinforced later with the massive city wall that surrounded Old San
Juan. Then, as now, the wall left the slum of La Perla unprotected, clinging to a strip of beach.

La Perla didn't look too bad when you were standing on the city
wall. The houses, tumbling down six or seven levels from the heights to
the sea, appeared substantial and fairly large until you knew that, inside,
they were all cut into several apartments. Anglos with any kind of sense
stayed out of La Perla but Jimmy was big and competent and known to
be Emilio's friend, and he was gratified to be greeted now and then as he
jogged down the cascade of stairways toward Claudio's tavern.

Sandoz was sitting in the far corner of the bar, nursing a beer. The
priest was easy to pick out of a crowd, even when he wasn't in clericals.
Conquistador beard, coppery skin, straight black hair that parted naturally in the center and fell over high, wide cheekbones, which narrowed
to a surprisingly delicate chin. Small-boned but nicely made. If Sandoz
had been assigned to Jimmy Quinn's old parish in South Boston, his exotic looks would surely have drawn the traditional title bestowed on attractive celibates by generations of Catholic girls: Father What-A-Waste.

Jimmy waved to Emilio and then to the bartender, who said hi and
sent Rosa over with another beer. Picking up the heavy wooden chair
opposite Sandoz and rotating it one-handed, Jimmy sat wrong-way

around and folded his arms on the chair back. He smiled up at Rosa as she handed him the beer mug and then pulled a long swallow, Sandoz watching him peaceably from across the table.

"You look tired," Jimmy remarked.

Sandoz shrugged expressively, momentarily a Jewish grandmother. "So what else is new?"

"You don't eat enough," Jimmy said. This was an old routine.

"Yes, Mama," Sandoz acknowledged obediently.

"Claudio," Jimmy yelled to the barkeeper, "get this man a sandwich." Rosa was already on her way from the kitchen with plates of food for both of them.

"So. You have come all this way to feed me sandwiches?" Sandoz asked. Actually, it was Jimmy who always got tuna sandwiches, bizarrely combined with a double side order of *bacalaitos fritos* and a half guava in the shell. Rosa knew that the priest preferred beans in *sofrito,* spooned over rice.

"Somebody's got to do it. Listen, I got a problem."

"Don't worry, Sparky. I hear you can get shots for it in Lubbock."

"De Niro," Jimmy said, wolfing a bite. Emilio made a sound like a game-show buzzer. "Shit. Not De Niro? Wait. Nicholson! I always get those two guys mixed up." Emilio never got anybody mixed up. He knew every actor and all the dialogue from every movie since *Horse Feathers.* "Okay. Be serious for ten seconds. You ever heard of a vulture?"

Sandoz sat up straight, fork in midair. Professorial now: "I presume you do not refer to the carrion-eating bird. Yes. I have even worked with one."

"No kidding," Quinn said, around his food. "I didn't know that."

"There's a lot you don't know, kid," Sandoz drawled. It was John Wayne, marred only by the barely perceptible Spanish accent that persisted during the quicksilver transformations.

Jimmy, who mostly ignored Sandoz's private games with language, continued to chew. "You gonna finish that?" he asked, after they'd eaten in silence for a little while. Sandoz swapped his plate for Jimmy's empty one and slumped against the wall again. "So what was it like?" Jimmy asked. "Working with the vulture, I mean. They assigned me one at the dish. Do you think I should cooperate? Peggy will have my guts if I do and the Japs will have 'em if I don't, so what's the difference? Maybe I should go for intellectual immortality and devote my life to the poor, which will include me, after the vulture picks my brains and they dump me at Arecibo."

Sandoz let him roll. Jimmy generally reached his own conclusions by talking, and Sandoz was accustomed to confessional musing. Instead, he wondered how Jimmy could eat so fast and still talk without sucking food into his windpipe.

"So what do you think? Should I do it?" Jimmy asked again, finishing off his beer and using a piece of bread to sop up the *sofrito*. He waved to Claudio for a second beer. "You want another?" he asked Sandoz.

Emilio shook his head. When he spoke this time, it was in his own voice. "Hold out for a while. Tell them you want someone good. Until the vulture does you, you still have some leverage. You have something they want, yes? Once they've got you stored, they don't need you. And if a vulture does a poor job on you, you're immortalized as mediocrity." Then he was gone again, embarrassed for giving advice, and Edward James Olmos appeared as a pachuco gangster, hissing, *"Horalé . . . ese."*

"Who did you?"

"Sofia Mendes."

Jimmy's eyebrows shot up. "Latina?"

Unexpectedly, Sandoz laughed. "Remotely."

"Was she good?"

"Yes. Quite. It was an interesting experience."

Jimmy stared at him, suddenly suspicious. When Emilio said interesting, it was often code for bloodcurdling. Jimmy waited for an explanation but Sandoz simply settled into the corner, smiling enigmatically. There was silence for a little while as Jimmy turned his attention back to the *sofrito*. The next time he glanced up, it was Jimmy who smiled. Down for the count. Sandoz fell asleep faster than anyone he'd ever met. Anne Edwards claimed the priest had only two speeds, Full Bore and Off.

Jimmy, an insomniac whose mind tended to run on a hamster wheel at night, envied the man's ability to catnap but knew it wasn't just a fortunate quirk of physiology that let Emilio crash at will. Sandoz routinely put in sixteen-hour days; he crashed because he was beat. Jimmy helped out as much as he could and wished sometimes that he lived closer to La Perla, so he could pitch in more often.

There was even a time when Jimmy had considered becoming a Jesuit himself. His parents, second-wave Irish immigrants to Boston, left Dublin before he was born. His mother was never vague about their motive for the move. "The Old Sod was a backward, Church-ridden Third World country filled with dictatorial, sexually repressed priests sticking their noses into normal people's bedrooms," she'd declare whenever asked. Despite this, Eileen admitted to being "culturally Catholic," and Kevin Quinn held out for Jesuit-run schools for the boy merely on the basis of the discipline and high scholastic standards. They had raised a son with a generous soul, with an impulse to heal hurts and lighten loads, who could not stand idly while men like Emilio Sandoz poured out their lives and energy for others.

Jimmy sat a while longer, thinking, and then went quietly to the debit station, punching in perhaps five times the amount needed to pay for their meals this evening. "Lunches all week, okay? And watch him while he eats, right, Rosa? Otherwise he'll give the food away to some kid." Rosa nodded, wondering if Jimmy noticed that he himself had just eaten half of the priest's meal. "I'll tell you his problem," Quinn continued, oblivious. "He's got two-hundred-pound ideas about getting things done, and a hundred and thirty pounds to do it with. He's gonna make himself sick."

Over in the corner, Sandoz, eyes closed, was smiling. "*Sí, Mamacita,*" he said, mingling sarcasm with affection. Abruptly, he hauled himself to his feet, yawned and stretched. Together, the two men left the bar and walked out into the soft sea air of La Perla in early spring.

IF THERE WAS anything that might have strengthened Jimmy Quinn's faith in the ultimate reasonableness of authority, it was the early career of Father Emilio Sandoz. Nothing about it made much sense until you got to the end and saw that the collective mind of the Society of Jesus had been working patiently in a direction mere individuals could not perceive.

Many Jesuits were multilingual but Sandoz more than most. A native of Puerto Rico, he'd grown up with both Spanish and English. His years of Jesuit formation tapped the rigorous riches of a classical education and Sandoz became nearly as proficient in Greek as in Latin, which he'd not just studied but used as a living language: for daily communication, for research, for the sheer pleasure of reading beautifully structured prose. That much was not far out of the ordinary among Jesuit scholastics.

But then, during a research project on the seventeenth-century missions to Quebec, Sandoz decided to learn French, in order to read the Jesuit Relations in the original. He spent eight intense days with a teacher, absorbing French grammar, then built vocabulary on his own. When his paper was complete at the end of the semester, he was comfortable reading in French, although he made no effort to learn to speak the language. Next came Italian, partly in anticipation of going to Rome someday and partly out of curiosity, to see how another Romance language had developed from the Latin stem. And then Portuguese, simply because he liked the sound of it and loved Brazilian music.

The Jesuits have a tradition of linguistic study. Not surprisingly, Emilio was encouraged to begin a doctorate in linguistics immediately after ordination. Three years later, everyone expected Emilio Sandoz, S.J., Ph.D., to be offered a professorship at a Jesuit university.

Instead, the linguist was asked to help organize a reforestation project while teaching at Xavier High School on Chuuk in the Caroline Islands. After only thirteen months of what would ordinarily have been a six-year assignment, he was moved to an Inuit town just below the Arctic circle and spent a single year assisting a Polish priest in establishing an adult literacy program, and then it was on to a Christian enclave in southern Sudan, where he worked in a relief station for Kenyan refugees with a priest from Eritrea.

He grew accustomed to feeling inexpert and out of his depth. He became tolerant of the initial frustration of being unable to communicate with grace or speed or humor. He learned to quiet the cacophony of languages competing for dominance in his thoughts, to use pantomime and his own expressive features to overcome barriers. Within thirty-seven months, he became competent in Chuukese, a northern Invi-Inupiak dialect, Polish, Arabic (which he spoke with a rather good Sudanese accent), Gikuyu and Amharic. And most important from his superiors' point of view, in the face of sudden reassignment and his own explosive temperament, Emilio Sandoz had begun to learn patience and obedience.

"There's a message from the Provincial for you," Father Tahad Kesai told him when he returned to their tent one sweltering afternoon, three hours late for what passed as lunch, a few weeks after the first anniversary of his arrival in Sudan.

Sandoz came to a halt and stared, tired and green-faced under the tent fabric. "Right on schedule," he said, dropping wearily onto a camp stool and flipping open his computer tablet.

"Maybe it's not a reassignment," Tahad suggested. Sandoz snorted; they both knew it would be. "Goat shit," Tahad said irritably, mystified by the way their superiors were handling Sandoz. "Why won't they let you serve out a full assignment?"

Sandoz said nothing so Tahad busied himself sweeping sand back out to the desert, to give the other priest a little privacy as he read the transmission. But the silence went on too long and when Tahad turned to look at Sandoz, he was disturbed to see that the man's body was beginning to shake. And then Sandoz put his face in his hands.

Moved, Tahad went to him. "You've done good work here, Emilio. It seems crazy to keep pulling you from hill to valley . . ." Tahad's voice trailed off.

Sandoz was, by this time, wiping tears from his eyes and making terrible whining sounds. Wordlessly, he waved Tahad in closer to the screen, inviting him to read the message. Tahad did, and was more puzzled than ever. "Emilio, I don't understand—"

Sandoz wailed and nearly fell off the stool.

"Emilio, what is so funny?" Tahad demanded, bewilderment turning to exasperation.

Sandoz was asked to report to John Carroll University outside Cleveland in the United States, not to take up a post as a professor of linguistics, but to cooperate with an expert in artificial intelligence who would codify and computerize Sandoz's method of learning languages in the field so that future missionaries would benefit from his wide experience, for the greater glory of God.

"I'm sorry, Tahad, it's too hard to explain," gasped Sandoz, who was on his way to Cleveland to serve as intellectual carrion for an AI vulture, *ad majorem Dei gloriam.* "It's the punchline to a three-year joke."

As MANY AS thirty or as few as ten years later, lying exhausted and still, eyes open in the dark long after the three suns of Rakhat had set, no longer bleeding, past the vomiting, enough beyond the shock to think again, it would occur to Emilio Sandoz to wonder if perhaps that day in the Sudan was really only part of the setup for a punchline a lifetime in the making.

It was an odd thought, under the circumstances. He understood that, even at the time. But thinking it, he realized with appalling clarity that on his journey of discovery as a Jesuit, he had not merely been the first human being to set foot on Rakhat, had not simply explored parts of its largest continent and learned two of its languages and loved some of its people. He had also discovered the outermost limit of faith and, in doing so, had located the exact boundary of despair. It was at that moment that he learned, truly, to fear God.

3

ROME:

JANUARY 2060

SEVENTEEN YEARS OR a single year later, on his way to see Emilio Sandoz a few weeks after their first meeting, John Candotti very nearly fell into the Roman Empire.

Sometime during the night, a delivery van had provided the last little bit of weight and vibration that could be withstood by a nineteenth-century street paved over a medieval bedroom constructed from the walls of a dry Roman cistern, and the whole crazy hollow thing collapsed. The road crew managed to extricate the van but hadn't gotten around to putting up barriers around the hole. John, hurrying as usual, almost walked right into it. Only the odd echo from his footsteps warned him that something wasn't right and he slowed down, his foot in the air, stopping just short of a historically interesting broken neck. This was the kind of thing that kept him constantly on edge in Rome but that he made comical in his messages home. His entire experience in this city sounded better than it lived.

John had decided to see Sandoz in the morning this time, hoping to catch him fresh after a night of rest and to talk some sense into him. Somebody needed to let the guy know exactly which rock and what kind of hard place he was between. If Sandoz was unwilling to talk about the mission, the crew of the ship that had sent him back, against all odds, had suffered from no such reticence. People who'd argued that interstellar travel was financially impractical had reckoned without the immense commercial possibilities of having a story to tell to an audience of over eight billion consumers. The Contact Consortium had played the drama for all it was worth, releasing it in tiny episodes, milking the interest and the money even after it was clear that their own people had probably perished on Rakhat.

Eventually, they got to the part of the story where they found Sandoz, and the shit hit the proverbial fan. The disappearance of the original Jesuit missionaries was transformed from a tragic mystery into an ugly scandal: violence, murder and prostitution, doled out in teasing, skin-crawling doses. The initial public admiration for the scientific expertise and swift decisiveness that made the mission possible wheeled 180 degrees, the news coverage as relentless as it was vicious. Sensing blood in the water, media sharks hunted down anyone still living who might have known members of the Jesuit party. The private lives of D. W. Yarbrough, Marc Robichaux and Sofia Mendes were dragged into the light and piously tittered over by commentators whose own behavior went unexamined. Only Sandoz had survived to be reviled and so he became the focus for the outrage, despite the fact that he was generally remembered with fondness or respect by people who'd known him before the mission.

It wouldn't have mattered if Sandoz had been as pure as a newborn baby here, John thought. He was a whore and a murderer there. No additional scandal was required to bring the pot to a boil.

"I have nothing to say. I shall withdraw from the Society," Sandoz still insisted, when pressed. "I just need a little time."

Maybe he thought he could keep quiet and the interest would die; maybe he thought he could stand the hounding and pressure. John doubted it; the media would eat Sandoz alive. He was known all over the world, and those hands were like the mark of Cain. There was no safe haven left on Earth for him but the Society of Jesus and even there he was a pariah, poor bastard.

John Candotti had once waded into a street fight simply because he thought the odds were too lopsided. He got his big nose broken for his trouble and the guy he helped wasn't notably grateful. Still, it was the right thing to do.

No matter how badly Sandoz stumbled on Rakhat, John thought, he needs a friend now, so what the hell? It may as well be me.

AT THAT MOMENT, Emilio Sandoz was not thinking about being eaten alive but about eating. He was considering the toast on the breakfast tray Brother Edward had just brought into his room. Edward must have thought it was time for him to try chewing something. His remaining teeth did feel steadier in his gums. And he was ashamed of having his food pureed, of drinking everything through a straw, of being an invalid . . .

Lost words came back to him, floating up like air through water, bursting into his mind. There were two meanings, two pronunciations of the word invalid. Null and void, he thought. I am invalid.

He stiffened, bracing for the storm, but felt only an emptiness. That's over now, he thought, and went back to the toast. Not yet trusting himself to speak without rehearsal, he worked the sentence out in advance. "Brother Edward," he said finally, "if you would be so kind as to break some bread into small pieces and then to leave me alone?"

"Of course, sir," Edward said, fussing with the tray, making sure everything was within easy reach.

"That was all English, yes?"

"Yes. And very good English at that, sir."

"If I mix things, you would tell me."

"Of course, sir."

It was often a sequel to torture and isolation: this disorientation, the confusion of languages. Edward Behr had a lot of experience with men like this—bodies shattered, souls reeling. Sizing up this particular situation and the man he found in it, Brother Edward had adopted a sort of British butler persona, which seemed to amuse Sandoz and which allowed him a certain dignity during his most undignified moments. Sandoz required careful handling. His physical condition was so distressing and his political position so difficult that it was easy to forget how many friends this man had lost on Rakhat, how quickly the mission had gone from promise to ruin, how recent it all was for him. A widower himself, Edward Behr recognized grief in others. "It will all come right in the end, sir," Edward said as he broke up the toast and moved the plate closer to Sandoz. "Try to be patient with yourself."

Edward turned to the window and reached up to pull the curtain open, stretching his portly body to its limit. His wife had called him Teddy Behr, from affection, and because he was built like a stuffed animal. "If you need anything," he said to Sandoz, "I'm near." And then he left.

It took half an hour to finish a single slice of toast and it wasn't a pretty process, but no one was watching and Sandoz managed. Then to his own continuing surprise, he felt the lethargy take over and fell asleep in the sunlight, slumped in the chair by the window.

A knock on the slightly open door woke him only minutes later. He was incapable of tying a handkerchief around the door lever, a venerable Jesuit custom that meant Do Not Disturb. He might have had Brother Edward do it for him but he hadn't thought of that. He hadn't thought of much lately. That was a mercy. The dreams, of course, were merciless . . . The knocking came again.

"Come in," he called, expecting it was Edward, come for the plates. Instead, he saw the Father General's oddly soft and rigid secretary, Johannes Voelker. Startled, he got to his feet and moved back, putting the chair between him and the other man.

JOHANNES VOELKER HAD a high, penetrating voice that rang in Sandoz's small bare room, and John Candotti heard it when he was still halfway down the hall. The door to the room was open as always, so John was spared the necessity of barging in without knocking.

"Of course, Dr. Sandoz," Voelker was saying as John entered the room, "the Father General would like to hear that you have decided to remain among us—"

"The Father General is kind," Sandoz whispered, glancing warily at John. He was standing in the corner, his back against the wall. "I need a little time. I won't trouble you longer than necessary."

"Ah. You see, Candotti?" Voelker said, turning to John. "He is determined. A pity but there are circumstances when a man leaves for the good of the Society," Voelker said briskly, returning to Sandoz, "and I shall commend such an honorable decision. Naturally, we will be happy to shelter you until you have fully recovered your strength, Dr. Sandoz."

Here's your hat, John Candotti thought, what's your hurry? Incensed, he was about to tell the Austrian to take a hike when he saw the shaking start. At first, John put it down to illness. Sandoz had almost died. He was still very frail. "Sit down, Father," John said quietly and went to the man's side to guide him back into the chair. He moved behind Sandoz and glared at Voelker. "Father Voelker, I think Father Sandoz could use some rest. Now."

"Oh, dear. I have tired you. Forgive me." Voelker moved without further prompting to the door.

"Voelker's a jerk," John Candotti said dismissively as the secretary's footsteps receded down the hall. "Don't let him rattle you. You can take all the time you need. It's not like we're waiting to rent your room out." He perched on the edge of Emilio's bed, the only other place in the room to sit. "Are you okay? You look a little—" Scared, he thought, but he said, "Sick to your stomach."

"It's . . . hard. To have so many people around."

"I can imagine," John said automatically but then he took it back. "I'm sorry. That was a stupid thing to say. I can't imagine it, can I?"

There was a brief bleak smile. "I hope not."

Sobered, John dropped all thoughts of lecturing this man on real life.

"Look, Father, I hope you don't mind but I was thinking about what might be a help with your hands," he said after a while, not quite sure why he was embarrassed about mentioning this. Sandoz himself had made no attempt to hide them. Probably, it was thinking about all the things the guy couldn't do for himself. Cut his toenails, shave, go to the can alone. Made you squirm, just considering it all. John rummaged around in his briefcase and pulled out a pair of thin leather gloves, fingers and thumbs removed, cut edges expertly turned and hemmed. "I mean, eventually, a surgeon could probably reconstruct the palms for you but, see, I thought gloves would sort of hold things together, for now. You still won't have a lot of dexterity, I suppose, but you might be able to grip things this way." Sandoz looked at him, wide-eyed. "I mean, you could try them. If they don't work, it's no big deal. Just a pair of gloves, right?"

"Thank you," Sandoz said in an odd voice.

Pleased, and relieved that Sandoz had not been offended by his offer, John helped him fit the impossibly long, scarred fingers into the gloves. Why the hell did they do this to him? John wondered, trying to be careful of the raw new tissue that had only recently reclosed. All the muscles of the palms had been carefully cut from the bones, doubling the length of the fingers, and Sandoz's hands reminded John of childhood Halloween skeletons. "Now that I think of it," John said, "cotton might have been better. It's okay. If this pair works out, I'll make another. I've got an idea for a way to fit a spoon into a little loop here, so it would be easier for you to eat. Sometimes the simplest solution is the best, you know?"

Shut up, John, you're babbling, he told himself. Occupied with putting the gloves on, he was for the moment completely unaware of the tears tracing the lines down Sandoz's worn and expressionless face. When he finished with the second glove, John looked up. Appalled, his smile faded.

Sandoz wept silently, still as an icon, for perhaps five minutes. John stayed with him, sitting on the bed, waiting until the man came back from wherever he'd been in memory.

"Father Candotti," Sandoz said at last, tears drying unacknowledged on his face, "if ever I should desire a confessor, I shall call upon you."

John Candotti, speechless for once, began to realize why he had been brought to Rome.

"Thank you for coming," Sandoz said.

Candotti nodded once and then again, as though confirming something, and left quietly.

4

ARECIBO, PUERTO RICO:
MARCH 2019

WHEN THE SOLUTION came to him, Jimmy Quinn was shaving, stooped over to see into a mirror hung, inevitably, too low to reflect his head. Most of his best ideas were like that. Sometimes, they occurred to him in the shower, crouched down trying to get his head under the water. He wondered if contorting his neck increased blood flow to his brain somehow. Anne Edwards would know; he'd have to ask her the next time he was over there for dinner.

This particular idea had taken its own sweet time in arriving. Jimmy had promised Peggy Soong that he'd find some way to balance the interests of the employees and the owners of Arecibo, but he'd come up dry. And that surprised him because he was generally able to find ways to please himself and, at the same time, to please his parents, his teachers, his buddies, his girlfriends. It wasn't that hard, if you put yourself in the other person's place. Jimmy liked to get along with people. So far, however, he'd found that the only way to get along with the Japanese management of the Arecibo Radio Telescope was to be quiet and do exactly as he was told.

His position at the dish was about as low as it could be, among the scientific staff. Whenever the telescope wasn't being used for something serious, Jimmy ran the standard SETI routines, monitoring the skies for alien radio transmissions. You could tell how low a priority the Search for Extraterrestrial Intelligence had become simply by noting that it was Jimmy who got stuck with the job. Most of the time, though, he processed requests to collect radio signals from targeted coordinates. A light astronomer would see something interesting and ask Arecibo to check out the same region of the sky so the two types of observations could be compared. Automated as Arecibo was, some actual real live person still had to receive the request, schedule the use of the dish, see that the work was done, take a look at the results and route the data back to whomever'd asked for it. It was not exactly secretarial; it wasn't Nobel Prize stuff either.

So the question was, why spend money on a first-rate vulture like Sofia Mendes when a perfectly adequate hack could automate his job for less?

After his master's at Cornell, Jimmy got the Arecibo job because he was willing to work cheap, because he'd been shrewd enough to study both Japanese and Spanish, and because he had some strengths in both light and radio astronomy. He loved his work and he was good at it. At the same time, he could see that much of what he did was amenable to automation. He understood that Masao Yanoguchi was under the gun to bring down costs at the dish because the lunar mining program looked like it was going to be a washout after all and the surest way to cut costs was to eliminate human beings from the process.

Yanoguchi had managed the Arecibo operation ever since ISAS, the Japanese Institute for Space and Aeronautical Science, purchased the radio telescope from the U.S. government. Arecibo was a frill, in the larger context of Japan's space industry, but Jimmy knew that there was vast Japanese satisfaction in owning it. Twice, the United States had attempted to force Japan to play by the West's rules with a decisive move to block Japan's access to raw materials and markets. Twice, the U.S. was stunned by the explosive reaction: the conquest of Asia in the first instance, the conquest of space in the second. And this time, there'd been no fatal mistake, like not bombing the shore facilities at Pearl Harbor.

Jimmy had taken a couple of courses in Japanese culture and he tried to apply what he learned but even after working at the Arecibo dish for almost a year, he found it hard to think of the Japanese as wild gamblers. And yet, his professors insisted, their entire history proved they were. Time after time, the Japanese had risked everything on a titanic throw of the dice. The horrific consequences of that single mistake at Pearl Harbor had made them the world's most calculating, meticulous and painstaking gamblers, but gamblers nonetheless. Westerners who understood this, one prof had commented in a wry aside, could occasionally propose a crap game and win.

Jimmy cut himself when the idea came at last, and laughed out loud and danced a little while he dabbed at the blood. Masao Yanoguchi was not going to fire him, at least not right away. Peggy the Hun would not eviscerate him and might even give him some credit for brains. He might get Sofia Mendes as his vulture, and he thought Emilio would be pleased. And hell, now that he thought of it, he might even have a topic for a doctoral thesis.

"You've done it again, Quinn," he crowed to his bloody reflection and finished up quickly in the bathroom, anxious to get to the dish.

"COME IN, MR. Quinn." Masao Yanoguchi waved Jimmy through his open office door. "Please, have a seat."

They each played the other's game: Yanoguchi, the friendly American-style boss; Quinn, the proper Japanese employee, uncomfortable sitting in the presence of a superior, letting his nervousness show. They chatted for a few minutes about the World Cup game coming up, but eventually Jimmy came to the point.

"Dr. Yanoguchi, I have been thinking about the AI program," Quinn began. "I know my job is pretty mechanical and I understand that it makes good business sense to automate what I do, so I've begun thinking about going back to school for a Ph.D., and it occurred to me that you and ISAS might be interested in the topic I hope to use for my thesis." Jimmy paused, brows up, looking for permission to continue. Yanoguchi nodded, apparently relieved that Quinn was not there to fight. Pleased with the sincerity of his own performance, Jimmy warmed to his topic. "Well, sir, I would like to attempt a little pilot project, a comparison of an AI astronomy program with the human subject it was based on. I'd like ISAS to use a first-rate AI analyst to develop the program. Then I'd do a side-by-side comparison of the program's data handling with my own, for perhaps two years." Yanoguchi sat up a millimeter straighter. Jimmy smoothly amended his proposal. "Of course, a year or even six months might be enough, and then I could work up a grant proposal. I might be able to come back to work here, on grant money, later on."

"Mr. Quinn," Yanoguchi said at last, "it could be argued that the results of such a comparison would be suspect because the subject held back critical information."

"Yes, that's true, sir. But that might be true of anyone who resented being the subject of an AI analysis, sir. I'm sorry, Dr. Yanoguchi, but it's common knowledge that most people do hope the programs will fail. I think that the use of a really good AI analyst would mitigate the possibility that the subject is holding back. Plus, since I'd be using the data myself in my thesis research, I'd have a personal motive to make sure the results were reliable." Yanoguchi said nothing but he didn't exactly frown, so Quinn continued. "It seems to me, sir, that it might be in ISAS's interests to have some kind of hard comparative data, to judge each AI program, wouldn't it? To see if a program misses things that humans pick up? And if that's not so, then the Institute can go on using artificial intelligence to eliminate low-level jobs like mine, knowing that it's truly as competent as the people it was based on. It's just one more aspect of the system that could be nailed down properly, sir." Jimmy waited a few moments and then said thoughtfully, "Of course, it's just a little pilot project. If it doesn't work out, you'll only have gambled six months' extra salary for me. If it comes to something, it would reflect well on Arecibo . . ."

And on Masao Yanoguchi. Who said nothing. Jimmy forged ahead.

"If you have no objection, sir, I wonder if we could get Sofia Mendes to do the analysis. I've heard she's very good and—"

"Very expensive," Yanoguchi pointed out.

"But I have a friend who knows her and he says she might be willing to do the project for the publicity. If her program beats me, her broker could use that to command higher fees. Maybe we could work something out with him. If she wins, ISAS could double the usual fee?"

"And if she loses, the broker gets nothing?" suggested Masao Yanoguchi thoughtfully.

It's worth considering, Jimmy urged Yanoguchi mentally. Very little downside risk. Take a chance, he prayed. But Jimmy didn't expect an answer and didn't press for one. Yanoguchi would never say yes until he'd gotten a consensus about the project from everyone in ISAS and maybe even beyond the Institute. A lot of people had a lot riding on artificial intelligence. And that was the beauty of the thing: the longer the Japanese took to make a decision on this, the longer he had a job. And if they said yes, he'd be around for the months it took the vulture to pick his brains and then for at least another six months to do the comparison. If he beat the program, he'd be able to stay on, and if it was a near thing, maybe ISAS would at least change the policy so that there was always a test period after an AI analysis, which should make Peggy happy because it bought a little time for people, some of whom might beat their AI counterparts in a fair test. And if the program beat him, then maybe he really would go back to school . . .

Masao Yanoguchi gazed at the open, innocent face and suddenly laughed. "Mr. Quinn," he murmured, not unkindly, "your subtlety is showing." Jimmy flushed, caught in the act. "Nevertheless, this is an interesting proposition," Yanoguchi said, standing up and walking Jimmy to the door. "Please put it in writing."

5

CLEVELAND, OHIO:
AUGUST 2014–MAY 2015

IF HIS RETURN from the Sudanese refugee station to the United States hadn't been so disorienting, Emilio Sandoz might have handled the impact of his first meeting with Sofia Mendes a good deal better. As it was, he took the brunt of it while jet-lagged and culture-shocked, and it was several weeks before he could establish custody of his reactions to the woman.

In the space of twenty hours, he had moved from a war zone in the Horn of Africa to the suburban campus of John Carroll University, set in the placid peace of a pretty neighborhood of old and well-kept houses, where the children screamed and ran but in play, laughing and robust, not stunned or desperate or starving or terrified. He was amazed at how shocking the children were to him. The gardens also startled him, on many levels—the soil, black as coffee grounds, the luxurious jumble of summer blossom and ornamental plants, the profligate use of rain and fertility . . .

He might have wished for a few days off but arrangements had already been made. He was to meet Sofia Mendes on his second day back, at a campus restaurant that served Turkish coffee—a fuel that, he would later learn, she required at regular intervals. Emilio got to the coffee shop early the next morning and sat in the back, where he could watch the door, silently taking in the ripples of laughter and witty, empty conversation all around him, getting used to English again. Even if he hadn't spent the past three years in the field and more than a decade before that studying for the priesthood, he would have felt a stranger among these students—the young men in brilliantly colored, intricately pleated coats that broadened shoulders and narrowed hips, the young women wasp-waisted and delicious in pale and shimmering fabrics the colors of peony blossoms and sherbet. He was fascinated by the beautiful grooming and attention to detail: the arrangement of hair, the delicacy of shoes, the perfection of cosmetics. And thought of shallow graves in the Sudan, and mastered the anger, knowing it was partly exhaustion.

Through this garden of artificial delights and into his inclement mood, Sofia Mendes strode purposefully. Catching sight of her, knowing somehow that this was the woman he was waiting for, he recalled the words of a Madrid dance mistress describing what she looked for in an ideal Spanish dancer. "Head up, a princely posture. The waist held high above the hips, the arms *suavamente articuladas*. The breasts," she said with absurd aptness that made him laugh, "like a bull's horns but *suave, no rígido*." Mendes carried herself so well that he was surprised to find when he stood that she was hardly over five feet tall. Her black hair drawn back severely from her face in the traditional manner, she was dressed plainly in a red silk blouse and a black skirt. The contrast with the students around her was unavoidable.

Brows up, she held out her hand to shake his briefly and then looked back toward the crowd she had just walked through. "As pretty as a vaseful of cut flowers," she remarked, accurate and cool.

At a stroke, the vigor of the boys, the loveliness of the girls looked temporary. He could see which ones would age badly and which would soon be shapeless and how many would give up their extravagance and dreams of glory. And he was startled by the precision with which the image matched his mood, chilled by his own harshness, and hers.

It was her last bit of small talk for many months. They met three mornings a week for what felt to Sandoz like a relentless interrogation. He found that he could stand only ninety minutes at a time; afterward, he was nearly ruined for the day and it was difficult to concentrate on the elementary Latin course and the graduate seminars in linguistics he was assigned to teach during his stay at John Carroll. She never wished him a good morning or engaged in any chitchat. She simply slid into the booth, opened her notebook and began questioning him about his steps in learning a language, about tricks he used, habits he'd formed, methods he'd developed almost instinctively, as well as the more formal and academic techniques he used to analyze and understand a language, on the fly, in the field. When he tried to leaven the sessions with jokes or asides or funny stories, she stared at him, unamused, until he gave up and answered her question.

Courtesies provoked outright hostility. Once, at the very beginning, he rose as she sat down and replied to her first demand for information with an elaborate and ironic bow worthy of Cesar Romero. "Good morning, Señorita Mendes. How are you today? Are you enjoying the weather? Would you care for some pastry with your coffee?"

She looked up at him, eyes opaque and narrowed, as he stood waiting for a slight unbending from her, a simple civil greeting. "The gentlemanly Spanish hidalgo act is tasteless," she told him quietly. She let the silence go on for a moment and then her eyes dropped to her notebook. "Let's get on with it, shall we?"

It didn't take much of that to exorcize the Jungian vision of her as the ideal Spanish woman from his mind. By the end of the month, he was able to see her as an actual person and began trying to figure her out. English was not her first language, he was sure. Her grammar was too precise and her dentals were a bit damped, the sibilants a little drawn out. Despite her name and appearance, her accent was not Hispanic. Or Greek. Or French or Italian, or anything else he could identify. He put her single-mindedness down to the fact that she was paid on a fee-for-project basis: the faster she worked, the more she made. It was an assumption that appeared to be confirmed when she berated him once for being late.

"Dr. Sandoz," she said. She never called him Father. "Your superiors are paying a great deal of money to have this analysis done. Do you find it amusing to waste their resources and my time?"

The only occasion she said anything about herself was toward the end of a session that embarrassed him so thoroughly he even dreamed about it once, and awoke cringing at the memory. "Sometimes," he told her, leaning forward over the table, speaking without realizing how it would sound, "I begin with songs. They provide a sort of skeleton grammar for me to flesh out. Songs of longing for future tense, songs of regret for past tense, songs of love for the present."

He blushed when he heard what he'd said, making it worse, but she took no offense; indeed, she seemed to miss any connection that might have been taken wrongly. Instead, she seemed struck by a coincidence and looked out the café window, her mouth open slightly. "Isn't that interesting," she said, as though nothing else he'd told her so far had been, and continued thoughtfully, "I do the same thing. Have you noticed that lullabies nearly always use a lot of command form?"

And the moment passed, for which Emilio Sandoz thanked God.

IF THE SESSIONS with Mendes were draining and faintly depressing, he found balance in an extraordinary Latin 101 student. In her late fifties, fine white hair drawn into a neat French braid, Anne Edwards was compact, quick and intellectually fearless, with a lovely pealing laugh she made frequent use of in class.

Two weeks into the course, Anne waited until the rest of the students cleared out of the room. Emilio, gathering his notes from the desktop, looked up at her expectantly.

"Are you allowed out of your room at night?" she asked. "Or do the cute ones like you have a curfew until they're senile?"

He flicked the ash off an air cigar and waggled his eyebrows. "What do you have in mind?"

"Well, I considered suggesting that we shatter our vows and run away to Mexico for a weekend of lust, but I've got *homework*," she said, shouting the last word, "because some sonofabitch Latin prof thinks we should learn ablative way too soon, in my humble opinion, so why don't you just come over for dinner on Friday night?"

Leaning back against his chair, he looked up at her with frank admiration. "Madam. How could I resist an invitation like that?" he asked. And leaning forward, "Will your husband be there?"

"Yes, dammit, but he's a very liberal and tolerant person," Anne assured him, grinning. "And he falls asleep early."

THE EDWARDSES' HOUSE was a square, sensible-looking structure, surrounded by a garden that, Emilio was delighted to see, mixed flowers with tomatoes and pumpkin vines, lettuces, carrot patches and pepper plants. Pulling off gardening gloves, George Edwards greeted him in the front yard and waved him in through the door.

A good face, Emilio thought, full of humor and welcome. Anne's age, with a full head of silver hair but with the alarming leanness one associated with chronic HIV or toxic hyperthyroidism, or aging runners. Running was the most likely explanation. The man looked very fit. Not, Emilio thought, smiling inwardly, the sort to fall asleep early.

Anne was in the large, bright kitchen, working on dinner. Emilio recognized the smell instantly but it was a moment before he could put a name to it. When he did, he collapsed into a kitchen chair and moaned, *"Díos mío, bacalaitos!"*

Anne laughed. "And *asopao*. With *tostones*. And for dessert—"

"Forget the homework, dear lady. Run away with me," Emilio pleaded.

"Tembleque!" she announced, triumphant, laughing but happy that she'd pleased a guest. "A Puerto Rican friend of mine helped with the menu. There's a wonderful *colmado* on the west side. You can get *yautía, batatas, yuca, amarillos*—you name it."

"You are probably unaware," Emilio said, face sincere, eyes glowing, "that there was a seventeenth-century Puerto Rican heretic who claimed that Jesus used the smell of *bacalaitos* to raise Lazarus from the dead. The bishop had him burned at the stake, but they waited until after dinner and he died a happy man."

George, laughing, handed Sandoz and Anne frosty shallow-bowled glasses, froth floating on creamy liquid. "Bacardi *añejo*," Sandoz breathed, reverent. George raised his glass and they toasted Puerto Rico.

"So," Anne said in a serious tone, delicate brows raised in polite interest, the soul of propriety but about to take a sip of her drink. "What's celibacy like?"

"It's a bitch," Emilio said with prompt honesty, and Anne exploded. He handed her a napkin to wipe her nose and, without waiting for her to recover, stood and created an earnest face to address a phantom crowd at an old-time Twelve Step meeting. "Hello. My name is Emilio and though I can't remember it, my unempowered inner child might have been a codependent sex addict, so I rely on abstinence and put my trust in a Higher Power. You're dripping."

"I am a highly skilled anatomist," Anne declared with starchy dignity, dabbing at her blouse with the napkin, "and I can explain the exact mechanism by which one blows a drink out one's nose."

"Don't call her bluff," George warned him. "She can do it. Have you ever thought about a Twelve Step program for people who talk too much? You could call it On and On Anon."

"Oh, God," Anne groaned. "The old ones are the best ones."

"Jokes or husbands?" Emilio asked innocently.

And so the evening went.

When he next showed up for dinner, Anne met him at the door, put her hands on both sides of his face, rose on tiptoe and planted a chaste kiss on his forehead. "The first time you're here, you are a guest," she informed him, looking into his eyes. "After that, my darling, you're family. Get your own damned beer."

He took the long enjoyable walk to the Edwardses' house at least once a week after that. Sometimes he was the only guest. Often there were others: students, friends, neighbors, interesting strangers Anne or George had met and brought home. The conversation, about politics and religion and baseball and the wars in Kenya and Central Asia and whatever else caught Anne's interest, was raucous and funny, and the evenings ended with people calling out last jokes as they walked off into the night. The house became his cave—a home where a Jesuit was welcome and relaxed and off-duty, where he could soak up energy instead of being drained of it. It was the first real home Emilio Sandoz had ever had.

Sitting in their screened-in back porch, sipping drinks in the dusk, he learned that George was an engineer whose last job had involved life-support systems for underwater mining operations but whose career had spanned the technological distance from wooden slide rules to ILIAC IV and FORTRAN to neural nets, photonics and nanomachines. New to retirement, George had spent the early weeks of freedom cutting a swath through the old house, catching up on every small repair, taking curatorial pride in the smoothly working wooden window casings, the tuck-pointed brickwork, the tidiness of the workroom. He read stacks of books, eating them like popcorn. He enlarged the garden, built an arbor, organized the garage. He sank into pillowy contentment. He was bored brainless.

"Do you run?" he asked Sandoz, hopefully.

"I went out for cross-country in school."

"Watch out, dear, he's trying to sucker you. The old fart's training for a marathon," Anne said, the admiration in her eyes contradicting her tartness. "We're going to have to rebuild his knees if he keeps this nonsense up. On the other hand, if he croaks doing roadwork, I'm going to be a tastefully rich widow. I believe very sincerely in overinsuring."

Anne, he found out, was taking his course because she'd used medical Latin for years and was curious about the source language. She'd wanted to be a physician from the start but chickened out, afraid of the biochem, and so she began her career as a biological anthropologist. After finishing her Ph.D., she got work in Cleveland, teaching gross anatomy at Case Western Reserve. Years of working with med students in the gross lab did nothing to sustain her awe of the medical curriculum and so, at forty, she went back to school and wound up in emergency medicine, a specialty that required tolerance for chaos and a working knowledge of everything from neurosurgery to dermatology.

"I enjoy the violence," she explained primly, handing him a napkin. "Would you like me to explain about how that nose thing happens? The anatomy is really interesting. The epiglottis is like a little toilet bowl seat that covers the larynx—"

"Anne!" George yelled.

She stuck out her tongue. "Anyway, emergency medicine is great stuff. In the space of an hour sometimes, you get a crushed chest, a gunshot wound to the head and a kid with a rash."

"No children?" Emilio asked them one evening, to his own surprise.

"Nope. Turned out, we don't breed well in captivity," George said, unembarrassed.

Anne laughed. "Oh, God, Emilio. You'll love this. We used the rhythm method of birth control for years!" Her eyes bulged with disbelief. "We thought it *worked*!" And they howled.

He loved Anne, trusted her from the beginning. As the weeks went by and his emotions became more tangled, he felt more strongly the need of her counsel and the conviction that it would be good. But disclosure was never easy for him; the fall semester was half over before, one night after he finished helping George clear up the dinner wreckage, he found the nerve to suggest a walk to Anne.

"Behave yourselves," George ordered. "I'm old, but I can shoot."

"Relax, George," Anne called over her shoulder, as they started down the driveway. "I probably flunked the midterm. He's taking me out to break the news gently."

They chatted amiably for the first block or two, Anne's hand on Emilio's arm, her silver head nearly level with his dark one. He started twice but stalled out, unable to find words. Amused, she sighed and said, "Okay, tell me about her."

Sandoz barked a laugh and ran a hand through his hair. "Is it that obvious?"

"No," she assured him, gentle now. "It's just that I've seen you with a gorgeous young woman at the coffee shop on campus a few times, and I put two and two together. So. Tell me!"

He did. About Mendes's adamantine single-mindedness. Her accent, which he could mimic to perfection but could not identify. The hidalgo remark, so out of proportion to his mild attempt to soften the relationship. The antagonism he sensed but could not understand. And finally, ending at the beginning, the almost physical jolt of meeting her. Not just an appreciation of her beauty or a plain glandular reaction but a sense of . . . knowing her already, somehow.

At the end of all this, Anne said, "Well, it's just a guess, but what occurs to me is that she's Sephardic."

He came abruptly to a halt and stood still, eyes closed. "Of course. A Jew, of Spanish ancestry." He looked at Anne. "She thinks my ancestors threw her ancestors out of Spain in 1492."

"It would explain a lot." She shrugged and they began to walk again. "Personally, I love the beard, darling, but it does make you look like central casting's idea of the Grand Inquisitor. You may be pushing a lot of her buttons."

Jungian archetypes work both ways, he realized. "Balkan," he said, after a while. "The accent could be Balkan."

Anne nodded. "Maybe. A lot of Sephardim ended up in the Balkans after the expulsion. She might be from Romania or Turkey. Or Bulgaria. Someplace like that." She whistled, remembering Bosnia. "I'll tell you something about the Balkans. If people there think they're going to forget a grudge, they write an epic poem and make the children recite it before bed. You're up against five hundred years of carefully preserved and very bad memories about imperial Catholic Spain."

The silence lasted a little too long to give credence to his next remark. "I only wanted to understand her better." Anne made a face that said, Oh, sure. Emilio went on doggedly. "The work we are doing is difficult enough. Hostility simply makes it harder."

Anne thought of an off-color comment. She didn't say it, but Emilio read it on her face and snorted, "Oh, grow up," and she giggled like a twelve-year-old who's just discovered smutty jokes. Anne took his arm then and they started back toward the house, listening to the sounds of the neighborhood buttoning up for the night. Dogs barked at them, the leaves rattled and whispered. A mother called out, "Heather! Bedtime! I'm not going to tell you again!"

"Heather. Haven't heard that one in years. Probably named after a grandmother." Anne suddenly stopped and Emilio turned back to look at her. "Shit, Emilio, I don't know—maybe God is as real for you as George and I are for each other . . . We were barely twenty when we got married, back before the Earth's crust cooled. And believe me, nobody gets through forty years together without noticing a few attractive alternatives along the way." He started to say something, but she held up her hand. "Wait. I intend to bestow upon you unsolicited advice, my darling. I know this will sound glib, but don't pretend you aren't feeling what you feel. That's how things slide into hell. Feelings are facts," she said, her voice a little hard, as she began to walk again. "Look straight at 'em and deal with 'em. Work it through, as honestly as you can. If God is anything like a middle-class white chick from the suburbs, which I admit is a long shot, it's what you *do* about what you feel that matters." They could see George now, sitting on the front stoop in a pool of light, waiting for them. Her voice was very soft. "Maybe God will love you more if you come back to Him with your whole heart later."

Emilio kissed Anne good-night, waved to George, and started back to John Carroll with a great deal to think about. Anne joined George on the porch, but before Emilio got beyond earshot, she called out, "Hey! What did I get on the midterm?"

"Eighty-six. You messed up the ablative."

"Shit!" she yelled. And her laugh sailed out toward him in the dark.

By Monday morning, he had come to some conclusions. He did not shave, feeling that would be too obvious, but he adjusted his manner, becoming as neutrally Anglo as Beau Bridges. Sofia Mendes relaxed fractionally. He permitted himself no small talk and fell into the rhythm of question and answer that suited her. The work went more smoothly.

He began meeting George Edwards on his training circuit and going part way with him. Emilio decided to run the 10K in the big spring race. George, who would be running the full marathon, was glad for the company. "Ten kilometers is nothing to be ashamed of," the older man assured him, grinning.

And he found work to do at a high school in a miserable neighborhood of East Cleveland. He brought the energy to God.

In the end, he was rewarded with something like a moment of friendship. Sofia Mendes had suspended their meetings for several weeks and then let him know she had something for him to look at. He met her at his office and she spoke to his system, calling the file in from the net. Waving him into a chair and sitting down next to him, she said, "Just start in. Pretend you are preparing for assignment to a mission where you'll use a language you have never studied and for which no formal instruction is available."

He did as he was told. After several minutes, he began skipping around, asking questions randomly, pursuing instruction at different levels. It was all there, the experience of years, even the songs. His best effort, ordered and systematized, seen through the prism of her own startling intellect. Hours later, he pushed away from the desk and met her eyes, which were shining. "Beautiful," he said ambiguously, "just beautiful."

And for the first time, he saw her smile briefly. The look of fierce dignity returned and she stood. "Thank you." She hesitated but then continued firmly. "This has been a good project. I enjoyed working with you."

He rose, as it was clear she intended to leave, just like that. "What will you do next? Take your fee and relax on a beach, perhaps?"

She stared at him for a moment. "You really don't know, do you," she said. "A very sheltered life, I suppose."

It was his turn to look at her, uncomprehending.

"You don't know the significance of this?" she asked, indicating the metal bracelet she always wore. He had noticed it, of course, a rather plain piece of jewelry, in keeping with her preference for simple clothing. "I receive only a living stipend. The fee goes to my broker. He contracted my services when I was fifteen. I was educated at his expense and until I repay his investment, it is illegal to employ me directly. I cannot remove the identification bracelet. It's there to protect his interests. I thought such arrangements were common knowledge."

"This can't be legal," he insisted, when he could speak. "This is slavery."

"Perhaps intellectual prostitution is nearer the mark. Legally, the arrangement is more like indentured service than slavery, Dr. Sandoz. I am not held for life. When I repay the debt, I am free to go." She gathered her belongings as she spoke and made ready to leave him. "And I find the arrangement preferable to physical prostitution."

That was altogether more than he could take in. "Where will you go next?" he asked, still stunned.

"The U.S. Army War College. A military history professor is retiring. Good-bye, Dr. Sandoz."

He shook her hand and watched her go. Head up, a princely posture.

6

ROME AND NAPLES:
MARCH–APRIL 2060

IN MARCH, A man with stolen Jesuit credentials managed to get past Residence security and into Emilio Sandoz's room. Fortunately, Edward Behr happened to be on his way there, and when he heard the reporter badgering Sandoz with questions he went through the door low and fast. The momentum of his drive slammed the intruder into a wall, where Brother Edward kept him pinned while shouting wheezily for assistance.

Unfortunately, the entire incident was broadcast live, transmitted by the man's personal AV rig. Even so, Edward thought afterward, it was rather gratifying to believe that the world might incidentally have gained some respect for the athletic abilities of short, fat asthmatics.

The intrusion was a setback for Sandoz, for whom the incident had been literally nightmarish. But even before the break-in, it was clear that he wasn't improving much mentally, despite the fact that his physical condition had stabilized. The worst symptoms of scurvy were under control, although the fatigue and bruising persisted. The doctors suspected that his ability to absorb ascorbic acid had been impaired by long exposure to cosmic radiation. There was always some kind of physiological or genetic damage in space; the miners did fairly well because they were shielded by rock, but the shuttle crews and the station staffs always had trouble with cancers and deficiency diseases.

In any case, Sandoz healed poorly. Dental implants were impossible; he'd been fitted with a couple of bridges so he could eat normally, but he had no appetite and remained underweight. And the surgeons wouldn't touch his hands. "There's no point in trying, as things stand," one of them said. "His connective tissue is like a spider web. It'll hold if you don't disturb it. Maybe in a year . . ."

So the Society brought in Father Singh, an Indian craftsman known for his intricate braces and artificial limbs, who fabricated a pair of near-prostheses to strengthen and help control Sandoz's fingers. Delicate-looking as spun sugar, the braces were fitted over his hands and extended back toward his elbows. Sandoz was courteous, as always, and praised the workmanship and thanked Father Singh for his help. And he practiced daily with an obstinate persistence that first worried and then frightened Brother Edward.

Eventually, they were told, Sandoz would learn to use only the wrist flexors to activate the servomotors that ran off electrical potentials generated in the muscles of his forearms. But even after a month, he couldn't seem to isolate the movement he needed, and the effort to control his hands took every bit of strength he had. So Brother Edward did his best to keep the sessions short, balancing the progress Emilio made against the price they both paid in tears.

TWO DAYS AFTER another reporter was caught climbing an outside wall near Sandoz's bedroom, the Father General called Edward Behr and John Candotti into his office, just after his regular morning meeting with his secretary. To John's dismay, Voelker stayed.

"Father Voelker has suggested that Emilio might benefit from a retreat, gentlemen," Vincenzo Giuliani began, glancing at Candotti with eyes that said quite clearly, Shut up and play along. "And he has kindly offered to conduct the Spiritual Exercises. I am interested in your views."

Brother Edward shifted in his chair and leaned forward, hesitant to speak first but with a definite opinion about this. Before he could form a sentence, Johannes Voelker spoke. "We are taught that we should make no decision in times of desolation. It's clear that the man is experiencing a darkness of the soul, and no wonder. Sandoz is spiritually paralyzed, unable to move forward. I recommend a retreat with a director who would help him focus on the task he has before him."

"Maybe if the guy didn't have people breathing down his neck, he'd do better," said John, smiling genially and thinking, You pedantic prig.

"Forgive me, Father General," Brother Edward broke in hastily. The animosity between Candotti and Voelker was becoming the stuff of legends. "With respect, the Exercises are a very emotional experience. I don't think Emilio's ready for them now."

"I'd have to agree with that," John said pleasantly. And Johannes Voelker is the last man on Earth I'd choose as a spiritual director for Sandoz, he thought. Shit or get off the pot, my son.

"Strictly from a safety standpoint, however," Edward Behr continued, "I'd like to see him elsewhere. He feels as though he's under siege, here in Rome."

"Well, in a manner of speaking, he is," the Father General said. "I agree with Father Voelker that Emilio must face up to his situation, but now is not the time and Rome is not the place. So. We are agreed that it's a good idea to take Emilio out of the Residence, even if we have different motives for the move, correct?" Giuliani rose from his desk and went to his windows, where he could see a morose crowd standing around under umbrellas. They'd been fortunate with the cold, wet weather, which had discouraged all but the most persistent reporters that winter. "The retreat house north of Naples would provide more privacy than we can guarantee here."

"The problem, I should think, is how to get Sandoz out of Number 5 without being detected," Edward Behr said. "The bread van won't work a second time."

"Reporters follow every vehicle," Voelker confirmed.

Giuliani turned from the windows. "The tunnels," he said.

Candotti looked puzzled. "I'm sorry?"

"We are connected to the Vatican by a complex of tunnels," Voelker informed him. "We can take him out through St. Peter's."

"Do we still have access to them?" Behr asked, frowning.

"Yes, if one knows whom to ask," Giuliani said serenely and moved toward the door of his office, signaling the end of the meeting. "Until our plans are in place, gentlemen, it is best, perhaps, to say nothing to Emilio. Or to anyone else."

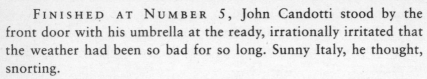

FINISHED AT NUMBER 5, John Candotti stood by the front door with his umbrella at the ready, irrationally irritated that the weather had been so bad for so long. Sunny Italy, he thought, snorting.

He shouldered his way through the media crowd that rushed at him as soon as he opened the door and took perverse pleasure in answering all the shouted questions with pointless quotations from Scripture, making a great show of piety. But as soon as he left the reporters behind, he turned his thoughts to the meeting that had just ended. Giuliani obviously agreed it was crazy to put Sandoz through the Exercises in his present state, John thought as he walked back to his room. So what was the point of that little show with Voelker?

It wasn't in John Candotti's nature to be suspicious of motives. There were people who loved to play organizational chess, to pit one person against another, to maneuver and plot and anticipate everyone else's next three moves, but John had no talent for the game and so he was nearly home before he got it, at the very moment that he managed to step into a fresh pile of dog droppings.

Crap, he thought, in observation and in commentary. He stood there in the rain, contemplating his shoe and its adornment and his own guileless good nature. This meeting, he realized, was part of some kind of good cop, bad cop balancing act Giuliani was encouraging. Gee, nice thinking, Sherlock! he told himself mordantly.

Obedience was one thing. Being used, even by the Father General, was another. He was offended but also embarrassed that he had taken so long to wise up. And even suspicious, now, because Giuliani had agreed so easily to find a way out of town for Sandoz. But, scraping the shit off his shoe and considering things, John was also sort of flattered; after all, he'd been brought here all the way from Chicago because his Jesuit superiors knew he was almost genetically programmed to despise assholes like his beloved brother in Christ, Johannes Voelker.

John was so anxious to get away from Rome himself that he didn't want to inquire too closely into the Father General's permission to leave. Just play the cards the way they lay, he told himself, and hope that God is on Emilio's side.

ON EASTER WEEKEND, the Vatican was packed with the faithful: 250,000 people, there to receive the Pope's blessing, to pray, to gawk, to buy souvenirs, to have their pockets picked. The Jihad promised bombs, and security was tight, but no one noticed a sickly man bent over his own lap, wrapped against the April chill, being wheeled out of the plaza by a big guy in a popular tourist jacket that proclaimed VESUVIUS 2, POMPEII 0. Anyone watching might only have been surprised at how easily they flagged down a central city taxi.

"Driver?" Sandoz asked as John belted him into the back seat. He sounded close to tears. The crowds, John supposed, and the noise. The fear of being recognized and mobbed.

"Brother Edward," John told him.

Edward Behr, in a cabbie's uniform, raised a dimpled hand in greeting from the front seat before turning his attention back to the streets. Outlawing private vehicles in the city had reduced the density of traffic but acted as Darwinian selection pressure for the most combative drivers. Edward Behr was, for good reason, an exceptionally careful driver.

John Candotti settled into the seat next to Sandoz and got comfortable, pleased with himself and with the day and with the world. "A clean getaway," he said aloud as Edward pulled onto the clogged autostrada to Naples. He turned to Sandoz, hoping that he'd caught the infectious, boyish spirit of getting away with something, of skipping school for a day of stolen freedom . . . And saw instead a desperately tired man, slumped in the seat beside him, eyes closed against a jarring, exhausting journey through the city, against new pain layered over scurvy's constant hemorrhagic ache and a damnable bone-deep weariness that rest could not remedy.

In the silence, John's eyes met those of Brother Edward, who had seen the same man in the rearview mirror, and he watched Ed's smile fade, just as his own did. They were quiet after that, so Brother Edward could better concentrate on feathering the turns and smoothing out the ride while driving as fast as he dared.

THE ROUTINELY AWFUL traffic through the Rome-Naples sprawl was made worse by additional security checkpoints, but Giuliani had eased their way and they got through relatively quickly, stopping only to let young soldiers mirror the undercarriage and make cursory searches through the luggage. It was just dusk when they arrived at the Naples house, a Tristano design from the early 1560s—uninspired but sturdy and practical. They were met at the door by a mercifully taciturn priest, who escorted them without fuss to their quarters.

Brother Edward accompanied Sandoz inside his room and watched as Emilio lowered himself to the bed and lay back, inert, an arm thrown across his eyes against the overhead light.

"I'll unpack for you, shall I, sir?" Edward asked, setting the valise on the floor.

There was a small sound of assent so Edward began putting clothes in the bureau. Taking the braces out of Sandoz's bag, he hesitated: it was he and not Emilio who had begun to look for excuses to avoid the practice sessions. "Skip them tonight, sir?" he suggested, straightening from the bureau drawer and turning toward the man on the bed. "Let me bring you something to eat and then you can get some sleep."

Sandoz gave a short hard laugh. " 'To sleep: perchance to dream.' No, Edward, sleep is not what I need tonight." He moved his legs over the side of the bed and sat up, holding an arm out. "Let's get it over with."

This was what Edward had come to dread: the moment when he had to help Emilio fit the terrible fingers into their wire enclosures and then tighten the harnesses around his elbows, making sure the electrodes were seated firmly against atrophying muscles now compelled to do double duty.

The bruises never went away. Often, as tonight, clumsy in his desire to be gentle, Edward took too long with the task and Emilio would hiss with pain, strain engraved in his face as Edward whispered useless apologies. And then there would be a silence until Sandoz opened his damp eyes and began the methodical process of activating the servos that brought thumb to finger, from smallest to largest, one by one, right hand and then left, over and over, as the microgears whirred spasmodically.

I hate this, Brother Edward thought again and again as he kept vigil. I hate this. And watched the clock so he could call a halt to it as soon as possible.

Sandoz never said a thing.

AFTER UNPACKING, JOHN Candotti found the refectory. Having ascertained that Brother Edward had already taken care of Emilio's meal and his own, John took a light supper in the kitchen, chatting with the cook about the retreat's history and what it was like to be there when the volcano erupted.

"There's a real wood fire lit in the commons," Brother Cosimo told John while he finished a plateful of mussels and pasta. "Illegal but not likely to be detected out here on the coast." The wind would disperse the evidence. "A brandy, Father?" Cosimo suggested, handing Candotti a glass, and since John could think of no sensible objection to this remarkably attractive idea, he followed the cook's directions to the hearth, where he intended to luxuriate in the warmth shamelessly.

The common room was dark, except for the flickering light from the fireplace. He could dimly see little groups of furniture around the edges of the room but headed straight for one of a pair of high-backed, upholstered chairs facing the fire and sank onto the nearest, settling into the comfort with no more thought than a cat. It was a beautiful room—mellow walnut paneling, an ornate mantel, carved centuries before but dusted and polished on this very day—and he found he could imagine a time when trees were so abundant that wood could be used freely like this, for decoration, for warmth.

He had just stretched his feet out toward the fire and was wondering idly if the next Pope's election would be signaled with a sign that said "White Smoke" when, as his eyes adjusted to the dark, he realized that Sandoz was standing near the tall mullioned windows, looking down at the shoreline far below, its rocks glimmering in the moonlight, waves lacing the beach.

"I thought you'd be asleep by now," John said quietly. "Rough trip, huh?"

Sandoz didn't reply. He began to pace, restless despite the obvious fatigue, sat down briefly in a chair far from Candotti, and then stood again. Close, John thought. He's very close.

But when Sandoz spoke, it wasn't what John hoped for or expected—a cleansing breakdown, a confession that could make way for the man to forgive himself, the pouring out of a story with a plea for understanding. Some sort of emotional release.

"Do you experience God?" Sandoz asked him without preamble.

Odd, how uncomfortable the question made him. The Society of Jesus rarely attracted mystics, who generally gravitated to the Carmelites or the Trappists, or wound up among the charismatics. Jesuits tended to be men who found God in their work, whether that work was scholarly or more practical social service. Whatever their calling, they devoted themselves to it and did so in the name of God. "Not directly. Not as a friend or a personality, I suppose." John examined himself. "Not, I think, even 'in a tiny whispering sound.'" He watched the flames for a while. "I would have to say that I find God in serving His children. 'For I was hungry and you fed me, I was thirsty and you gave me to drink, I was a stranger and you welcomed me, naked and you clothed me, sick and you cared for me, imprisoned and you came to me.'"

The words lingered in the air as the fire popped and hissed softly. Sandoz had stopped pacing and stood motionless in a far corner of the room, his face in shadows, firelight glittering on the metallic exoskeletons of his hands. "Don't hope for more than that, John," he said. "God will break your heart." And then he left.

AND WENT ALONE to the room he'd been given and stopped short, seeing that the door had been closed. He felt a volcanic anger well up as he struggled with his hands but forced himself to beat the rage down, to concentrate on the simple tasks of opening the door and then leaving it open a hand's breadth behind him, the horror of being caged now only barely stronger than the urge to kick it shut. He wanted very badly indeed to hit something or to throw up and tried to control the impulses, sitting in the wooden chair, hunched and rocking over his arms. The overhead light had been left on, making the headache worse. He was afraid to stand and walk to the switch.

The nausea passed and when he opened his eyes, he noticed an old ROM periodical with a windowed memo overlaying the text, lying on the night table next to the narrow bed. He stood to read it. "Dr. Sandoz," the memo said, "there has been a reconsideration of Mary Magdalene in the years of your absence. Perhaps you will be interested in the new thinking. —V."

The vomiting went on long past the point when there was anything left to bring up. When the sickness abated, he stood, sweating and trembling. Then he willed his hands to grasp and smash the ROM tablet against the wall, wiped his mouth on his sleeve, and turned toward the door.

7

CLEVELAND AND SAN JUAN:
2015–2019

FINISHED AT JOHN Carroll and asked for a preference, Emilio Sandoz requested that he be sent back to La Perla in Puerto Rico. The request should have gone through the Antilles Province for administrative review, but Emilio was not surprised when Dalton Wesley Yarbrough, the Provincial in New Orleans, called him.

"Milito, you sure? We got a professorship for you up at Le Moyne, now we done jerkin' you around. Ray's been chewin' everybody's ear off 'bout getting you for that linguistics position," D.W. said. The Texas twang was nearly impenetrable unless you knew him well. D.W. could speak standard English when he pleased but, as he told Emilio once, "Son, with the vows we take, there's a limited range of opportunity for eccentricity. I get my laughs where I can."

"I know," Emilio said, "and Le Moyne's got a great department but—"

"Weather ain't that bad in Syracuse," D.W. lied cheerfully. "And La Perla ain't forgot nothin', son. Won't be no welcome-home parties."

"I know, D.W.," Emilio said seriously. "That's why I should go back. I need to put some ghosts to rest."

Yarbrough thought that over. Was it affection that made him want to agree, or guilt? D.W. had always felt about half responsible for the way things had turned out, good and bad. That was arrogant; Emilio had made his own decisions. But D.W. had seen the potential in the boy and hadn't hesitated a minute when he'd gotten a chance to pull the kid out of La Perla. Emilio had more than lived up to his expectations; still, there'd been a price to pay. "Well, okay then," D.W. said finally. "I'll see what I can do."

Entering his office two weeks later, Emilio spotted the glowing message light. His hands shook a little as he opened the file and he was tempted to blame this on the Turkish coffee he'd developed an unholy taste for, but he knew it was nerves. Once he admitted that, he was able to bring himself back to calmness. *Non mea voluntas sed Tua fiat,* he thought. He was prepared to do as he was bidden.

His request had been accepted without comment by the provincials concerned.

IN DECEMBER, HE called Anne and George Edwards from San Juan, spending the extra money for a viewer because he wanted to see their faces and them to see his. "Come and work with me," he said. The clinic was losing its National Service doctor and no one was willing to replace him. Would Anne? George, with the omnicompetence of a life-long engineer and householder, could renovate buildings, teach kids a hundred practical arts, reactivate the net that would link Anne with the larger hospitals and the kids with outside teachers.

Before they could react, he told them about La Perla, in stark statistical detail. He had no illusions and refused to let the Edwardses harbor any. All they could hope for was a chance of salvaging a few lives out of the thousands of souls cramming the slum.

"Well, I don't know," Anne said doubtfully, but he could see her eyes, and he knew. "Promise me there'll be lots of knife fights?"

Hand raised, he swore, "Every weekend. And gunshot wounds, too. And car wrecks." They all knew it was gallows humor. There would be babies born to thirteen-year-olds who would show up at the clinic with "stomachaches." Backs and shoulders wrenched, wrists damaged, knees torn at the kapok factory. Hands opaline with infected cuts, gone bad from the bacteria and toxins in the offal at the fish-processing plant. Sepsis, diabetes, melanomas, botched abortions, asthma, TB, malnutrition, STDs. Liquor and drugs and hopelessness and rage pounded deep into the gut. "The poor you will always have with you," Jesus said. A warning, Emilio wondered, or an indictment?

He saw Anne look at George, who sat thinking awhile. "The whole damned baby boom is retiring. Sixty-nine million old farts playing golf and complaining about their hemorrhoids." George snorted. "It's only a matter of time until someone opens up Funerals 'R' Us."

"I can't see either of us taking up golf," Anne said. "We may as well go, don't you think?"

"Right. We're outta here," George declared.

And so, in May of 2016, Anne and George Edwards moved into a rented house in Old San Juan, eight flights of stairs up the hill from the clinic Anne took over. Emilio took some time off to help them settle in. Once they had a bed, their first concern was finding a big wooden table with an assortment of chairs to go around it.

EMILIO BEGAN HIS own work simply: cleaning up the mission's physical plant, organizing and surveying things, quietly getting acquainted with the neighborhood again. He worked within the existing programs, at first—the baseball league, the after-school stuff.

But he was always alert to the possibility that this child or that one could climb out and escape, if someone cared. He bought a lot of *bolita* tickets, giving the numbers away but keeping track of children with a talent for statistics, luring them to George, who let them play with his web links and who began tutoring a couple of kids who might do well in math. He found a child, a young girl, weeping over a dog hit by a car, and brought Anne her first assistant, Maria Lopez, eleven and good-hearted and ready to learn.

And there was a little horror named Felipe Reyes who hawked stolen goods right outside the clinic, a boy with the foulest mouth the widely experienced Anne Edwards had ever encountered. Emilio listened to the kid using two languages to excoriate passersby who wouldn't buy from him and said, "You are the worst salesman I ever met but 'mano, can you talk!" He taught Felipe to curse in Latin and eventually got him to serve Mass and help around the Jesuit Center.

Anne spent the first months in the clinic reading through the records, getting a grim feel for the kind of medicine practiced here. She dealt with the business of inventories and inspections, upgrading the equipment, restocking the supplies, while tending to the immediate calls for care: the severed finger, the infections, high-risk pregnancies and pre-mature births, the giardiasis, the gunshot wounds. And she gradually learned who among her medical colleagues on the island was willing to take referrals from her.

George settled in as well, making endless lists, changing the locks on every door, window and storage cabinet in the clinic, overhauling the software linking the Jesuit Center with webs and libraries, installing the used but serviceable medical equipment Anne ordered. For his own sat-isfaction, he signed up at the Arecibo Radio Telescope as a docent, in-dulging his own long-latent interest in astronomy.

That was where he met Jimmy Quinn, who would lead them all to Rakhat.

"GEORGE," ANNE ASKED at breakfast one morning, a few months after they'd moved to Puerto Rico, "has Emilio ever said any-thing to you about his family?"

"No, I don't believe so, now that you mention it."

"Seems like we should have met them by now. I don't know. There are undercurrents in the neighborhood I don't understand," Anne ad-mitted. "The kids adore Emilio, but the older people are pretty distant." More than distant, really. Hostile, she thought.

"Well, there're a lot of little evangelical churches in La Perla. Maybe it's some kind of religious rivalry. Hard to tell."

"What if we gave a party? At the clinic, I mean. Might break the ice."

"Sure," George shrugged. "Free food is always a good draw."

So Anne took care of the refreshments with the help of a few women in the neighborhood she'd made friends with. To her surprise, the very unpaternal George waded into the preparations and the fiesta it-self with great enthusiasm, handing out sweets and little toys, setting off homemade rockets, blowing up balloons and generally being silly with the kids. And Emilio astonished her as well, doing magic tricks, of all things, working the crowd of children with the timing of a professional, provoking screams and peals of laughter, drawing in the mothers and grandmothers, the aunts and older brothers and sisters as well.

"Where the hell did you learn to do magic tricks?" she whispered to him afterward, as shoals of kids passed around and between the legs of adults dishing out ice cream.

Emilio rolled his eyes. "Do you have any idea how long the nights are near the Arctic Circle? I found a book. And I had a *lot* of time to practice."

When it was all over, Anne walked back into the office after seeing the last of the children off and found herself in the midst of an argument between her two favorite men.

"He believed you," Emilio cried, sweeping up the colored paper and confetti.

"Oh, he did not! He knew I was kidding," George said, stuffing trash into a bag.

"What? Who believed what?" Anne asked, going to work on the ice cream debris. "There's a dish under that desk, sweetheart. Can you get that for me?"

Emilio fished the bowl out and stacked it with the others. "One of the kids asked George how old he was—"

"So I told him I was a hundred and sixteen. He knew it was a joke."

"George, he's only five! He believed you."

"Oh, swell. Nice way to get to know people in the neighborhood, George. Lie to their kids!" Anne said, but she was grinning and laughed as the two men launched into a good-natured dispute over the moral distinction between lying to children and stand-up comedy. Both of these guys should have been daddies, Anne thought, watching them, alight with the simple satisfaction of pleasing children. It saddened her a little, but she didn't dwell on it.

The first fiesta was such a success that others, larger and even more fun, followed. There was always some health issue tied in. Anne handed out condoms and birth-control information to everyone over the age of eleven, or did immunizations for kids under six, or checked for head lice or took blood-pressure readings. The week after a fiesta always brought in more patients than usual, people with "little questions," which often turned out to be serious medical problems they'd endured for years. George started spending more time at the J-Center and a couple of new kids began to meet him there. It was small stuff but enough to make them feel they were making some headway. People seemed glad they had come.

As time went on, Anne heard pieces of Emilio's story, which seemed to involve a seriously screwed-up family and a fair bit of ugly commerce. Not terribly surprising, considering. As a member of a generation that spilled its guts in public with unedifying displays of Olympic-level whin-

ing, Anne had mixed feelings about Emilio's silence. Unexamined nasti-
ness could fester and poison lives; on the other hand, she admired the
ability to shut up and carry on. Emilio was certainly within his rights not
to reveal the sordid details of his childhood even to his friends. Or perhaps especially to his friends, whose good opinion of him, he might feel,
would not survive the revelations. So, while she was curious, Anne felt
her interest was intrusive and never asked him about his family.

Of course, that didn't keep her from looking for people in the neighborhood who resembled him. To her anthropologist's eye, Emilio's face
had a distinctive changeable quality. One minute, he could look like a
Hollywood Spaniard—black beard and imperial eyes, his face vivid and
alive with intelligence; the next, all she could see was the enigmatic
structure hard beneath the skin, the Taino endurance bred in the bone.
She saw the same qualities in a dignified woman at the flower market
who could have been his older sister. But Emilio had never even mentioned if he had sisters or brothers, and Anne knew that when someone
is that reticent about something so ordinary, there is usually good reason. So she was not completely unprepared for the way she found out
that Emilio did indeed have a brother. What took her by surprise was her
own response to the priest himself.

She was alone at the house that night, doing a literature search on
clubfoot for one of her patients, when Emilio called and asked her to
meet him at the clinic. His speech was slurred, and she could not believe
him drunk. "Emilio, what's happened? What's wrong?" she asked, startled by how frightened she was.

"Splain when you get here. Hard to talk."

George was up at the Arecibo telescope for some kind of late-night
shoot he was interested in. Anne phoned to let him know what was going on, not that she knew much herself, and asked him to come home
right away. Then she hurried down the eighty stairs to the clinic. The office looked deserted when she got there, and she wondered if she'd misunderstood what Emilio had wanted her to do. But she found to her
relief that the door was unlocked and Emilio was waiting inside, sitting
alone in the dark.

Anne touched on the light, drew one breath at the sight of him and
in the next, drew on clinical detachment as deliberately as she did her
gown and gloves. "Well, Father," she commented dryly, taking his chin
in her hand and inspecting his face from side to side, gentleness belying

her tone, "I see you turned the other cheek. Repeatedly. Don't laugh. You'll split the lip open again."

She'd seen enough of this kind of thing to stoop down and check his knuckles for abrasions and broken bones. His hands were unmarked. She frowned up at him, still holding his hands, but his eyes slid away. Sighing, she stood and unlocked the supply room, where she opened a cabinet, getting out what she needed. His pupils had reacted properly and he had been able to call her; the slurred speech was not neurological in origin; there was no concussion, but his face was a mess. As she assembled the supplies, he spoke quietly from the next room.

"I think a rib broke. I heard something crack."

She hesitated a moment and then returned to him, loading the pressure-injection gun with a dose of an immune-system booster. "Because of the cuts," she told him, holding the gun up for him to see. "Can you unbutton your shirt or do you need help?"

He managed the buttons but couldn't pull the bloodied shirt out of his jeans. Maybe whoever beat him up didn't know he was a priest, she thought, wondering if it would have made a difference. She helped him with the shirt, pulling it down off his arms, careful not to touch him unnecessarily. He was the color of maple syrup, she decided, but she said merely, "You're right about the rib." She could see the bruise on his back where the blow had landed and popped the bone outward. Kicked him when he was down, whoever it was. Aiming for a kidney but a little high. The lungs sounded clear, but she helped him move to the portable imager and did a torso scan to check for internals. While she waited for the image, she used the injection gun on him and then sprayed anesthetic on the cut over his eye. "This is going to need stitches but I can do the rest with bioadhesive."

The scan looked okay. Greenstick fracture in the right sixth rib, hairline in the seventh. Painful, not dangerous. The anesthetic took hold quickly. He sat there silently, letting her clean his face up and pull the cuts together.

"Okay, here's the hard part. Put your arms up and let me get the ribs wrapped. Yeah, I know," she said softly, when he gasped. "This is going to be wicked for the next week or so. I don't recommend sneezing anytime soon."

She was honestly surprised at how difficult she found it, being so close to him. Until that moment, she'd have sworn that she had long ago come to terms with getting old, and being childless. This beautiful man made her reassess both assumptions. He kept going in and out of focus: son, lover. It was completely inappropriate. But Anne Edwards was not given to self-deception and she knew what she was feeling.

She finished taping him up and let him catch his breath while she reloaded the gun. Without asking permission, she pressed the nozzle against his arm for the second time and told him, "You can offer up your suffering tomorrow. Tonight, you're going to sleep. We've got about twenty minutes to get you into a bed." He didn't argue; it was too late, in any case. She put the gun back and helped him into his shirt, letting him button it himself while she put things away.

"Want to tell me about it?" she asked finally, perching on the edge of her desk. He looked up at her through the hair falling over his forehead, black against the bandages. The bruise on his cheek is going to be spectacular, Anne thought.

"No. I don't think so."

"Well," she said quietly, steadying him as he got to his feet, "I'll assume you didn't get into a fight over a girl in a bar, but I can come up with more lurid explanations if you don't want to indulge my vulgar curiosity."

"I went to see my brother," he said, glancing into her eyes.

So he has a brother, she thought. "And he said, Welcome back, Emilio, and beat the shit out of you?"

"Something like that." There was a silence. "I tried, Anne. I gave it an honest try."

"I'm sure you did, sweetheart. Come on, let's go home."

They left the clinic and started up the stairs, the priest already too dopey to be aware of the stares and questions that Anne shook her head at. George met them about halfway. Light as Emilio was, it took both the Edwardses to get him up the last flight of stairs and into the house. He stood swaying as Anne turned down the guest bed while George got him undressed. "Sheets?" he asked blurrily, apparently worried about getting blood on the linens.

"Nobody gives a damn about the sheets," George told him. "Just get into bed." He was asleep before the covers settled over him.

ANNE CLOSED THE guest-room door and, in the dark hallway, she reached out for George's familiar arms. Neither of them was entirely surprised that she cried. He held her for a long time and then they went into the kitchen. While she heated up their supper, Anne told him about some of it, and he guessed more than she might have given him credit for.

They moved into the dining room, pushing the clutter on the table off to one side, and ate in silence for a while.

"Do you know what made me fall in love with you?" George asked suddenly. Anne shook her head, puzzled that he should ask her this now. "I heard you laugh, down the hall, just before I got to Spanish class that first day. I couldn't see you. I just heard this fabulous laugh, like a whole octave, top to bottom. And I had to hear it again."

She put her fork down gently and came around the table to stand by his chair. His hands went around her hips and she pulled his head to her belly, cradling it against her body. "Let's live forever, old man," she said, smoothing the silver hair away from his face and bending to kiss him. He grinned up at her.

"Okay," he agreed amiably, "but only because it'll really piss off that insurance guy you bought the annuities from."

And she laughed, a full octave, descending from high C like chimes.

THE NEXT MORNING, Anne got up early after a bad night, pulled on a white terry robe and went to look in on Emilio. He was still sleeping heavily, in almost the same position they'd left him in. She could hear George in the kitchen making coffee, but she wasn't ready to face him yet. Instead, she went into the bathroom and closed the door. Dropping the robe off her shoulders, Anne turned to a full-length mirror.

There she inspected the results of a lifetime of disciplined diet and decades of rigorous ballet classes. Her body had never been thickened by childbearing. At menopause, she'd begun hormone replacement, ostensibly because she was at risk for heart trouble and osteoporosis—a small-boned blue-eyed blonde who'd smoked for twenty years before giving it up in med school. In reality, without the compensation of children, she'd clung to the illusion of relative youth with the artificial extension of middle age. It was okay to be old, as long as she didn't look it. All in all, she was pleased with what she saw.

And so she forced herself to imagine Emilio's eyes on her, to work through in thought any conceivable scenario in which he could come to her as she was now. She did not look away from the mirror: an act of will.

At last she turned from her image, done with the exercise, and ran the shower. A son-in-law, she thought as the water beat down on her shoulders. A Sagadese son-in-law, with whom an old woman could flirt and joke outrageously across a clear generational distance. That came close to the need she felt. Anthropology to the rescue, after all these years.

Then she stopped moving and wondered what Emilio needed. Son, then, she thought. Like a son.

She turned off the water and stepped out onto the rug, dried herself, and dressed in jeans and a T-shirt. Occupied with morning rituals, she nearly forgot the night's distress. But before Anne left the bathroom, she took one last look at herself in the mirror. Not bad for an old bat, she thought briskly, and startled George by grabbing his ass when she passed him in the hallway.

THE HOUSE WAS empty when Emilio awoke. He lay quietly for a long while, getting his bearings, remembering how he came to be in this bed. Finally, the dull pounding in his head convinced him he'd feel better upright. Using his arms and stomach muscles, trying to keep his chest still, he sat. And then stood, holding on to the headboard.

There was a bathrobe on the chair next to his bed, with a new toothbrush stuck prominently in the pocket, where he'd be sure to see it. His clothes had been cleaned and were stacked, folded, on a bureau. There was a bottle of tablets sitting on the nightstand with a note from Anne. "Two when you wake up. Two before bed. They won't make you groggy. There's coffee in the kitchen." He wondered briefly what *groggy* meant. Nauseous, he guessed from context, but made a mental note to look it up.

Standing in the bathroom, he decided against a shower, not sure what to do about the tape holding his rib in. He cleaned up as best he could and stared blankly at his reflection, noting the flamboyant colors and the swelling. A sudden wave of panic overcame him as he wondered what day and time it was, afraid it was Sunday and that his small congregation had been let down by his failure to appear. No, he remembered. It must be Saturday. Young Felipe Reyes would have been the only one at the chapel, ready to serve. He laughed, anticipating the fantastic Latin dressing down he was in for from Felipe, but the pain in his chest stopped him cold and he realized that raising the Host was going to be a real struggle the next day. He remembered Anne's voice the night before. "You can offer up your suffering tomorrow." She was being sarcastic, but she understood.

He dressed slowly. In the kitchen, Anne and George had left fresh bread and oranges for him. He was still a little sick to his stomach, so he took only a cup of black coffee, which helped the headache.

It was about two in the afternoon when he was ready to leave. Emilio permitted himself one heartfelt obscenity and steeled himself for a very public walk back to his little apartment, down near the beach.

He gave a different story to each person who stopped him, the explanations becoming funnier and more extravagantly improbable as he worked his way home. People who'd never spoken to him before now laughed at his replies and shyly offered help. The kids rallied and ran errands for him, bringing offers of food from their mothers. Felipe was jealous.

He was able to use only his left arm to raise the consecrated bread and wine, but Mass the next morning was the best attended since he'd returned to Puerto Rico. Even Anne came.

8

ARECIBO:

MAY 2019

THAT SPRING, JIMMY Quinn's written proposal to Dr. Yano-guchi was routed through the ISAS channels, discussed and approved. Sofia Mendes was hired by arrangement with her broker, who agreed to the competitive aspect of the proposition. Mendes herself laid out crystalline criteria for how success or failure would be judged. There was a period of negotiation but in the end, ISAS accepted her terms. If she won, her broker was to receive three times her normal fee, enough to clear her debt. If she lost, ISAS could accept the program with its limitations known, but pay nothing. Her broker could then legally extend her contract for treble the time it took her to do the ISAS project. Jimmy was delighted.

Sofia Mendes, wrapping up her Singapore project in late April and preparing for the ISAS job, was not delighted. She maintained a cold neutrality, concentrating on what was, blocking out what might be. She had survived because, by heritage and experience, she knew how to see reality unclouded by emotion. It was a talent that had served her family well for centuries.

Before the expulsion of the Jews from Spain in 1492, the ancient Mendes were bankers, financiers to royalty. Hounded out of Iberia, they were welcomed by the Ottoman Empire, which gladly accepted the Sephardic merchants and astronomers, physicians and poets, archivists, mathematicians, interpreters and diplomats, the philosophers and the bankers like the Mendes, whom their Catholic majesties, Ferdinand and Isabella, drove from Spain. The Sephardim quickly became the most productive and energetic people in the empire, their society adorned at the top by notables who served successive sultans, as their forebears had served in Spanish courts. The culture that gave the world the Talmud and the towering physician-philosopher Maimonides once again became influential and respected.

But things change. The Ottoman Empire became merely Turkey. The Mendes were represented in the twentieth century by quiet, accomplished people who did not speak of their historic glory to outsiders but did not let their children forget those days either. They wasted no time mourning the past; they did their best in the circumstances in which they found themselves, and their best was commonly superb. In that, Sofia was their heir. The money and influence were gone; the pride and clearheadedness and intelligence were not.

When Istanbul began tearing itself to rubble in the insanity that grew out of the Second Kurdish War, Sofia Mendes was thirteen. Her mother, a musician, was dead before Sofia's fourteenth birthday: a random mortar shell in the afternoon. Within weeks, her father, an economist, was missing, probably dead as well; he went to find food and never came back to the remains of their home. Her childhood, which had been books and music and love and learning, was finished. There was no way out of the city, sealed off by U.N. troops, left to devour itself in isolation. She was alone and destitute in a world of pointless carnage. By an eight-hundred-year-old Sephardic tradition, she had been since the age of twelve and a half *"bogeret l'reshut nafsha"*—an adult with authority over her own soul. The Torah taught, Choose life. And so, rather than die of pride, Sofia Mendes sold what she had to sell, and she survived.

Her clients were mostly half-grown boys crazed with violence and men who might have been decent husbands and good fathers once but who were now militiamen in a hundred vicious factions, all that remained of the brilliant cosmopolitan society that had once gloried in its diversity, as had San Francisco, Sarajevo, Beirut. She learned to get the money or the food first and she learned to take her mind elsewhere when her body was used. She learned that mortal fear resolves into lethal anger, that the men who cried in her arms were likely to try killing her before they left, and she learned to use a knife. She learned what every-one learns in war. Living through it is all that matters.

The Frenchman picked her from the line of girls at the corner because even after a year and a half on the streets, she was still beautiful. Jean-Claude Jaubert was always attracted by contrasts: in this case, the pale skin and the black hair, the well-marked brows; the aristocratic carriage and the dirty schoolgirl uniform; youth and experience. He had money, and there were still things to be had in Istanbul if you could pay. He in-sisted on dressing her properly, providing a hotel room with running wa-ter, where she could bathe, and a meal, which she did not bolt down despite evident hunger. She accepted all this and what came after, without gratitude or shame. He found her a second time and afterward, at dinner, they discussed the war, the outside world and Jaubert's business.

"I am a futures broker," he told her, leaning back from the table and settling his stomach over his belt. "I represent a group of investors who sponsor promising young people in difficult circumstances."

He had made his fortune in the Americas, where he'd mined slums and orphanages for bright, determined children whose feckless or dying parents could provide neither an environment nor an education ade-quate to develop their offsprings' potential. "Brazil, of course, was the first to privatize their orphanages," he told her. Burdened by hundreds of thousands of children, abandoned or orphaned by HIV and TB and cholera or just running wild, the government had finally given up pre-tending that it could do anything with these kids. Jaubert's backers had another way.

"Everyone wins," Jean-Claude Jaubert explained. "The taxpayers' burden is reduced, the children raised in a proper manner, fed and edu-cated. In return, the investors receive a percentage of the children's earn-ings for life."

A lively secondary market had developed, a bourse where one could invest in an eight-year-old who'd tested extraordinarily high in mathematical ability, where one could trade rights to the earnings of a medical student for those of a talented young bioengineer. Liberals were horrified, but men like Jaubert knew that the practice gave children a monetary value, which made them less likely to be shot during street-cleaning sweeps through the slums.

"And yet," Jaubert told her, "I think that the most promising and spirited young people are depressed by the lifelong contracts they are held to. They burn out, refuse to work. You can see perhaps what a waste this is." Jaubert proposed that a more equitable contract be drawn, lasting perhaps twenty years, which would include the years of training provided by the investors. "Brokers, such as I, will find work for the talent, who will receive a decent living wage. When released from the contract, mademoiselle, you would have a reputation, experience and contacts—a firm foundation upon which to build." It was necessary that Sofia be tested for various diseases and disabilities that might affect her work, of course. "Should anything untoward be detected," Jaubert told her, "you would be treated if possible and with your consent, naturally, *ma cherie*. The medical costs are added to the contracted debt."

It was Sofia herself who negotiated the clause allowing her to buy Jaubert out if she were able to earn his backers' investment, plus four percent over projected inflation, compounded annually over the contract life, in less than twenty years. Jaubert was delighted. "Mademoiselle, I applaud your business sense. It is a pleasure to work with someone as practical as she is beautiful!" The clause provided her with a motive to earn the highest fees as quickly as possible, a benefit to them both.

Their relationship from that time on was cordial. After the handshake that sealed their agreement, he never touched her again: Jaubert had his own code of ethics. Her tutors and trainers found her a machine for learning. Polyglot from childhood, she spoke Ladino, classical Hebrew, literary French, commercial English, as well as the Turkish of her neighbors and schoolmates. To these, the investors determined, she should add Japanese and Polish, to widen her sphere of usefulness. She had a natural bent toward AI analysis, which the investors lost no time in developing. In the great Sephardic tradition, her programs were distinguished by their strict logical clarity, the transitions from one subject to the next graceful and simple.

Jaubert was congratulated, and prospered along with his backers. He himself felt he had rescued something very fine when he found Sofia Mendes. Jaubert had seen self-possession and intelligence under the dirt and hunger, and his perception paid off handsomely.

What Sofia Mendes saw now, with vision unclouded by emotion, was an end to a time of bondage. All she had to do was learn an astronomer's job and then do it faster, cheaper and more accurately than he could do it himself. She resisted both hope and fear. Either could weaken you.

DR. YANOGUCHI INTRODUCED her to George Edwards on her first day at the dish. "Mr. Edwards is our most knowledgeable volunteer," Yanoguchi told her, as she shook the hand of a lean, silver-haired man the age her father would have been, had he lived. "We get quite a few tourists and school groups. He'll give you the standard tour, but don't hesitate to ask questions. George knows everything! And when you're finished, you can get started with Jimmy Quinn."

She was startled by the size of the Arecibo dish—three hundred meters in diameter, a vast aluminum bowl set into a natural depression in the mountains. Above the bowl, hundreds of tons of steerable antennae hung from cables connected to support towers anchored in the surrounding hills.

"It works just like an old-fashioned TV satellite dish," George said, wondering for a moment if she was too young to remember TV. It was hard to tell; the girl might have been twenty-four or thirty-four. "A radio telescope focuses every radio wave that hits it down toward a central collection point. The signals bounce off the dish to a system of amplifiers and frequency converters suspended above the bowl." He pointed things out as they walked along the edge of the dish. "From there, the signals travel down to the building that houses the processing equipment." The wind made it hard to hear, and George had to shout. "The astronomers use what's essentially a very fancy spectrometer to analyze the polarization, intensity and duration of the radio waves. Jimmy Quinn can explain how all that works, or you can ask me if you like."

George turned to her before they went inside. "Have you ever done anything like this system before?"

"No," she admitted, shivering. She should have realized it would be chilly in the highlands. And one had a sense of being overwhelmed at the beginning of a project. She was always starting from scratch and there was always the chance that, this time, she wouldn't be able to understand, that something would simply be beyond her. Sofia straightened her back. I am Mendes, she thought. Nothing is beyond me. "I'll manage," she said aloud.

George looked at her sideways for a moment and then reached past her to open the door to the main building. "I'm sure you will. Listen, if you don't have any plans next weekend, why not come down to San Juan for dinner . . ." And they went indoors.

Upon meeting Mr. Quinn for the first time, Sofia Mendes noted privately that it was evidently her day for being startled by the size of things. She was accustomed to being the smallest adult in nearly any gathering but she had never stood next to anyone as tall as Jimmy Quinn before. She had to reach up to shake his hand and momentarily felt herself to be ten years old, meeting a friend of her father's.

She followed him to his work space, Quinn ducking under doorways and pipes as they passed through aisles flanked by cubicles constructed from old-fashioned movable panels. As they walked, he pointed out the locations of the coffee machine and the WC, not seeming to notice that she could not see over the half-walls that rose only chest-high for him. When they arrived at his cubicle, Sofia noticed that he'd removed the middle drawer of his desk, probably to keep his knees from being bruised, she decided.

For his part, Jimmy was half in love with Sofia Mendes before they sat down. For one thing, she was the most beautiful girl he'd ever seen, in real life. And she'd made the first cut in his mind already by not saying anything about his height. If she managed to go one more minute without asking any stupid basketball questions or the odious "How's the weather up there?" he swore he'd marry her, but before he could propose, Sofia opened her notebook and asked him for an overview of his job.

Emilio had warned him that she was not much for small talk, so Jimmy began by walking her through the process of collecting data from a bright region called 12-75. "There's a stable configuration near the central engine of the system, with two very powerful jets at right angles to it, throwing off material at half the speed of light." He sketched on the screen as he spoke, using an open display so she could take notes while he talked. "Elizabeth Kingery is a light astronomer who thinks she's got a new way of finding out if there are two galaxies surrounding two black holes locked in orbit around each other, like this, see? And she wants to compare the data to quasars, which people think used to be twinned galaxies like 12-75. Are you following this?"

Mendes looked up from her notes and impaled him with a stare. Very bright, Emilio had told him. Don't underestimate her. Jimmy cleared his throat. "So, the idea is to map this region of the sky using both radio and light astronomy in synchronized observations. The as-

tronomer who originates the request gives the observatories at least two
or three times when we can do the work. We have to work around the
celestial conditions and the weather on Earth."

"Why not use orbiting observatories?"

"Liz doesn't have enough funding or clout for access. But you can
do a lot with land-based data. So. Anyway, you get a consensus on the
schedule and then you hope it doesn't rain or something, because that
messes things up. Sometimes if there's a narrow window, we gut it out
and do the work even if conditions are bad. Do you want to know about
that now?"

"Later, please. Just an overview for now."

"Sure. Let's see. Once we decide to go ahead, I have to check the
noise floor." She looked up. "That means I see if the target region is
emitting a signal strong enough to be detected above the background
noise. All electrical equipment generates electrical noise—electrons
banging around in the metal of the equipment itself. We chill the re-
ceivers down in liquid helium to keep them really cold, because cold
slows down the movement of the electrons and that reduces the noi—"
The stare again. "Right. You know that. Okay. If the target signal is really faint, we go around turning stuff off. Computers we aren't using for
the shoot, lights, air conditioners, whatever. Then I choose a calibration
signal—a known radio source. I shoot that to tune the system up."

"How do you choose the calibration target? Briefly, please."

"There's a huge catalog on-line and we pick one near the target signal. Usually I just look at the signal using a virtual oscilloscope. We
know what a signal from a calibration source is supposed to look like."

"And if the signal differs from expected?"

All business, Emilio said. Well, she has to eat . . .

"Mr. Quinn. If the signal differs from the expected?" she repeated,
dark brows raised, stylus poised.

"That's where the art comes in. Each one of these dishes is essentially handmade. They all have quirks—cabling problems, grounding
problems. The weather affects them, the time of day, the ambient noise.
You have to get to know a piece of equipment like this. And then when
you've eliminated everything, you have to use your intuition about what
could be causing distortions or interference or stray signals. One time,"
he said, warming up again, "we thought we had an ET signal, extraterrestrial. We got it every few months but nobody else could confirm.

Turned out it was the ignition of this one old school bus and we heard it every time the kids from that school came up here on a field trip."

The Stare. It already had a capital letter in his mind. "Listen," he said seriously, "I'm not just wasting your time telling funny stories. You have to know about stuff like this or your program is going to claim it's found intelligent life on Mars. And everyone knows there's only Australians there, right?"

She smiled, in spite of herself. "Ah," said Jimmy shrewdly. "I see you've worked with Australians."

For a moment, she struggled to return to sobriety but finally laughed. "There's no such thing as beer too warm to drink," she said with a very good Australian accent. Jimmy laughed then as well but, wisely, did not press his luck.

"HOW'S IT GOING?" George Edwards asked her, a month or so after she started. They met for lunch frequently, Sofia saving up questions to ask him on the days when he came to the dish.

"Slowly. Mr. Quinn is very cooperative," Sofia conceded, looking up at George from the thick coffee mug she held in both small hands, "but easily distracted."

"By you," George ventured, to see how she'd react, knowing that Jimmy was miserably besotted with a woman whose only interest seemed to be a relentless deconstruction of his brain, cell by cell. Sofia simply nodded. No blush, George noted, no compassion. She's not a romantic, that's for sure.

"It makes things difficult. Animosity is easier to deal with," she said, glancing across the cafeteria at Peggy Soong. George grimaced: Peggy could be a pain in the ass. "On the other hand, infatuation is preferable to condescension. I appreciate that you treat me as a competent professional, Mr. Edwards. It's nice to work without being patronized. Or chatted up."

"Well, I hope this doesn't count as chatting you up," George said dryly, "but that dinner invitation is still open. What do you say?"

She had decided, upon reflection, to accept his invitation if he repeated it. People were often hostile to her work and, by extension, to her; she had not been invited to anyone's home since childhood. "I'd be happy to come, Mr. Edwards."

"Good. Anne's been wanting to meet you. Sunday afternoon? About two?"

"That will be fine. Thank you. I have some questions about weather effects on radio reception, if you wouldn't mind," she said, setting her plate aside and pulling out her notebook. And they went on to business.

ON SUNDAY, SHE drove to San Juan, allowing time for the dreadful traffic. She parked with difficulty, found a flower stall with ease, and bought a bouquet for Dr. Edwards. She liked Puerto Rico, actually, and had been pleasantly surprised to find how close Spanish and Ladino were. There were spelling differences, divergences in vocabulary, but the basic words and grammar were often identical. She asked the flower vendor the way to the Edwardses' address and climbed the stair-street to the shell-pink stucco house she was directed to. The doors to an ironwork balcony overlooking the street were open, as were the windows, and she clearly heard a woman's voice call, "George? Did you get that pump fixed down in the clinic?"

"No, I forgot all about it." She recognized Mr. Edwards's voice. "Hell. I'll get to it. It's on the list."

A peal of laughter rang out. "So's world peace. I need the pump working tomorrow."

Sofia knocked. Anne Edwards, white hair pulled into a messy bun, flour up to her elbows, answered the door. "Oh, no!" she cried. "Not just brilliant but good bones as well. I do hope you have a terrible personality, dear," Anne Edwards declared. "Otherwise, I shall lose faith in a just God."

Sofia hardly knew how to respond, but George Edwards called from the kitchen, "Don't let her fool you. She gave up believing in a just God when Cleveland blew the World Series last year. The only time she ever prays is the ninth inning."

"And the night before a presidential election, for all the good it does. God is a Republican from Texas," Anne asserted, bustling Sofia into the living room. "Come into the kitchen and keep us company. Dinner's almost ready. The flowers are lovely, dear, and so are you."

They passed through the living room, a pleasing jumble of books and watercolors and prints, with mismatched but comfortable-looking furniture and quite a good Turkish rug. Anne noticed Sofia take it all in and waved her floury hands at the place dispiritedly. "We've only been here a year. I keep thinking I should do something about this place but there's never any time. Oh, well, maybe someday."

"I rather like it as it is," Sofia said honestly. "It looks like someplace where you could fall asleep on the sofa."

"Aren't you splendid!" Anne cried delightedly. Emilio often did exactly that. "Oh, Sofia, that is so much nicer than thinking it's just a plain mess!"

They joined George in the kitchen. He directed Sofia to what Anne called the Kibitzer's Stool and handed her a glass of wine, which she sipped as George finished slicing vegetables for the salad and Anne went back to whatever it was that involved flour. "George does all the knife work," Anne explained. "I can't afford to get cut. Too much risk of infection. I dress like an astronaut when I'm in the ER or the clinic but it's better to keep my hands out of harm's way. Do these cookies look familiar?"

"Why, yes. My mother used to make those," Sofia said, a little startled by the memory of meringue-topped sweets.

"Ah, lucky guess," Anne murmured. The menu had been easy and Anne had enjoyed putting it together. Sephardic cuisine was basically Mediterranean—light, sophisticated, emphasizing vegetables and spices. She'd found a recipe for *pandericas,* "rich lady's bread" served by Sephardim on Rosh Hashanah and other festive occasions. Peach melba, with the cookies, for dessert. "You'll have to tell me if the recipe's any good. I got it from a book."

THEY TOOK TURKISH coffees into the living room after dinner, and the conversation turned to music. It was George who noticed Sofia looking at the old piano against the wall. "It doesn't get a lot of use," he told her. "The last tenant left it in the house. We were going to give it away but then we found out that Jimmy Quinn can play, so we had the thing tuned last week."

"Sofia, do you play?" Anne asked. It was a simple question. The girl's hesitation was surprising.

"My mother was a music teacher so, of course, I had lessons when I was little," Sofia said finally. "I can't remember when I sat at a piano last." But she could remember. The time of day and the way the sunlight slanted through the window in the music room and her mother nodding and commenting and sitting down to demonstrate a different phrasing;

the cat jumping onto the keyboard only to be dumped unceremoniously onto the carpet, the practice session punctuated by occasional gunfire and the thud of a mortar shell landing somewhere nearby. She could remember everything, if she let herself. "I'm terribly out of practice."

"Well, give it a try," George said.

"Anyone who can make her own music is way ahead of me. All I can play is the radio. Sit down, Sofia," Anne urged, glad of some activity that might replace the fits and starts of conversation. Sofia was an appreciative but quiet guest, and the dinner was more subdued than Anne was used to or entirely happy with, although it was pleasant enough. "Did the tuner do a decent job or did we simply contribute to the general reek of Puerto Rican corruption?"

"No, truly, I can't recall a single piece," Sofia pleaded.

Her demurrer was dismissed, firmly but kindly, and although she was rusty, pieces came back to her. She lost herself for a few minutes, becoming reacquainted with the instrument, but only for a few minutes. She rose and would have made an excuse to leave, but George reminded her of the peach melba and she decided to stay a bit longer.

As they ate dessert, Anne urged her to come back any time to use the piano but knowing Sofia's attitude, she added, "I have to warn you. Jimmy Quinn comes down for dinner now and then, so you may run into him after hours." And then, as though it hadn't been on her mind all afternoon, "We have another mutual acquaintance, by the way. Do you remember Emilio Sandoz?"

"The linguist. Yes, of course."

"That was your cue to exclaim 'Small world!' He's the reason we're here actually," George said, and he sketched out the story of their coming to Puerto Rico.

"You are missionaries, then," Sofia said, trying not to sound as horrified as she was.

"Oh, God, no! Just plain old bleeding-heart, pain-in-the-ass liberal do-gooders," Anne said. "I was brought up Catholic but I drifted away from the Church years ago."

"Anne can still work up some Catholicism, with a couple of beers in her, but I'm a flat-out atheist. Still," George admitted, "the Jesuits do a lot of good work . . ."

They spoke for a little while about the clinic and the Jesuit Center. But then the talk veered off toward Sofia's work at the dish, Anne falling uncharacteristically silent as George explained a series of technical procedures to the young woman. There was a lightning brightness to the girl when she was working that made an interesting contrast to a rather appealing awkwardness in social things.

Yes, Anne thought, watching them, there it is. Now I see the attraction.

LATER THAT NIGHT, in bed, Anne nestled in close to George, who found himself a little breathless. Damn, he thought, I've got to start running again.

"Oh, sweet mystery of life at last I've found you," Anne sang. George laughed. "Lovely girl," Anne remarked, her mind shifting suddenly to Sofia, who was one of the few women Anne had ever met who merited the word exquisite: tiny and perfect. But so closed. So guarded. She had expected more warmth in a girl who'd attracted both Emilio and Jimmy. And probably George as well, if Anne was any judge, and she was. "Very bright. I can see why she set Emilio back on his heels. And Jimmy, too," she added as an afterthought.

"Hmmm." George was almost asleep.

"I could be a Jewish mother, if I put my mind to it. The real trouble with Jesus," Anne decided, "was that he never found a nice Jewish girl to marry and have a family with, poor thing. That's probably blasphemy, isn't it."

George got up on an elbow and looked at her in the dark. "Keep out of it, Anne."

"Okay, okay. I was only kidding. Go to sleep."

But neither of them did for a while, each thinking thoughts in the dark.

9

NAPLES:
APRIL 2060

J OHN C ANDOTTI WAS awake and dressing when he heard the knock, just after dawn.

"Father Candotti?" It was Brother Edward, calling quietly but urgently in the hallway. "Father, have you seen Emilio Sandoz?"

John opened the door. "Not since last night. Why?"

Behr, rumpled and pudgy, looked almost angry. "I just came from his room. His bed wasn't slept in and he's sicked up and I can't find him."

Pulling on his sweater, John pushed past Brother Edward and headed for Sandoz's room, unable to believe the man wasn't there.

"I cleaned up the mess. Lost everything he ate yesterday," Edward called behind him, wheezing, as they hurried down the hallway. "Although that was little enough. I already checked in the lavatories. He's not in there, I tell you."

John stuck his head into the room anyway and caught the lingering odor of vomit and soap. "Damn," he whispered fiercely. "Damn, damn, damn. I should have expected something like this! I should have been nearby. I would have heard him."

"It was my place to be here, Father. I don't know why I didn't insist on the room next door. But he doesn't usually need me at night anymore," Edward said, trying to explain his lapse to himself as much as to Candotti. "I would have looked in on him last night but I didn't want to interfere if he was— He told me he wanted to talk to you. I thought he might—"

"I thought so, too. All right, look. He can't be far away. Have you checked the refectory?"

Trying not to panic, they searched the building, John, for one, half-expecting to find Sandoz's body at each turn. He'd begun to wonder about contacting the Father General, or the police, when it occurred to him that Sandoz was from an island and might be down by the water. "Let's look outside," he suggested, and they left the main building on its western side.

The sun had hardly begun to climb and the stone balcony was still in shadow, as was the shoreline far below. Stunted trees, contorted by the prevailing winds off the Mediterranean, were covered with a gold and green haze, and farmers were already plowing, but the spring had been gray and cold—Vesuvius, everyone said. Anxiety and chill combined and John began to shiver as he leaned over the wall, eyes sweeping the coast.

Then, awash with relief, he spotted Sandoz and shouted against the wind, "Brother Edward? Brother Edward!" Edward, hunched against the cold with round arms crossed over his barrel chest, had headed for the garage to count the bicycles. He heard Candotti's voice indistinctly and turned back. "I see him," John yelled, motioning downward. "He's on the beach."

"Shall I go down and bring him back?" Edward called on his way back to the balcony.

"No," John yelled. "I'll get him. Grab a coat for him, okay? He must be freezing."

Brother Edward trundled off to get three coats. Returning minutes later, he helped John into the biggest one, handed him another to bring to Sandoz and pulled one on himself as John started down the long line of stairs that zigzagged downhill to the Mediterranean. Before he'd gotten far, Brother Edward stopped him with a shout.

"Father? Be careful."

What an odd thing to say, John thought, wondering for a moment if Brother Edward was concerned about his slipping on the damp stone stairs. Then John remembered the way Sandoz had come at him, that first day, back in Rome. "I will. It'll be okay." Brother Edward looked doubtful. "Really. If he hasn't done anything to himself, I don't think he'd hurt anyone else."

But he sounded more sure of that than he was.

THE WIND WAS carrying the sound of his footsteps away from Sandoz. Not wanting to startle him, John cleared his throat and made as much noise as he could, scuffling through the gravelly sand. Sandoz didn't turn but he stopped moving and waited near a large stone outcropping, part of the geological formation that had tithed its substance to the ancient buildings on the hill behind them.

John stopped as he drew even with the man and looked out over the water himself, watching shorebirds wheel and dip and settle on the gray water. "I have been suffering from horizon deprivation," he declared conversationally. "Feels good to be able to focus on something that's far away." John's own face and hands ached with cold. He was shuddering now and did not understand how Sandoz could be so still. "You gave us a scare, man. Next time, let somebody know when you're going out, okay?" He took a step closer to Sandoz, the jacket held casually in one outstretched hand. "Aren't you freezing? I brought you a coat."

"If you come near me," Sandoz said, "you'll bleed for it."

John let his arm drop, the coat brushing the rocky sand, unnoticed. Closer now, he saw that what he had taken for stillness was a coiled tension, wound too tightly to be seen from a distance. Sandoz turned away and reached out toward a line of fist-sized stones placed along the edge of a natural shelf in the rocks, the brace gleaming suddenly as the sunlight came at last over the bluff. His own body tensing in sympathetic concentration, John watched the muscles in Sandoz's back, outlined by sweat-dampened cloth, knotting convulsively as he worked to bring his fingers around a stone.

Sandoz turned back toward the Mediterranean, sparkling now in the morning light, and with the grace of an old ballplayer, cocked and threw. The fingers did not loosen in time and the rock thudded into the sand. Methodically, he went back to the shelf and once again gripped a stone, turned, stanced and threw. When he exhausted his supply of rocks, he went out to collect them again, leaning from the waist, grasping them with his left hand, gasping sometimes with the effort, but releasing them carefully one by one, in a row on the rocky shelf.

Most of the stones, heartbreakingly, were only a few steps from where he stood to throw them.

BY THE TIME the sun was overhead, Candotti had discarded his own coat, and he now sat on the beach, watching silently. Brother Edward had joined him and he watched as well, the tears rolling down his plump cheeks drying quickly in the wind off the sea.

Around ten o'clock, when the bruises had broken through to frank bleeding, Edward tried to talk to Sandoz. "Please, Emilio, stop now. That's enough." The man turned and looked through him as though one of them did not exist, the dark eyes unfathomable. John saw then that there was nothing to do except bear witness, and gently drew Ed away.

For two hours more, he and Brother Edward marked the painful progress Sandoz made, his fingers working more consistently for him, the stones beginning to land in the water more often than not, new ones taking their place on the rocky shelf. Finally, he was able to whip off a dozen in sequence, each sinking into the water a good distance beyond the shoreline. Shaking and gray-faced, Sandoz stared out at the sea a moment longer and then walked past the two men who had shared this morning with him. He did not pause or even glance at them as he drew near, but he spoke in passing.

"Not Magdalene," he said. "Lazarus."

IF VINCENZO GIULIANI was moved by what he witnessed that morning from the balcony, there was no sign of it in his face as he watched the three men make their way along the stone steps leading upward from the beach. Emilio stumbled badly, twice, on the way up. The white heat of anger that had seen him through the dawn had burned down to a dangerous snarling resentment and Giuliani could see him shake off the help he was offered by John Candotti and Brother Edward when he fell.

The men below had no idea that the Father General was not in Rome. He had, in fact, preceded them to the Naples house, taking up residence in the room next to the one given to Sandoz, where he waited patiently for the breakdown he was engineering. In the thirteenth century, the Dominicans proposed that the end justifies the means, Giuliani mused. The Jesuits took up that philosophy in their turn but multiplied the means, doing what seemed necessary in the service of God, for the good of souls. Deception, in the case before him, he deemed justifiable, preferable to a direct approach. So Vincenzo Giuliani had signed the note "V," knowing that only Voelker addressed Sandoz as "Doctor." Emilio's reaction tended to confirm the Contact Consortium's allegations about what had happened on Rakhat. And as Giuliani had gambled, the very idea that Voelker knew was enough to snap Emilio's brittle self-control.

It took almost half an hour for the little party to climb to the top of the cliff. As they approached, the Father General stepped back into the shadows, waiting to speak until they were near enough to be startled by the soft and unexpected words.

"Really, Emilio," Vincenzo Giuliani said in a dry, bored voice, "why not stumble again, in case someone has missed the symbolism? I'm sure Brother Edward has been meditating on Golgotha all the way up, but Father Candotti is a practical man and may have been distracted by the fact that he's long overdue for breakfast." He saw, without unseemly satisfaction, the fresh anger he had provoked and he continued in the same light, ironic tone. "I'll see you in my office in fifteen minutes. And get cleaned up. The carpets in that room are quite valuable. It would be a pity to bleed all over them."

THE MAN USHERED into Giuliani's office twenty minutes later had indeed been cleaned up, Giuliani observed, but he had not eaten since vomiting the previous evening and had not slept at all, after an exhausting trip out of the city. Sandoz looked waxen, the skin beneath his eyes purplish. And he had put himself through a hellish ordeal this morning. Good, Giuliani thought.

He did not invite Sandoz to sit but rather left him standing in the center of the room. Giuliani sat motionless behind the vast desk, outlined by the light from the window at his back, his face unreadable. Aside from the ticking of an ancient clock, there was no sound. When the Father General finally spoke, his voice was quiet and mild.

"There is no form of death or violence that Jesuit missionaries have not met. Jesuits have been hanged, drawn and quartered in London," he said quietly. "Disemboweled in Ethiopia. Burned alive by the Iroquois. Poisoned in Germany, crucified in Thailand. Starved to death in Argentina, beheaded in Japan, drowned in Madagascar, gunned down in El

Salvador." He stood and began to circle the room slowly, an old habit from his days as a history professor, but stopped for a moment by the bookcase to select an old volume, which he turned idly over and over in his hands as he spoke, strolling again, placing no special emphasis on any of his words. "We have been terrorized and intimidated. We have been reviled, falsely accused, imprisoned for life. We have been beaten. Maimed. Sodomized. Tortured. And broken."

He came to rest now in front of Sandoz, close enough to see the man's eyes glittering. There was no change in Emilio's face but the tremor was visible. "And we, who are vowed to chastity and obedience," he said very softly, holding Emilio's eyes with his own, "have made decisions, alone and unsupported, that have given scandal and ended in tragedy. Alone, we have made horrifying mistakes that would never have occurred in a community."

He had expected the shock of recognition, the look that comes when the truth is spoken. For a moment, Giuliani wondered if he had misjudged. But he saw shame, he was certain, and despair.

"Did you think you were the only one? Is it possible that you are so arrogant?" he asked, in tones of wonderment. Sandoz was blinking rapidly now. "Did you think you were the only one ever to wonder if what we do is worth the price we pay? Did you honestly believe that you alone, of all those who have gone, were the single man to lose God? Do you think we would have a name for the sin of despair, if only you had experienced it?"

Give the man credit for courage. He did not look away. Giuliani changed tactics. He sat down at the desk once more and picked up a notescreen. "The last report I received on your health tells me that you are not as sick as you seem. What was the term the physician used? 'A psychogenic somatic retraction.' I do hate jargon. I suppose he means you are depressed. I would put it more bluntly. I think you are wallowing in self-pity."

Emilio's head snapped up, face carved in wet stone.

For an instant, Sandoz looked like a bewildered child, slapped for weeping. It was so brief, so out of expectation, that it almost didn't register. Months later, and for the rest of his life, Vincenzo Giuliani would remember that instant.

"I, for one, am tired of it," the Father General continued matter-of-factly, sitting back in his chair and contemplating Sandoz like a master of novices. How strange, to be both a year younger and decades older than this man. He tossed the notescreen aside and straightened, hands folded on the desk in front of him, a judge about to pass sentence. "If you treated anyone else as you have treated yourself during the past six hours, you would be guilty of assault," he told Sandoz flatly. "This will cease. From this moment on, you will show your body the respect it deserves as God's creation. You will allow your arms to heal and then you will embark on a sensible and moderate course of physical therapy. You will eat regularly. You will rest properly. You will care for your own body as you would for that of a friend to whom you are indebted. In two months' time, you will appear before me and we will examine in detail the history of the mission upon which you were sent," Giuliani said, his voice hardening suddenly as he pronounced each word separately, "by your superiors."

And then, mercifully, Vincenzo Giuliani, Father General of the Society of Jesus, took back the awful burden that belonged to him and his predecessors by right. "During these months and for all time," he told Sandoz, "you will cease to arrogate to yourself responsibility that lies elsewhere. Is that clear?"

There was a long moment, but Emilio nodded almost imperceptibly.

"Good." Giuliani rose quietly and went to the door of his office. He opened it and was not surprised to see Brother Edward waiting, his anxiety plain. Candotti was seated a little way down the hall, hunched over, hands together between his knees, tense and tired.

"Brother Edward," the Father General said pleasantly, "Father Sandoz will be having some breakfast now. Perhaps you and Father Candotti would like to join him in the refectory."

10

SAN JUAN, PUERTO RICO:
AUGUST 2–3, 2019

LOOKING BACK ON what happened that warm August night, Anne Edwards always wished she'd dug out horoscopes for everyone at the dinner. It would have been an excellent test of astrology, she thought. Somewhere, under someone's sign, there should have been a warning: "Brace yourself. Everything changes tonight. Everything."

Emilio, when she asked him over for dinner on Saturday, had suggested with telling casualness that George might invite Jimmy Quinn and Sofia Mendes as well. Sure, Anne agreed, putting misgivings aside. The more, the merrier.

Emilio had not seen Sofia since Cleveland, and it was beginning to seem as though he was deliberately avoiding her, which was probably uncomfortably close to the truth. Well, Anne knew what it took to convert attraction to valued friendship and believed Emilio capable of it; she was willing to provide neutral ground for the task. And Sofia? An emotional anorexic, Anne diagnosed privately. That, perhaps, along with her beauty, was what drew men. Jimmy had long since confessed to his infatuation, unaware that Sofia'd had a similar effect on Emilio. And George, for that matter. And I'm in no position to complain, she thought. My God, all this misplaced sexual heat! The house is going to be flooded with pheromones tonight.

So, she decided, locking up the clinic on Saturday afternoon, my job is to make the evening feel like a family gathering, make the kids feel like cousins, maybe. Above all, she understood, it was necessary to avoid treating Emilio and Sofia, or even Jimmy and Sofia, as a couple. Keep it fun, she told herself firmly, and then keep out of it.

ON FRIDAY OF that week, Jimmy Quinn had begun explaining to Sofia the portion of his job involving the Search for Extraterrestrial Intelligence.

"The SETI work is similar to the rest of the observations but it's on the back burner," he told her. Headsets and gloves on, they felt themselves to be sitting in front of an old-fashioned oscilloscope, some VR engineer's idea of a joke. "When we aren't using the dish for anything else, SETI does a systematic scan for radio signals from other planets. The program flags anything that looks like a possible ET message—anything with a constant frequency that's not one of the known sources like registered radio broadcasts or military transmissions, things like that."

"I understand there are already very sophisticated pattern-recognition programs in place," Sofia said.

"Yeah. The SETI programs are old but they're good, and ISAS updated the signal-processing equipment when they took Arecibo over. So the system already knows how to screen out junk signals from things we know are nonsentient sources like hydrogen atoms vibrating or stars making noise." He pulled up an example. "See how crazy this looks? This is a star's radio signal. It's completely irregular and it sounds like this in audio," he said, making a breathy crackly noise through his teeth. He pulled up a new display. "Okay. Radio used for communication uses a constant frequency carrier with some kind of amplitude modulation. See the difference?" Sofia nodded. "SETI scans over fourteen million separate channels, billions of signals, looking for patterns in the noise. When the system picks out something interesting, it logs the time, the date, the source location, the frequency and the duration of the signal. The problem is the backlog of transmissions the SETI tech has to look at."

"So your job is to disprove the standing hypothesis that a transmission is intelligent communication."

"Exactly."

"So—" Stylus raised, flipping up one eyepiece, she settled herself to take in the next load of information. Jimmy took off his headset and gazed at her, until she cleared her throat.

"Can I ask you something first? It'll be quick," he assured her when she sighed. "Why do you take notes in longhand? Wouldn't it be easier to record these sessions? Or to type directly into a file?"

It was the first time anyone had asked her about her own methods. "I don't just transcribe what you tell me. I'm organizing the information as I listen. If I recorded the session, I'd have to take the same amount of time listening to it later as the original interview took. And over the years, I've developed a personal shorthand. I write faster than I can type."

"Oh," he said. It was the longest she'd ever talked. Not exactly a date but sort of a conversation. "Are you going to George and Anne's tomorrow night?"

"Yes. Mr. Quinn, please, can we move on?"

Jimmy replaced his headset and dragged himself back to the display. "Okay, I begin by taking a look at the flagged signals. A lot of them nowadays turn out to be coded transmissions from dope factories about five hundred kilometers out. They're always moving around, and they change frequencies all the time. Usually the software screens them out because they're so close to Earth, but sometimes the transmissions take an odd bounce off an asteroid or something and the signal looks as if it's coming from far away."

Jimmy began working his way through the log, becoming absorbed in the process, talking more to himself than to Sofia. Watching him with one eye, she wondered if men ever figured out that they were more appealing when they were pursuing their own work than when they were pursuing a woman. Slavering was hardly attractive. And yet, she was surprised to recognize, she had begun to like Jimmy Quinn very much. She shook the thought off. There was no place for it in her life and she had no wish to foster whatever fancies he might be nurturing. Sofia Mendes never promised what she could not deliver.

"That's interesting," Jimmy said. Sofia concentrated on the eyepiece image and saw a table-shaped signal. "See? There's a signal that comes out of the background noise, stays around for—lemme look up the duration. Here. It was there for about four minutes and then it dropped off." He laughed. "Well, hell, it's got to be something homemade. This part right here?" He pointed to the tabletop portion of the signal.

"A constant carrier frequency with amplitude modulation," she said.

"Bingo." He laughed. "It's gotta be local. We're probably picking up some religious broadcast from Tierra del Fuego bouncing off that new hotel Shimatzu is building. The one with the microgravity stadium?"

She nodded.

"Well, anyway, this gives me a chance to show you how I'd play around with a possible ET. See, the whole signal looks like a pulse when it's displayed like this," he said, tracing the tabletop shape with an electronic finger. "Now. I can focus on just this section along the top of the pulse, like this, and change the amplitude scale." He did so. The formerly straight horizontal line now looked jagged. "See? The amplitude varies . . . quite a bit, actually." His voice trailed off. It looked sort of familiar. "Got to be local," he muttered.

Sofia waited a few minutes as Jimmy fiddled with the signal. Triple time, she thought. "Mr. Quinn?" He flipped up an eyepiece to look at her. "Mr. Quinn, I'd like to begin with the details of the existing pattern-recognition software, if you please. Perhaps there is documentation I can work from."

"Sure," Jimmy said, killing the display, pulling off the VR equipment, and getting up. "We haven't transferred all that old stuff. The working programs are here but nobody does much with the documentation, so it's still archived on the Cray. Come on, I'll show you how to access it."

WHEN SOFIA MENDES arrived at the Edwardses' on Saturday evening, precisely on time and bearing a bottle of Golan Heights cabernet, Jimmy Quinn was already there, wired up and too loud, in stylishly bloused trousers, resplendent in a vividly colored shirt that would have fit Sofia like a bathrobe. She smiled in spite of herself at his patent pleasure in seeing her, thanked him for his compliment to her dress, and then to her hair, and not giving him any time to go further, handed the wine to Mr. Edwards and took shelter in the kitchen.

"Emilio might be a little late," Dr. Edwards told her, kissing her cheek. "Baseball game. Don't be alarmed if he shows up in a full-body cast, dear. His team's in second place and when it's that close, Father Sandoz plays ball for keeps."

But Sofia heard his voice only ten minutes later, announcing the score, clearly pleased with the result. Greeting George and Jimmy on the run, Sandoz came straight to the kitchen, hair still damp from his shower, shirttails flying, with flowers for Dr. Edwards, upon whom he bestowed a brief courtly kiss. Obviously at home, he reached past Anne for a vase on one of the shelves, filled it with water and put the flowers into it, arranging them a little before turning from the sink to take them out to the table. Then he saw Sofia, sitting on the stool in the corner, and his eyes warmed while his face remained gravely dignified.

Drawing one flower from Anne's bouquet, he tapped the moisture from it and inclined his head in a short, formal bow. *"Señorita. Mucho gusto. A su servicio,"* he said with exaggerated courtesy, a parody of the Spanish aristocrat who had so offended her before. Familiar now with the squalor of his childhood, she understood the joke this time and, laughing, accepted the flower. He smiled and, his eyes slowly leaving hers, turned to Jimmy, who'd just come into the kitchen, effectively jamming it with humanity. Anne hollered for everyone to clear out so she could move and Emilio pushed Jimmy back out of the room, picking up the thread of an argument Sofia couldn't follow about something they evidently fought over frequently and to no useful purpose. Anne handed her a platter of *banderillas* and they began ferrying food out to the table. The conversation quickly became general and lively. The meal was good and the wine tasted of cherries. It all contributed to what happened.

After dinner, they moved into the living room and Sofia Mendes felt herself relaxing in a way that she had never experienced as an adult. There was a kind of safety here that she found as exotic as a dogwood and as beautiful. She felt that she was wholly welcome, that people in this home were prepared to like her, no matter who she was or what she'd done. She felt she could tell Anne, or even George, about the days before Jaubert, and that George would forgive her and Anne would say that Sofia had been brave and sensible to do what she had to.

As dusk deepened into night, the conversation trailed off and Anne suggested that Jimmy play something, an idea that met with universal approval. He looked like a child looming over a toy piano, Sofia thought, his knees splayed to the outside, almost level with the keys, feet angled in toward the pedals. But he was a graceful and fluid player, his big hands easily dominating the keyboard, and she tried not to be embarrassed as he sang a rather obvious love song.

"Jimmy, I know you adore me, but try to be discreet," Anne said in a stage whisper, glancing at Sofia and hoping to change the mood before the boy dug himself in too deeply. "George is standing right here! And anyhow, this stuff is too damned sentimental."

"Come on, punk, get out of there," George ordered, laughing, waving Jimmy away from the piano. "Sofia, your turn."

"You play?" Jimmy asked, knocking over the piano bench in his haste to vacate for her.

"A little," she said and added honestly, "not so well as you."

She began with a small piece by Strauss, not too difficult but pretty. Gaining confidence, she tried some Mozart but got lost in one of the more complicated passages and gave up, despite the encouragement mixed with good-natured razzing. "I think I must be very nervous, to play like this," she said smiling ruefully, turning toward the room.

She meant to apologize for her ineptitude after Jimmy's lovely playing and to yield the instrument to him, but then her eyes fell on Sandoz, sitting in a chair in the corner, at a little distance from the rest of them, withdrawn by choice or by nature or by circumstance. Unclear about her own motives, warmed by the wine and the company, she began something she thought would be familiar to him, a very old Spanish melody. To everyone's surprise, probably even his own, Emilio left his corner, came to the side of the piano, and began to sing in a clear light tenor.

Judging him, Sofia changed keys and then the tempo as well. His eyes narrowed slightly but he started the second verse in the minor key she was using, following her lead. Pleased that he'd understood her intent, holding his eyes with hers, she began to sing a different song, in counterpoint.

She had a grainy contralto and the voices were gorgeous together, despite or perhaps because of the oddity of a male taking the higher notes, and for a little while there was no other sound in the world than the song Emilio Sandoz and Sofia Mendes sang.

Jimmy looked sick with envy. Anne moved behind him, bending over the sofa to put her thin, strong arms around his big shoulders and rest her head next to his. When she felt the rigidity give way, she tightened her embrace briefly and let him go, straightening up and standing quietly as the song went on. Ladino, she thought, recognizing elements of Spanish and Hebrew. Sofia's song was a Sephardic variation on the Spanish tune, perhaps.

Anne looked at George and saw him come to his own conclusion, suspecting the outcome, but not from the music, only from a feeling of inevitability about these two people. And then her silent analysis fell away and she listened, trying not to shiver, as the two songs diverged and interwove until, at the very end, the harmony and counterpoint resolved: lyrics and melodies and voices coming together, across the centuries, to a single word and note.

Tearing her eyes away from Emilio's face, Anne led the chorus of praise, restoring a fragile equilibrium. Jimmy did his best, but ten minutes later he made excuses about having work to catch up on and, calling out his good-byes, headed for the door. This was the cue for a general exodus, as though all of them needed to put space between themselves and a kind of intimacy no one had planned or anticipated. Anne hesitated, feeling that as hostess she should wait until Emilio and Sofia left as well. But it was taking them a few minutes to get organized, so she covered herself with a plausible excuse and followed Jimmy out the door.

He was more than halfway to the plaza when Anne caught up with him in the dark. The neighborhood was quiet, although there were snatches of music coming in with the sea breeze from La Perla, where things went on later. Hearing her footsteps, he turned, and she stopped two stairs upward of him, so she could look him in the eye. It wasn't cold but Jimmy was shaking, a gigantic Raggedy Andy doll with his spiraling yarnlike hair, mouth drawn up in his silly crescent smile.

"Do you suppose suicide is a viable option?" he joked lamely. Anne didn't dignify that with a reply, but her eyes were compassionate. "Why didn't you stop me sooner when I was playing? I don't know if I can stand to be in the same time zone with her after tonight," he moaned. "God, she must think I'm a complete idiot. But, Jesus, Anne," he cried out quietly, "he's a priest! Okay, okay, he's a really good-looking priest, not a big ugly Mick with shit for brains—"

Anne stopped him with a finger on his lips. She could think of dozens of things to say: that nobody can make anyone else love them, that half the world's misery was wanting someone who didn't want you, that unavailability was a powerful aphrodisiac, that Jimmy was a sweet, intelligent, dear man— None of it would help. She joined him on his step, laid her head against his chest and put her arms around him, marveling again at the sheer size of the boy.

"Jesus, Anne," he whispered above her. "He's a priest. It isn't fair."

"No, my darling, it never is," she assured him. "It never, ever is."

THAT TIME OF night, it was less than an hour's drive back to Arecibo. By the time he pulled into the apartment parking lot, Jimmy was done crying and almost past the desire to get drunk, which he'd rejected as too dramatic a response to the situation. Sofia had never given him any encouragement. The whole thing had been a fantasy, and that was that. And really, what did he know about Emilio? Priests were just men, Eileen Quinn had always reminded him when he'd come home from school full of hero worship and awe. Ordination doesn't make you a saint. And anyway, in other religions, priests married and had children.

Shit, he thought. It was just a song. I've got them married, with kids! It's none of my business.

But he couldn't get the sound of them together out of his mind. It was like watching . . . Sleep was out of the question. He tried a few pages of the book he was reading but ended up tossing it across the room, unable to concentrate. He rooted around in the cupboards and wished he'd taken Anne up on her offer when she asked him if he wanted to take some leftovers home with him. Finally, he decided to make good on the excuse he'd used to leave early and connected with the dish system. He opened the SETI log, picking up where he'd left off with Sofia on Friday afternoon, deciding to bull his way through the hideously embarrassing prospect of seeing her again by going straight at the topic he'd cover with her on Monday.

AT 3:57 A.M. on Sunday, August 3, 2019, James Connor Quinn pulled off his headset and sat back in his chair, sweating and sucking air, sure now, but hardly able to believe what he alone in all his world knew.

"Jesus Christ," Jimmy breathed, meeting the future by turning to the ancient past. "Holy Mother of God."

He rubbed his eyes and combed his fingers through his tangled, scribbly hair and sat, staring blankly, for a few moments longer. Then he called Anne.

11

ARECIBO, PUERTO RICO:
AUGUST 3, 2019

"YOU'RE JOKING," ANNE whispered. "Sweet pea, if you have called me at four o'clock in the goddamned morning and this isn't for real—"

"I'm serious."

"Have you told anyone else yet?"

"No. You're the first. My mother will kill me, but you're who I wanted to tell." Anne, standing naked in the dark, smiled and sent a mental apology to Mrs. Quinn. She heard Jimmy's urgent voice again. "Wake George up and get him on the VR net. I'm going to call Emilio and Sofia, too."

Anne didn't say anything, but Jimmy understood her silence.

"It was the song that did it. I couldn't stop thinking about it and when I looked at the signal, it just reminded me of music. I figured if it was music, I'd recognize it and then I could figure out where it was coming from. So I washed it through a digital sound program. Anne, it's like nothing I've ever heard before."

"Jimmy, are you certain it's not just some kind of music you're not familiar with—South Ossetian or Norwegian or something? I mean, it's a big world."

"Anne, I just spent three hours verifying and checking and trying to disprove and it is really, truly, absolutely not local. It's not a bounce, it's not a pirate station, it's not drug ships, it's not military. It is ET and I got a confirm from Goldstone's files, but nobody there has looked at it yet. It's music, Anne, and it's ET and you know what else?"

"Jesus, Jimmy, don't tease! What?"

"They're neighbors. We're picking up an amazingly loud party near Alpha Centauri. They're only about four light years from here. That's practically next door."

"Holy shit. Wow. Jimmy, shouldn't you tell somebody official?"

"Not yet. Right this minute, it's mine. I want my friends to know first. So for crying out loud, wake George the hell up and get on the net."

"No, listen. If this is real, then virtual reality isn't good enough. I want real reality. Tell Emilio to come here to the house. We'll swing by to pick up Sofia and then go on up to the dish. We'll be on the road in, say, twenty-five minutes. We should be there by—" She found she couldn't add. Her mind just went blank. God. Music. Four light years away.

"About six o'clock," Jimmy supplied. "Okay, I'll be there. And Anne?"

"Yeah, I know, bring food. We'll hit Señor Donut's on the way."

"No. Well, that, too. But—thanks. That's what I wanted to say. For last night."

"Hey, if news like this is the thanks I get for giving you a hug, you are entirely welcome, darling boy. We'll see you in a couple of hours. And Jimmy? Congratulations. This is fantastic."

IT WAS A clear chilly morning, the light still pale, when the Edwardses and their passengers pulled in. Jimmy's little Ford was the only car in the dish parking lot besides the guard's. "Private tour, Mr. Edwards?" he asked as they signed in.

"No, there's something Jimmy Quinn wanted to show us and we figured it was better to come by when the place isn't busy," George said. Anne, smiling innocently, handed the guard a couple of donuts on the way by.

Awake all night, Jimmy was bleary-eyed but too strung up on his nerves to notice he was tired. As they squeezed into his little cubicle, he grabbed the donut Anne held out to him and ate it in two bites, setting up the playback while he chewed.

It was vocal, mainly. There was a percussive underlayment and possibly wind instruments as well, but it was hard to tell about that—there was still a lot of noise, although Jimmy had already filtered some out. And it was unquestionably alien. The timbre of the voices, the harmonics were simply different, in some way that Jimmy couldn't describe in words. "I can display sound signatures that would show the differences between their voices and ours graphically," he told them, "the way you can see that a violin sounds different from a trumpet. I don't know how to say it."

"I know it's not scientific, but you can just tell," Anne agreed, shrugging. "It's like you could tell Aretha Franklin's voice from anyone else's, from a single note. It's just *different*."

At first, they simply listened to the fragment of music over and over, each time groaning as the signal fell off to static just as the music began to build to something wonderful. Then, after the third hearing, Anne said, "Okay. What can we tell about them? They sing in groups, and there is a lead singer. So they have a social organization. Can we assume they breathe air because their music can be heard like this?"

"We can assume they have some kind of atmosphere that propagates sound waves," George said, "but not necessarily anything we could breathe."

"So they've got something like lungs and mouths and they can control expelled air, or whatever it is they breathe," Anne listed.

"And they can hear, or there'd be no point to singing, right?" said Jimmy.

"The language doesn't sound tonal to me," Emilio said, "but it's difficult to tell when people are singing. There is a sentence structure. There are consonants and vowels and something in the throat, like glottal stops." It didn't occur to him to wonder if they had throats. "Jimmy, may I hear it again, please?"

Jimmy replayed it. Sitting at the edge of the group, almost in the hallway just beyond Jimmy's little space, Sofia watched Sandoz, seeing in action the process she had abstracted while working for the Jesuits in Cleveland. He was already beginning to mouth a little of it, picking up phrases sung by the chorus, trying out phonemes. Without a word, she handed him her notebook and stylus. "I could learn this, I think," he said to no one in particular, distracted, half-convinced already. He began making notes. "Jimmy, may I?" Jimmy rolled his chair out of the way and let Emilio take the console.

"Jim, have you changed the frequency much?" George asked. "Is this what it really sounds like, or is it more like insects chirping or whales singing in real time?"

"No, as near as I can figure, this is what it sounds like. Of course, it would depend on the density of their atmosphere," Jimmy told him. He thought for a while. "Well. They've got radio. That implies vacuum tubes at least, right?"

"No," George disagreed. "Vacuum tubes were actually kind of a fluke. You could just as easily go straight to solid state. But they would have to understand electricity." There was a short pause, everyone chewing on the ideas, the only sound that of the music as Emilio slowed it down and repeated sections, correcting his notes. "And chemistry, for sure," George continued. "They'd have to know something about metals and nonmetals, conductors. Microphones need carbon or some kind of variable resistor. Batteries—zinc and lead."

"A theory of wave propagation," Jimmy said. "Radio implies a lot."

"Mass communications," Anne suggested. "And a segment of the population with the leisure to sit around thinking up wave theories. So: probably a stratified society with economic divisions."

"Metallurgy," Jimmy said. "You wouldn't start with radio, right? You'd work metal for other stuff first. Jewelry, weapons, metal tools."

"All possible," George said. He laughed and shook his head, still stunned. "Well, chalk one up for the Principle of Mediocrity, boys and girls." Sofia raised her brows in question, so George explained. "That's the idea that Earth is nothing special, DNA is a pretty easy molecule to make and life is fairly abundant in the universe."

"My goodness," Anne sighed, "what a fall. We thought we were the center of the universe and now look! Just another bunch of sentients. Ho-hum." Her face changed and she leaned over to hug Emilio with wicked glee. "Whom do you suppose God loves best, Father? Ooh, there's a nasty little idea. Sentient rivalries! Think of the theology, Emilio!"

Emilio, who had played the music again and again, catching more of it each time, finding a pattern or two, suddenly sat very still. But before he could say anything, Anne spoke up again. "Jim, you said this was Alpha Centauri. What's the system like?"

"Pretty complicated. Three suns. A yellow one that's a lot like Sol and two others, red and orange. People have thought for years that the system was a good candidate for having planets. But it isn't easy to sort things out when you've got three stars to contend with, so I guess it never seemed worth the effort. Jeez, it's going to be a hot prospect now."

The discussion went on for some time, with George, Anne and Jimmy extrapolating, deducing and arguing. Emilio, thoughtful, went back to the music again, playing it through softly once more, but then he turned the playback off.

Sofia alone had neither comment on the music itself nor any speculation about the singers, but when the talk finally slowed to a halt, she asked, "Mr. Quinn, how did you decide to run the signal through an audio output?"

In the excitement, Jimmy had forgotten the embarrassment of the previous evening, and now he was feeling too good to care. "Well, there was all the music last night," he said evenly. "And when I was in school, I had a part-time job cleaning up old recordings from a Soviet archive for digitizing. The signal just looked like music to me. So I decided to give it a try."

"It would be fair to say that you used your intuition."

"I guess so. It was a hunch."

"Would another astronomer have known what a musical signal looks like and come to the same conclusion?"

"Hard to say. Probably. Sure—somebody would have thought of it eventually."

"Would it ever have occurred to you, do you think, to suggest to me that the AI system wash all signals through an audio output to screen for transmissions such as this?"

"Only to eliminate them as ETs," Jimmy admitted. "See, we always expected a string of primes, some kind of mathematical sequence. I think I'd have suggested that anything that looked like music was definitely not ET. Remember? Yesterday?" He yawned enormously and stood to stretch, which required Anne to duck out of his way and George to move into a corner. "Day before yesterday, now. I sort of recognized that the signal was music then, so I assumed it was local. If I'd been sure it was ET, I might never have considered music. I don't know why but I always thought it was either music or ET, but not both."

"Yes. Odd, isn't it. That would have been my assumption as well," she said without emotion, but she was twisting the metal bracelet around and around. Triple time. She'd be perhaps thirty-seven or thirty-eight. Not forever. Hubris, to have made the wager. "Mr. Quinn, your job is secure. My system would not have picked this up. I will recommend that the project be scaled back. I can automate the request-and-return segments of the work. And coordination of scheduling. That could be finished in one or two months."

"We could go, couldn't we . . . if we wanted to?" Emilio said in the silence that followed her remarks. "I mean, there'd be a way to get there, if we decided to try."

The others looked at him blankly, still thinking about Sofia's unenviable position.

"We could use a meteor—no, an asteroid, yes?" he corrected himself, looking directly at Sofia. "It wouldn't be any worse than the little wooden ships people used to cross the Atlantic in the 1500s."

At first, only Sofia saw what he was driving at. "Yes," she said, glad to be distracted by him for once. "The asteroids aren't bad, really. The miners' quarters can be rather comfortable—"

"Yeah, sure," George said. "You've already got the mass-drivers grafted on and the lifepod in place. Get a big enough asteroid and you could just keep feeding slag into the engines. We do it now on a small scale to bring the rocks into Earth orbit from the asteroid belt. I thought years ago that you could go as far as you wanted, if you got a big enough rock. There just wasn't any reason to leave the solar system."

"Until now," Emilio said.

"Until now," George agreed.

"Did I miss something?" Anne said. "Asteroids?"

But George was starting to laugh and Emilio looked positively beatific. "Sofia," George said, "tell Anne about that contract you had—"

"—with Ohbayashi," Sofia finished for him. She looked at Anne and then the others, and gave a small astonished laugh before saying, "It was just before working with Dr. Sandoz in Cleveland. I did an expert system for Ohbayashi's asteroid mining division. They specified an AI program that could take into account the cost of remote assaying and the costs of capturing an asteroid, mining and refining the minerals in space, versus the projected market values of the product at delivery, Earthside. Very little intuition involved, except projecting future metals prices," she said wryly. "You're right, Dr. Sandoz. A partially mined asteroid could be used as a vehicle."

Emilio, who had been leaning forward and watching her carefully as she spoke, clapped once and sat back in his chair, smiling broadly.

"But it would take four years, wouldn't it?" Anne objected.

"Four years isn't so bad," Emilio said.

"Whoa," Jimmy said, looking at Sofia and Sandoz. "Okay, first off, it's four point *three* and it's *light* years, not plain solar years. Even a third of a light year is a nontrivial distance. And anyway, that's the time it takes for light and radio waves to travel the distance, not a ship. It would take a ship a lot longer . . . but even so . . ." he said, starting to think about it now.

George gestured for Sofia's notebook and stylus. Emilio saved his file and handed it over. "Okay, so do the problem," George said, blanking the screen so he could sketch the idea out on the tablet. "At thirty-two feet per second per second, you'd have one G of gravity. Say you accelerate for half the trip and then rotate the rock a hundred and eighty degrees and decelerate for the second half . . ."

For a while there was no sound except the muttering of numbers and the tapping of a keyboard, Jimmy beginning the calculations on-line as George continued them by hand. George finished his estimate first, to Jimmy's irritation. "You'd need about seventeen years to get there, not four." Emilio looked both crestfallen and startled by the difference. "Hell," George told him, "Anne was in graduate school longer than that!" Anne snorted but George went on, "What if you kept a normal sleeping and waking schedule and bumped the engines up for two Gs while the crew's flat in bed? That would cut the time down and get you closer to light speed, so you'd get some help from relativity. Make the trip seem faster to the people onboard."

Jimmy continued to work on his own line of calculation. "No, wait. It might seem to the crew more like six or seven months."

"Six or seven months!" Emilio exclaimed.

"Jeez," Jimmy said, staring at the numbers. "You could get real close to light speed in less than a year or so, even at one G, constant acceleration. Like maybe ninety-three percent. Anybody want to take on Einstein? I wonder if you'd run out of rock . . . How big would the asteroid have to be?" he asked himself and went back to the calculations.

"Wait a minute. I don't understand about people sleeping," Anne said. "Wouldn't you have to have somebody awake all the time to steer?"

"Nah—navigation would be mostly automated, at least until you got near the system," George told her. "You'd just launch yourself in the right direction—"

"And pray," said Emilio, laughing a little crazily.

They fell quiet, talked out for the moment. "What do we do now?" Jimmy asked. It was almost eight o'clock, and he was beginning to think about what kind of trouble he could be in for not calling Masao Yanoguchi first.

It was Emilio Sandoz, face solemn and eyes alight, who answered him. "Start planning the mission," he said.

There was silence and then Anne laughed uncertainly. "Emilio, sometimes I can't tell when you're joking. Do you mean a mission or do you mean a mission? Are we talking science or religion?"

"Yes," he said simply, with a kind of hilarious gravity that kept the rest of them off balance. "Sofia, George, Jimmy. I was only speculating before—but this is a serious possibility, yes? Fitting out an asteroid for such a trip?"

"Yes," Sofia confirmed. "As Mr. Edwards said, the idea has been around for some time."

"It would cost hell's own money," George pointed out.

"No, I don't think so," Sofia said. "I know of bankrupted wildcatters who'd be pleased to sell off hulks that didn't pan out, with the engines in place. It wouldn't be cheap but neither would it be prohibitive, for some kind of corporation . . ." Her voice trailed off and she looked at Sandoz, as everyone else was. For some reason, he found what she had just said very funny.

None of them could have known what he was thinking, how much this reminded him of that evening in Sudan when he read the Provincial's order sending him to John Carroll. Where he met Sofia. And Anne and George, who found Jimmy. Who brought them all here, now. He ran his hands through the dark, straight hair that had fallen into his eyes and saw them all staring at him. They think I've lost my mind, he thought.

"I wasn't listening closely enough before," he said, back in control. "Tell me again how this could be done."

In the next hour, George and Jimmy and Sofia outlined the ideas for him: how wildcatters selected and obtained suitable asteroids and outfitted them with life support, how the engines broke down silicates to use as fuel to move the asteroids to Earth-orbit refineries, how twenty-ton loads of refined metals were aimed, like the old Gemini capsules, at recovery sites in the ocean off Japan's coast. How you could scale the system up for long-range travel. Trained as a linguist and a priest, Emilio had a hard time understanding the Einsteinian physics that predicted that the transit time elapsed on Earth would be around seventeen years, while the effect of traveling near light speed would make it seem closer to six months for the crew onboard the asteroid.

"Nobody understands this the first time they hear about it," George assured him. "And most people who think about it at all just accept that the math works out this way. But let's say you go to Alpha Centauri and come straight back. When you get home, the people you left would be thirty-four years older but you'd only have aged about a year, because time slows down when you're near light speed."

Jimmy explained how they could plot the course, and Emilio found that even less intelligible. And then there was the problem of making landfall. There were a lot of loose ends, George and Jimmy and Sofia acknowledged. Even so, it could be done, they thought.

Anne listened as closely as Emilio, but she was skeptical to the point of dismissing the whole business as silly. "Okay, granted," she said at last, "I personally have a hard time understanding how maglev trains stay up. But look, there are half a million things that will go wrong. You'll use up the whole asteroid before you get there—the fuel will run out. The asteroid will crack apart if you mine it out wrong. You'll hit some random piece of interstellar shit and get smashed to atoms. You'll fall into one of the suns. You'll crash trying to land on the planet. You won't be able to breathe once you get there. There'll be nothing you can eat. The singers will eat you! Emilio, quit it. I'm serious."

"I know," he laughed. "So am I."

She looked around the room for allies and found none. "Am I the only one who sees how nuts this is?"

"'God does not require us to succeed. He only requires us to try,'" Emilio quoted quietly. He was sitting very still, in the farthest corner of the cubicle, elbows on his knees, hands clasped loosely, looking up at her with merry eyes.

"Oh, sure. Wave Mother Teresa in my face," Anne said, getting angry. "This is stupid. You guys are crazy."

"No," George insisted. "It can be done, at least in theory."

"Anne, we have, in this room, much of the expertise needed to make a go of this, or at least to attempt it," Emilio said. "Jimmy, could you navigate such an asteroid, using the same skills you use to locate astronomical targets?"

"Not this morning, but I could start working on it now and by the time everything's ready to go, I could be ready. There are very good astronomical programs that we can use. You don't just aim at where Alpha Centauri is now. You have to aim at where the system will be in however many years it'll take your craft to get there. But that's just celestial mechanics. You just have to decide to work the problem out. And you'd have to find the planet once you got to the star system. That might be harder, really."

Emilio turned to Sofia. "If you had freedom of choice, would you find it objectionable to work again for the Society of Jesus? Perhaps as a general contractor, to acquire and organize the material elements needed to put such a mission together? You have contacts in the mining industry, yes?"

"Yes. The project would be different from the kind of AI analysis I ordinarily do, but no more demanding. I could certainly pull together the materials, if I were authorized to do so."

"Even if the mission were, at its heart, religious in nature?"

"My broker would have no objections. Jaubert's done business with the Jesuits before, obviously."

"I cannot speak for my superiors," Emilio told her, dark eyes opaque now, "but I will propose that they buy out your contract, terminate it and work with you directly as a free agent. Your choice, not the broker's."

"My choice." She had not had a choice in so many years. "There is no objection. That is, I have none."

"Good. George, how different is the life-support system used for mining asteroids from the underwater system you are familiar with?"

George didn't answer right away. All the technology he'd mastered, he was thinking. All the miles he'd run. Everything—his whole life was an apprenticeship for this. He looked at Sandoz and said, steady-voiced, "Same things. Only instead of extracting oxygen from water, they use rock. The oxygen is a by-product of the mining and fuel production for the engines. And, like Jimmy said, by the time we're ready to go, I could be up to speed."

"Oh, now, stop right there," Anne said flatly and looked straight at Emilio. "This has gone far enough. Are you seriously proposing that George get involved in this?"

"I am seriously proposing that everyone in this room be involved with this. Including you. You have anthropological expertise, which would be invaluable when we make contact—"

"Oh, come on!" Anne yelled.

"—and you are a physician as well, and you can cook," he said, laughing, ignoring the howl, "which is a perfect combination of skills because we can't afford to have a doctor along who would only wait around for someone to break a leg."

"Peter Pan. You guys are all set to go to Never-Never-Land and I get to be Wendy. Fabulous! There is a rude gesture that comes to mind," Anne snapped. "Emilio, you are the most sensible, rational priest I've ever met. And now you are telling me that you think God wants us to go to this planet. Us personally. The people in this room. Am I getting this straight?"

"Yes. I am afraid I think I do believe that," he said, wincing. "I'm sorry."

She looked at him, helpless with exasperation. "You are demented."

"Look, Anne. Perhaps you're right. The whole idea is mad." He moved from his corner to her perch on a table behind Jimmy's terminal, took her hands and went down on one knee, not in an attitude of prayer but with an odd playfulness. "But, Anne! This is an extraordinary moment, is it not? Entertain, for this extraordinary moment, the notion that we are all here in this room, at this moment, for some reason. No, let me finish! George is wrong. Life on Earth is unlikely," he insisted. "Our own existence, as a species and as individuals, is improbable. The fact that we know one another appears to be a result of chance. And yet, here we are. And now we have evidence that another sentient species exists nearby and that they sing. They sing, Anne." She felt his hands squeeze hers. "We have to find out about them. There is simply no alternative. We have to know them. You said it yourself, Anne! Think of the theology."

She had no reply. She could only look at him, and then at the others, one by one. Sofia, who was knowledgeable and brilliant and who seemed to think there was no insurmountable economic or technical difficulty in launching a mission. Jimmy, who was already working out the astronomical problems. George, whom she loved and trusted and believed in, and who thought they should be part of this. Emilio. Who spoke of God.

"Anne, at least, shall we not try?" Emilio pleaded. He looked about seventeen years old to her, a teenager trying to convince his mom that he'd be fine driving across the country on a motorcycle. But he was not seventeen, and she was not his mother. He was a priest, pushing middle age, and he was alive with something she could hardly imagine.

"Let me propose the idea to my superiors," he said, his voice reasonable. He stood but kept her hands in his. "There are a hundred, a thousand ways the idea can prove itself impossible. I am willing to let God decide. We could call it fate, if that makes you feel more rational."

Still, she did not reply but he could see her eyes change. Not capitulation but a sort of worried, reluctant assent was forming. A willingness to suspend judgment, perhaps.

"Someone will go, sometime," he assured her. "They are too close not to go. The music is too beautiful."

There was a part of Anne Edwards that was thrilled about the discovery, that gloried in being this close to history in the making. And deeper, in a place she rarely inspected, there was a part of her that wanted to believe as Emilio seemed to believe, that God was in the universe, making sense of things.

Once, long ago, she'd allowed herself to think seriously about what human beings would do, confronted directly with a sign of God's presence in their lives. The Bible, that repository of Western wisdom, was instructive either as myth or as history, she'd decided. God was at Sinai and within weeks, people were dancing in front of a golden calf. God walked in Jerusalem and days later, folks nailed Him up and then went back to work. Faced with the Divine, people took refuge in the banal, as though answering a cosmic multiple-choice question: If you saw a burning bush, would you (a) call 911, (b) get the hot dogs, or (c) recognize God? A vanishingly small number of people would recognize God, Anne had decided years before, and most of them had simply missed a dose of Thorazine.

She took her cold hands out of Emilio's warm ones and crossed her arms over her chest. "I need coffee," she muttered and left the cubicle.

12

EARTH:
AUGUST 3–4, 2019

AT 9:13 A.M., Sunday, August 3, 2019, the guard at the Arecibo Radio Telescope signed out Jimmy Quinn's visitors. Leaving his desk for a few minutes to stretch a little, the guard strolled to the front door and returned the waves of George and his passengers. Masao Yanoguchi arrived at Arecibo half an hour later. As he signed in, the guard remarked, "You must have passed George on the way up." Yanoguchi nodded pleasantly but headed directly for Jimmy Quinn's cubicle.

By 10:00, as George Edwards was pulling out of the parking lot of Sofia Mendes's apartment building in Puerto Rico, Dr. Hideo Kikuchi was called in from his early-morning golf game, just outside Barstow, California, to take a call from Masao Yanoguchi. Within forty-five minutes, the staff of the Goldstone Station was assembled and the Arecibo discovery was confirmed. Several individuals at Goldstone considered seppuku. The shift boss, who should have noticed the discovery before Jimmy, resigned immediately, and while he did not actually kill himself, his hangover the next morning was very nearly lethal.

By 10:20, that Sunday morning, Sofia Mendes had brewed a pot of Turkish coffee, closed the cheap, ugly curtains over the window of her one-room efficiency apartment to block out distractions, and sat down to code the AI system that would automate request scheduling for the Arecibo Radio Telescope. She put Dr. Sandoz's speculations out of mind. *Arbeit macht frei,* she thought grimly. Work could buy her freedom, sooner or later. So she worked, to make it sooner.

Emilio Sandoz, back in La Perla by 11:03, called D. W. Yarbrough in New Orleans and spoke to him for some time. Then he sprinted to the chapel–cum–community center, where he threw on the simple vestments he used and celebrated Mass for his small congregation at 11:35. The homily was on the nature of faith. Anne Edwards was absent.

At 5:53 P.M., Rome time, a video transmission from D. W. Yarbrough, New Orleans Provincial, interrupted the late-afternoon nap of Tomás da Silva, thirty-first General of the Society of Jesus. The Father General did not return to his room, nor did he appear for his evening meal. Brother Salvator Rivera cleared up the untouched dishes at nine P.M., muttering darkly about the waste of food.

The Japanese ambassador to the United States left Washington on a chartered plane at 11:45 A.M. local time and arrived in San Juan three and a half hours later. While he was in flight, news of the discovery flashed from system to system around the astronomical world. Virtually all radio astronomers dropped whatever they were doing and aimed telescopes at Alpha Centauri, although there were a few who were working on the origin of the universe and did not care greatly about planets, inhabited or otherwise.

Waiting for the world press to converge on Arecibo, an archivist for ISAS posed the Arecibo staff with various dignitaries as they assembled at the dish to grace history with their presences. Jimmy Quinn, more than a little overwhelmed by what was happening, was nevertheless able to appreciate the humor of once more finding himself standing in the exact center of the back row. The tallest kid in every class since preschool, he had a large collection of group pictures in which, in every single solitary one, he was standing in the exact center of the back row. After the pictures were taken, Jimmy asked permission to call his mother. Better late than never.

The news conference was carried live, worldwide, at 21:30 G.M.T. In Boston, Massachusetts, Mrs. Eileen Quinn, recently divorced, watched it alone. She wept and laughed and hugged herself and wished someone had told Jimmy to get his hair cut or at least to comb it. And that shirt! she thought, dismayed as always by Jimmy's taste in clothes. When the conference was over, she called everyone she knew, except Kevin Quinn, the bastard.

By 5:56 P.M., before the news conference in Arecibo had ended, two enterprising fifteen-year-old boys had broken into Jimmy Quinn's home system by way of his public web address and pirated the code needed to reproduce the music electronically. The Arecibo system was secure but it had never occurred to Jimmy, an honest man, to put a serious lock on his own. It would be weeks before he realized that his inability to imagine theft had led to the vast enrichment of an illegal offshore media company that bought the code from the kids.

It was 8:30 on Monday morning in Tokyo when the conference ended. Legitimate bids to reproduce and market the ET music began to flood in to ISAS almost immediately. The Director of the Institute for Space and Astronautical Science deferred to the Secretary General of the United Nations, pointing out that there was a long-standing agreement that any transmission received by the SETI program was the possession of all humankind.

Anne Edwards, hearing this on the radio as she and George fixed supper, was disgusted. "We paid for the damned program. We put all of the real money into it. The whole idea of SETI was American. If anybody makes any money off this, it should be the U.S., not the U.N., and certainly not Japan!"

George snorted. "Yeah, well, we're about as likely to collect as Carl Sagan is, and he's been dead for years. Of course," he said, wheedling slightly, "that's why it would be so great if we—"

"Don't start with me, George."

"No guts."

Anne turned very slowly from the sink and looked narrowly at her beloved husband of over forty years. After drying her hands on a towel, she folded it neatly and laid it on the counter. "Eat shit," she suggested, smiling prettily, "and die." George laughed, which irritated her further. "Oh, George, be serious! You'd be leaving everyone you know and love behind—"

"Right. And even if you got back alive, everyone you knew would be dead!" he admitted belligerently. "So what? They'll be dead anyway. You want to hang around and watch?" Anne blinked. "Look. When your great-grandparents got on the boat from Europe, they may as well have been going to another planet. They left everyone behind, too! And

Anne—who would we be leaving? Our parents are dead. We've got no kids. We don't even have a *cat,* for chrissakes."

"We have each other—" Anne said, a little defensively.

"Exactly, which is why it would be so great—"

"Oh, God. Just stop. Okay? Just stop." She turned back to the sink. "They aren't going to offer the job to a couple of old farts like us anyway."

"Wanna bet?" George asked, and she could hear the self-satisfied smile in his voice. "The priests won't be kids either. And, anyway, sixty ain't what it used to be."

"Dammit, George! I've really had enough of this!" Anne said, spinning around furiously. "So help me, if you say I'm beautiful when I'm angry, I will eviscerate you," she snarled, brandishing a dessert fork. He laughed and she cooled off. "All right. Enjoy the fantasy. Have fun. But, George," she said, eyes serious, "if they do make the offer? The answer is no, as far as I'm concerned. And that's the end of it."

Supper was unusually quiet in the Edwards household that evening.

AT THE END of that long Sunday, Jimmy was called into the office of Masao Yanoguchi, who took note of the ludicrous rumpled clothing and the red-rimmed eyes and estimated that the boy had been awake for almost thirty-six hours. He waved Quinn into a chair and watched the comically elongated framework fold itself into a sitting position. The guard's log was open on Yanoguchi's desk.

"Mr. Quinn, I recognize the names of Ms. Mendes and Mr. Edwards. I assume Dr. Edwards is the wife of Mr. Edwards. Who is E. J. Sandoz, please?"

"A friend, sir, a priest. They are all friends of mine. I'm sorry. I should have called you first but it was four in the morning and I wasn't really sure, not a hundred percent . . ."

Yanoguchi let the silence fill the room. Jimmy twisted his watch around and around his wrist in unconscious mimicry of Sofia, hours earlier. He stared at the floor for a few moments and then glanced at Yanoguchi but looked away almost immediately. "I was afraid I was wrong and I wanted someone else to listen—" Jimmy stopped and this time when he looked up, he didn't turn away. "That's not true. I knew. I was sure. I just wanted to share it with my friends first. They're like family to me, Dr. Yanoguchi. That's no excuse for poor judgment. I'll resign, sir. I'm sorry."

"I accept your apology, Mr. Quinn." Yanoguchi closed the guard's book and lifted a single small sheet of paper from his desk. "Ms. Mendes left this memo for me. She recommends that the AI project be restricted to request and return. I believe I agree. This will be carried out at considerable savings to ISAS because of your suggestion that the project be done as a wager." Yanoguchi put the memo aside. "I would like you to continue to cooperate with her, although you will no longer be required in your former position." He watched Quinn master his reaction and, pleased with the young man's self-discipline, went on to say, "Starting tomorrow morning, you will be in charge of a full-time effort to monitor the source of the transmission. You will supervise a staff of five. Round-the-clock coverage, two people per shift. I'd like you to coordinate the effort with similar crews at Barstow and the other telescopes."

He stood, and Jimmy got to his feet as well. "Congratulations, Mr. Quinn, on a historic discovery." Masao Yanoguchi, arms at his sides, bowed briefly; later, Jimmy would realize he was more surprised by this gesture than by anything else that had happened that day. "Permit me to give you a lift home," Yanoguchi suggested. "I don't think you should be driving. I'll have my chauffeur pick you up tomorrow morning as well. You can leave your car here overnight."

Jimmy was too dazed to say anything. Masao Yanoguchi laughed and led the boy out toward the parking lot.

THAT NIGHT, FOR the second time in as many nights, Emilio Sandoz had trouble falling asleep.

He used this apartment gratis because the house was too close to the encroaching ocean; no one else dared to stay in it anymore and the landlord had given up trying to rent it out. Tonight, alone as always in the little bedroom, Emilio stared at the cracked and patched ceiling made beautiful by moonlight reflected off the sea, and listened to the hypnotic sound of waves nearby. He knew sleep would not come easily and did not close his eyes to coax it.

He'd been prepared, to some extent, for nights like the one he'd passed the previous evening. "Lotta people in this ole world," D. W. Yarbrough had warned him once. "Sometime, somewhere, one or two of 'em gonna ring some bells for a man. Count on it, son." So even before he met Sofia Mendes, he understood that he'd have to reckon with someone like her. He no longer denied the turmoil she aroused in him; he simply accepted that it would take time to bring a natural response into congruence with his vows.

He'd never really questioned the vows. He accepted them as essential to the Apostolate—for making him readily available to work for the good of souls—and when the time came, he took them wholeheartedly. But at fifteen, when it all began? He'd have laughed himself stupid at the idea of becoming a priest. Oh, sure, D.W. got the charges dropped and got him off-island before anyone else took a shot at him, and he was grateful in a half-articulate way but in the beginning, he only intended to lie low until he was eighteen and could do as he pleased. Go to New York. Break into the minors. Box, maybe. Flyweight. Welterweight, if he filled out more. Sell again, if he had to.

The first months in the Jesuit high school were a shock. He was as far behind the other students scholastically as he was ahead of them in raw experience. Few of the boys talked to him, except to goad him, and he returned the favor. D.W. made him promise one thing: not to hit anyone. "Just master your hands, *'mano*. No more fighting. Get a grip, son."

Nobody from his family ever wrote or called, much less visited. His brother beat the rap, D.W. told him toward the end of the first semester, but still blamed Emilio for what happened. Well, fuck him, who gives a shit? he thought savagely and swore he'd never cry again. He went over the wall that night. Found a whore, got wrecked. Came back defiant. If anybody noticed he was gone, no one said anything about it.

The tide began to turn for him about eight months into his sophomore year. The quiet orderliness of life in the boarding school began to seduce him. No crises, no sudden terror, no gunshots and screaming in the night. No beatings. Each day planned, no surprises. Almost in spite of himself, he did well at Latin. Won a prize, even. "For excellence." He liked the sound of that. Rolled the word around in his mind.

He did better junior year, despite the fact that he spent nearly all of it arguing with the priests. So much of what he knew about religion struck him as total bullshit; he was disarmed when the fathers freely admitted that some stories were in fact pious fictions. But, judging his character, they dared him to cut through what he called the crap: to find the core of truth, carefully preserved and offered to all comers through the centuries.

As the months passed, he began to feel as though something in his chest were loosening, as though something that had kept a grip on his heart had begun to let go. And then one night, the image of a full-blown rose unfolding petal by petal from its tightly wrapped bud came to him in a brief wordless dream and he woke from it, shattered, face wet with tears shed in sleep.

He told no one of this dream, tried hard to forget it himself. But when he was seventeen, he entered the novitiate.

Many were surprised, but as D. W. Yarbrough pointed out, Emilio had a good deal in common with the Basque soldier who had founded the Society of Jesus in the sixteenth century. Like Ignatius of Loyola, Emilio Sandoz had known brutality and death and stinking fear, and as the days of silence during the Long Retreat passed, he had a past worthy of the name to reconsider and to turn away from.

Things that drove other young men from the path to priesthood were balm to him: the *ordo regularis,* the liturgical cadences, the quiet, the purposefulness. Even the celibacy. For, looking back on his chaotic youth, Emilio had no experience of sex that was not about power or pride or lust undiluted by affection. It was easy to believe that to live as a celibate was a charism—a special kind of grace. And so, it began: after the novitiate, classical and humane studies, and then philosophy. Regency, when the scholastic was sent out to teach in one of the Society's high schools. Then years of theology with ordination at last, and from there further: to tertianship and final vows. Perhaps three out of ten who began Jesuit formation stayed the course. Emilio Sandoz, to the astonishment of many who'd known him as a boy, was among them.

And yet, in all those years of preparation, the prayer that had resonated most strongly in his soul was the cry, "Lord, I believe. Help me in my disbelief."

He found the life of Jesus profoundly moving; the miracles, on the other hand, seemed a barrier to faith, and he tended to explain them to himself in rational terms. It was *as though* there were only seven loaves and seven fishes. Maybe the miracle was that people shared what they had with strangers, he thought in the darkness.

He was aware of his agnosticism, and patient with it. Rather than deny the existence of something he couldn't perceive himself, he acknowledged the authenticity of his uncertainty and carried on, praying in the face of his doubt. After all, Ignatius of Loyola, a soldier who had killed and whored and made a thorough mess of his soul, said you could judge prayer worthwhile simply if you could act more decently, think more clearly afterward. As D.W. once told him, "Son, sometimes it's enough just to act less like a shithead." And by that kindly if inelegant standard, Emilio Sandoz could believe himself to be a man of God.

So, while he hoped someday to find his way to a place in his soul that was closed to him now, he was content to be where he was. He never asked God to prove His existence to little Emilio Sandoz, just because he was acting less like a shithead nowadays. He never asked for anything, really. What he'd been given was more than enough to be grateful for, whether or not God was there to receive or care about thanks.

Lying in bed, that warm August night, he felt no Presence. He was aware of no Voice. He felt as alone in the cosmos as ever. But he was beginning to find it hard to avoid thinking that if ever a man had wanted a sign from God, Emilio Sandoz had been hit square in the face with one this morning, at Arecibo.

He slept, after that. Sometime just before dawn the next morning, he had a dream. He was sitting in the dark, in a small place. He was alone and it was very quiet and he could hear himself breathing, the blood singing in his ears. Then a door he had not suspected was there began to open: and he could see a flare of light beyond it.

This dream first sustained and then haunted him for many years afterward.

13

EARTH:
AUGUST–SEPTEMBER 2019

ANNE EDWARDS WAS finishing up her morning appointments when she saw Emilio hanging around the clinic's open door. She stopped midstride but then continued out of her office into the tiny reception area.

"You angry with me?" he asked quietly, not coming in.

"I'm angry with somebody," she conceded waspishly, drying her hands and stepping to the door. "I'm just not sure with whom."

"With God, perhaps?"

"I liked you better when you didn't bring God into every damned conversation," Anne muttered. "Do you want lunch? I'm going home for half an hour. There's leftover pasta."

He shrugged and nodded and stood out of her way as she locked up. They climbed the eighty steps to the house, Anne breaking the silence only to return the greetings of people they passed. Once inside, they moved to the kitchen and Emilio perched on the stool in the corner, watching Anne steadily as she rummaged around, putting together a light lunch for both of them.

"It is often hard to tell from the way people behave whether or not they believe in God," he remarked conversationally. "Do you, Anne?"

She started the ancient microwave and then turned to him, leaning against the counter and meeting his eyes for the first time since noticing him at the clinic. "I believe in God the way I believe in quarks," she said coolly. "People whose business it is to know about quantum physics or religion tell me they have good reason to believe that quarks and God exist. And they tell me that if I wanted to devote my life to learning what they've learned, I'd find quarks and God just like they did."

"Do you think they're telling the truth?"

"It's all rock and roll to me." She shrugged and turned away to pull the plates out of the oven and carry them to the table. He hopped off the stool lightly and followed her to the dining room. They sat down and began to eat, the sounds of the neighborhood drifting in with the breeze through the open windows.

"And yet," Emilio said, "you behave like a good and moral person."

He expected an explosion and he got it. She threw her fork down with a clatter on the plate and sat back. "You know what? I really resent the idea that the only reason someone might be good or moral is because they're religious. I do what I do," Anne said, biting off each word, "without hope of reward or fear of punishment. I do not require heaven or hell to bribe or scare me into acting decently, thank you very much."

He let her simmer down enough to pick up her fork and resume eating. "A woman of honor," he observed, inclining his head with respect.

"Damned straight," she muttered around a mouthful of food, glaring at her plate and spiking a piece of rigatoni with her fork.

"We have more in common than you might suppose," Emilio said mildly but did not elaborate when her head came up. As she struggled to swallow, he set his plate aside and became businesslike. "There has been a great deal of work done in the past few weeks. Our physicists have confirmed the practicality of using an altered asteroid for transport, and Alpha Centauri can in fact be reached in under eighteen years. I am told that if Jupiter and Saturn had been big enough to produce sustained fusion, our solar system might have looked like the three suns of Alpha Centauri. So the plan is to come in above the plane of the system and look for solid planets in the same relative orbit as Earth or Mars, between the sun and the gas giants." She grunted: sounds reasonable. Watching her reactions carefully, he continued, "George has already proposed an imaging technique that would help us identify planetary movement, which he can coordinate with radio monitoring, once we reach the system."

He expected surprise and anger. He saw resignation. It suddenly came to him that George might leave Anne and that she might be willing to let him go. The possibility made him go cold. Beyond their broad and useful professional qualifications, Anne and George Edwards were possessed of a fair degree of wisdom and a joint total of more than 120 years of alert experience of the world, combined with physical toughness and emotional stability. It had never occurred to him that one of them might stay behind.

Since proposing the mission, Emilio had been taken aback by the pace of things. What had begun in laughter, almost as a joke, was snowballing, changing lives. Already, time and money were being spent in quantities that staggered him. And if the speed of events scared him, the precision with which the pieces were falling into place was even more unnerving. He went sleepless, unable to decide which was harder to live with: the idea that he had started all this, or the possibility that God had. The only way he could reassure himself during these midnight debates was to believe that wiser heads than his were making the decisions. If he could not put his faith directly in God, who remained unknowable, he could place it in the structure of the Society and in his superiors—in D. W. Yarbrough and in Father General da Silva.

Now he felt himself rocked again by doubt. What if the whole thing was a mistake and it cost the Edwardses' marriage? And as quickly as that passed his mind, he caught another glimpse of the serenity that sometimes came to him lately. Anne and George, he felt sure, were meant to be a part of the mission, if the mission was meant to be. And when he spoke again, Anne heard only calm and reason.

"The Society would never permit a suicide mission, Anne. If the voyage could not be undertaken now with a reasonable chance of success, we would simply wait until it seems sensible to make the attempt. Already, the plans call for provisions sufficient for ten years, just in case the subjective travel time does not contract as much as the physicists predict. The specifications call for an asteroid more than sufficiently large to provide fuel for a return trip, plus a one hundred percent safety margin," he told her. "Who knows? The atmosphere may be unbreathable or it may be impossible to land. In such cases, we would gather as much information as possible and return home."

"Who's we? Is it definite now? Are you going?"

"There has been no decision about the crew as yet. But the Father General is, in fact, a religious man," Emilio said ironically, "who seems to believe that God is involved with this discovery." He saw that set her off again and laughed. "In any case, it would be logical to assign someone like me to the mission. If it is possible to make contact with the Singers, a linguist will presumably be useful." He wanted to tell her how much it meant to him to think that she would be part of this, but Emilio suspected he'd taken the subject as far as he could. He pushed his chair from the table and stood, picking up their plates and taking them to the kitchen. Out of sight, he called to her, "Anne. May I ask a favor?"

"What?" she asked suspiciously.

"I have an old friend coming in to visit. May I offer him your hospitality?"

"Dammit, Emilio! Aren't there any restaurants in Puerto Rico? Between you and George, I end up feeding every stray cat on this island."

He came out of the kitchen and leaned against the doorjamb, arms across his chest, grinning, not fooled for a moment.

"All right, who's coming?" she demanded ungraciously, refusing to be charmed.

"Dalton Wesley Yarbrough, New Orleans Provincial of the Society of Jesus, from Waco, Texas, Vatican City of the Southern Baptists," he announced with ceremony, standing at attention, a butler introducing the next guest to enter a ballroom.

She put her head in her hands, defeated. "Barbecue. Hush puppies. Collard greens, red beans and watermelon. With Carta Blanca. I can't seem to help myself," she said in tones of wonderment. "I have this compulsion to cook for strangers."

"Well, ma'am," said Emilio Sandoz with a Texas twang, "they don't come a whole hell of a lot stranger'n D. W. Yarbrough."

She laughed, reached behind her to the bookcase, and pitched a hardcover novel at him. He caught it with one hand and flipped it back at her. They spoke no more about the mission, but a truce had been reached.

"DR. QUINN, ELAINE Stefansky says the ET transmission is a hoax. Do you have a comment on that?"

Jimmy was no longer startled to find reporters waiting outside his apartment at eight in the morning and no longer amused that they routinely promoted him to doctor. He pushed past the crowd and made his way to the Ford. Murmuring "No comment," Jimmy got into the car, the crowd closing around the vehicle, shouting questions, aiming AV pickups at him. Jimmy let the window down. "Look, I don't want to run over anybody's foot here. Could you back off a little? I have to get to work."

"Why haven't there been any other transmissions?" someone called out.

"Is it that they're not sending or we're not listening?" asked another.

"Oh, we're listening," Jimmy assured them. With the entire scientific community and a goodly portion of the world's population looking over his shoulder, Jimmy Quinn had coordinated a concentrated effort by radio astronomers to listen for additional transmissions. There weren't any. "We're even sending, but it will take nearly nine years, minimum, before we find out if they notice us yelling and waving our arms," he said, starting to raise the window. "Listen, I gotta go. Really."

"Dr. Quinn, have you heard the Mongolian Humi singers? Stefansky says their music may have been altered and planted in the SETI file. Is that true?" "What about the Sufis, Dr. Quinn?"

Skeptics had begun to flood the nets with alternate explanations for the music, experimenting with obscure folk traditions, running the music backward or playing with the frequency, to show how alien human music could sound, especially when modified electronically.

"Well, sure, all that stuff sounds strange." Jimmy still found it hard to be rude enough to drive away abruptly, but he was learning. "But none of it sounds like what we picked up. And I'm not a doctor, okay?" Apologizing, he eased the car out of the crowd and drove to the Arecibo dish, where another mob was waiting.

THE MEDIA EVENTUALLY went on to other things. Radio telescopes around the world returned one by one to projects that had been under way before August 3rd. But in Rome, coded transmissions continued to move along the clear-cut Jesuit chain of command, from Father General to Provincial to Rector to individual priest given an assignment. There were practical decisions to be made, many scientific teams to organize.

Tomás da Silva, thirty-first General of the Society of Jesus, remained convinced of the authenticity of the signal. The theological rationale for this mission had been worked out decades before there was any evidence of other sentient species in the universe: mere considerations of scale suggested that human beings were not the sole purpose of creation. So. Now there was proof. God had other children. And when it was time for Tomás da Silva to make a decision about acting on this knowledge, he quoted the bald and artless words of Emilio Sandoz, to whom he had spoken on the evening of the discovery. "There is simply no alternative. We have to know them."

His private secretary, Peter Lynam, questioned this on August 30, 2019, but Father General da Silva smiled and dismissed the troubling slenderness of the reed that supported all their deliberate and complex plans to contact the Singers. "Have you noticed, Peter, that all the music that sounds most similar to the extraterrestrial music is sacred in nature?" the Father General asked. He was a man of great spirituality and almost no business sense. "Sufic, Tantric, Humi. I find that very intriguing."

Peter Lynam did not argue but it was clear that he thought the Father General was chasing wild geese. Lynam was, in fact, losing his nerve about the whole expensive business.

Seeing his secretary's barely concealed misgivings, Tomás da Silva laughed and, raising a didactic finger, declared, *"Nos stulti proptur Christum."*

Yes, well, Lynam mused silently, perfect humility might require that one be "a fool for Christ," but that does not rule out the possibility of being a plain fool.

Four hours later, to Peter Lynam's astonished chagrin and Tomás da Silva's pure delight, a second transmission was detected.

Despite the recent decline in interest, there were several radio telescopes set to receive the signal when it came. The word "hoax" was permanently retired from discussion of the songs. And around the world, those few who knew the extent of the plans for a Jesuit mission to the source of the music were greatly relieved, and began to be very excited indeed.

IN THE END, it was not George or Emilio who convinced Anne Edwards to sign on to the plan. It was a bus accident.

A trucker going east on the coast road swerved briefly onto the shoulder to avoid a chunk of rock in the road but then overcooked his return to the pavement. For a few moments, the truck went into the oncoming lane and sheared the side off a westbound bus that had just rounded the curve. The truck driver was killed. Among the bus passengers, there were twelve DOA, fifty-three others more or less badly hurt, and quite a few hysterical. By the time Anne took the call and got to the hospital, its lobby was filled with distraught relatives, and lawyers.

She helped first with triage and then moved to a trauma theater, part of the team trying to save a woman in her sixties with extensive head injuries. Anne had talked to the husband in the lobby. They were tourists from Michigan. "I gave her the window seat, so she could see. I was sitting right next to her." He kept putting his hand to the side of his face, where his wife's head had been hurt. "This trip was my idea. She wanted to go to Phoenix to see the grandkids. No, I said, let's do something different. We always go to Phoenix."

Pressed, Anne had murmured something about doing their best for his wife and moved on to the next task.

At dawn, the crisis was over and the patients who had passed through Emergency were distributed to their waiting relatives, to the wards, to the ICU, to the morgue. By chance, Anne glanced into an open door on her way out of the hospital and saw the man from Michigan seated at the foot of his wife's bed, his face striped and stippled with glowing readouts from the machinery surrounding them. Anne wanted to say something comforting, but the punch-drunk reaction to hours on her feet was beginning and the only thing that came to mind was, "Next time, go to Phoenix," which was clearly inappropriate. Then, oddly, the final scene of *La Bohème* came to her and, instructed by Puccini's librettist, she put a hand on the man's shoulder and whispered, "Courage."

When she got home, George was awake and dressed and offered her coffee, but she decided to clean up and catch a few hours of sleep. Standing in the shower, soaping herself, she glanced down at her own nakedness and a vision of the woman with the head trauma came back to her. The woman had been in good shape; her body might go on for decades, but she'd never know the grandkids were all grown up. One minute, she was in the State of Puerto Rico and the next minute, she was in the State of Persistent Vegetables. Jesus, Anne thought, shuddering.

She rinsed off and stepped out of the shower. Towel wrapped around her wet hair and terry robe wrapped around her durable dancer's body, she padded into the dining room and sat across the table from George. "Okay," she said. "I'm in."

It took him a few moments to realize what she was agreeing to.

"What the hell," Anne said, seeing that he understood. "It's gotta be better than not quite dying in a bus wreck on vacation."

ON SEPTEMBER 13, Jean-Claude Jaubert received a message asking for an AV appointment to discuss a buyout of the remaining time on Sofia Mendes's contract. The individual making the request gave no name and, seeing no referral, Jaubert denied video access but agreed to open an electronic meeting, which he would encrypt and route through several networks. Jaubert was not a criminal but his was a business subject to jealousies, hard feelings, tedious disputes; one could not be too careful.

Reestablishing contact on his own terms, he pointed out that he had recently taken a loss on Ms. Mendes's behalf. Her association with Jaubert had been extended somewhat in compensation. Was the negotiant in a position to purchase rights to seven and a half years? He was. Jaubert named a price and interest rate, assuming that the man would amortize the cost with a ten-year note. The reply stated a lower price, to be paid in cash. A mutually agreeable sum was found. Jaubert mentioned that he preferred, of course, Singaporean dollars. There was a slight delay. Zlotys were offered. This time it was Jaubert's turn to hesitate. Poland was volatile, but there was an interesting possibility of making a quick profit on the currency aspect of the deal.

Done, he agreed. And watching the ensuing flood of numbers wash over the screen, Jean-Claude Jaubert became a modestly richer man. *Bonne chance, ma cherie*, he thought.

ON SEPTEMBER 14, a third transmission from Alpha Centauri was picked up, fifteen days after the second. In the midst of the jubilation, the Arecibo staff put aside their initial reactions to the small, icy woman whose profession threatened their jobs and a little farewell party for Sofia Mendes was incorporated into the general exuberance. George Edwards arranged to have food delivered to the cafeteria and quite a few people dropped by to have some pizza or cake and to wish her good luck. Elsewhere. Far from Arecibo, they hoped, laughing good-naturedly, but serious all the same. Sofia took these ambivalent farewells with cool grace but seemed anxious to leave. Her contractual relationship with Dr. Yanoguchi discharged, she said good-bye to Jimmy Quinn and thanked George Edwards, asking him to relay her best wishes to his wife and to Dr. Sandoz. George, smiling mysteriously, suggested that they'd all be seeing one another again sometime, one way or another.

Arriving at her apartment that afternoon, wrung out from the unremitting labor of the previous weeks, Sofia fell onto the bed and fought tears. Nonsense, she told herself, just get on with it. But she conceded the need for a day of rest before informing Jaubert that she was ready for the next assignment. He had contacted her in August about the Jesuit asteroid project. It would be interesting work. There were compensations for her situation, she reminded herself.

To Sandoz's intense dismay, the Jesuits had only been willing to contract her services through Jaubert. She was surprised at the depth of his shock. Business is business, she told him and reminded Sandoz that he'd said himself that he had no authority to speak. She'd harbored no hopes, she assured him, and consequently had none to be dashed. That seemed to make him feel worse. A strange man, she thought. Intelligent, but naive. And slow to react to changed circumstances, she felt. Then again, most people were.

Releasing her hair from its habitual chignon, she ran a bath, planning to soak in it until the water was tepid. Idly, waiting for the tub to fill, she checked her messages to see what, if anything, was awaiting her attention.

She read the transcript of the negotiations twice and still found it impossible to believe. The sheer viciousness of Peggy Soong's practical joke choked her. Hands shaking, stunned by the violence of her outrage, Sofia turned off the bathwater, tied her hair back and went to work on breaking the file's intervening encryption, hoping to trace it to Soong, trying to imagine what she could do to the woman that was terrible enough to repay her for this pointless, heartless—

It took only minutes to realize that Peggy was not involved with this at all. It was, in fact, Jaubert's code. Sofia had written it herself, early in their association. It had been modified over the years, but her style was unmistakable.

Working through the transcript, she confirmed that the transaction had taken place. She accessed the international monetary exchange and saw that Jaubert had made a 2.3 percent gain overnight by hanging on to the zlotys. Singapore was down; Jaubert's luck was intact. But she could not pry from the network the origin of the money. Who on earth would have done such a thing? she wondered, very nearly frightened now. Jaubert had been a reasonable man to work for, had never asked her to do anything illegal or distasteful. But the possibility had always existed.

There had to be a legal transfer of rights to her. She combed through the civil records covering her contract, registered in Monaco, thinking over and over, Who owns me now? What bloodsucking vampire owns me now? Finding the correct file, she read the final entry and sat back, hand to her mouth, throat so tight she thought she might suffocate.

Contract terminated. Free agent. Inquiries: contact principal directly.

As though from a distance, she heard a wail. She walked numbly to the window and pushed the curtain away, looking outside for the child who was sobbing somewhere nearby. There was no one there, of course, no one else anywhere to be heard. After a while, she walked to the bathroom to blow her nose and wash her face and think about what she might do next.

WHEN THE BELL rang two nights later, Anne Edwards went to the door and saw Emilio looking like a boy again, standing behind a tall, lean priest in his fifties. Late that night, alone at last in their bedroom, Anne, eyes bulging, confessed to George in a tiny, strangled voice, "That is the butt-ugliest man I ever met. I don't know what I expected but—wow!"

"Well, hell, a Texas Jesuit! I pictured the Marlboro man dressed up like Father Guido Sarducci," George admitted in a whisper. "Jesus. Which eye are you supposed to look at?"

"The one that looks back at you," Anne said decisively.

"I like D.W., I really do, but all during dinner I kept wondering if he'd be offended if I put a bag over his head," George said, suddenly breaking up. That set Anne off, and pretty soon they were hanging on to each other, appalled and ashamed, laughing helplessly, but trying to be as quiet as they could, since the subject of their merriment was in the guest room, right down the hallway.

"Oh, God, we're bad!" Anne gasped, struggling to sober up and losing the battle. "This is awful. But, shit! That one eye, wandering off on its own recognizance!"

"The poor bastard," George said quietly, getting ahold of himself momentarily, trying to sound sympathetic. There was a fleeting silence, as they each pictured D.W., his long broken nose almost as badly askew as his cast eye, loose-lipped grin displaying teeth just as disheveled.

"I'm not a cruel woman," Anne whispered, pleading for understanding. "But I kept wanting to kind of tidy him up, you know?"

"Maybe if we wear the bags?" George asked. Anne, whining and holding her stomach, fell onto the bed and buried her face in a pillow. George, completely undone, followed her.

It had been an evening of laughter, in fact, and none of it at D.W.'s expense until the Edwardses reached their bedroom after midnight.

"Dr. Anne Edwards and Mr. George Edwards," Emilio had said, formally introducing his guest at their door, "I would like to present to you Dalton Wesley Yarbrough, New Orleans Provincial of the Society of Jesus."

"From Waco, Texas, ma'am," D. W. Yarbrough began.

"Yes, I know, Vatican City of the Southern Baptists," Anne said. If she was startled by him, there was no hint of it then. She took the hand he offered, knowing what was coming but ready for him.

"I sure am pleased to meet you, ma'am. Milio has told me a lot about you," D.W. said, smiling, purest malice dancing in his variously arranged eyes. "An' I want straight off to extend to you the profound sympathy of the entire state of Texas on the humiliating loss Dallas handed Cleveland in the World Series last year."

"Well, we all have our crosses to bear, Father." Anne sighed bravely. "It can't be easy for a Texan to say Mass while the entire congregation is praying, Oh, Jesus, just give us one more oil boom—this time we promise we won't piss it all away."

D.W. roared, and they were off and running. Emilio, anxious that these people who meant so much to him should like one another, unleashed a smile like sunrise, went to his chair in the corner and settled in to watch the show. The dinner conversation, as hot and colorful as the barbecue sauce, soon found its center of gravity around politics, there being a presidential-election campaign heating up in which a Texan figured prominently, as usual.

"The country's already tried Texans," George protested.

"And you cowards keep throwin' 'em back to us after just one term!" D.W. hollered.

"Lyndon Johnson, George Bush," George soldiered on.

"No, no, no. You can't blame Bush on Texas," D.W. insisted. "Real Texans never use the word 'summer' as a verb."

Wordlessly, Emilio handed a napkin to Anne, who wiped her nose.

"Gibson Whitmore," George continued.

"Awright. Awright. I admit that was a mistake. He couldna poured water out a boot if the instructions was on the heel. But Sally's good people. Y'all're gonna love her, I guarantee."

"And if you believe that," Emilio said informatively, "D.W. has a very nice piece of the True Cross you might like to invest in."

It was three hours after they sat down to eat when Yarbrough pushed himself reluctantly away from the table, declared that he was stuffed insensible, and then told three more stories that left everyone else at the table worn out and breathless, stomachs and cheeks aching. And it was yet another hour before the four of them got up and started moving glasses and dishes into the kitchen. But there, finally, in the hard bright light of that room, the real reason for D. W. Yarbrough's visit came out.

"Well, folks, where I come from the only thing in the middle of the road is yellow stripes and dead armadillos," D.W. announced, hooking his hands over the top of the door frame and stretching like a gorilla. "So I'll tell y'all right now, I plan to recommend to the Father General, bless his narrow ole Portugee ass, that Emilio go ahead on this asteroid bidness and that the two of you go along, if you're willin'. I talked to the Quinn boy this mornin' and he's okay, too."

George stopped putting plates into the dishwasher. "Just like that? No tests, no interviews? Are you serious?"

"Serious as snakebite, sir. Y'all been researched, I guarantee. Public records, and so forth." There had, in fact, been hundreds of man-hours expended in studying their qualifications, and a rancorous in-house debate over including non-Jesuits in the party. There was ample historical precedent for a mixed crew and solid logic in selecting people with a broad range of experience, but with that established, Father General da Silva had, in the end, simply decided the issue in favor of what appeared to him to be God's will.

"And tonight was the interview," Anne said shrewdly.

"Yes, ma'am. You could say that." The accent and color abated somewhat as D.W. continued, "Emilio had it straight from the start. The skills are mostly all there. The relationships are already in place. We could dick around some, pickin' nits and lookin' at ever' kind of possibility, but I think she'll fly. Assumin' y'all can stand lookin' at me for months on end."

Anne pirouetted abruptly, finding that the glassware in the sink suddenly required her undivided attention. She tried not to let her shoulders shake.

"You're coming?" George asked, with admirable restraint.

"Yessir. That's part of what makes the Father General so sure this bidness is ordained, so to speak. See, somebody's got to get the crew up and down, couple-three times. You recall, there's still the open problem of landin' on the planet. If we find it."

"We could ask Scotty to beam us down," Anne suggested brightly, finally able to face her guest as Emilio, carrying a load of plates into the kitchen, ducked under D.W.'s arm.

"I thought it pretty much has to be a standard Earth-to-dock space-plane," George said. "Of course, just because the Singers've got radio, there's no reason to assume they've got airports—"

"So, the task becomes findin' some kind of flat land or desert to land on because they ain't no guarantee of a runway. And then the undercarriage might collapse from landin' on soft ground and the crew would be stranded." D.W. paused. "So we might do well to use a vertical lander, wouldn't you say?"

"D.W. was in the Marines," Emilio remarked, picking up a dishtowel to dry the stemware Anne was washing. The old trick of keeping a straight face was failing him these days. More and more, his face matched his eyes. "I don't think I ever mentioned that."

Anne looked sideways at D.W. "I have this terrible feeling that you aren't going to tell us that you were a chaplain."

"No, ma'am, I wasn't. This was back in the late eighties, early nineties you unnerstan', 'fore I signed up as a lifer in Loyola's outfit. I flew Harriers. 'Magine that."

Anne, who didn't quite see the point of this information, nevertheless tried imagining that and wondered how D.W. managed depth perception with a cast eye. Then she remembered LeRoy Johnson, a major-league ballplayer with a similar cast in one eye who consistently batted over .290, and she guessed their brains compensated for the problem somehow.

"It couldn't be a stock plane," George said. "You'd have to special-order one with a biphasic skin like the spaceplanes use, so it could take the reentry heat."

"Yeah, folks're workin' on that." D.W. grinned. "Anyhow, turns out, landin' a jump jet's real similar in some ways to flyin' an asteroid docker, 'cause they ain't no runways on space rocks neither. So I expect an ole Harrier pilot may be the very thing for the job at hand."

This time even Anne realized the implications.

"Kinda spooky, ain't it. Hell of a lot of coincidences. Like we say back home, when you find a turtle settin' on top of a fencepost, you can be pretty damn sure he didn't get there on his own." D.W. watched Anne and George look at each other and then continued. "Tomás da Silva, the General his own self, he thinks maybe God's been goin' around puttin' turtles on fenceposts. I don't know about that but I hafta admit, this's kept me up some long nights, thinkin'." D.W. stretched again and smiled crookedly at them. "I'm still in the Reserves and I've kept up my flight hours. I'll be spendin' the next little bit of time qualifyin' on a docker. Oughta be real interestin'. Which way is it to this guest room you've been so kind as to offer me, Dr. Edwards?"

"WELL, FUCK ME dead!" cried Ian Sekizawa, vice president of the Asteroid Mining Division of Ohbayashi Corporation, headquartered in Sydney. "It's Sofie! What a treat to see you again, girl! What's it been? Three years?"

"Four," Sofia said, withdrawing a bit from her screen, not feeling safe from Ian's bear hug even across the electronic distance between them. "It's good to see you, too. Are you still happy with the system? It still suits your requirements?"

"Fits like a finger in a baby's bum," Ian said, grinning when her eyes widened. His grandparents were from Okinawa but he and his language were pure Australian. "Our blokes could be pissed as a newt and still bring back the goods. Profits are up almost twelve points since you did that work for us."

"I'm pleased to hear it," she said, genuinely gratified. "I have a favor to ask of you, Ian."

"Anything, my beauty."

"This is confidential, Ian. I have an encrypted business proposition for you to consider."

"Jaubert doing a dirty?" he asked, eyes narrowed in speculation.

"No, I'm independent now," she told him, smiling.

"Fair dinkum? Sofie! That's beaut! Is this your own little project or are you fronting?"

"I represent clients who wish to remain anonymous. And Ian," she said, "if you are interested, I am hoping you can take this step on your own authority."

"Send the proposal and I'll do me dash," he told her forthrightly. "If it's buggered, I'll trash the code and no one's the wiser, right, love?"

"Thank you, Ian. I appreciate your help," Sofia said. She ended the video conference and sent the code.

LOOKING HER PROPOSITION over, Ian Sekizawa lapsed into thoughtfulness. She wanted a good-sized rock, junk, ice-bearing, with a lot of silicates, more or less cylindrical around the long axis; crew quarters for eight, engines and mining robots included, used if possible, installed if necessary. He tried to reckon who would want such a thing and for what. A drug factory? But then why ask for the mining equipment? Sure, ice, but why so much silicate? He turned it around in his mind for a while but came up with nothing that struck him as practical.

From his own point of view, it was sweet. Before Sofia's AI wizardry, Aussie wildcatters had gone from rock to rock, hoping to make the one big strike that could pay off the equipment mortgages they owed to Ohbayashi and set them up for life. Ninety-nine out of a hundred wildcatters went broke or crazy or both and abandoned their last asteroid with the equipment in situ. Rights reverted to Ohbayashi, which recovered the hardware whenever it was profitable to do so. He had a dozen or more rocks that could do for Sofia's client.

"Oh shit, oh fuck, oh dear, cried the fairy princess as she waved her wooden leg in the air," he recited blandly, alone in his office.

Sofia was offering a fair price. He could bury the transaction in "Obsolete equipment sales," maybe. The rocks were worth fuck-all as things stood. Why not sell one off? he thought. And who gives a damn what it's used for?

WAITING IN HER small rented room for Ian Sekizawa's response to the proposal, Sofia Mendes stared out the window at the Old City of Jerusalem and asked herself why she had come here.

In her first hours of freedom, she had decided simply to carry on as before. She informed the Jesuits in Rome of her new status, assured them of her willingness to act as general contractor on the previously negotiated terms, and made arrangements to have the agreement rewritten in her own name. There was a 30 percent advance payment and, realizing that she could fulfill the contract from anywhere in the world, she had used the money to buy passage to Israel. Why?

Without her mother to light the Sabbath candles, without her father to sing the ancient blessings over the bread and wine, she'd lost touch with the religion of her truncated childhood. But after years of wandering, she felt a need to go home somehow, wanted to see if she was capable of belonging somewhere. There was nothing left for her in Istanbul—peaceful now, exhausted from achieving its own destruction. And her ties to Spain were too tenuous, too faint and historical. So. Israel. Home by default, she supposed.

On her first day in Jerusalem, shyly, never having done so before, she'd sought out a *mikveh,* a place of ritual cleansing. She chose a place at random, unaware that it catered to Israeli brides preparing for their weddings. The *mikveh* lady who took care of her assumed at first that she was about to be married and was distressed to find that Sofia did not even have a sweetheart. "Such a beautiful girl! Such a lovely body! What a waste!" the woman exclaimed, laughing at Sofia's blush. "So, you'll stay here! Make aliyah, find a nice Jewish boy and have lots of beautiful babies, naturally!"

It was hopeless to contradict the good-natured advice, and she wondered why she wanted to, as she allowed herself to be preened and cleaned—hair, nails, everything rinsed, smoothed and shined, her body made free of cosmetics, of dust, of the past. Why not stay? she asked herself.

Wrapped in a white sheet, she was escorted to the *mikveh* itself and then left alone to descend the tiled steps, with their intricate mosaic designs, into the warm, pure water. The *mikveh* lady, standing discreetly behind a half-closed door, helped her remember the Hebrew prayers and urged her, "Three times. All the way under, so every bit of you is immersed. There's no rush, dear. I'll leave you now."

Breaking the surface of the water for the third time, smoothing her hair away from her forehead and pressing the moisture from her eyes, Sofia felt weightless and suspended in time as the words of the old prayers drifted through her mind. There was a blessing for tasting the first fruit after a winter of want, now said for new beginnings, she recalled, when some turning point had come to a life. Blessed art Thou, O God, Ruler of the Universe, for giving us life, for sustaining us, for enabling us to reach this season . . .

Perhaps it was the *mikveh* lady's talk of marriage and children that brought Emilio Sandoz to mind. Sofia Mendes had kept her distance from men since that final night with Jaubert—too much, too early. Even so, she found the idea of priestly celibacy barbaric. What she knew of Catholicism was repellent, with its persecutions, its focus on death, on martyrdom, its central symbol an instrument of Roman criminal justice, appalling in its violence. In the beginning, it was an act of heroic self-control to work with Sandoz: a Spaniard, dressed for mourning, heir to the Inquisition and the expulsion, the representative of a pirate religion that took the bread and wine of Shabbat and turned it into a cannibalistic rite of flesh and blood.

She had challenged him on this point one night at Anne and George's, inhibitions weakened by Ronrico: "Explain this Mass to me!"

There was a silence as he sat still, apparently looking at the dinner plates and chicken bones. "Consider the Star of David," he said quietly. "Two triangles, one pointing down, one pointing up. I find this a powerful image—the Divine reaching down, humanity reaching upward. And in the center, an intersection, where the Divine and human meet. The Mass takes place in that space." His eyes lifted and met hers: a look of lucid candor. "I understand it as a place where the Divine and the human are one. And as a promise, perhaps. That God will reach toward us if we reach toward Him, that we and our most ordinary human acts— like eating bread and drinking wine—can be transformed and made sacred." Then the sunrise smile appeared, transforming his dark face like dawn. "And that, Señorita Mendes, is the best I can do, after three shots of rum at the end of a long day."

It was possible, she admitted to herself, that one had misjudged. Out of ignorance. Or prejudice. Sandoz had made no move to convert her. He was a man of impressive intelligence who seemed to her clear-souled and fulfilled. She had no idea what to make of his belief that God was calling them to contact the Singers. There were Jews who believed that God is in the world, active, purposeful. After the Holocaust, it was difficult to sustain such an idea. Certainly her own life had taught her that prayers for deliverance go unheard, unless she wanted to believe Jean-Claude Jaubert was God's agent.

Still, Israel rose from the ashes of the six million. Jaubert got her out of Istanbul. She was alive. She was free now.

Sofia left the *mikveh* that day with a strong sense of purpose, and when she got back to her room, she contacted Sandoz in San Juan and spoke plainly, without false modesty or bravado. "I should like to be a part of your project. I want not merely to make arrangements for the voyage but to be a member of the crew," she told him. "My former broker, who is in a position to make valid comparisons, can provide references that will establish my intellectual suitability for a project such as this. I respond quickly to new situations and have unusually broad experience, technically and culturally. And I would bring a rather different perspective to the problems the crew may encounter, which may prove useful."

He did not seem at all surprised. Correct and respectful, he told her that he would relay her offer to volunteer to his superiors.

Then came a meeting with the bizarre Yarbrough. He told stories and asked sly, shrewd questions and got her to laugh twice and at the end, he said in his unfathomable dialect, "Well, darlin', the Company hired you a while back cause you was smarter'n hell and very damn quick on the uptake, and we already know you work harder'n six mules, and you get along fine with all these other folks who're goin', and I expect you can learn anything you put your mind to, which is gonna count for a whole lot if we ever meet these Singers. But what decides *me*, bein' as ugly as two warthogs in a mud ditch personally, is that havin' you around while we live for six, eight months inside a rock would prolly keep everyone else from pullin' their own eyes out by the roots. I'll have to check with the boss, but far's I'm concerned, you're in, if you're game."

She stared at him. "Does that mean 'yes'?"

He grinned. "Yes."

Standing at the window now, she could see the Kotel, the Western Wall. Too far away to hear the murmur of prayers, she could watch the tidal ebb and flow of tourists and pilgrims, pointing, davening, weeping, placing small pieces of paper bearing petitions and prayers of gratitude into the spaces between the ancient stones. And she knew why she was here. She had come to Israel to say good-bye to the past.

She heard her system's message signal and opened the file, read Ian Sekizawa's one-word reply and smiled.

"Done," the screen said.

THAT YEAR, SEVERAL superb works of Renaissance art were sold without publicity to private investors. At an auction in London, a price was found for what had previously been considered a priceless collection of seventeenth-century Oriental porcelains. Long-held pieces of property and stock portfolios quietly went on the market at calculated times and in carefully selected locations where considerable gains were available upon sale.

It was a matter of taking profits, liquidating some assets, redeploying capital. The total needed, as Sofia Mendes predicted, was not an inconsiderable amount of money, but it did not beggar the Society by any means and did not even affect Jesuit missions and charitable projects on Earth, which were operated under current cash flow from educational and research facilities, leasing agreements and patent licenses. The sum accumulated in this way was deposited in a reliably discreet Viennese bank. Jesuits around the world were instructed to monitor the public news media and private data nets for any mention of Jesuit financial activity and to relay that information to the Father General's office at Number 5. No pattern was detected, all that year.

14

NAPLES:

MAY 2060

Not even Vesuvius could delay spring forever. As the weather moderated, Emilio Sandoz found he could sleep more easily in the open, lulled by waves and bird cries, his back against sun-warmed rock. He thought perhaps it was the sunlight on his closed eyes that banished the darkness even in sleep; he was less likely to awaken sweating and nauseated. Sometimes the dreams were merely puzzling, not terrifying. Or vile.

He was on a beach, with a child from La Perla. He was apologizing because, though his hands were unharmed in the dream, he couldn't seem to do the magic tricks any longer. The child looked at him with the strange and beautiful double-irised eyes of the VaRakhati. "Well," she said, with the confident practicality of the half-grown, "learn some new tricks."

"Padre, c'è qualcuno che vuol vedervi."

He sat up, breathing hard, disoriented. He could still hear the dream-child's words and it seemed important to him not to forget what they were before he'd had time to think about them. He rubbed his eyes with the back of his forearm, resisting the impulse to shout at the boy for waking him.

"—un uomo che vuol vedervi."

A man who would see you, the boy was saying. What was his name? Giancarlo. He was ten. His mother was a local farmer who sold produce to restaurants in Naples. Sometimes the retreat house ran short when there were extra people in the refectory, and Giancarlo brought vegetables to the kitchen. He often hung around, hoping to be sent on an errand, to bring a message to the sick priest, perhaps, or to help him up the stairs sometimes. *"Grazie,"* Emilio said, hoping this was *thanks* in Italian, but unsure. He wanted to tell the boy that he could manage the stairs on his own now but couldn't find the words. It was so long ago, so many languages ago.

Pulling himself together, he stood carefully and climbed slowly off the huge weathered rock that was his sanctuary, using his bare feet to find purchase, startling badly when Giancarlo suddenly produced a stream of treble Italian. It was too fast, too complicated, and Emilio was whipsawed between fury at being asked to understand something that was beyond him and despair that so much was beyond him.

Slow down, he told himself. It's not his fault. He's a good kid, probably just curious about a man wearing gloves but no shoes . . .

"I don't understand. I'm sorry," he said finally, moving again, hoping the sentiment would get through. The boy nodded and shrugged and offered him a hand he didn't dare accept, to steady him on the last jump to the ground. He wondered then if Giancarlo knew about his hands, and if he'd be frightened by them. It would be another week before he could try the braces again. In the meantime, he wore Candotti's fingerless gloves, which had been, as John predicted, a good and simple solution to some problems: concealment, for example.

Emilio leaned against the rock for a time, and then smiled and jerked his head across the beach toward the long stone stairway. Giancarlo smiled back and they walked along in companionable silence. The boy stayed close as they worked their way up the bluff, killing time by hopping with two feet from step to step, spending his energy with the profligacy of the young and healthy, uncomfortable in the presence of enfeeblement. It was slow going but they got all the way up the stairs without pausing more than a few moments now and then.

"Ecco fatto, padre! Molto bene!" Giancarlo said, in the encouraging if slightly patronizing tone used by well-meaning adults addressing small children who succeed at something very simple.

Recognizing both the words and the attitude, Emilio realized in time that the child would pat him on the back; expecting the touch, he was able to tolerate it and gravely gave the child his thanks again, sure now that *grazie* was Italian. And once again, he veered unsteadily, warmed by the good-heartedness of this child, staggered by mourning for another. With a gesture and a smile that took a great deal of effort, he gave the boy leave to go. Then he rested on a stone bench at the top of the stairs, to give himself time to recover before going in.

The habit of obedience was not extinguished in him; summoned, he appeared, even if the fear made his heart pound. It took him longer to get a grip on his feelings than it did to get over the climb from the beach. Regular hours, regular food, regular exercise, on orders from the Father General. Given half a chance, his body was healing, repairing itself. Hybrid vigor, Anne would have said, half-seriously. The strengths of two continents.

He thought sometimes of the peculiar peacefulness he'd experienced toward the end of the voyage back, watching blood seep from his hands and thinking, This will kill me, and then I can stop trying to understand.

He wondered then if Jesus expected gratitude as Lazarus emerged, stinking, from the crypt. Maybe Lazarus was a disappointment to everyone, too.

THE SHORT, STOCKY man waiting for him was almost past middle age, wearing a black skull cap and a dark plain suit. A rabbi, Emilio thought, his heart sinking. A relative of Sofia's, a second cousin perhaps, here to demand an accounting.

The man had turned at the sound of Emilio's footsteps. Smiling a little sadly through a full and curling beard mostly gone to gray, he said, *"No me conoces."*

A Sephardic rabbi might use Spanish but would not have addressed a stranger so familiarly. Emilio felt himself slide into helpless frustration and looked away.

But the man saw his bewilderment and seemed to sense his fragile state of mind. "I'm sorry, Father," he said. "Of course, you wouldn't recognize me. I was only a kid when you left, not even shaving yet." He laughed, pointing to his beard. "And now, as you see, I still don't shave."

Embarrassed, Emilio started to apologize and back away when the stranger suddenly let rip a torrent of Latin insults and taunts, the grammar flawless, the content appalling. "Felipe Reyes!" Emilio breathed, mouth open with astonishment. He stepped back, the surprise was so great. "I can't believe it. Felipe, you're an old man!"

"Things like that happen, if you wait long enough," Felipe said, grinning. "And only fifty-one! Not so old. Mature, we like to call it."

For a few moments, they stood and looked at each other in wonderment, taking in the changes, visible and implied. Then Felipe broke the spell. Waiting for Emilio to appear, he had drawn a couple of chairs to either side of a small table near a window in the large open room and, laughing again, he motioned Emilio across and pulled out a chair for him. "Sit down, sit down. You're too thin, Father! I feel like I should order you a sandwich or something. Don't they feed you here?" Felipe almost said something about Jimmy Quinn but thought better of it. Instead, he fell quiet as they sat together, beaming at Sandoz, giving him time to get over the shock.

Emilio finally burst out, "I thought you were a rabbi!"

"Thank you," Felipe said comfortably. "As a matter of fact, you made a priest out of me. I am a Jesuit, old friend, but I teach at the Jewish Theological Seminary in Los Angeles. Me! A professor of comparative religion!" And he laughed delightedly at Emilio's amazement.

For the next hour, in the language of childhood, they reminisced about La Perla. It was only five or six years ago for Emilio and he found to his surprise that he could recall more names than Felipe, but Reyes knew what had happened to everyone and had a hundred stories, some funny, some sad. Of course, it had been almost forty years since Emilio had left; he shouldn't have been surprised that so much of the narrative came down to a litany of deaths, and yet . . .

His parents were long gone but there was his brother to find out about. "Antonio Luis died a couple of years after you left, Father," Felipe told him.

"How?" he made himself ask.

"Just like you'd expect." Felipe shrugged and shook his head. "He was using product, man. Always screws them up in the end. He had no judgment. He was skimming cash and the Haitians laid him down."

His left hand hurt like hell and the headache was making it hard to concentrate. So many dead, he thought. So many dead . . .

". . . so Claudio sold the restaurant to Rosa, but she married this *pendejo* who drove the place into the ground. They lost it a few years later. She divorced him. Never got back on her feet again, really. But remember Maria Lopez? Who worked for Dr. Edwards? Father? Do you remember Maria Lopez?"

"Yes. Sure." Squinting now against the light, Emilio asked, "Did Maria end up going to medical school?"

"No way." Felipe paused to smile thanks at a brother who brought them both cups of tea, unasked for. Neither drank. Hands in his lap, Felipe continued, "But she got out. Dr. Edwards left her a pile of money, did you know that? Maria went to the University of Krakow Business School and ended up making an even bigger pile of money. Married a Polish guy. They never had children. But Maria set up a scholarship fund for La Perla kids. Your work is still bearing fruit, Father."

"That wasn't my doing, Felipe. That was Anne." It came to him that it must have been Anne and George who'd bought out Sofia's contract. He remembered Anne laughing about how much fun it was to give away money they'd saved for retirement. He remembered Anne laughing. He wanted Felipe to leave.

Felipe saw the distress but went on, voice quiet, insistent on the good that Sandoz had done. The trees planted on Chuuk Island had matured; a man who'd learned to read and write as a teenager in the Jesuit literacy program became a revered poet, his work illuminated by Arctic beauty and the souls of his people. "And remember Julio Mondragón? That kid you got to quit defacing buildings and paint the chapel? He is a tremendous big deal now! His stuff goes for amazing prices and it is so beautiful, sometimes even I think it's worth the money. People come to the chapel to see his early work, can you imagine?"

Emilio sat, eyes closed, unable to look at the man he had inspired to take up the burdens of priesthood. That of all things he did not wish responsibility for. The words of Jeremiah came to him: "I will not mention God or speak anymore in his name." And then Reyes was kneeling in front of him and through the roaring in his head, he heard Felipe say, "Father, let me see what has been done to you."

Let me see: let me understand. Emilio held out his hands because, hideous as he found them, they were far easier to display than what was inside him. Gently, Felipe pulled the gloves away and as the mutilation was revealed, there was the familiar whir of servomotors and microgears, the metallic susurration of mechanical joints, but strangely muffled by the overlayment of extraordinarily lifelike artificial skin.

Felipe took Emilio's fingers in his own cool mechanical hands. "Father Singh is brilliant, isn't he. It's hard to believe now but I actually made do with hooks for a while! Even after he made the prostheses, I was pretty depressed," Felipe admitted. "We never did find out who sent the letter bomb, or why. But the strange thing is, after a while, I was even grateful for what happened. You see, I am happy where I am today, so I am thankful for each step that took me here."

There was a silence. Felipe Reyes's hips were beginning to get arthritic and he suddenly felt like the old man he was becoming, getting to his feet and watching the bitterness transform Emilio's face.

"That bastard! Did Voelker send for you?" He was up now, moving away from Felipe, pacing, putting distance between them. "I wondered why he didn't leave a biography of Isaac Jogues next to my bed. He had something better, didn't he. An old friend of mine who's got it worse. That sonofabitch!" Sandoz said, incredulous, fluent in his fury. He suddenly stopped and turned on Felipe. "Did you come here to tell me to count my blessings, Felipe? Am I supposed to be inspired?"

Felipe Reyes pulled himself to his full, if modest, height and looked frankly at Emilio, whom he had idolized in youth and whom he still wanted to love, in spite of everything. "It wasn't Voelker, Father. The Father General asked me to come."

Sandoz went very still. When he spoke, his voice had the quiet, nearly calm sound of viciously controlled anger. "Ah. Your task then is to shame me for making such a fuss. For wallowing in self-pity."

Felipe found there was nothing he could say and, helpless, let the silence linger, Sandoz watching him like a snake. Suddenly, the man's eyes lit up dangerously. Comprehension dawning, Felipe knew.

"And the hearings, too?" Sandoz asked, the voice caressing now, brows up, mouth open slightly, waiting for confirmation. Felipe nodded. To bitterness, Sandoz added amused contempt. "And the hearings. Of course! God!" he cried, in direct address. "It's perfect. Just the sort of creative touch I've come to expect. And you here as devil's advocate, Felipe?"

"It's not an inquisition, Father. You know that. I'm just here to help—"

"Yes," Emilio said softly, with a smile that left his eyes untouched. "To help find the truth. To make me talk."

Felipe Reyes endured Emilio's gaze as long as he could. He looked away finally, but he could not close out the soft savage voice.

"You can't imagine the truth. I lived it, Felipe. I have to live with it now. You tell them: the hands are nothing. You tell them: self-pity would be an improvement. It doesn't matter what I say. It doesn't matter what I tell you. None of you will ever know what it was like. And I promise you: you don't want to know."

When Felipe looked up, Sandoz was gone.

VINCENZO GIULIANI, BACK in his Rome office, was informed of the fiasco within the hour.

In truth, the Father General had not summoned Felipe Reyes to serve as Emilio Sandoz's prosecutor. There would be no trial, no devil's advocate, not even in the loose colloquial sense that Emilio had used. The aim of the coming inquiry was to help the Society plan its next moves regarding Rakhat. Reyes was a well-respected specialist in comparative religious studies whom Giuliani expected to be of use as Sandoz worked his way through the details of the Rakhat mission. But there was no use denying it. The Father General had also hoped that Felipe Reyes, who had known Sandoz in better days and who himself had been maimed while studying at a Pakistani university, might give Emilio a healthier perspective on the apparent uniqueness of his experience. So it was with a good deal of chagrin that Giuliani learned how badly he'd misread Sandoz on this score.

Sighing, he rose from his desk and walked to the windows to stare out at the Vatican through the rain. What a burden men like Sandoz carried into the field. Over four hundred of Ours to set the standard, he thought, and remembered his days as a novice, studying the lives of sainted, blessed and venerated Jesuits. What was that wonderful line? "Men astutely trained in letters and in fortitude." Enduring hardship, loneliness, exhaustion and sickness with courage and resourcefulness. Meeting torture and death with a joy that defies easy understanding, even by those who share their religion, if not their faith. So many Homeric stories. So many martyrs like Isaac Jogues. Trekking eight hundred miles into the interior of the New World—a land as alien to a European in 1637 as Rakhat is to us now, Giuliani suddenly realized. Feared as a witch, ridiculed, reviled for his mildness by the Indians he'd hoped to gain for Christ. Beaten regularly, his fingers cut off joint by joint with clamshell blades—no wonder Jogues had come to Emilio's mind. Rescued, after years of abuse and deprivation, by Dutch traders who arranged for his return to France, where he recovered, against all odds.

Astonishing, really: Jogues went back. He must have known what would happen but he sailed back to work among the Mohawks, as soon as he was able. And in the end, they killed him. Horribly.

How are we to understand men like that? Giuliani had once wondered. How could a sane man have returned to such a life, knowing such a fate was likely? Was he psychotic, driven by voices? A masochist who sought degradation and pain? The questions were inescapable for a modern historian, even a Jesuit historian. Jogues was only one of many. Were men like Jogues mad?

No, Giuliani had decided at last. Not madness but the mathematics of eternity drove them. To save souls from perpetual torment and estrangement from God, to bring souls to imperishable joy and nearness to God, no burden was too heavy, no price too steep. Jogues himself had written to his mother, "All the labors of a million persons, would they not be worthwhile if they gained a single soul for Jesus Christ?"

Yes, he thought, Jesuits are well prepared for martyrdom. Survival, on the other hand, could be an intractable problem. Sometimes, Vincenzo Giuliani suspected, it is easier to die than to live.

"I'M REALLY STARTING to hate those stairs," John Candotti called, walking across the beach. Sandoz was sitting on the rocks as usual, his back against the stone, hands exposed and loose, dangling between his drawn-up knees. "I don't suppose you could brood in the garden? There's a real nice spot for brooding, right next to the house."

"Leave me alone, John." Emilio's eyes were closed and he had what John was beginning to recognize as the look of a man with a crushing headache.

"I vass only followink awdahs. Father Reyes sent me." He expected an epithet, but Sandoz was back in control, or past caring. John stood on the beach, a few feet from Sandoz, and for a while looked out over the sea. There were sails in the distance, brilliant in the slanting sunlight, and the usual fishing boats. "It's times like this," John said philosophically, "when I remember what my old dad always used to say."

Emilio's head came up and he looked at John wearily, resigned to another assault.

"'What the hell are you doing in the bathroom day and night?'" John shouted suddenly. "'Why don't you get out of there and give somebody else a chance?'"

Emilio lay his head back against the rock, and laughed and laughed.

"Now, that is a good sound," John said, grinning, delighted by the effect he'd had. "You know what? I don't think I've ever heard you laugh before, not really."

"*Young Frankenstein!* That's from *Young Frankenstein!*" Emilio gasped. "My brother and I knew that whole movie by heart. We must have watched that thing a hundred times when we were kids. I loved Mel Brooks."

"One of the greats," John agreed. "*The Odyssey. Hamlet. Young Frankenstein.* Some things never die."

Emilio laughed again, wiping his eyes on his sleeve and catching his breath. "I thought you were going to tell me things would look better in the morning or something. I was preparing to murder you."

John checked at that but decided it was only a figure of speech. "Heavens! Then I suppose my presence constituted the near occasion of sin, my son," he said prissily, mimicking Johannes Voelker. "May I join you on your rock, sir?"

"Be my guest." Emilio moved over to make room, shaking off the lingering reaction to seeing Felipe again.

Preceded by his prowlike nose, John clambered up, all elbows and knees and big feet, envying Emilio's compact neatness, the athletic grace evident even now. John made himself fairly comfortable on the unyielding surface of the rock, and the two men admired the sunset for a while. They'd be climbing the stairs in darkness but they were both familiar with every step.

"The way I see it," John said, breaking the silence as the light deepened to blue, "you've got three choices. One: you can leave, like you said you wanted to, in the beginning. Leave the Society, leave the priesthood."

"And go where? And do what?" Sandoz demanded, his face in profile as hard as the bald stone outcropping they sat on. He had not spoken of leaving since the day the reporter burst into his room, when the reality of life on the outside had shouted in his face. "I'm trapped. And you know it."

"You could be a rich man. The Society was offered an immense amount of money just for permission to interview you." Emilio turned to him and, in the dusk, John could almost taste the bile rising in the other man's throat. He waited, to give Sandoz a chance to say something, but Emilio turned back to the sunless sea. "Two: you can see the inquiry through. Explain what happened. Help us decide what to do next. We'll stand by you, Emilio."

Elbows on his drawn-up knees, Emilio raised his hands to his head and rested the long, bony fingers there, pale and skeletal against his hair. "If I start talking, you won't like what you hear."

He thinks the truth is too ugly for us, John had thought, coming down the stairs after a hurried conference with Brother Edward and Father Reyes. Ed thought perhaps that Sandoz didn't realize how much of his story had been made public. "Emilio, we know about the child," John said quietly. "And we know about the brothel."

"No one knows," Sandoz said, his voice muffled.

"Everybody knows, Emilio. Not just Ed Behr and the people at the hospital. The Contact Consortium released the whole story—"

Sandoz stood suddenly and climbed off the rock. He took off down the darkened beach, heading south, arms crossed over his chest to keep the hands tucked under his armpits. John jumped down after him and followed at a run. Overtaking Sandoz, he grabbed the smaller man's shoulder and twisted him around, shouting at him, "How long do you think you can hold all this in? How long do you plan to carry it all yourself?"

"As long as I can, John," Sandoz said grimly, wrenching his shoulder out of Candotti's grip and backing away from him. "As long as I can."

"And then what?" John yelled as Emilio turned away from him. Sandoz spun to face him.

"And then," he said with quiet menace, "I'll take the third option. Is that what you want to hear, John?" He stood there, trembling slightly, flat-eyed, skin drawn taut over the bones of his face.

John, his anger draining away as quickly as it had risen in him, opened his mouth to say something, but Sandoz spoke again.

"I'd have done it months ago but I'm afraid I still have enough pride to deny God the punchline for whatever sick joke I'm playing out now," he said lightly, but his eyes were awful. "That's what's keeping me alive, John. A little bit of pride is all I've got left."

Pride, yes. But also fear: *For in that sleep of death what dreams may come.*

15

SOLAR SYSTEM:
2021

THE <u>STELLA MARIS</u>:
2021–2022, EARTH-RELATIVE

"ANNIE, IT IS so cool! Wait until you see it. The rock looks like this giant potato. And all I could think of when I saw it was the *Muppet Show*. Spuds in spa-a-a-ce!"

Anne laughed, amused by the image and relieved to have George home, if only for a few days while he and D.W. collected additional equipment. The past four weeks had been an anxious time for a woman whose faith in technology was more by practical default than informed conviction, but George had come back to her ebullient and confident, burying her misgivings in an avalanche of enthusiasm as she drove him home from the San Juan airport.

"The engines are on one end and the remote cameras and so forth are on the other end, but recessed and kind of cross-eyed, so they don't point directly in the line of travel—"

"Why's that?"

"To keep them from getting abraded by 'interstellar shit' as you so delicately put it, my dear. The cameras focus on a set of mirrors—the mirrors are exposed but we can sort of peel layers off as the images degrade, the way you peel a layered face shield off a motorcycle helmet in a dirt race. God, you look fabulous!" She kept her gaze on the road but the delicate fan of lines around her eyes deepened with pleasure. Her hair was piled in some kind of style George could only identify as "up" and she was wearing pearls and cream silk. "So anyway," he said, "if you think of the potato, we dock on the long side, like where you'd put the butter—"

"Or the soy-based butteroid nonfat substance, with the taste of real margarine," Anne muttered, eyes on the traffic.

"You fly into this tube and then there's an airlock, but you have to suit up to go from the docker to the airlock. Then you go down this little rock corridor with the wall surfaces all sealed up and there's another airlock just in case—"

"Just in case what?" Anne wanted to know, but he hardly heard her.

"Then you get to the living quarters, which are right in the center where the shielding is best and Annie, it's beautiful inside. Kinda Japanese-looking. Most of the walls are really light panels, so we don't go nuts from the dark. They're sort of like shoji screens." She nodded. "So. There're four concentric cylinders inside, okay? The bedrooms and the toilets are around the outer cylinder. The rooms are pie-shaped—"

"Did you set aside one for the exercise and medical equipment?"

"Yes, Doctor. I put the stuff in there, but you'll have to set it up the way you want it when you get there." George closed his eyes, picturing the rest, then stared straight ahead, not seeing the traffic or San Juan, but the unique and wonderful vessel that would be their home soon, which felt cozy and nautical to him, everything in its place, neat and organized and surprisingly comfortable. "The next inner cylinder has a big common room with built-in tables and benches and the kitchen, which is good, you'll like it. Did you know Marc Robichaux can cook? French stuff. Lot of sauces, he says—"

"I know. Marc's a honey. We've been in touch on the net a lot."

"—but we're eating out of tubes until we've got gravity. Oh! And I had the robots hollow out an extra room with a stone tub, like a Japanese bathroom, where you soap up and rinse off in a little water and then soak."

"Oooh, now that sounds seriously okay," Anne purred. "How big is it?"

He leaned over and planted a kiss on her neck. "Big enough. Now. In the center, there are two more concentric cylinders for the Wolverton tube, right? Column of plants stuck in holes all around the outer cylinder. Leaves coming out into the living area, roots converging toward the center, right? All the air and almost all the wastes get filtered through the plant cylinder. I've seen them before but *God,* this one is beautiful! Marc has been working on the plant mix for months—"

There was more about the plants and then George went on to tell her about the bridge and how the mining robots fed the mass-drivers. And Anne gathered that he and Sofia and Jimmy would be working on AI programs that would make the asteroid self-navigating on the return trip, locking onto Earth broadcasts and Sol's radio frequency, so the system could do the kind of calculations Jimmy was doing on the trip out, in case he was killed. And there was also a VR flight simulator for the docker-lander they'd all train on, in case D.W. was . . .

Anne nosed the car into a parking space at that point and shut off the motor. There was a long silence, both of them sobered by the knowledge that casualties were likely. They were all being cross-trained, to build redundancy into the final crew of eight.

"The ship will just about fly itself on the way back," George said finally.

"That's the part I like," Anne said firmly. "The 'on the way back' part."

ANNE STILL PLAYED Official Skeptic, but the past eighteen months had worked a surprising internal change in her. Time after time, it looked as though the entire mission would be scrubbed; each time, Anne marveled as Jesuit industry and Jesuit prayer were brought to bear on the problems.

The first asteroid turned out to have a faultline likely to give way under one G of acceleration. The second appeared perfect until a remote assay showed too high an iron content, which would foul the engines over the long term. A few nights later, the evening prayers of a Jesuit physicist were interrupted by the sudden realization that his load-bearing calculations were unduly limited by the specification of a roughly cylindrical rock. He finished his prayers, rapidly rethought his assumptions, and woke up Jesuit colleagues in several different time zones. Twelve hours later, Sofia Mendes was authorized to contact Ian Sekizawa and instruct him to broaden the search to include asteroids of nearly any shape, as long as they were roughly symmetrical around the long axis. Within days, the reply from Ian came: he'd located a rock that was more or less ovoid, would that do? It did, nicely.

There was a similar crisis over the biphasic cladding for D.W.'s docker. The material used to sheathe spaceplanes had to function in the unimaginable cold of space as well as in the blast-furnace heat of entry and exit from an atmosphere. Military orders, being the most lucrative contracts, took precedence over civilian projects. Intense prayer, along with astute technical and diplomatic skill, was dedicated to this problem. Unexpectedly, the military government in Indonesia fell and the Indonesian Air Force's order for a spaceplane was canceled, freeing up material for the private order that had been placed months earlier by Sofia Mendes on behalf of an anonymous group of investors.

After a while it became hard to ignore how, against odds, the dice kept coming up in favor of the mission. The crew members went on with their training, their work unaffected by the waxing and waning of confidence, but they all experienced varying degrees of amazement. Even the Jesuits were divided. Marc Robichaux and Emilio Sandoz smiled and said, "See? *Deus vult,*" while D. W. Yarbrough and Andrej Jelačić shook their heads in wonder. George Edwards and Jimmy Quinn and Sofia Mendes remained agnostics on the question of whether these events were minor miracles or major coincidences.

Anne said nothing but as the months passed, it was increasingly difficult to resist the beauty of belief.

AND SO, AS fate or chance or God would have it, nineteen months and twelve days after Anne began compiling her list with "1. Bring nail clippers," she was able at last to cross off the wry final entry: "Vomit in zero G." Unable to stomach even playground swings as a child, she was resigned to the idea that having the contents of her abdomen drift lungward would probably be sufficient to set off the space sickness that still afflicted 15 percent of all travelers, despite medical advances. Not completely pessimistic about her chances of avoiding this, she wore the antinausea transdermal patch that D. W. Yarbrough swore by, and swore at it when she could breathe again.

On the whole, however, she was able to congratulate herself. Everyone had expected her to be frightened so, of course, she decided to confound their expectations by enjoying the ride. And she did. The vertical liftoff was incredibly noisy but there was very little sense of motion. Then there was the thrill of building to four Gs, of being plastered against her couch as they roared along toward Mach 1, when suddenly the noise dropped off behind them. The sky quickly got blacker and blacker and then D.W. turned the afterburner off and she was thrown forward against the belts so hard she thought she'd ruptured her heart. Then she caught sight of the moon and the turquoise rim of the Earth against the dense darkness, straight out the cockpit window ahead of her. As Asia rolled under them into a sunset of great and memorable beauty, Anne felt herself drift away from the couch and begin to float.

It was then that she experienced an instant of unprecedented clarity, a moment of wholly unanticipated certainty that God was real. The sensation fled almost as quickly as it came but left in its wake the conviction that Emilio was right, that they were meant to be here, doing this impossible thing. She looked to him in astonishment, shaken, and was irrationally infuriated to see that he was asleep.

They had been up about two and half hours when Sofia floated by to make a navigational sighting. Turning her head to follow the movement was probably what did it. Anne's inner ears, not her guts, betrayed her. Without warning, her body revolted against its bizarre situation, and she spent the next few hours retching and blowing her nose. When it was over, she realized she was famished and, unfastening her straps, pushed off toward the cockpit, feeling like Mary Martin on a wire until she bumped into a bulkhead so hard that she exclaimed, "Ouch!" and then "Damn," without thinking. She glanced back at Emilio, hoping that she hadn't disturbed him, but he opened his eyes and grinned greenly at her, and she realized that he'd been awake all along and was just this side of blowing breakfast.

D.W. chose that moment to holler back to them, "Hey, anybody hungry?" The effect of the question was immediate and impressive.

At his own firm if garbled request, Anne left Emilio alone to cope with the revolting experience as she had, without a solicitous audience. She joined D.W. and Sofia for lunch, which featured an excellent vichyssoise, packaged in bags like toothpaste tubes. With her stomach settling and a surprisingly decent meal in her, Anne's spirits rose all the way up to okay. This was sufficient improvement for her to decide morosely that even while suffering from the Fat Face, Chicken Legs syndrome that was affecting them all in zero G, Sofia at thirty-two looked better than Anne had on her wedding day, fresh-faced and twenty. Not even a radical redistribution of blood plasma and lymph was able to dim Sofia's looks entirely, the fluid in her face smoothing it into an ivory oval, dark brows arched and tranquil over egg-shaped eyelids, the lips pursed in calm self-possession: an emotionless Byzantine portrait.

D.W., on the other hand, was even more unsightly than usual.

Beauty and the Beast, Anne thought, watching them work head to head over some navigational task. It was a friendship she found odd and pure and touching in a way she didn't quite understand. With Sofia, D.W. dropped most of his elaborate Good Ole Boy act and seemed to take up less of the oxygen in a room; Sofia, for her part, seemed less wary in D.W.'s company, more at home in her skin. Remarkable, Anne mused. Who'd have thunk it?

THERE HAD BEEN resistance to the escalation in Sofia's involvement with the mission, not from the other crew members, but from the Father General's office, which had been willing to employ her as a contractor but balked at her inclusion in the crew. It had taken D. W. Yarbrough's direct intercession to bring her in and the Texan was pretty damned pleased with himself for pushing it through.

For one thing, Sofia had turned out to be a natural pilot; nerveless and precise, with a logical approach to complex systems, she picked up the skills from her instructors with the cool competence that once profited Jean-Claude Jaubert and now delighted D. W. Yarbrough. "Learning curve like a jump jet's flight path—all but straight up," D.W. declared to the Father General, and continued cheerfully, "I could drop dead any time now and she'd get 'em all up and down, no problem. 'S a load off my mind, I guarantee."

But there was more to it than that. D.W. made no claim to saintliness, only to a certain talent for bringing people into their own—for finding God in them. A master of disguise himself, Yarbrough knew when he was looking at a facade. If nothing else was accomplished on this crazy-ass mission, he told himself first and the Father General last, he intended to take a shot at helping this one soul patch itself up and make itself whole. Long ago, John F. Kennedy proposed that America go to the moon, not because it would be easy but because it would be difficult, and that was the gift D. W. Yarbrough offered Sofia Mendes: the opportunity to do something so difficult that she'd be stretched to her limits, feel her own possibilities, find something in herself to rejoice in.

And if it was a shock that Sofia was as wise to his ways as he was to hers, he reckoned that might be to the good. For all his folksy cowboy shtick, Yarbrough was, at fifty-nine, a careful, competent leader whose slipshod personal style masked a relentless, fastidious attention to detail. Once an air squadron commander, he knew there were many things one could not control when engaged in battle, and that knowledge dictated an iron-willed insistence that what could be controlled must be brought to perfection. And in this, Sofia was his match.

As the two generalists on the team, D. W. Yarbrough and Sofia Mendes had grappled with the coordination and supervision of the greatest voyage into the unknown since Magellan left Spain in 1519. Together, they had gone over every detail of the mission, collecting and absorbing the results of the work of several hundred independent task forces, reconciling differences, making command decisions, insisting on additional thought, better solutions, more thoroughly considered plans. They had to allow for every imaginable contingency: desert heat, tropical rain, arctic cold, plains, mountains, rivers, and do it with as much overlap in equipment as possible, to minimize bulk. They studied food-storage systems, considered possible means of overland transport, argued fiercely over whether they should bring coffee or learn to do without it, discussed the ecological impact of bringing seeds in hopes of establishing gardens, brainstormed about trade goods, shouted, fell out, made up, laughed a good deal and, despite the accumulated odds against such an outcome, came to be fond of each other.

Finally the day arrived when they were ready to begin loading the asteroid for the trip. D.W. and Sofia ferried George Edwards and Marc Robichaux up to the rock first, so they could inspect and fine-tune the life-support system onboard the asteroid and stow the first shipment of supplies.

Marc Robichaux, S.J., was a naturalist and watercolorist from Montreal. Blond hair graying at forty-three, he remained one of those perennially youthful looking men, soft-spoken and gentle-eyed. "The quintessential Shy, Cute Guy," Anne pegged him, the kind of boy who was simultaneously a high school heartthrob and a teacher's pet, adorable but with an obnoxious tendency to turn his papers in early and get A's on them. Marc was in charge of the Wolverton tube plant colony and the tilapia tank, which would produce fresh food to supplement the packaged stuff they were bringing. George Edwards was responsible for the software control of the Wolverton tube as well as for the software and mechanical aspects of the allied air- and water-extraction systems. The two men had spent the last year learning each other's specialties, Marc's quiet carefulness a good balance for George's exuberant try-anything approach to life.

Next up were James Connor Quinn, twenty-eight, mission specialist for navigation and communications, and the musicologist Alan Pace,
S.J. At thirty-nine, Father Pace was a willowy Englishman who gave the
sleepy-eyed impression of someone who had seen it all and who quite
possibly knew it all as well. It was a trait that worried D.W.; Pace was a
last-minute replacement for Andrej Jelačić, who'd suffered a heart attack during a stress test. Andrej, still mourned, was a hard act to follow.
But Alan was well qualified—a remarkable musician, if kind of a pain in
the ass. Like many musicians, he had a precise and orderly mind and
had, in fact, minored in mathematics. He cross-trained with Jimmy
Quinn, an amateur pianist, and they had spent the months of preparation studying the growing collection of alien song fragments, along with
the technical skills needed to navigate the rock to Alpha Centauri.

That left Emilio Sandoz, forty, and Anne Edwards, who like her
husband was sixty-four, as the last ones up to the rock. They had remained in Puerto Rico while the others dispersed for training. A new
priest was assigned to take over Emilio's work in La Perla, and he'd
shifted his effort to the clinic, where Anne supervised him in an accred-
ited physician's assistant course, with an emphasis on the kinds of medical emergencies they might face off Earth, without benefit of hospitals,
pharmacies or elaborate equipment. For his part, Emilio once again became Anne's language teacher, this time using Sofia's AI program to help
Anne prepare for learning the Singers' language. Together night after
night, they transcribed and studied the intercepted transmissions. They
were handicapped by the utter lack of referents but picked out recurring
phrases and accustomed themselves to the rhythm of the language.

They had a fair amount of material to work from, as did Alan Pace.
Once established, the reception pattern became reliable. By June of
2021, most radio astronomers had returned to other projects and telescope operators simply turned toward Alpha Centauri in alternating 15-
and 27-day cycles, tuning in for what seemed to be regularly scheduled
concerts. The music never lasted long, the signals falling off to noise
after only a few minutes. The songs always differed from one another,
although a theme was repeated once. Sometimes there was the call-and-
response pattern of the first song. Sometimes there was a soloist. Sometimes the music was choral.

Most exciting, in some ways, was that individual Singers came to be
recognized, after a time. Of these, the most compelling had a voice of

breathtaking power and sweetness, operatic in dimension but so plainly used in hypnotic, graceful chant that the listener hardly noticed its gorgeousness except to think of beauty and of truth.

This was the voice of Hlavin Kitheri, the Reshtar of Galatna, who would one day destroy Emilio Sandoz.

IF THE ANTINAUSEA patches did not entirely eliminate space sickness, they did seem to limit its duration. Both Anne and Emilio were fine by the time D.W. called out, some twelve hours after liftoff, "Thar she blows!" Floating cautiously toward the cockpit windows, they caught their first glimpse of the asteroid.

Emilio, who'd also been the recipient of George's enthusiastic description, made a disappointed face. "What? No sour cream? No chives?"

Anne giggled and pushed off to return to her place in the cargo bay. "And no gravity," she said over her shoulder. She was grinning.

"Is that significant?" Emilio asked in a low voice, joining her in the back.

"Strap in, you two," D.W. ordered. "We still got mass and you can still bust your neck if I blow the docking."

"Shit. What does he mean, blow the docking? He never said anything about that before," Anne muttered, taking her position and fastening the straps that held her to her couch.

Emilio, also buckling up, had not forgotten the look on Anne's face. "So, what was that about no gravity?" he pressed. "C'mon. What? What!"

"How shall I put this?" She was blushing but went on very quietly in tones of great propriety. "George and I have been married almost forty-five years and we've done it about all the ways it can be done, except in zero G."

He put his hands over his mouth. "Of course. It never occurred to me, but naturally—"

"It isn't supposed to occur to you," Anne said severely. "I, on the other hand, have thought of very little else since I stopped throwing up."

THE DOCKING PROCEDURE went smoothly. D.W. and Sofia went almost directly to their quarters, having worked continually during the flight. Even Emilio and Anne were tired simply from being passengers, and despite the excitement of seeing the living quarters for the first time, neither of them protested being sent to "bed"—sleeping bags suspended in midair.

While the newcomers slept, George, Marc, Alan and Jimmy moved the last few hundred items off the docker. A lot of thought had gone into the geometry of the storage areas; it was hard to anticipate how the load would shift under acceleration. Indeed, all aspects of the living quarters had been planned for function in first weightlessness and later with a definite down, which would be aft, toward the engines, once they were fired. So everything had to be carefully secured before the first of two shakedown burns D.W. planned for the next day.

The work took hours, which was partly why Jimmy Quinn was so late waking up the next morning, but only partly. Eileen Quinn once observed that getting Jimmy up for school was more like performing a resurrection than providing a wake-up call; never a willing early riser, Jimmy hated mornings even in space. So when he floated into the common room after dealing with the aggravating complexities of weightless hygiene, he was ready to apologize for delaying the shakedown burn. To his surprise, Anne and George were still missing from breakfast, so he wasn't the latest after all. He went about his business, silent as usual at that time of day, sucking down a tube of coffee and some lobster bisque he'd discovered in the food bins. It was only after the caffeine began to work that he realized that everyone was kind of waiting for something to happen.

He was about to ask D.W. what time the burn was scheduled for when the laughter from Anne and George's room got noticeable and he turned to say, "What do you suppose they're up to?" He meant it as an innocent question, but Emilio cracked up and D.W. put his hands over his face. Alan Pace was clearly trying very hard not to notice anything, but Marc was laughing and Sofia's shoulders were shaking, although Jimmy couldn't see her face because she'd gone off to a corner of the galley.

"What—?" he started to ask again, but now Anne was audibly convulsed and then George's voice rang out from their cabin. "Well, sports fans, we're talking a major disappointment here in Fantasy Land."

That set D.W. off, but Alan was still quite composed and remarked, "Ah, I expect this is a difficulty somehow attributable to Newton's Third Law," which Jimmy, in his morning fog, had to think about for a moment before he said vaguely, "For every action, there is an equal and op-posite reaction . . ." And then it began to dawn on him.

"Ole George is prolly having a little trouble gettin' a purchase," D.W. commented, which made even Alan Pace laugh. But Marc Ro-bichaux pushed off purposefully toward a storage cabinet and floated back moments later, smiling seraphically, a middle-aged Angel Gabriel holding a two-inch-wide roll of silver adhesive tape. This he delivered by cracking open the door to Anne and George's room and holding it inside one-handed, the way one might deliver toilet paper to a discommoded guest. Meanwhile, Karl Malden's sonorous TV voice, marred by a slight Spanish accent, called out to them, "Duct tape! Don't leave home with-out it."

Anne shrieked with laughter, but George yelled, "I don't suppose we could get a little gravity around here?" and D.W. hollered back, "Nope. All we got is levity."

And thus began the first morning of the Jesuit mission to Rakhat.

"WELL, LADIES AND gentlemen, the *Stella Maris* is on her way out of the solar system," Jimmy called out from the bridge, a remarkably short time after they got under way.

A ragged cheer went up. Knobby hands wrapped around a cup of coffee, D.W. leaned over the table and said archly, "Miz Mendes, I 'magine this qualifies you as the all-time champi'n Wanderingest Jew in history." Sofia smiled.

"He's been waiting for months to use that line," George snorted, watching the clocks and seeing the first discrepancies appear.

"Are we there yet?" Anne asked brightly. There were boos and groans.

"Well, I thought it was funny, Anne," Emilio told her earnestly, as he set the table, "but I have really low standards."

From the moment the engines were fired, they had full gravity, and it very quickly seemed normal to be inside an asteroid traveling toward Alpha Centauri, no matter how crazy the idea was objectively. The only indication that they were doing anything extraordinary came from two clock-calendar readouts mounted in the common room, which George was watching with open-mouthed fascination. The ship's clock, hand-labeled US, appeared normal. The Earth-relative clock, labeled THEM, was calibrated as a function of their computed velocity.

"Look," George said. "You can see it already." The seconds were ticking by noticeably faster on the Earth clock.

"I am still confused about this," Emilio said, glancing up at the clocks as he laid out napkins that Anne and D.W. had had a big argument about several months earlier. Anne's logic was, "I refuse to spend half a year watching you guys wipe your mouths on your sleeves. There is no reason to make this trip into some kind of nasty macho endurance test. There'll be plenty of time to wallow in hardship when we get where we're going." "Table linens are a silly-ass waste of cargo capacity," had been D.W.'s counter. Finally, Sofia had pointed out that cloth napkins would weigh about eight hundred grams and weren't worth shouting about. "Coffee," Sofia said, "is worth shouting about." And, thank God, Emilio thought, the women had won that argument, too.

"The faster we go, the closer we approach the speed of light," George explained again patiently, "and the faster time will roll by on the Earth clock. At our peak velocity, halfway through the voyage, it will be our impression that one year is passing on Earth for every three days spent on the ship. Of course, on Earth, if anyone knew what we're up to, it would seem that time on the ship slowed down so that each day takes four months to pass. That's relativity for you. It depends on your point of view."

"Okay, I've got that. But why? Why does it work that way?" Emilio persisted.

"*Deus vult, mes amis,*" Marc Robichaux called cheerfully from the galley. "God likes it that way."

"As good an answer as any, I suppose," George said.

"Praise! We require lavish praise!" Anne announced as she and Marc brought out the first meal they'd managed to cook normally in space: spaghetti with red sauce, a salad made with Wolverton veggies and reconstituted Chianti concentrate. "Oh, I am so glad we're done with weightlessness!"

"Really? I rather enjoyed zero G," Sofia said, taking a seat at the table. George leaned over to Anne and said something inaudible. Everyone smiled when she hit him.

"Only because it didn't make you sick!" Emilio retorted, ignoring the Edwardses, although Anne heard and seconded his sentiment.

"Well, that may be part of it," Sofia admitted, "but I very much liked being any height I pleased."

Walking in from the bridge right on cue, Jimmy Quinn plummeted into a chair with comic suddenness. Even sitting, he towered over her. "Sofia and I have a deal," Jimmy told them. "She doesn't say anything about basketball and I never mention miniature golf."

"Well, Miz Mendes, we may have quite a spell of zero G to look forward to," D.W. said. "You'll get another shot at bein' tall when we get where we're goin' and have to stop and look around."

"And when we reverse the engines halfway there," George pointed out. "We'll be in freefall while we come about."

"You and Anne gonna try it again?" Jimmy asked. Anne slapped him in the back of the head as she passed behind him to get the pepper from the galley. "You know, George, if you aren't going to share, it's not fair to the rest of us."

Alan Pace looked pained, but there was a chorus of hoots from the rest of them, as they settled around the table. They paused for grace and then passed the food around, laughing and ragging at one another. It was easy to feel they were all back at George and Anne's place, having dinner. Pleased at how the group was gelling, generally, D.W. listened and let the conversation drift a while, before holding up a hand. "Okay, listen up, rangers and rangerettes. Here's the *ordo regularis,* startin' to-morrow."

The days were divided hour by hour. There would be free time for the four civilians, as D.W. called them, while the four Jesuits convened for the Mass, although anyone was welcome to join them. Classes were scheduled for three hours per day, nominal Sundays excepted, to give further depth to their training and maintain mental discipline, and to make sure that each crew member gained at least a passing knowledge of every other's specialty. In addition, they were each scheduled for a daily hour of physical training. "Gotta be ready for anything," said the old squadron commander. "Nobody slacks off."

There were routine maintenance operations and a rotating duty ros-ter. There were clothes and dishes to be cleaned even in space, filters to be changed, plants and fish to be tended, hair and crumbs and unidenti-fiable orts to be vacuumed, even when traveling at a substantial portion of the speed of light toward God only knew what. But there would also be time for them to pursue private projects. The ship's computers con-tained pretty close to the sum of Western knowledge in memory and a fair bit of non-Western data as well, so there was plenty to work with. And each day after lunch, D.W. proposed, they would work together on a joint project. "I have consulted with Miz Mendes, here, on this one,"

he said, aiming an eye in her direction. "Father Pace is going to teach us
to sing the whole of Handel's *Messiah*."

"It's quite nice music," Sofia said, shrugging in response to the
muted surprise around the table. "I have no objection to learning it in
anticipation of the appearance of the Messiah. I simply argue that Handel was somewhat premature."

Another chorus of hoots and whistles broke out, punctuated by
George's "Go get 'em, Sofia!" and Anne's blissful cry, "We've got another duelist at the table!" And D. W. Yarbrough grinned, beaming at
Sofia like she was his own personal triumph. Which in some ways she
was, Anne thought.

"Seriously, however, music is why we are here. The one thing we
know for certain about the Singers is that they sing," Alan Pace pointed
out, accurately if a trifle pedantically, trying to introduce some sort of serious discussion into the conversation. "Music may very well afford us
our only means of communication."

The clink of forks and dishes became audible in the quiet, and Anne
was about to say something tart when Sofia Mendes spoke.

"Oh, I shouldn't think so. Dr. Sandoz has mastered thirteen languages, six of them in the space of a little over three years," she said
coolly, passing the salad to Jimmy, whose own mouth had dropped open
at Pace's comment. "Would you be interested in a wager? If we make
contact successfully, I am willing to bet that he'll have the basic grammar
worked out in under two months." She smiled pleasantly at Pace and
watched him, brows raised expectantly, as she took another bite of
spaghetti.

"I'll take a piece of that action, Alan," D.W. said comfortably, looking somewhere in the vicinity of Alan Pace but quite possibly at Sofia or
Emilio instead. "You lose, we can call you Al for a month."

"Ah. Stakes are too high for me," Pace said, backing down
smoothly. "I stand corrected, Sandoz."

"Forget it," said Emilio a little stiffly, and he left the table carrying
a plate of half-eaten food to the galley, evidently finished with his meal.

HE WAS GRATEFUL to hear Anne pick up the conversation after
he left, and put himself to work cleaning the pots. Intent on mastering
his reaction, he was startled when he heard Sofia Mendes's voice behind
him, and that infuriated him further.

"Which is worse," she asked levelly, reaching past him to put her dishes on the counter, "to be insulted or to be defended?"

Emilio stopped scrubbing, not used to having his mind read, and rested his hands on the sink but resumed resolutely a moment later. "Forget it," he said again, without looking at her.

"It is said that the Sephardim taught pride to the Spaniards," she commented. "I apologize. That was inappropriate. It won't happen again."

When he turned, she was gone. He swore violently under his breath and wondered, not for the first time, what had ever made him believe he might have the temperament of a priest. Finally, he straightened his shoulders, ran wet hands through his hair and walked back into the common room.

"I am not a complete jerk," he informed the table formally, and having caught their attention with that, he assured them, "but I could be if I made an honest effort." Through their surprised laughter, he begged pardon of Father Pace for taking offense and Alan reiterated his own regrets as well.

Emilio took his place at the table again and waited until the others seemed engrossed in the after-dinner talk before he leaned slightly toward Sofia, sitting on his left. *"Derech agav,"* he said quietly, *"yeish arba-esrei achshav."*

"I stand corrected," she said, echoing Alan Pace. Her eyes were sparkling, although she didn't look at him directly. "You're rolling the r's a little but otherwise the accent is quite good." By the way, he'd said casually in Sephardic Hebrew that would almost have passed for that of an Israeli native, it's fourteen now.

And if Jimmy Quinn and Anne Edwards and D. W. Yarbrough noticed Sofia's face, because they were all alert to such things for different reasons, they also realized later that this was the last time Emilio Sandoz sat next to the young woman for nearly a year.

16

THE STELLA MARIS:
2031, EARTH-RELATIVE

IT WAS FIVE months into the voyage when Emilio heard a knock at his door after dinner one night. "Yes?" he called quietly.

Jimmy Quinn stuck his head into the room. "Got a minute?"

"Let me check my schedule." Emilio sat up cross-legged on his bed and consulted an appointment book made of air. "Tuesday? Eleven-fifteen?"

Grinning, Jimmy came all the way in, closing the door behind him. He looked around the little room, never having been inside it before. "Same as mine," he commented. A narrow bunk, a desk and chair, a terminal networked to the ship's backup computer system. One difference: a crucifix on the wall. "Jeez, you keep it bright in here! Hot, too. I feel like I'm at the beach."

The priest narrowed his eyes sensuously and shrugged. "What can I say? Latinos like it sunny and warm." But he turned down the light panels to make Jimmy more comfortable and flicked off the display on the ROM tablet he'd been reading, setting it aside. "Have a seat."

Jimmy swiveled the chair away from the desk and sat looking around for a while. "Emilio," he said, "can I ask you something? A personal question?"

"Of course, you may ask," Sandoz said a little warily. "I don't promise I will answer."

"How do you stand it?" Jimmy suddenly burst out in a strangled whisper. "I mean, I'm going crazy! Look, I hope this doesn't embarrass you, because I sure as hell am embarrassed, but even D.W. is starting to look good to me! Sofia made it real clear that she's not interested and—"

Emilio held up a hand, not wanting further details. "Jim, you knew what the crew complement was when you volunteered. And I'm sure you did not believe that Ms. Mendes was included for your convenience—"

"Of course not!" Jimmy said, indignant because he *had* entertained a certain low-level expectation of life's possibilities in that direction. "I just didn't know how hard it would be."

"So to speak," Sandoz murmured, eyes sliding away, a smile flickering on his lips.

"So to speak. God, this is awful!" Jimmy laughed, wrapping his long arms around his head and contracting into a coil of mortification. Then his limbs uncurled and he looked back at the priest and asked frankly, "Look, seriously, what do you do? I mean, what am I supposed to do?"

He expected something along the lines of Zenlike self-mastery and Rosaries, so he almost didn't understand when Emilio looked him in the eye and said, "Take care of yourself, Jim." At first, from the way it was said, with the intonation used to say good-bye to someone, Jimmy thought he was being dismissed. It took a moment to sink in. "Oh. Well, yeah. I do, but . . ."

"Then take care of yourself more often. Until it's not right in the front of your mind all the time."

"Is that what you do? I mean, maybe after a while, you don't feel the need anymore, I guess, huh?"

Emilio's face closed. "Even priests have private lives, Jim."

For the first time since meeting the man, Jimmy felt he'd crossed some line and he backpedaled as quickly as he could. "I'm sorry. Really. You're right. I shouldn't have asked that. Jesus."

Sandoz sighed, clearly uncomfortable. "I suppose, under the circumstances . . . All right. In answer to your first question, I can tell you that in a survey of five hundred celibates, four hundred and ninety-eight of them said that they masturbated."

"What about the other two?"

"Elementary, Watson. From their response we may deduce that they had no arms." Before Jimmy had recovered, Emilio continued dryly, "As for your second question, I can only say that after twenty-five years, the need persists."

"God! Twenty-five *years*."

"The first part of your exclamation explains the second part." Emilio ran his fingers through his hair, a nervous habit he had never been able to break. He let his hands fall and rested them on his knees. "You are actually in a more difficult situation than a priest or a nun is. Celibacy is not the same as deprivation. It is an active choice, not simply the absence of opportunity." Jimmy said nothing, so Emilio went on, voice quiet, face and eyes serious. "Look, I'll be honest with you. Priests differ in their ability to hold themselves to the vow. This is common knowledge, yes? If a priest goes secretly to a woman once a month, he may be stretching his self-control to its limit and he may also be having sex more often than some married men. And yet, the ideal of celibacy still exists for him. And as time goes on, such a priest may come closer and closer to consolidating his celibacy. It's not that we don't feel desire. It's that we hope to reach a point, spiritually, that makes the struggle meaningful."

Jimmy was quiet. He looked at the grave and unusual face of the man opposite him and when he spoke, he sounded older, somehow. "And you've gotten to that point?"

Unexpectedly, Emilio's face lit up and he seemed about to say something, but then the fingers combed through the dark hair again and his eyes slid away. "Even priests have private lives," was all he said.

THAT NIGHT, AS Jimmy lay in his bunk, he remembered a conversation with Anne one evening, back in Puerto Rico. He'd been over at their place for dinner, and George, who always seemed to know when somebody needed to talk to Anne alone, went to bed early. It was three weeks after the first ET radio signal and Jimmy was depressed because everyone thought he'd screwed up, or that Elaine Stefansky was right and he had been the victim of a hoax after all or, worse yet, was responsible for the hoax himself. He still saw Sofia quite often at work and he found himself uncomfortable with Emilio, wondering if they were lovers. He felt jealous and judgmental. And he was troubled by the mixture.

He beat around the bush for a while, but Anne knew what he was getting at. "No, I don't think there's anything going on," she told him plainly. "Not that I'd disapprove, you understand. I think it would do him good to love her and I think it would do her good to be loved, if you want my opinion."

"But he's a priest!" Jimmy protested, as though that settled something. "He's taken vows!"

"Oh, God, Jimmy! Why are we so damned hard on priests when they find someone to love? What exactly is the crime here?" she demanded. "What is so terrible about loving a woman! Or even just needing to get laid once in a while, for crying out loud."

He'd been speechless at that. Anne had a directness that shocked him sometimes. She reached out for her glass of wine but only twirled the stem in her fingers, rotating it slowly, watching the burgundy glow in the low light. "We all make vows, Jimmy. And there is something very beautiful and touching and noble about wanting good impulses to be permanent and true forever," she said. "Most of us stand up and vow to love, honor and cherish someone. And we really truly mean it, at the time. But two or twelve or twenty years down the road, the lawyers are negotiating the property settlement."

"You and George didn't go back on your promises."

She laughed. "Lemme tell ya something, sweetface. I have been married at least four times, to four different men." She watched him chew that over for a moment before continuing, "They've all been named George Edwards but, believe me, the man who is waiting for me down the hall is a whole different animal from the boy I married, back before there was dirt. Oh, there are continuities. He has always been fun and he has never been able to budget his time properly and—well, the rest is none of your business."

"But people change," he said quietly.

"Precisely. People change. Cultures change. Empires rise and fall. Shit. Geology changes! Every ten years or so, George and I have faced the fact that we have changed and we've had to decide if it makes sense to create a new marriage between these two new people." She flopped back against her chair. "Which is why vows are such a tricky business. Because nothing stays the same forever. Okay. Okay! I'm figuring something out now." She sat up straight, eyes focused somewhere outside the room, and Jimmy realized that even Anne didn't have all the answers and that was either the most comforting thing he'd learned in a long time or the most discouraging. "Maybe because so few of us would be able to give up something so fundamental for something so abstract, we protect ourselves from the nobility of a priest's vows by jeering at him when he can't live up to them, always and forever." She shivered and slumped suddenly. "But, Jimmy! What unnatural words. Always and forever! Those aren't human words, Jim. Not even stones are always and forever."

He had been taken aback by her vehemence. He thought that because she and George had been married so long, she'd have high standards for everyone. A promise is a promise, he wanted her to say, so he could be angry with Emilio and hate his father for leaving his mother and believe that it would be different for him, that he'd never lie or cheat or run out on his wife or have an affair. He wanted to believe that love, when it came to him, *would* be always and forever.

"Until you get the measure of your own soul, Jim, don't be quick to condemn a priest, or anyone else for that matter. I'm not scolding you, sweetheart," she said hurriedly. "It's just that, until you've been there, you can't know what it's like to hold yourself to promises you made in good faith a long time ago. Do you hang in there, or cut your losses? Soldier on, or admit defeat and try to make the best of things?" She'd looked a little sheepish then and admitted, "You know, I used to be a real hardass about stuff like this. No retreat, no surrender! But now? Jimmy, I honestly don't know if the world would be better or worse if we all held ourselves to the vows of our youth."

He tried to think about all that, lying in his bunk. The divorce had been awful but then his mother found Nick, who loved her something fierce, and she was surrounded now by Nick's kids, who thought the world of her. Things had worked out okay.

And he thought about Emilio and Sofia. He knew very little about Sofia, only that she had lost her family in Istanbul during the U.N. quarantine and that she'd gotten out by contracting to a broker. And, of course, that she was Jewish, which had thoroughly surprised him when he first found out. It didn't seem to bother her to be the only non-Catholic in the crew and she was respectful of the priests' commitments, even if she had picked up a healthy dose of irreverence from Anne. Sofia, he realized then, had almost apprenticed herself to Anne during these long months, studying the nuances of affection: the quick hugs, the way to cup a chin in the hand or brush back the hair while making some acerbic, narrow-eyed, comic comment. And if Sofia was still pretty formal, it was clear that she was trying to recapture something that might have been hers by right if her life had been different. There was a promising warmth in her, which Jimmy had misinterpreted as an invitation. And now understood to be a simple offer of friendship.

Well, he'd blown that by looking for more than she was willing to give. So he adjusted his sights. If Sofia ever felt safe enough to offer friendship again, he decided, friendship would be enough for him. It could happen. When you live in close quarters for months, a certain amount of familiarity is unavoidable. And he wondered then how hard that was on Emilio.

After that first real dinner onboard the *Stella Maris,* Emilio started calling everyone but Anne and D.W. by their last names. "Mendes," he'd call out, "did you already take care of this filter? I thought I was supposed to do that this week." Sofia had persisted in Doctoring and Mistering everyone, but shortly after Emilio made his change, she took up the practice and it was, "You have to purge some files, Sandoz. We're running low on op-RAM." It gave them a way of speaking to and about each other without first names but without unnatural formality. It was probably Emilio's way of turning the intensity down, to make the relationship more comradely.

Even so, Jimmy was convinced, the sexual tension was still there. Where two people working together might have brushed hands during a task or stood closely, Emilio took pains to prevent contact: an awkwardly held wrist, a slight movement away. By chance alone, they might have sat together sometimes, and so it was significant that they never did. And for all the music and singing that went on in the *Stella Maris,* there had been no second song, no repetition of the heart-stopping intimacy of that evening in August.

Emilio could be so casual and funny that you forgot sometimes that he was a priest and it came as a surprise when you saw his face during the Mass, or watched him doing something ordinary extraordinarily well, in that Jesuit way of making everyday labor a form of prayer. But even Jimmy could see that Emilio and Sofia would be good for each other and that their children would be beautiful and bright and beloved. And, following in the footsteps of centuries of compassionate Catholics before him, Jimmy now wondered why guys like Emilio had to make a choice between loving God and loving a woman like Sofia Mendes.

He asked himself how he'd feel if he found out someday that Emilio had kept his vow, always and forever. To his surprise, he leaned toward sad. And he knew that Anne, who used to be such a hardass about stuff like this, would approve.

IT WOULD NOT have surprised Emilio Sandoz that his sex life was discussed with such candor and affectionate concern by his friends. The single craziest thing about being a priest, he'd found, was that celibacy was simultaneously the most private and most public aspect of his life.

One of his linguistics professors, a man named Samuel Goldstein, had helped him understand the consequences of that simple fact. Sam was Korean by birth, so if you knew his name, you knew he was adopted. "What got me when I was a kid was that people knew something fundamental about me and my family just by looking at us. I felt like I had a big neon sign over my head flashing ADOPTEE," Sam told him. "It's not that I was ashamed of being adopted. I just wished that I had the option of revealing it myself. It's got to be something like that for you guys."

And Emilio realized that Sam was right. When wearing clericals, he did feel as though he had a sign over his head flashing NO LEGITIMATE SEX LIFE. Lay people assumed they knew something fundamental about him. They had opinions about his life. Without any understanding of what celibacy was about, they found his choice laughable, or sick.

Oddly, it was men who'd left the active priesthood to marry who were most eloquent about celibacy. It was as though, having given up the struggle themselves, they could more freely acknowledge the value of it. And it was in the words of one such priest that Emilio had found the clearest description of the Pearl of Great Price: a humaneness beyond sexuality, love beyond loneliness, sexual identity grounded in faithfulness, courage, generosity. And ultimately, a transcendent awareness of creation and Creator . . .

There were as many ways to lose one's balance and sense of purpose as there were people who engaged in the struggle. He had himself gone through a time when avoidance of sex became so consuming he thought of nothing else, like a starving man who dreams of food. Finally he had simply accepted masturbation as a way station, for by then he'd known men who made compromises that brought nothing but grief to the women who loved them or who dissolved loneliness in alcohol or, worst of all, who denied that they felt desire and split their lives: paragons in the light, predators in the dark.

To persist, to find a way through and beyond the rigidity, the pitfalls and the confusion, Emilio had with painful care carved out an unflinching self-awareness and honesty. He found a way to live with the aloneness, to say "Yes" when he asked himself if the Pearl would be worth the price he paid, day after day. Night after night. Year after year.

Who could speak of such things? Not Emilio Sandoz who, for all his facility with many languages, remained tongue-tied and inarticulate about the center of his soul.

For he could not feel God or approach God as a friend or speak to God with the easy familiarity of the devout or praise God with poetry. And yet, as he had grown older, the path he had started down almost in ignorance had begun to seem clearer to him. It became more apparent to him that he was truly called to walk this strange and difficult, this unnatural and unutterable path to God, which required not poetry or piety but simple endurance and patience.

No one could know what this meant to him.

17

NAPLES:
JUNE 2060

SEEING SANDOZ ENTER the Father General's office on the first day of the inquiry into the Rakhat mission, Johannes Voelker winced and gave thanks that this was all taking place in seclusion, away from Rome, far from the prying of the media, which feed off beauty and vice. How many of the others did this evil man corrupt, Voelker wondered bitterly, before they died? Did he kill them, too, as he did the child?

Candotti and Behr had come in with Sandoz, Behr opening the door, Candotti pulling out a chair for him. Partisans certainly, under the spell. Even Giuliani seemed to make allowances, to coddle Sandoz, who had done incalculable damage to the reputation and material position of the Society of Jesus— Voelker looked up, and realized Giuliani was staring at him.

"Good afternoon, gentlemen," Vincenzo Giuliani said pleasantly, warning Voelker wordlessly to govern his attitude as the three newcomers entered the room. "Emilio, I'm pleased to see you looking so well."

"Thank you, sir," Sandoz murmured.

Slender and elegant in black, the dark hair longish now and outlined in silver, Emilio appeared less frail than he had been two months earlier. He was steadier on his feet, and his color was much better. What his mental state was, Giuliani had no idea. Sandoz had hardly spoken since Felipe Reyes's arrival, beyond courtesies and the shallowest of dinner-table conversations; not even John Candotti had been able to draw him out. A pity, Giuliani thought. It would have been helpful to know what was going on in the man's mind.

The Father General moved from his desk and took his place at the head of the superb eighteenth-century table they would use during the hearings. The tall office windows were open to the June air, gauzy curtains moving prettily in the breeze. After a wet, gray spring, the summer promised to be cooler than usual, rainier, but quite enjoyable, Giuliani thought, watching the others settle into their places. Felipe Reyes left a chair in the corner of the office and hesitated before taking a seat, as though considering what position to take, relative to Sandoz. Voelker stood and pulled out the chair next to his own, putting Reyes directly opposite Candotti, who sat next to Emilio. Edward Behr took a seat near the windows where he could observe without being noticed, and where Emilio could see him.

"Gentlemen," Giuliani began, "I would like to make it clear at the outset that this is neither a trial nor an inquisition. Our purpose is to establish a clear picture of events that took place during the mission to Rakhat. Father Sandoz has a unique perspective and a degree of insight into these events that we hope will clarify our partial knowledge. For our part, we have information to share that, I believe, may be new to Father Sandoz." Never able to speak from a sitting position, Giuliani rose and began to circle the office. "Some of us are old enough to recall that approximately a year after the *Stella Maris* left the solar system, Mr. Ian Sekizawa of the Ohbayashi Corporation publicized his suspicions that the Society had sent a ship to Rakhat. There was a great outcry, Emilio, which was to be expected. Sekizawa went to his own people first and they approached the United Nations with a detailed plan to follow the *Stella Maris* into space using much the same technology. The U.N., faced with a fait accompli, authorized a consortium of commercial interests to make direct contact with the Singers. A diplomatic element was added to the Contact Consortium's crew, to represent all humankind." Giuliani stopped his slow circuit of the room and looked at Sandoz. "You may remember Wu Xing-Ren and Trevor Isley, Emilio."

"Yes."

If Giuliani had expected a reaction, he was disappointed. "The Contact Consortium's ship, the *Magellan,* left for Rakhat about three years after the *Stella Maris*. And, at this point, I'm afraid things become rather tangled. While it takes seventeen years in Earth-time for humans to travel between Earth and Rakhat, radio signals require only four and a third years, so there is a confusing overlap and it's hard to sort out the sequence of events. I must remind you that we lost all communication from your party about three years after your landing on Rakhat, Emilio." Nothing. No reaction at all. "When the *Magellan* arrived near the planet, her crew didn't know that you were all presumed dead. They attempted to contact you by radio. When they couldn't raise any response, they boarded the *Stella Maris* and gained access to the records, which gave them every reason to believe that your contact with the sentient species was successful . . ."

Sandoz continued to gaze out the windows. Irritated, Giuliani found himself reacting as though Emilio were a daydreaming graduate student. "Excuse me, Father Sandoz, if this is failing to hold your attention—"

Sandoz raised his eyebrows and turned his head to look at the Father General. "I'm listening, sir," he said. The voice was even and firm, without a trace of insolence. Nevertheless, the eyes returned to the hills beyond the courtyard.

"Good. Because this is important. Our understanding is that the *Magellan* party landed near the last coordinates reported by your party before your transmissions ended. They located you after about twelve weeks, and took considerable trouble to remove you from your predicament and to tend to your injuries." Again, there was no reaction. "Our understanding is that you were then taken to the *Stella Maris,* which was programmed to return you to solar orbit, and you were sent home alone." Giuliani paused and his tone changed. "I'm sure the voyage was very difficult."

For the first time, Emilio Sandoz had a comment. "It was," he said, almost to himself, still looking out the windows, "unimaginable."

The words hung in the room, distant and thin as birdsong.

"Quite," the Father General said at last, thrown off momentarily. "In any case, the radio transmissions from the *Magellan* party continued for an additional three and a half months. At that point, all contact was lost. We have no idea what happened to them, nor do we understand why the transmissions from Ours stopped after only three years. And we trust that you will be able to explain some of these mysteries, Emilio."

The Father General nodded to Voelker, who placed a tablet in front of Sandoz, the surface blanked. This, Voelker thought, is going to be exceedingly interesting to watch.

"But our first order of business, I'm afraid, is to deal with the very troubling allegations made by Wu and Isley." Emilio looked up, and Giuliani was forced to stop and consider him for a moment. The puzzlement looked genuine. "We have, naturally, waited until you were strong enough to speak in your own defense. Rakhat is far beyond any civil jurisdiction. No criminal charges have been brought against you but the accusations are disturbing, and there have been serious repercussions even in the absence of trial or proof." Voelker leaned over the table and brought up the display. Giuliani spoke again. "These allegations were sent by radio, so they arrived and were made public over twelve years ago. Please take your time and read them carefully. We are hoping to hear you refute them."

IT TOOK EMILIO about ten minutes to make his way through the document. Toward the end, it was difficult to see clearly and he had to reread portions to be sure he understood, which was distressing.

The Contact Consortium's story didn't take him completely by surprise. "We know about the child," John had said, "and we know about the brothel." But it was so absurd, so unfair, that he hadn't taken in the implications, not really. The mind tries to protect you that way, he supposed. Until this day, he had not known what everyone else in this room, what the whole world had heard over twelve years earlier, nor could he have imagined how damning it would sound.

And yet, it explained some things, and for that Emilio was grateful. He'd begun to wonder if the headaches were because of a brain tumor, because there was so much that made no sense to him. This, at least, made the animosity and revulsion explicable: the way Isley and Wu looked at him, what they must have been thinking . . . But he found other parts of the report both mystifying and an outrage. He tried again to make sense of it all and wondered if he'd said something wrong or had been misunderstood. There is a clue here somewhere, Emilio thought, hoping to remember that later, when things were not so pressured. Then the headache tightened its grip and things began to flicker past his mind.

Often in the past months, he had found himself suspended between screaming hysteria and black humor. Screaming, he had determined on the voyage back, only made the headaches more devastating.

"It could be worse," Emilio said at last. "It could be raining."

Black humor, on the other hand, made everyone else angry. Giuliani and Reyes were not amused. Voelker was outraged. John got the joke, but even he thought the timing was pretty poor. Emilio, his vision very distorted now, looked for Edward Behr but saw only that the man was no longer next to the window.

"It is time that someone explained to you, Sandoz, that this is not simply your private disgrace," Voelker rapped, his voice hammering in Emilio's ears. "When these charges were made public, the reputation of the Society was all but destroyed. We now operate only fourteen novitiates worldwide! And there are hardly enough new men to fill even those—"

"Oh, come on, Voelker! That's the worst kind of scapegoating!" It was John's voice shouting back. "You can't blame Emilio for every problem we've had for—"

Then Felipe's voice added to the din, and Emilio began to feel that his head would shatter, that the bones of his skull would go to pieces. He tried to escape from the yelling somehow, to go inside himself away from all this, but found no place to hide. For weeks, he'd prepared singlemindedly, building walls brick by brick, deciding which questions to answer, which to turn aside and how. He'd been sure he could get through the hearings, that he had some distance from everything now, but the carefully constructed defenses were crumbling, and he felt as flayed and raw and exposed as if it were all happening again.

"That's enough." Giuliani's words cut through the argument and the room fell silent abruptly. His voice was very mild when he spoke again. "Emilio, is there any truth to these charges?"

Brother Edward, having spotted the whiteness around the eyes that signaled migraine, was already on the way to Sandoz, hoping to get him out of the room before the vomiting started. But he stopped and waited for Emilio to speak.

"It's all true, I suppose," Emilio said but the roaring in his head made it hard now to hear his own voice. And then everyone was shouting again, so probably no one heard him say, "But it's all wrong."

He could feel Edward Behr taking him under the arms, pulling him to his feet. There was more talk, Edward's voice close to his ear, but he didn't understand what anyone was saying. He thought it must have been John Candotti who half-carried him out of the office, and he tried to protest that there was nothing wrong with his legs. They managed to

get him into the stone-paved hallway before he lost control; he was glad
he hadn't spoiled the carpets. When it was over, there was the sting of
the injection and the brief terrible sensation of falling and falling even as
he was being carried up the stairs.

It's all true, he thought as the drug took hold. But it's all wrong.

THE LANDER FROM the *Magellan* had set down near the village of Kashan, where the Jesuit party had lived for over two Rakhati
years. The humans were met not by priests but by a terrifying mob of individuals they later learned to call Runa. The Runa were very big, very
agitated, and Wu had expected to be killed on the spot. The *Magellan*
party was about to retreat to their lander when a smaller person, whom
they believed to be quite young, made her way through the crowd and
went directly to Trevor Isley, whom she addressed, astonishingly, in English.

She introduced herself as Askama and asked Trevor if he had "come
for Meelo?" Askama seemed convinced that Isley was a relative of Father Emilio Sandoz—or Meelo, as she called him—a family member
come to fetch the priest. When they asked about any others like Sandoz,
Askama said that the other foreigners were gone but told them over and
over, "Meelo is not dead," that he was in the city of Gayjur now. Gradually the *Magellan* party understood that Askama meant to take them
there. It seemed wise to go with her. They hoped that Sandoz would be
able to explain the situation once they reached Gayjur.

They went by river barge to the city. Along the route, Runa villagers
shouted from the banks and, once, rocks were thrown. Trevor Isley, who
happened to be wearing black, was obviously the target of that assault
and it seemed clear that the missionaries had somehow poisoned the atmosphere, the very thing the *Magellan* crew had expected and feared.

The city population was not openly hostile but the humans were
watched silently as they made their way through the streets. Askama
brought them to Supaari VaGayjur, whom they found to be something of
a scholar. Supaari, they learned, had studied with Sandoz for a long
while and his English was surprisingly good, although more heavily accented than Askama's. He was also a member of the ruling Jana'ata, a
person of apparent wealth and a gracious host, although Askama was
dismissed rather abruptly. She was not allowed to stay with them but she
was permitted to remain in the compound somewhere and the humans

saw her often. While Supaari confirmed Askama's story that Emilio Sandoz had once been accepted as a member of his household, he informed the *Magellan* party that Sandoz no longer resided with him. Why? they asked. Where was he now? Supaari was indirect. Other living arrangements had been made for the Foreigner Sandoz that were "more suited to his nature," Supaari told them, and changed the subject.

Over the next few weeks, the *Magellan* party was entertained lavishly, Supaari showing off his knowledge of their lingua franca and doing his best to answer their questions. At their request, he introduced them to other Jana'ata of influence. Everyone seemed cool and distracted, uninterested in trade or cultural exchanges. It became obvious that something ugly was brewing. Even the normally urbane Supaari became upset one afternoon, telling them that the Runa had attacked and killed several Jana'ata on a riverway near the city. Nothing like this had ever happened previously. Supaari assured them that relations between the Runa and the Jana'ata had always been good before. Supaari was of the opinion that the foreigners, as everyone called the Jesuits, were responsible for this. Balance had been lost. Traditions had been broken.

The *Magellan* party brought up Sandoz's name repeatedly, hoping for a more complete explanation of the situation from him, but Supaari seemed in no hurry to produce the man. In the end, it was not Supaari VaGayjur but the child Askama who located Sandoz and took Wu and Isley to him.

Father Emilio Sandoz was found in a state of shocking degradation in what was obviously a whorehouse, where he was employed as a prostitute. His first act when found was to kill Askama, a child who had clearly been devoted to him. Upon questioning, the priest became hysterical and then refused to speak. The Jana'ata, preoccupied with larger affairs, pressed no charges and released Sandoz to the custody of the Consortium. Wu and Isley were not in a position to conduct any kind of investigation, so they decided to send Sandoz back to Earth and let the authorities there deal with him. The priest was transported to the *Stella Maris*, along with a cargo of remarkable gifts from Supaari VaGayjur, and the *Magellan* party turned their attention to repairing relations with the VaRakhati.

In the weeks that followed, there were reports of additional Runa attacks on Jana'ata civilians near the city. Fearing that they would be caught up in the civil war that seemed imminent, Wu and Isley thanked Supaari for his hospitality and aid, and made plans to take their party back up to the *Magellan,* where they could either sit out the unrest or try a different region of the planet. Wu's last transmission reported his group's plan to head back toward their lander with an escort provided by Supaari VaGayjur. The *Magellan* party was never heard from again.

And so it was that the only person to return from Rakhat alive was the priest and whore and murderer Emilio Sandoz, who had very much wanted to die.

THE BREATHING HAD steadied now and Edward Behr knew that the medication had finally taken hold. It was much more effective if it could be taken orally when the headaches began. Edward tried to be alert to their onset, but Emilio hid a great deal. This time the pain had come screaming in with startling suddenness, and no wonder: to sit and read an indictment like that, minutely observed, the tiniest reaction analyzed for what clues might be given away.

Edward Behr had seen this kind of thing before—the body punished for what the soul could not encompass. Sometimes it was headache, as with Emilio. Sometimes excruciating back pain, or chronic stomach trouble. You saw it in the alcoholics, often, drinking to dull the sensitivity, to mute the hurt. So many people buried the soul's pain in their bodies, Edward thought. Even priests who, one would have thought, might have known better.

Brother Edward had spent many hours sitting like this, watching Emilio sleep, praying for him. Of course, he'd known the stories about Sandoz before being assigned to care for him. And he had tended the man's body, was well aware of the injuries, which were not merely those to his hands and which silently told the sordid story. The original release of the information came when Edward Behr was married, before he ever thought of his present life or imagined he might meet one of the principals, but he'd been interested, naturally. It was the news story of the century, after all. He recalled the teasing insinuations, the dramatic revelations, the scandalized reactions overshadowing the scientific and philosophical importance of the mission to Rakhat. Then there was, for the second time, a mysterious end to the transmissions and the long wait for Sandoz to return, bringing with him the only hope for some kind of explanation.

Emilio's very survival had been improbable, not to say miraculous. Alone for months, in a crude vehicle, navigated by only slightly less crude computers, he had been found in the Ohbayashi sector of the asteroid belt when a support ship investigated the automatic distress signal. By that time, he was so malnourished that the healed scars of his hands had reopened, the connective tissue going to pieces. He would have bled to death if the Ohbayashi people hadn't picked him up when they did.

Brother Edward realized that he might be the only one who believed wholeheartedly that it was a good thing Emilio had been found alive. Even John Candotti was ambivalent, if only because death seemed kinder and God was merciful.

Edward didn't know what to think about the killing of Askama or the violence said to have been triggered by the Jesuit missionaries. But if Emilio Sandoz, maimed, destitute, utterly alone, had turned to prostitution, who could condemn him? Not Edward Behr, who had some measure of the man's strength and of what it must have taken to bring him to the state he'd been found in, on Rakhat. Johannes Voelker, by contrast, was convinced that Sandoz was simply a dangerous rogue, gone to appalling excess in the absence of external controls. We are what we fear in others, Edward thought, and wondered how Voelker spent his time off.

There was a quiet knock at the door. Edward rose silently and went into the hallway, pulling the door almost but not quite closed behind him.

"Asleep?" the Father General asked.

"Yes. It'll be hours," Brother Edward said softly. "Once the vomiting starts, I have to inject the Prograine, and that knocks him out."

"The rest will do him good." Vincenzo Giuliani rubbed his face with both hands and let out a long uneven sigh. He looked at Brother Edward and shook his head. "He admits it's all true. But I could have sworn he was dumbfounded."

"Sir, if I may speak frankly?"

"Of course. Please."

"I can't say anything about the murder. I've seen real anger. To be honest, I've seen potential for violence, although he's always turned it on himself. But, Father, you only read the medical reports. I saw—" Brother Edward stopped. He'd never spoken of this to anyone, not even Emilio, silent always in the early days when he'd been too ill to move from bed. Perhaps the reports had been too clinical. Perhaps the Father General hadn't understood what the sodomy had done, how desperate Sandoz must have been . . .

"It was brutal," Brother Edward said plainly, and he looked at the Father General until Giuliani blinked. "He does not enjoy pain. If he worked as a whore, it gave him no pleasure."

"I don't suppose the work ever does give much pleasure, Ed, but your point is taken. Emilio Sandoz is not a depraved libertine."

Giuliani walked to the doorway and hesitated before taking a step into the room. Most men were simple. They were looking for security, or power, or a feeling of usefulness or of certainty or competence. A cause to fight for, a problem to solve, a place to fit in. There were many possibilities but once you grasped what a man was looking for, you had the beginnings of understanding. At a loss, he studied the exotic face, half-hidden by dark hair and bed linens, and whispered, "So what, in the name of Jesus, is he?" It was a question he'd pondered, one way or another, off and on, for sixty years. He didn't expect an answer, but he got one.

"A soul," said Edward Behr, "looking for God."

Vincenzo Giuliani stared at the fat little man standing in the hallway and then at Sandoz, sleeping drugged against an assault on his own body, and wondered, What if that's been it, all along?

IT WAS WELL into the night before Emilio stirred. He became aware that the small reading lamp by the chair was on and said quietly, his voice blurred with sleep, "I'll be okay, Ed. You don't have to sit up. Go to bed." When he heard no response, he roused himself and turned over, rising onto an elbow, and saw not Edward Behr but Vincenzo Giuliani.

Before Sandoz could spit out the words that were forming in his mind, Giuliani spoke. "Emilio, I am sorry," he said, the calm conviction in his voice concealing the calculated risk he was taking. "You were condemned in absentia by men who had no right to judge. I can't think of any adequate way to apologize. I don't expect you to forgive me. Or any of us. I am sorry." He watched the words sink in, rain to parched ground. So, he thought, that's how he sees it. "If you can bring yourself to it, I'd like to begin again. I know it won't be easy, but I think you need to tell us your side of all this, and I know we need to hear it."

The face closed to him, pride warring with an exhaustion that had nothing to do with sleep.

"Get out," Emilio Sandoz said at last. "And shut the door."

He did, and was about to go to his own room when he heard something that gave the Father General pause. It had been, simply, a gamble: a guess at how Sandoz might have felt. But hearing this, Vincenzo Giuliani required himself to remain in the hallway. Head against the wooden door, hands gripping the frame, he listened until the weeping was over, and learned the sound of desolation.

18

"NONE FOR ME, thanks," Emilio said.

Sofia sighed. "Three."

"I got a hand that looks like a foot," said D.W., staring at his cards with disgust.

"I'm a skilled surgeon," Anne said. "I could help you with a problem like that." Emilio laughed.

"Nothing's gonna help this mess. Fold."

"One for me," Anne told Alan.

"Dealer takes three. You know, Sandoz, it's draw poker. You don't always have to stand pat," Alan Pace explained patiently, dealing out his own three cards. "You can draw."

"Robichaux's the artist," Emilio said serenely. "He draws. I stand pat."

"Leave me out of this," Marc yelled from the little gym off the commons.

"Nice that you guys have nothing better to do than play cards," Jimmy called from the bridge, where he and George were processing sequential images of the vast region between the center sun and the two outliers, hoping to detect some telltale difference—a smeared line or a displaced dot—that would indicate a planet moving in orbit. They'd been circling at .25 G high above the plane of the Alpha Centauri system for weeks and were collectively bored witless. "Some people around here are actually working."

"Anne and I could take your appendix out if you like," Emilio offered, raising his voice slightly. He looked back at his cards. "See your two and raise you two."

Sofia and Anne folded. Alan tossed in two more Wolverton tube peanuts. George, taking a break, strolled buoyantly into the common room and reached over Anne's shoulder to look at the cards she'd thrown down. "No guts!" he said. "I'd have played that!" She glared at him, but he planted a noisy kiss on the back of her neck. Quarter G was a lot of fun.

Emilio added four peanuts and then four more and leaned back in his chair, squinting through imaginary cigarette smoke. "Cost you eight legumes to find out what I've got, Pace."

Alan ignored the Bogart impression and took the bet. Sandoz would play with anything or nothing. "Fives? You stood pat with a pair of fives?" Alan cried when they laid the cards down. "Sandoz, I will never understand you! Why didn't you draw three cards?"

Emilio smiled delightedly and shrugged. "Fives are good enough to beat fours, yes? My deal. Ante up, ladies and gentlemen, ante up." The cards went out again, Emilio's infectious merriment spreading around the table as they each looked at the hands he dealt them.

"The perfect poker face," D.W. said, shaking his head. "He laughs at everything he gets. The good hands are funny and so are the lousy ones."

"This is true," Emilio agreed amiably. "Alan, just for you. Pick a card at random and I'll draw."

Alan pulled a card from the middle of Emilio's hand and Emilio dealt himself a new one off the top of the deck. Predictably, he found it hilarious, and it was impossible to tell if he'd just gotten four of a kind or busted a flush. When the bets came around to him, he pushed his whole pile of peanuts into the center. "Winner takes all. Come on, Pace," Emilio urged.

They laid their cards down again and Alan roared with indignation. "I don't believe it! A straight."

Emilio was practically crying now. "And the worst part is, you filled it. I was holding nothing!" He pushed the peanuts over to Alan and held up a hand, becoming before their eyes the very Buddha, soul of disinterest. "The trick is not to care. I have a perfect indifference to winning."

There were cries of "Liar!" and dark mutterings about confession from Anne and Sofia and D.W., who'd all seen Emilio take the skin off his face maniacally sliding into home, and wide eyes from Alan, amazed by the eruption.

"He is completely full of shit, Alan," George told him. "He doesn't care about poker because he doesn't like peanuts. But he'll cut your heart out at second base if he thinks you're going to steal third."

"This is also true," Emilio acknowledged peaceably, gathering up the deck while the others vilified him. "And if we were playing for raisins, it would be different. I like raisins."

"Raisins make a mess of the cards," Sofia pointed out.

"Do you ever get tired of being practical?" Emilio demanded.

"Bingo," they heard Jimmy say quietly.

"No, poker," Emilio corrected him. "Bingo is with those square cards, and you put beans on the numbers . . ." He fell silent as Jimmy came into the common room. One by one, they turned to look and went motionless, waiting.

"A planet," Jimmy said, dazed. "We found it. We found a planet. Might not be the Singers' planet, but we found a planet."

SINCE ROTATING THE asteroid at the halfway point, to turn the engines around and begin deceleration, they'd stopped every two weeks to do periodic broad-spectrum imaging, engines off, and to listen for radio signals, which became relatively strong but remained strangely intermittent. As the *Stella Maris* passed out of the plane of the Alpha Centauri system, rising "above" it in order to image the system at right angles, there was something far odder than interval to worry about: they lost the radio signals completely. It was generally unnerving, although the reactions ranged from Marc's faith that everything would come right in the end to George's palpable frustration at being unable to figure out what could account for it. But Emilio seemed strangely relieved, almost giddy, suggesting cheerfully that they turn around and go home, an idea that provoked howls of rejection.

Now they all crowded around the bridge display as Jimmy ran the images back and forth in sequence, so they could see a point of light, varying in brightness from image to image, moving slightly. "Look," he said, "you can even see the difference in the reflected sunlight. It's sort of gibbous here."

Marc Robichaux, who'd come out of the tiny gym when he heard the uproar, leaned around Jimmy and pointed to a smear, somewhat closer to the central sun. "And here. Another one."

"Good eye, man," Jimmy said. "Sure enough. That's one, too."

"Can you enlarge these regions, Jimmy?" Marc asked, towel hung over his neck, still breathing fast, but not from treadmill work any longer.

"No point in it. Real-time observation, folks. We can just plain look at them with the telescope." A few minutes later, they could see the first planet directly, appearing now as a fuzzy ball, grayish and lumpy. And then the second, the one Marc had spotted, much larger and with two substantial companion bodies.

"Moons," George said softly, putting his arm around Anne and pulling her close. "Moons!"

"Forget the first one. There's our planet," Marc said, with complete confidence. "A good-sized moon keeps a planet's precession steady enough for stable weather patterns to develop. If there's open water, moons make tides, and tides breed life." Anne looked at him, brows up, the question unasked. The naturalist smiled. "Because that's the way God likes it, Madame."

And then everyone was talking at once, congratulating Jimmy and George and Marc, discussing how long it would take to get to the planet with the moons, excitement swamping the funk they'd been in as the sterile weeks had dragged by. The buzz of conversation halted when D.W. looked around for Emilio and then called out sharply, "Sit down 'fore you fall down, son," and pushed past the little crowd around the display, making his way through the common room benches and tables. He wasn't quite quick enough to catch Emilio before he hit the floor.

There was, at first, a burst of laughter because Emilio looked so comical, going down like a puppet with the strings cut, but in slow motion because of the low gravity. Alan Pace thought impatiently that he'd only done it as a joke and was irritated as usual at the man's habitual frivolity.

Anne was right behind Yarbrough. "It's okay," she said matter-of-factly as the laughter died and turned to consternation. "He's just fainted." She could have lifted Emilio off the floor herself; at .25 G, he only weighed about thirty pounds. But intellectual equality aside, Anne

Edwards retained a certain deference toward male sensibilities, so she looked up at D.W., intending to ask him to carry Emilio into his cabin for her. She was astonished to see that Yarbrough was trembling. Then it clicked and many things became clearer to her.

"Jimmy, would you lug him into his room for me, please?" she called out in a slightly bored voice, to minimize the drama. D.W. opened the door to Emilio's room and stepped out of the way as Jimmy went by, a giant Raggedy Andy carrying Emilio, who looked like a rag doll himself, limp in the big man's arms. Anne gave the situation about three seconds' consideration and then gave D.W. a firm and reassuring hug, brief but forthright, before squeezing past Jimmy into the little cabin. Jim left and she closed the door behind him.

Emilio was already coming out of it. Anne could hear D.W. just outside the door, in full East Texas cry, making everyone laugh and steering the conversation back to the planet. The voices receded, and Anne looked back to Emilio, who was now sitting up, feet over the side of the bed, eyes wide and blinking.

"What happened?" he asked.

"You passed out. Must have been the surprise about the planet. The autonomic nervous system will do that to you. You can feel your arms and legs get cold and then everything turns white."

He nodded. "That never happened to me before. What a strange sensation." He shook his head to clear it and his eyes widened again.

"Whoa. Just sit there a while. Takes a little time for your blood pressure to get settled." She was leaning against the bulkhead, arms crossed, watching him with a clinical eye but thinking about what she'd just seen. He laughed a little and then sat still, letting his equilibrium reassert itself.

"I am surprised," Anne said judiciously, "that you were surprised."

"About the planet?"

"Yes. I mean, this whole thing was your idea. I thought you had some kind of direct line to God about this." She wasn't as sarcastic as she might have been. In fact, she said this with a straight face, almost, with only a hint of insincerity to protect herself.

He was silent for a long time, starting twice to say something and then stopping again. Finally, he said, "Anne, may I tell you something? In confidence?" She slid down the wall, as controlled in her drop to the floor as Emilio had been boneless, and sat cross-legged, looking up at him. "I've never told anybody this, Anne, but—" He stopped again and laughed nervously. "This must be some kind of record, yes? A man who can be completely inarticulate in fourteen languages."

"You don't have to tell me if you don't want to."

"No. I need to talk to someone about this. Not someone. You. I need to talk to you about this. Anne, I'm just getting somewhere that everyone thinks I've been all along."

There was another silence, as he tried to decide how much to tell her, where to start. She waited, watching him, pleased to see the color come back and then touched to realize that he was blushing. Self-disclosure is almost like sex, she thought. It isn't easy to bare your soul.

"You have to understand, Anne, I'm not one of those guys who decided to be a priest when he was seven. I started out—well, you've seen La Perla, right? But you can't imagine what it's like to grow up there." There was another pause, as the memories crowded in. "Anyway, the Jesuits, D.W. especially, they showed me a different kind of life. I'm not saying that I became a priest because I was grateful. Okay, I admit, that was probably part of it. But I wanted to be like them. Like D.W."

"Not a shabby ambition," she said, eyes steady.

He took a deep breath. "No. It was a good ambition. And it wasn't all hero worship. I wanted this life and I have no regrets. But—Anne, do you remember when I said that it's difficult to tell from the way people behave whether or not they believe in God?" Emilio watched her carefully, looking for shock or disappointment, but she didn't seem horrified or even terribly surprised. "You'd make a good priest, you know."

"Except for that celibacy shit," she laughed. "And the popes keep saying I have too many X chromosomes. Don't change the subject."

"Right. Right." He hesitated again, but finally the words began to come for him. "I was like the physicists you talked about. I was like a physicist who believes in quarks intellectually, but doesn't feel quarks. I could make all the Thomist arguments about God and discuss Spinoza and say all the right things. But I didn't feel God. It was not a thing of the heart for me. I could defend the idea of God but it was all from hearsay evidence, a lawyer would call it. None of it had any emotional truth for me. Not like it does for guys like Marc." He hugged himself and leaned forward over his knees. "I mean, there was a place in me that wanted God to be in it, but it was empty. So, I thought, Well, not yet. Maybe someday. And to be honest, I sort of looked down on that kind of thing. You know how there are people who'll tell you that Jesus is a close personal friend of theirs, yes?" His voice was very low and he made a face that said, Who are they kidding? "I always thought, Sure, right, and you probably see Elvis at the laundromat."

"Hey! What's wrong with that!" Anne cried, offended. "I have personally seen Keith Richards at a grocery store in Cleveland Heights."

He laughed and moved back onto the bed so he could sit against the wall. "Okay. So, one day, I get this call at four in the morning. And then we're all sitting in Jimmy's office, listening to this incredible music and I say, I wonder if we could go there? And George and Jimmy and Sofia say, Sure, no problem, just do the math. And you thought we were crazy? Well, so did I, Anne. I mean, at first, it all was sort of a game! I was just toying with the idea of it's being God's will, really." Anne remembered the playfulness. It had seemed so strange at the time. "I kept expecting the game to stop, and everyone would have a good laugh at my expense, and I'd go back to trying to get Ortega to give me that house for the preschool and arguing with Richie Gonzales and the council about the sewers in the east end and all the rest of it, right? But it just kept going. The Father General and the asteroid and the plane and all these people working on this crazy idea. I kept waiting for someone to say, Sandoz, you idiot, what a lot of trouble for nothing! But everything kept happening."

"Like D.W. said, a whole hell of a lot of turtles showing up on a whole hell of a lot of fenceposts."

"Yes! So I'm lying in bed, night after night, and I can't sleep anymore, and you know me—I used to fall asleep in the middle of a sentence. All night long, I would be thinking, What is happening here? And part of me would say, God is trying to tell you something, you dumb bastard. And another part of me would say, God doesn't talk to punks from Puerto Rico, you know?"

"What makes you say that? I ask as one semicommitted agnostic to another, you understand."

"Well, okay, I take it back about Puerto Rico, but it's not fair for God to play favorites. What makes me so special that God would bother to tell me anything, right?"

He ran out of steam for a while, and Anne let him stare and gather his thoughts. Then he looked at her and smiled and climbed down off the bed to sit next to her on the floor, their shoulders touching, knees drawn up. The difference in their ages seemed less important than their near equality of size. Anne had a flashing memory of sitting like this with her best friend when they were both thirteen, telling secrets, figuring things out.

"So. Things kept happening, just like God was really there, making it all happen. And I heard myself saying *Deus vult,* like Marc, but it still seemed like some kind of huge joke. And then one night, I just let myself consider the possibility that this is what it seems to be. That something extraordinary is happening. That God has something in mind for me. Besides sewer lines, I mean . . . And a lot of the time, even now, I think I must be a lunatic and this whole thing is crazy. But, sometimes—Anne, there are times when I can let myself believe, and when I do," he said, voice dropping to a whisper and his hands, resting on his knees, opening, as though to reach for something, "it's amazing. Inside me, everything makes sense, everything I've done, everything that ever happened to me—it was all leading up to this, to where we are right now. But, Anne, it's *frightening* and I don't know why . . ."

She waited to see if he had more but when he fell silent, she decided to take a shot in the dark. "You know what's the most terrifying thing about admitting that you're in love?" she asked him. "You are just *naked.* You put yourself in harm's way and you lay down all your defenses. No clothes, no weapons. Nowhere to hide. Completely vulnerable. The only thing that makes it tolerable is to believe the other person loves you back and that you can trust him not to hurt you."

He looked at her, astounded. "Yes. Exactly. That's how it feels, when I let myself believe. Like I am falling in love and like I am naked before God. And it is terrifying, as you say. But it has started to feel like I am being rude and ungrateful, do you understand? To keep on doubting. That God loves me. Personally." He snorted, half in disbelief and half in astonishment, and put his hands over his mouth for a moment and then pulled them away. "Does that sound arrogant? Or just crazy? To think that God loves me."

"Sounds perfectly reasonable to me," Anne said, shrugging and smiling. "You're very easy to love." And saying it, she was pleased to hear how natural it sounded, how unburdened.

He reared away to look at her and his eyes softened, doubts set aside for a truth he was sure of. *"Madre de mi corazón,"* he said quietly.

"Hijo de mi alma," she replied, as softly and as certain. The moment passed and they were back together, staring at their knees, com-

panionable again. Then the spell was broken, and he laughed. "If we stay in here much longer, we shall give scandal."

"Do you think so?" she asked, eyes wide. "How flattering!"

Emilio got to his feet and offered Anne a hand up. She stood easily in the low gravity but held onto his hand a moment longer than necessary, and they embraced and laughed again because it was hard to decide whose arms should go over whose shoulders. Then Anne opened the door and called out wearily, "Okay, somebody get this man a sandwich."

Jimmy yelled, "Sandoz, you jerk! When's the last time you ate? Do I have to think of everything?" And Sofia said, "Maybe we should play for raisins next time," but she and Jimmy already had a meal ready for him. And things went back to as normal as they could get, inside an asteroid, above Alpha Centauri, looking for signs from God.

"MY DADDY HAD a Buick once, drove like this," D. W. Yarbrough muttered at one point. "Sumbitch handled like a damn pig in a wallow."

Nobody dared laugh. During the past two weeks, D. W. Yarbrough and Sofia Mendes had worked nonstop, dropping the *Stella Maris* closer and closer to the planet. The process was dangerous and frustrating, and D.W. was sometimes startlingly short with people.

Everyone was irritable, and after D.W. finally managed to wrestle the ship into an acceptable orbit, they went into freefall and things got even worse. For over three years, they'd worked like mules to be here, within sight of the planet they had come to investigate. In a small place together for over eight months, they'd gotten along remarkably well, but there were accumulated tensions and anxieties and a grinding restlessness that did not surface in shouting matches very often but was evident in sudden silences as people swallowed retorts.

Of all of them, D.W. was most likely to snarl, dressing people down for minor mistakes or lapses in attention to detail or ill-timed remarks. Emilio, no worse than any of the others, nevertheless caught hell most often. When Yarbrough laid down the law to reestablish the regular order, Emilio threw out a little joke about the *disordo irregularis*. D.W. stared at Sandoz until his eyes dropped and then told him, "If you can't be serious, be quiet." Which shut Emilio up for days. Another time, after the Father Superior left everyone feeling ruffled by issuing a string of abrupt commands at breakfast, ending with a particularly sharp decree aimed at Sandoz, Emilio tried to take the sting out of it by asking, "You want fries with that order?" Yarbrough just about took his head off with a barrage of very rapid, very colloquial, heavily accented Spanish no one else could follow, but whose meaning they could guess at by the effect.

Anne might have approached D.W. to see if she could provide a little perspective on the general topic of overcompensation but within an hour, she herself was on the receiving end of a lecture, having forgotten to cover a salt shaker, whose contents had then drifted out of the holes over several days. D.W. opened the storage cabinet and a miniature snow squall resulted. There was an unpleasant exchange and George got involved, and it took both Sofia and Jimmy's intervention to calm everyone down.

Eventually the adjustment to zero G was over, nausea had abated all round, the *ordo* was back in place, and everyone was once again working with reasonable efficiency. They did a full survey to begin with, launching several satellites to encircle the planet, collecting atmospheric and geographic data. At this distance, the patterns of ocean and landmass were clear. The overall impression was of greens and blues running to purple, broken by areas of red and brown and yellow, frosted with the white of clouds and very small ice caps. It wasn't Earth but it was beautiful, and it had a powerful pull on their emotions.

The biggest surprise was the sudden reappearance of the radio signals. Whenever they moved between the moons and the planet, the ship received bursts of incredibly strong radio waves. "They're aiming at the moons," Jimmy realized as he sketched the system and worked out what was happening physically. There was no indication of any indigenous life or colonies on the moons. "Why would they be aiming radio at the moons?"

"No ionosphere!" George announced triumphantly one afternoon, floating into the common room from his cabin, where he'd been going over the atmospheric data. It came to him out of the blue, when he wasn't thinking about the radio problem. "They're using the moons to bounce the signals off."

"That's it!" Jimmy yelled from the bridge. He shot into the common room, hooked a hand around a support pole like a gigantic orangutan, and friction-spiraled to a halt. "That's why we only got the signals every fifteen and twenty-seven days back home!"

"You lost me with that one," Anne called from the galley, where she and Sofia were getting lunch ready.

"Without an ionosphere to contain radio waves, you could only use line-of-sight signals, like microwave towers at home," George explained. "If you wanted to broadcast over a wider region, you could aim a really strong signal at the moons, and it would bounce back in a cone that would cover a lot of the planet's surface."

"So what we were picking up at home was the scatter around the moons, every time they moved into line with Earth," Jimmy said, crowing with happiness at clearing up that little mystery.

"What's an ionosphere?" Anne asked. Jimmy gaped at her. "Sorry. I've heard the word but I don't know what it is, really. I'm a doctor, Jim, not an astronomer!" George broke up but Jimmy, too young for the first *Star Trek,* didn't get it.

"Okay: solar radiation knocks electrons off atmospheric molecules at the top of the atmosphere, right? That makes them ions," Jimmy began.

"Listen up," D.W. cut in, as he pushed himself into the common room from the bridge. "Be ready to give a summary of everything you've learned tomorrow at nine. I got decisions to make."

Then he was gone, disappearing into his cabin, leaving people shaking their heads and muttering. Anne watched him go and rotated toward Sofia. "What do you think? PMS?"

"It's a form of affection," Sofia smiled. "The squadron commander is back on duty. He doesn't want his people killed by enthusiasm and cabin fever, but no one wants to come this far and then go back without visiting the surface, especially not D.W. There's a great deal of pressure on him."

"I see your point," Anne said, impressed by the analysis, which she considered precisely one brick shy of the full load, and wondered if Sofia was unaware or very discreet. Discreet, Anne decided. Sofia didn't miss much and she knew D.W. very well. "Which way is he leaning? Do you know?"

"He keeps his own counsel. From what I've gathered, we could survive on the surface. Maybe D.W. will go down alone or with one or two others and leave the rest on the ship."

Anne closed her eyes, sagging as much as one could while weightless. "Oh, Sofia, I think I would literally rather die than stay inside here one minute longer than I have to."

Sofia was surprised to see the woman look every day of her age for once, and for a dreadful moment she thought that Anne would burst into tears. Sofia reeled her in for the kind quick embrace she had received in the hundreds from the older woman. It was not an impulsive act, for hardly anything Sofia Mendes did was impulsive. But now, at last, she'd soaked up enough affection to give some back.

"Oh, Sofia, I love you all," Anne said, laughing and taking a quick swipe at her eyes with a sleeve. "And I am mortally sick of every last one of you. Come on. Let's get these guys fed."

THE NEXT MORNING was as tense and demanding as anything Anne had ever sat through. Or floated through, in this case. She meant to follow it all but found herself distracted and savagely restless during a long debate about whether the lander fuel would combust properly in the atmosphere of the planet. The air was breathable, and the weather was stinking hot but wouldn't kill them. There were a lot of thunderstorms and cyclones going on at any given time, which could have been due to the season or to the amount of energy pouring into the system from the three suns.

Marc's presentation was thorough but frustrating. He could delineate boundaries between ecological regions but who knew what that predominantly lavender stuff was? It might be something like a deciduous forest in summer or something like grasslands or something like conifer forest or even an enormous algae mat. "Whatever it is," Marc pointed out with a shrug, "there is a great deal of it." Terrain was easier for him to interpret with confidence. Open bodies of water were sometimes plain, but Marc warned that they could be confused with swampy areas. Tidal zones were remarkably extensive—not surprising with multiple moons. There were obvious oxbow lakes and many river systems. He believed there were areas of cultivated land but told them, "It is quite easy to confuse agricultural plantations with mixed species forest."

Let's just go, Anne thought as Marc droned on. Fuck this shit. Let's just do it. Pack some sandwiches, get in the goddam lander, and go down and throw open the doors and just live or die.

Startled by her own fretfulness, she looked around and saw it in the others as well, but then Marc said, "And this is the source of the radio transmissions." There was an exhalation and a murmur all around. Marc outlined an area near the coast. "This appears to be a city in a high valley ringed by several mountains. There is not the confluence of roads I expected, but these lines here may be canals leading from the two rivers you can see, here and here. This may be a port. I would guess that this semicircular area could be a good harbor."

There were other regions showing features that suggested cities elsewhere on the continent, but they'd come because of the music, so there was no serious discussion of landing near those. Despite this unanimity, an argument broke out over how close to the transmitter city they should approach initially.

Alan Pace was astonished that there was any question at all. He wanted to make contact with the city inhabitants immediately and directly. "With respect to Sandoz, the musical communication could be drawn on at the very beginning, just as we used music to make contact with the Guarnari in the eighteenth century. Also, there are the precedents of Xavier and Ricci, who determined to go as quickly as possible to the cities of Japan and China, and worked with the educated classes first."

"You don't think we'd scare the lights out of 'em, just showin' up in all our alien glory some afternoon?" D.W. asked Alan.

"We could tell them we're from France," Emilio suggested thoughtfully. Even Alan cracked up.

"Maybe we won't be all that big a surprise to them. Human beings have been speculating about alien species for hundreds of years," Jimmy Quinn said, ignoring Emilio but grinning. "With all the moons and suns, these folks have got to be interested in astronomy."

"Do you think so, Jim?" Anne asked, joining the discussion for the first time. "With three suns, very little of the planet is in darkness at any one time, or for very long. They might not pay any attention at all to the night sky."

"They're aiming radio at the moons," Sofia and Jimmy said simultaneously. Everyone laughed, and Anne shrugged and nodded, admitting defeat.

"Anyway, it seems to me that we'd do best to go where the high tech is. I'm willing to bet that this here"—George pointed to a lake in the mountainous area near the city—"is a hydroelectric dam. See? This could be the spillway. If they can build stuff like this and figure out how to bounce radio off their moons, they've got to be at least as technologically advanced as nineteenth- or twentieth-century Earth. So they're probably reasonably sophisticated. I say we go for it. Land in the center of town."

Marc was very much disturbed by this line of reasoning and appealed directly to D.W. "Father, it seems to me that we should learn something of the planet before we deal with the intelligent species, if for no other reason than to send basic ecological data back for the next party, in case something happens to us. We need to get our bearings first."

D.W. turned to Anne. "How long do you expect it to take us to get used to gravity again?"

"George says the planet is a little smaller than Earth, so we expect the gravity to be a little lighter than we were used to. That's a plus. But we've all lost muscle mass and bone density, and our feet are too soft to walk very far. And frankly, everyone is strung out," she said. "Alan, I know you're just dying to see the instruments and to sing with the Singers, but making contact is going to be very risky. Do you honestly feel you're ready to cope with any kind of crisis at this point?"

Pace grimaced. "I suppose not."

"Me, neither," Anne said. "I should think we could take two to three weeks getting used to conditions on the surface, building up strength and readapting to sunlight."

"That would also give us time to study the flora and fauna at least in a limited region," Marc said. "And we could find out if we can eat or drink anything safely—"

The discussion went on for hours but ultimately D.W. decided that they would attempt to land in an area that appeared to be uninhabited, with supplies for a month's stay, to assess the conditions and plan their next move. And later they all realized that in the end, the decision to go had once again come down to the words of Emilio Sandoz.

"I agree with Marc and Anne about a cautious approach, but there are logical arguments either way and no empirical means of choosing between them," he'd said. "So, I suppose, at some point, we must simply make a leap of faith." Then, to his own surprise, he added, "If God brought us this far, I don't think He will fail us now."

And if the statement was not entirely unconditional, only Anne noticed.

19

LANDFALL, RAKHAT:
OCTOBER 13, 2039, EARTH-RELATIVE

THE FOLLOWING DAYS were the worst they'd experienced, physically and mentally. From the tonnage of stored matériel, they had to select the equipment, clothing and food that seemed likely to be most immediately useful and stow it on the lander. The asteroid systems had to be locked down for their absence. The radio transceivers had to be set up to receive, encrypt and relay their reports to Earth. The onboard computers had to be left in a condition to be accessed remotely.

D.W. double-checked everything, catching errors, correcting mistakes. Having nursed a certain amount of resentment about his high-handedness, Anne began to reassess. D.W. was right to have gotten a grip on things when he did. Even with his steadying influence, the activity verged on frantic toward the end. They were all secretly scared they'd forgotten something or made a mistake that would result in some disaster or get someone killed. So when D.W. finally called a halt and brought them all together, there was a sense of being pulled back from the brink of hysteria.

"Finish what you have to do by five o'clock this afternoon," he told them. "Then let it go. Stop thinkin' about what can go wrong. It's more important right now to calm down. Y'all're too strung out for your own good. Go to bed early tonight. Just rest if you can't sleep. We'll say Mass at nine. And then we'll go down." D.W. smiled into the eyes of all his tired people, one by one. "You'll do fine. I'd trust any of you, apart or together, with my life and my soul. And when you bed down tonight, I want y'all to think about what Emilio said: God didn't bring us this far to let us down now."

THAT NIGHT, ANNE left George and pushed herself across the commons to D.W.'s door. She knocked softly, not willing to wake him if he was asleep but wanting to talk to him in private if he wasn't.

"Who is it?" he called quietly.

"Anne." There was a little delay, and then the door opened.

"Evenin'. C'mon in. I'd offer you a chair but . . ."

She smiled and tried to find a place to float that felt properly situated. A paper for some graduate student, she thought. *Maintenance of Culturally Based Distancing Norms in Zero G.* "This won't take long, D.W. You need rest, too. I just wanted to ask if you'd consider letting Emilio be the first one out of the lander tomorrow."

In the silence that fell, Anne watched him work it through in his mind. There was no place in history at stake here, no plan to record this event. No reporters, no photography or AV feed to the nets. From a culture gone mad with documentation, publicity, broadcast, narrowcast and pointcast, where every act of public and private life seemed to be done for an audience, the voyage of the *Stella Maris* had begun in privacy, and its mission would be carried out in obscurity. Jesuits being as they are, there would be no mention of who set foot on this planet first, not even in the internal report relayed back to the Father General, whoever he might be when the news got back. Even so, as their leader by nature and by Order, it was D.W.'s risk to take and his privilege to claim. If Emilio Sandoz had first suggested this endeavor, it had nevertheless become D. W. Yarbrough's mission. No one had worked harder or longer, no one had given more thought to it or slaved over its details more single-mindedly. Anne knew that and she honored it.

He looked up at her after a long time, almost bringing both eyes into alignment with the intensity of his gaze. She could see him making one of the decisions involved in discussing this with her and she maintained a strict neutrality, so as not to influence him. When he spoke, his voice was as empty of accent as his face was naked of defense. "And you think that this would be appropriate? There would be no suspicion," he said and then hesitated before saying, "of favoritism?"

"D.W., I wouldn't have asked if I thought there was even a possibility of that." It's okay, she wanted to say. He's easy to love. I understand. "I think the others would approve and I believe it will mean a great deal to him. Spiritually." She cleared her throat then, embarrassed even to have said that word. "I hope you don't mind my venturing into your purview here—"

D.W. waved that off. "Oh, hell, no. Course not. I trust your judgment. You're much closer to him than I ever was, Anne." He looked at her to see if she accepted that and then rubbed his eyes, red-rimmed and bloodshot in his pale, disheveled face. "Okay. Fine by me. He goes first. Assumin' it looks safe to get out! We may get down there and decide it's too damn dangerous for anyone to risk it."

"Oh, D.W.! Oh, my darling man!" Anne cried. "If you even think about not letting us out of the lander, I will *chew* straight through that plane. You just try to stop me."

D.W. laughed, and she decided against hugging him but held out her hand. He took it and, to her complete astonishment, brought it to his lips and kissed it, looking crookedly at her the whole time. "Good night, Miz Edwards," he said, Southern and gallant as he could be, dressed in sweats and floating in midair. "Sleep well, y'hear?"

ALL OF THEM, in their own ways, prepared that night both for death and for a kind of resurrection. Some confessed, some made love, some slept exhausted and dreamed of childhood friends or long-forgotten moments with grandparents. They all, in their own ways, tried to let their fear go, to reconcile themselves to their lives prior to this night, and to what might come tomorrow.

For some of them, there had been a turning point that now seemed justified, however painful the decision might have been. For Sofia Mendes, a way to make peace with what, even now, she could only think of as "the days before Jaubert." For Jimmy Quinn, the end of worry that he was wrong to leave his mother, and right to claim his life as his own.

For Marc Robichaux and Alan Pace, there was a sense that they had lived their lives the right way and confidence that God had recognized their artistry as the prayer they had always meant the work to be, and there was hope that He would let them serve Him now.

For Anne and George Edwards, for D. W. Yarbrough and Emilio Sandoz, this voyage had given meaning to random acts, and to all the points where they had done this and not that, chosen one thing and not another, to all their decisions, whether carefully thought out or ill considered.

I would do it all again, each of them thought.

And when the time came, each of them privately felt a calm ratification of those reconciliations, even as the noise and heat and buffeting built to a terrifying violence, as it seemed less and less likely that the plane would hold together, more and more likely that they'd be burned alive in the atmosphere of a planet whose name they did not know. I am where I want to be, they each thought. I am grateful to be here. In their own ways, they all gave themselves up to God's will and trusted that whatever happened now was meant to be. At least for the moment, they all fell in love with God.

But Emilio Sandoz fell hardest of all, letting his fear and doubt go almost physically, his hands opening as everyone else clutched at controls or straps or armrests or someone else's hand. And when the mind-numbing scream of the engines diminished and then fell off to a silence almost as deafening, it seemed only natural that he should move into the airlock and open the hatch and step out alone, into the sunlight of stars he'd never noticed while on Earth, and fill his lungs with the exhalation of unknown plants and fall to his knees weeping with the joy of it when, after a long courtship, he felt the void fill and believed with all his heart that his love affair with God had been consummated.

Those who saw his face as he pushed himself to his feet, laughing and crying, and turned back to them, incandescent, arms flung wide, recognized that they stood witness to a soul's transcendence and would remember that moment for the rest of their lives. Each of them felt some of the same dizzying exultation as they emerged from the lander, spilling from their technological womb wobbly and blinking, and felt themselves reborn in a new world.

Even Anne, sensible Anne, allowed herself to enjoy the sensation and didn't spoil it by speculating aloud that it was probably plain relief at cheating death combined with a sudden drop in blood pressure to the brain, consequent to the reversal of Fat Face, Chicken Legs. None of them, not even George who had no wish to believe, was entirely exempt from transcendence.

❀

THERE FOLLOWED DAYS of rapture and hilarity. Children on a field trip to Eden, they named everything they saw. The eat-me's and the elephant birds, hoppers and walkies, the all-black Jesuits and the all-brown Franciscans, scummies and crawlers, hose-noses and squirrel-tails. Little green guys, blue-backs and flower-faces, and Richard Nixons, which walked bent over looking for food. And then black-and-white Dominicans, to round out their collection of orders. And turtle trees, whose seed pods resembled turtle shells; peanut bushes, whose brown blossoms were double-lobed; baby's feet, with foliage soft as rose petals; and pig plants, whose leaves were like sows' ears.

The niches were all there. Air to fly through, water to swim in, soil to burrow under, vegetation to exploit and hide behind. The principles were the same: form follows function, reach high for sunlight, strut your stuff to attract a mate, scatter lots of offspring or take good care of a precious few, warn predators that you're poisonous with bright colors or blend into the background to escape detection. But the sheer beauty and ingenuity of the animal adaptations were breathtaking and the gorgeousness of the plant life staggering.

Anne and Marc, their eyes informed by their study of evolution and Darwinian selection, were beside themselves with delight in everything they saw. They said it with different inflections but they both exclaimed repeatedly, "My God, this is so great!" And long past the point when the others wanted to drop exhausted to the ground, Anne's voice or Marc's could be heard calling softly but urgently, "You've got to see this! Come quick before it moves!" until they were all sated with beauty and novelty and astonishment.

D.W. had come in over ocean and flown low as a drug smuggler over what might as well be called treetops. He spotted a clearing and made a snap decision to land there rather than further on, in the plain Marc had chosen. Surrounded by the tall, heavy-stemmed vegetation that filled the niche of trees, they felt safe and unobserved. If the weather promised to be mild, they slept in the open, weaponless, too ignorant or trusting to worry about major carnivores or aggressive poisonous things. They had tents and took shelter during the sudden rainstorms, but they were frequently drenched. No one cared. The nights were so brief and the days so warm, they dried out quickly and napped in the leaf-filtered sunlight, drowsing in the warmth, contented and lazy as dogs by firelight.

Even dozing, they were suffused with their surroundings. The wind-borne fragrance of a thousand plants as varied as stephanotis, pine, skunk cabbage, lemon, jasmine, grass, but unlike any of them; the heavy dank odor of vegetation decayed by another world's bacteria; the oak-like musky bass notes of the crushed herbs they lay on overwhelmed their ability to perceive and categorize such things. As three dawns and three dusks came and went, the sounds of the long day changed, from chorus to chorus of trilling, shrieking, whirring things. Sometimes they could match the sound to the animal that made it: a shrilling that belonged to the lizardlike creatures they called little green guys, an amazingly loud rasping noise that was made by a small scaly biped staking out its territory in the forest's ground litter. Most often, the sounds were full of mystery, as was the God that some of them worshiped.

THEIR FORAYS BEYOND the clearing were limited, made in pairs, kept always within sight and call of the lander and encampment. But after so much time together, they all broke D.W.'s rule once in a while and sought time alone, to come to grips with the experiences, to think and absorb and then move ahead again, into wonder. So Sofia was not surprised when she found Emilio sitting alone, his back against a boulder that had formed in layers, like sandstone. His eyes were closed. He might have been sleeping.

There are moments, she thought later, when reality seems to shift suddenly, like shards of colored glass in a kaleidoscope. Looking down at Sandoz, seeing him at rest and unaware, she realized, simply, that he was no longer young. And was astonished at the wave of feeling that swept over her.

He was always working or laughing or studying, and his intensity and humor made him seem ageless. She knew something of his life, having worked with him, and recognized him as one of her own kind: an eternal beginner, starting over and over in a new place in new circumstances, with new languages, new people, a new commission. They had this in common: the continual rushed confrontation with change, the feeling of being hothoused, forced to bloom early, the exhausting exhilaration of doing the unreasonable not just adequately but well and with grace.

Flexible, then, and adaptable but not authoritative. He felt himself to be a skilled tradesman, perhaps, doing work to order. She wondered if he had ever given an outright command in his life and thought that if she depended on Emilio Sandoz to teach her a language, she might never even suspect that the imperative mood existed. All this, perhaps, contributed to what she had always perceived as a certain unfledged quality, made more striking by a willingness to submit to authority, odd in a grown man of intelligence and energy, but part and parcel of Jesuit formation. Not childish, but certainly childlike. And yet, she could see now the skin of the eyes pleating, the mouth bracketed by deeper grooves than she had noticed the first time she'd seen him. Half his life, she thought, given to this jealous God of his.

And perhaps a third of my own life given to Jaubert, she thought, and before that . . . Who am I to judge a life misspent?

She drew closer to him, the humus and herbage cushioning her step and absorbing the sound of her approach, and dropped silently almost to her knees. Her hand was drawn to a lock of hair near his face, silver against the black, and she reached out tentatively, as though to touch a butterfly. Sensing her movement, his eyes opened, and she took cover behind Anne's unwitting lessons.

"Sandoz!" she cried, lightly seizing his hair and pulling it playfully toward his eyes, "Look at this! You're getting gray, old man."

He laughed. She smiled back and stood again, looking around, as though there were something, anything in this world, that was of more interest to her now than the man she'd just turned away from.

"So. You are pleased with your choice?" When she said nothing, Emilio asked again, "Happy that you came here?"

"Yes, I am happy with my choice." Sofia gazed at the forest, her hands gesturing toward it all, before turning to look at him. "This makes everything worthwhile, doesn't it." She was aware, always, that he knew what she had been and wondered with fresh interest how this shadowed his thoughts of her.

"I had a dream last night," Emilio told her. "I was floating in the air. And in the dream, I said to myself, I wonder why I never tried this before? It's so easy."

"REM-mediated dendrite formation," she told him. "Your brain is trying to organize a response to prolonged weightlessness followed by all this new sensory input."

Emilio regarded her through narrowed eyes. "You spend entirely too much time with Anne. What is it with the women on this mission?" he demanded suddenly. "If I looked up *prosaic* in the dictionary, it would probably say, 'Immune to poetry. See also *Mendes* comma *Sofia.*' I happen to believe that dream was a religious revelation."

He had been praying, Sofia realized, not sleeping. His voice was light and ironic, but she had seen his face that day and knew he meant it. She tried hard to identify the feeling, to name what swept her, and realized that it was tenderness. This is impossible, she thought. I can't let this happen.

"Aside from exasperating me," he continued, "did you have some reason for—?"

She blinked. "Oh. Yes, actually, it's time for work. Anne sent me for you."

"No one is hurt?" he asked, getting to his feet.

"No. But Robichaux is ready to begin the experiments with local food sources. Anne wants you to help monitor the responses."

They walked back to the encampment, bantering amiably on the way. But she was careful to keep her distance, and believed she gave no sign that she had at last taken up a burden that Emilio had long carried for both of them, without her conscious knowledge. Sofia Mendes, after all, had survived by sealing off emotion, her own and others'. It was an old skill, employed in times past to protect herself and now honorably exercised on behalf of another. I am Mendes, she thought. Nothing is beyond me.

ANNE LOOKED UP from her notebook as Emilio and Sofia joined the others. It's happened, Anne thought, but she turned immediately to the work at hand.

"We'll start with a little meat," she told the group sitting in a circle in front of the lab tent. "Marc wants to go first, but he's just spent a lot of time throwing up in zero G so I don't want to put him under any further stress. Jimmy's big and healthy and he'll eat anything that gets near his mouth. I expect he'll survive if the stuff here turns out to be poisonous to us." Jimmy laughed but looked a little nervous. Anne wasn't joking. "Emilio, you and I are going to watch him in shifts for the next twenty-four hours," Anne continued. "I'll take the first three hours and then you're on."

"What are we looking for?" Emilio asked, sitting on the ground between Alan and George.

"Vomiting within the first hour or so. Then abdominal pain. Then intestinal pain, and then diarrhea ranging from annoying to bloody and life threatening. And then," she said seriously, looking at Jimmy the whole time, "there's the possibility of strokelike bleeding in the brain and a whole range of damage to the intestines and liver and kidneys, which could be either temporary or permanent."

"You'd never get permission from the National Institutes of Health to run this experiment," Jimmy said.

"Not even if the lab rats signed their consent forms with perfect penmanship," Anne agreed. "But we're not applying for a research grant. Jimmy, you know the risks. Marc and I have run a hundred tests, but there are endless chemical compounds in anything as complicated as a plant or an animal. Alan has volunteered to go first if you want to back out."

He didn't, and they began with a small amount of roasted little green guy because the animals were abundant and easy to catch. Everyone watched as Jimmy got ready to take his first bite.

"Simply hold it in your mouth for thirty seconds and then spit it out, please," Marc instructed him. "Any tingling or numbness around the lips or in the mouth?"

"No. It's not bad," Jim told them. "Could use some salt. Tastes just like chicken." There were moans, as he knew there would be, and he beamed happily at the response.

"So. Another bite and this time swallow," Marc told him. Jimmy sucked the rest of the meat from the little pair of legs. And was shouted at by Marc, to everyone's surprise, since they didn't know Marc had shouting in him. "Never again, do you understand? There is a protocol and you will observe it!"

Sheepish, Jimmy apologized but, despite the risk he took, suffered no ill effects, either immediately or at any time during the next twenty-four hours. Like the rainwater they'd drunk, little green guy meat seemed harmless.

They went on from there, with Jimmy taking the first taste of each item they sampled. If it didn't make Jimmy sick, Alan and D.W. tried it next and then George and Marc, and finally Sofia, with Anne and Emilio acting as controls, recording the foodstuffs they tested and tracking the responses, ready to do what they could if someone reacted badly. Marc's protocol was observed to the letter after Jimmy's rashness. If anyone experienced the tingling or numbing that indicated potential poison, the item was described carefully for the record and not tried again. If there was no numbing and if the item was reasonably palatable, then they'd take another small bite and swallow. Wait fifteen minutes and try some more. Then finish a good-sized sample an hour later and hope to be as lucky as Jimmy had been.

They rejected many things on the basis of taste. Most of the leaves they tried were too bitter, and many of the fruits were too sour, although one that tasted great gave even Jimmy the shits. Alan broke out in a rash once, and Marc threw up after one meal. But slowly they compiled a list of things that didn't seem to damage them, even if it was still unclear whether or not they were deriving any useful nutrients from the food. That would require time and a gradual shift from a diet made up primarily of food brought from Earth to one comprising native elements.

THE PLANET SEEMED so welcoming and their contentment was so thorough that the weeks came and went without a return to the *Stella Maris*. Having admired its extravagant beauty, warmed by its suns, sheltered by its forest, at least potentially nourished by it, they began to feel at home on this planet whose name they did not know and to trust its benevolence and welcome.

The first and only sign of trouble was simply that Alan slept late one morning. In the relaxed discipline of those days, D.W. let him but finally decided to roust him out for breakfast. First with humor and then with concern, he jostled Alan with a toe and then shook his shoulder. Getting no response, he called to Anne, who knew from the tenor of his voice to bring her kit.

Shouting Alan's name, talking to him constantly, she surveyed his condition. Airway open. Breathing and heartbeat irregular. "Alan, honey, come on back. Come on, sweetheart, we know you're in there," she said in what she hoped was a mother's voice as D.W. began the ritual anointing. Pupils dilated and fixed. "Father Pace!" she yelled. "You'll be late for services!" Anything. Try to engage him, find a way into wherever he was now, pull him back. Pulse thready. In the ER, she'd have had a team all over him, intubating, charging the paddles. Death, in her experience, was never peaceful. Her training was to resist until flat-line, and beyond. After fifteen minutes, someone took hold of her shoulders and drew her back, ending the CPR. Understanding, she gave

Pace up, but sat and held his limp hand until D.W. took it from her and crossed it over Alan's still and cooling chest.

"You'll want an autopsy," she said. D.W. nodded numbly: they had to know. "I'll have to do it right away. Without preservatives, with this heat—"

"I understand. Go ahead."

George, who knew more than he liked about Anne's work, lashed together a waist-high table for her and curtained off an enclosure, using tarps from the lander. Then he filled containers of water from a nearby creek so she could rinse off as she worked, as well as all the tough, black plastic showerbags, setting them in the sunlight to warm the water, knowing that she'd want to scrub when she was done. Sofia finally roused herself from shocked immobility and went to help George as he took down his and Anne's tent and set it up again, away from the rest of the encampment. He thanked her and explained quietly as they worked, "She's hard to be around when a patient dies under her hands like this. You never get used to that. It'll be better if we can be off by ourselves for a while afterward."

Emilio, meanwhile, helped lift Alan's body onto the crude table and stayed behind after D.W., Jimmy and Marc left the enclosure. "Do you want me to assist?" he asked, willing but already pale.

"No," she said abruptly. Then she softened. "You don't want this in your mind. Don't even stay close enough to hear. I've done a thousand bodies, sweetheart. I'm used to it."

But not bodies like this. Not fresh; not friends. It was, in fact, among the worst, the most distressing things she'd done in a lifetime of grisly experience. And it was among the most futile. Hours later, she made the corpse presentable and called for the priests, who dressed it in vestments and wrapped it in another tarp, the plastic shroud garishly yellow, as inappropriate and unacceptable as the death it concealed.

It was dusk by then. Sitting around the small fire, the others listened to the nearby sound of falling water as Anne showered the blood and brains and excrement and stomach contents from her body, soaped away the smell, and tried unsuccessfully to put the images and sounds from her mind. When she emerged, wet-haired but dressed and appar- ently composed, it was too dark for D.W. to see how tired she was and how upset. He thought, perhaps, that this was not difficult for her, that she was a professional, hardened, unsusceptible to breakdown. So he called her to the fire and asked her the results.

"Let her alone," George said, putting an arm around Anne and turning her toward their tent. "Tomorrow is soon enough."

"No, it's okay," Anne said, even though it wasn't. "It won't take long. There was no obvious cause of death."

"There was the rash, Doctor. Perhaps an allergic reaction to the fruit he ate?" Marc suggested quietly.

"That was days ago," Anne said patiently. "And the rash was probably a contact dermatitis. There was no indication of elevated histamine levels in his blood, but we should take whatever he ate yesterday off our list." She turned again to go to the tent, to lie down with George and to remind herself in his arms that she was alive, and glad of it.

"What about an aneurysm?" Emilio asked. "Maybe he had a blood vessel that was ready to rupture all along and this was just chance."

They were taking refuge in the concrete. Anne realized that. Faced with death, people looked for reasons, to protect themselves from its arbitrariness and stupidity. She'd been up for twenty hours. So had the others, but they'd only waited. Anne put her hands on her hips and stared at the ground, breathing deeply to control the anger. "Emilio," she said softly but precisely, "I have just completed as thorough an autopsy as can be done under these conditions. How much detail would you like? There was no evidence of internal bleeding anywhere. There was no blood clot in the heart or lungs. There was no inflammation of the gut or stomach. The lungs were clear of fluid. The liver was in remarkably fine condition. The kidneys and the bladder were not infected. There was no stroke. The brain," she said, working hard now to keep her voice steady, for the brain had been the hardest to retrieve and inspect, "was fine. There was no physical sign that allows me to declare a known cause of death. He just died. I don't know why. People are mortal, okay?"

She turned to walk away again, looking for someplace to sit down and cry by herself, and nearly screamed when she heard D.W. ask, "What about the bite on his leg? It didn't look like much and we've all been bitten, but maybe . . . Anne, there's got to be a reason—"

"You want a reason?" she asked, rounding on him. He stopped talking, startled by her tone out of his own reverie. "You want a reason? *Deus vult, pater.* God wanted him dead, okay?"

She said it to shock D.W., to shock them all, to shut them up, and she was bitterly glad to see it work. She saw D.W. stop in midsentence, motionless, his mouth open slightly, Emilio wide-eyed, Marc blinking with the violence of it, the way she'd turned his habitual cry of faith against them.

"Why is that so hard to accept, gentlemen?" Anne asked with a flat stare. "Why is it that God gets all the credit for the good stuff, but it's the doctor's fault when shit happens? When the patient comes through, it's always 'Thank God,' and when the patient dies, it's always blame the doctor. Just once in my life, just for the sheer fucking *novelty* of it, it would be nice if somebody blamed God when the patient dies, instead of me."

"Anne, D.W. wasn't blaming you—" It was Jimmy's voice. She felt George take her arm and she shook him off.

"The hell he wasn't! You want a reason? I'm giving you the only one I can think of, and I don't care if you don't like it. I don't know why he died. I didn't kill him. Dammit, sometimes they just die!" Her voice broke on the words and that made her more furious and desolate. "Even when you've got all the medical technology in the world and even when you try your goddamnedest to bring them back and even if they're wonderful musicians and even if they were healthy yesterday and even when they're too damned young to die. Sometimes they just die, okay? Go ask God why. Don't ask me."

George held her while she wept through her rage and told her quietly, "He wasn't blaming you, Anne. Nobody blames you," and she knew that, but for the moment it did feel like it was all her fault.

"Oh, shit, George!" she whispered, wiping her nose on her sleeve, and trying to stop crying and failing. "Crap. I didn't even like him all that much." She turned helplessly toward Jimmy and Sofia, who had moved to her side, but it was the priests Anne was looking at. "He came all this way for the music and he didn't even get to hear it once. How is that fair? He never even got to see the instruments. What is the point of bringing him all this way, just to kill him now? What kind of stinking goddam trick is this for God to play?"

IN THE LONG months aboard the *Stella Maris,* many stories were told. They all still had secrets to keep, but some childhood memories were shared and Marc Robichaux's were among them.

Marc was not one of those guys who knew he wanted to be a priest when he was seven, but he was very close to it. Diagnosed with acute lymphoblastic leukemia at five, he was lucky enough to be a Canadian when universal health care was available. "Leukemia is not that bad," he told them. "Mostly you are just very, very tired and you feel you need to die as a tired child needs to sleep. The chemo, on the other hand, was very terrible."

His mother did her best, but she had other children to care for. So it fell to his paternal grandmother, perhaps compensating for the way her son had deserted the family under cover of the stress of Marc's illness, to sit by his bed, to regale him with stories of old Quebec, to pray with him and assure him with perfect confidence that a new kind of operation, an autologous bone marrow transplant, would cure him. "Only a few years earlier, the kind of leukemia I had would surely have killed me. And the transplant itself very nearly did," he admitted. "But a few weeks later— it was like a miracle. My grandmother was convinced it was in fact a literal miracle, God's plan for me."

"What about you, Marc?" Sofia asked. "Did you think it was a miracle, too? Is that when you decided to become a priest?"

"Oh, no. I wanted to be a hockey star," he told them, through a burst of surprised laughter. And when they refused to believe this, he insisted, "I was a very good goalie in high school!" The talk moved on to sports at that point and never came back to Marc's childhood. But Sofia was not far wrong, although it was almost ten years before Marc Robichaux found a focus for his clear sense that life was God's gift, to give or take.

His grandmother's rosary had come with him to Rakhat, and so did his conviction that all life is fragile and evanescent, that God alone endures. And yet he knew that Anne would find such an answer to her unanswerable question inadequate and unsatisfying. Why? she would ask. Why does it have to be that way?

In the brief hours before the first of the Rakhati dawns, as Marc kept vigil with Alan's body, he watched Jimmy Quinn moving quietly from tent to tent, listening, agreeing, finding common ground and relaying messages. There had been times, Marc knew, when each of the mission members had thought privately that Alan Pace might cause trouble, but none of them had anticipated that it would come about like this or that Anne of all people would drive a wedge into the group.

Finally, with the night noises quieting and the orange sun's chorus tuning up, Jimmy came across the clearing toward Marc. "Blessed are the peacemakers," Marc said quietly. "Has the diplomacy gone well?"

Jimmy stared toward what they called east because that's where daybreak began, and ticked off the summaries with his fingers. "George thinks it's D.W.'s fault for pushing Anne past her limits. Anne is ashamed of herself for blowing up and says it was twenty years of frustration coming to a head. D.W. understands that and wishes he'd waited until Anne was rested up. Emilio also understands about Anne but he's afraid your feelings were hurt. Sofia says not even Job got an answer to Anne's question and Job got to ask God to His face."

Unexpectedly, Marc smiled. The orange sunlight filtered through the eastern edge of the forest and reached his silvering hair, restoring to it the golden tint of his youth. He had been a spectacularly beautiful child and even in middle age, the lovely lines of his face softening, he could be a treasure to look at. "Tell Father Yarbrough I should like to be the celebrant, please. And be sure that Dr. Edwards comes to Mass, *oui*?"

Jimmy waited to see if Marc had anything more to say but Robichaux turned away. The beads of an antique rosary began again to slip through his fingers in the gentle rhythm only Marc, and perhaps God, could hear.

THERE WAS A brief, tight discussion before the Requiem about whether they should bury Alan, cremate the corpse or take it back to the *Stella Maris*. The issue was whether or not the bacteria in his body would contaminate the local ecosystem. To Anne's considerable relief, she and Marc found themselves on the same side of the argument.

"The moment we stepped out of the lander, we affected this ecosystem," Anne said, voice husky from crying. "We have breathed and vomited and excreted and shed hair and skin cells. This planet has already been inoculated with whatever bacteria we're carrying."

"Have no illusions," Marc Robichaux added. "Our presence is now a part of this planet's history."

So a grave was dug and the yellow tarp's shrouded contents were carried to its edge. The Liturgy of Resurrection was begun, and when the time came, Marc spoke of Alan Pace and of the beauty of his music and the delight he had taken in hearing whole songs only a few weeks earlier.

"The voyage was not without reward for Alan," Marc said. "But we are left with Anne's question. Why would God bring him all this way, only to die now?" He paused and looked at Sofia before continuing. "The Jewish sages tell us that the whole of the Torah, the entirety of the first five books of the Bible, is the name of God. With such a name, they ask, how much more is God? The Fathers of the Church tell us that God is Mystery and unknowable. God Himself, in Scripture, tells us, 'My ways are not your ways and My thoughts are not your thoughts.'"

The noise of the forest was quieting now. Siesta was the rule in the heat of midday, when three suns' aggregate light drove many animals to shelter. They were all, priests and lay, tired and hot, and wanted Marc to finish. But Marc waited until Anne lifted her eyes to his. "It is the human condition to ask questions like Anne's last night and to receive no plain answers," he said. "Perhaps this is because we can't understand the answers, because we are incapable of knowing God's ways and God's thoughts. We are, after all, only very clever tailless primates, doing the best we can, but limited. Perhaps we must all own up to being agnostic, unable to know the unknowable."

Emilio's head came up and he looked at Marc, his face very still. Marc noted this and smiled, but continued. "The Jewish sages also tell us that God dances when His children defeat Him in argument, when they stand on their feet and use their minds. So questions like Anne's are worth asking. To ask them is a very fine kind of human behavior. If we keep demanding that God yield up His answers, perhaps some day we will understand them. And then we will be something more than clever apes, and we shall dance with God."

20

NAPLES:
JUNE 2060

"REYES, RELAX! WE'RE in far less danger out here."

"Far less is not the same as none," Felipe Reyes told the Father General sourly. They were out of sight of land now and unlikely to run onto rocks, which Giuliani knew to be the real hazard while sailing in the bay, but Reyes was unconvinced. "I was a lot happier when we could see the shoreline."

Giuliani grinned into the sun, as they sailed close-hauled on a starboard tack. He'd put Reyes on the tiller, figuring that the man could control it using his upper arm and elbow. Usually he gave virgins the jib sheet and taught them how to keep the sail from luffing so he could take the tiller himself, but Reyes didn't have a secure enough grip to handle rope.

"This is the first day, including Sundays, in almost ten years that I haven't been in at least four meetings," the Father General said. He was stripped to the waist, tanned and big-shouldered, in remarkable condition for a man of his age. Felipe Reyes, stocky and unathletic, kept his shirt on. "It's getting so I always make a sincere Act of Contrition before I go into a meeting. Statistically, it's a good bet I'm going die during one. Prepare to come about."

Reyes ducked far lower than necessary as the boom passed over his back. He had a vision, as vivid as anything Santa Teresa de Avila ever experienced, of being swept overboard and sinking like a stone.

"I'm sorry it has to come at Emilio's expense," Giuliani continued, "but I'm delighted by the chance to get out on the water."

"You love this, don't you," Reyes said, watching him.

"Oh, yes. Yes, I do. And I am, by God, going to take a year off when I'm eighty and sail around the world!" he declared. The wind was coming up and there was weather to port. "Sailing is the perfect antidote for age, Reyes. Everything you do on a sailboat is done slowly and thoughtfully. Most of the time, an old body is entirely capable of doing whatever needs to be done while you're cruising. And if the sea is determined to teach you a lesson, well, a young back is no more capable than an old one of resisting an ocean, so experience counts more than ever. Coming about."

They sailed on in silence for a while, passing and saluting a couple of men on a fishing boat. Reyes had lost track in all the jibes and tacks of which way they were going, but he had the impression that they might be circling the bay. There were a lot of fishermen out. Funny, for so late in the afternoon.

"I tried to get Sandoz to come out here with me yesterday. Thought he'd enjoy it. He looked at me like I was suggesting a suicide pact."

"Probably scared to be out in a boat," Felipe said, hoping it wasn't obvious that he was actually pretty frightened himself.

"But you guys are from an island! How can you be scared of the sea?"

You guys, Felipe noted. Plural. So much for not being obvious. "Easy. Hurricanes and pollution. Toxic tides and sharks. Nothing like living on an island to convince you that land is the correct place to be." Felipe looked out at the horizon and tried not to notice the storm clouds. "I never learned to swim, myself. I doubt that Emilio ever did either. Too late now, in any case," he said, holding up his prostheses.

"You won't need to swim, Reyes," the Father General assured him. He was quiet for a while and then said casually, "Tell me about Emilio. I knew him as a kid—he was one of my *secundi* during formation, you know. God's best beloved, we *primi* used to call him. Only a matter of time until he leads a revolt of angels . . . Had to be the best at everything, from Latin to baseball." Sandoz had turned the joke around and grown a beard that made him look like Satan in a bad religious painting; it was a neat and soundless answer to the ribbing, now that Giuliani thought of it. "And later, I knew him by reputation, as an academic. Brilliant in his field, I understand. What was he like, as a parish priest?"

Reyes blew out a breath and sat still. Just as he'd suspected. That was what this invitation was about. "He was a good priest. Very likable guy. Young. Great sense of humor. Athletic." Hard to believe it was the same man. All the warmth and fun gone. Not surprising, under the circumstances. The hearings were not going well. Emilio answered questions in monosyllables or got lost trying to recall technical discussions he said he'd only half-listened to. Reyes was embarrassed for him. He seemed inarticulate and confused at times, got angry and defensive when pressed.

They came about again and sailed toward another fishing boat. This time, the fisherman called out to the Father General. Felipe could patch together enough Italian to understand that Giuliani was confirming that he'd be attending a wedding in July. The Father General seemed to know a lot of the fishermen.

"Did you ever hear about the Basura Brigade?" Felipe asked suddenly.

"No. What was that? *Basura* means garbage, right?"

"Right. That was typical Sandoz, now that I think of it. It was at the beginning, when he first got back to La Perla. The neighborhood—well, it was a slum, you understand. A lot of squatters. There was a sort of shanty town in the east end. And it was never incorporated, so there was no garbage pick up. People threw stuff into the sea or dumped it over cliffs. Emilio just started picking trash up in the streets. Bags and bags of it. And he'd carry it up to Old San Juan and leave it in front of the Edwardses' house so the city would haul it. He got in trouble with city council, but the Edwardses claimed it was their trash. So they got away with it for a while."

"Coming about."

Felipe ducked under the boom again, letting it pass inches above his head, taken up with his story. "At first the kids would just kind of follow Emilio around—he was terrific with kids. Anyway, they'd follow him around, and he'd hand them each a bag, and pretty soon there'd be this whole parade of little kids with big bags of garbage, trailing up the stairs behind Emilio and leaving this incredible pile of trash in front of the Edwards place. And that was a very fancy tourist neighborhood, so there were tons of complaints."

"Let me guess. The city finally decided it was better to pick up the garbage in the neighborhood than to make an issue about it with a very telegenic priest."

"You bet. I mean, he could be so charming, but you just knew he would keep bringing the garbage up until hell froze over. And he pointed out that the kids were doing something constructive and let the council figure out that those same kids could be picking pockets in San Juan, so . . ."

Giuliani waved to another fisherman. "You know, I have never been able to reconcile the stories I hear about Emilio with the man I know. The last word I'd choose to describe him is charming. He was the grimmest man I ever met, in formation. Never smiled. Worked like a dog. And just ferocious about baseball."

"Well, you know, Latino boys still aspire to the F's. They want to be *feo, fuerte y formal.*" He looked to see if the Father General had enough Spanish. "Ugly, strong and serious. The macho ideal. I imagine Emilio took a lot of abuse as a kid because he was small and good-looking, so he made up for it by being very serious, very correct."

"Well, I'd have said sullen and hostile rather than serious and correct. You know, I'm not certain I've ever seen him smile. Or heard him say more than three words in a row. When I hear people describe him as charming or funny, I think, Are we talking about the same person? Coming about." Giuliani motioned toward another boat and Felipe nodded and changed the tiller position. "And then I hear he does impressions and magic tricks, he's great with kids—" He fell silent but Reyes offered nothing further, so he mused, "I have always found him stiff and standoffish, but he has an uncanny ability to make friends! Candotti and Behr would walk over hot coals for him."

"Can I sit on the other side of this thing?" Felipe asked. "This arm's getting tired."

"Sure. You want me to take it? I sail alone quite a bit when I get the chance."

Felipe was surprised to find he didn't want to give the tiller up. "No. Actually, if I can just switch sides, I'll be fine," he said and gingerly stood to move. He sat down rather abruptly, the slap of the waves pushing him off balance, but settled into the tiller again. "I'm beginning to see the attraction of this sailing business," he admitted. "This is my first time in a boat, you know. When did you start sailing?"

"When I was a kid. My family had a thirty-two-foot cutter. My dad had me working out celestial navigation problems when I was eight."

"Father General, may I speak frankly?"

There was a silence. "You know, Reyes," Giuliani said at last, squinting at the horizon, "one thing I hate about this job is that everyone always asks permission to speak frankly. Say whatever you want. And call me Vince, okay?"

Taken aback, Felipe gave a short laugh, knowing himself to be utterly incapable of calling this man Vince, but then he asked, "When did you get your first pair of shoes?"

It was Giuliani's turn to be taken aback. "I have no idea. When I was a toddler, I suppose."

"I got my first pair of shoes when I was ten. Father Sandoz got them for me. When you were growing up, was there ever any question about your going to school? I don't mean college. I mean, did anyone ever imagine that you wouldn't go to high school?"

"I see what you're driving at," Giuliani said quietly. "No. There was no question at all. It was absolutely assumed that I would be educated."

"Of course," Felipe said, shrugging good-naturedly, accepting the naturalness of such an attitude for families like Giuliani's. He didn't have to say, You had a mother who knew who your father was, you had educated parents, money for a sailboat, a house, cars. "I mean, if you hadn't gone into the priesthood, you'd have been a banker or a hospital administrator or something, right?"

"Yes. Possibly. Something like that, perhaps. The import business or finance would have come pretty easily."

"And you'd feel perfectly entitled to be whatever you wanted to be, right? You're smart, you're educated, you work hard. You deserve to be who you are, what you are, where you are." The Father General didn't reply, but he didn't deny the observation's truth. "You know what I'd be, if I weren't a priest? A thief. Or worse. I was already stealing when Emilio took an interest in me. He knew about some of it, but he didn't know I was already busting into cars. Nine years old. I would have graduated to grand theft auto before I was thirteen."

"And if D. W. Yarbrough hadn't taken an interest in Emilio Sandoz?" Giuliani asked quietly. "What would Emilio have been?"

"A salesman," Reyes said, watching to see if Giuliani knew the code. "Black tar heroin, out of Mexico via Haiti. Family tradition. They all did time. His grandfather was assassinated in prison. His father's death touched off a minor gang war. His brother was killed for skimming profits."

Felipe paused and wondered if he had any right to tell Giuliani this.

Some of it was a matter of public record; Emilio's file probably contained at least this much information and perhaps a great deal more.

"Look," Felipe said, caught up now in the stark contrast between his life, Emilio's life, and the lives of men like Vincenzo Giuliani, who were born to money and position and security, "there are still times when the thief I started out to be feels more authentic to me than the priest I've been for decades. To be pulled out of a slum and educated is to be an outsider forever—" He stopped talking, deeply embarrassed. Giuliani could never understand the price scholarship boys paid for their education: the inevitable alienation from your uncomprehending family, from roots, from your own first person, from the original "I" you once were. Angry, Felipe decided to say nothing more about Emilio Sandoz. Let Giuliani ask the man directly.

But the Father General said, "So you memorize the rules and you try not to expose yourself to humiliation."

"Yes."

"And you are stiff and formal in direct proportion to how completely you feel out of your element."

"Yes."

"Thank you. That explains a lot. I should have realized—"

They were interrupted by another shouted conversation in Italian as they hove back in toward Naples and came near another boat. Reyes caught something about the bambinos. Irritably, he asked, "Don't any of these people actually fish?"

"No, I don't think so," Giuliani said genially. "They certainly know their way around boats, but they don't fish."

Puzzled now, Felipe looked at him. "You know all these guys, don't you?"

"Yes. Second cousins, mostly." Giuliani grinned as Reyes worked it out.

"I don't believe it. Mafia! They're Mafia, aren't they," said Felipe, eyes bulging.

"Oh, goodness. I wouldn't say that. One never says that. Of course, I don't know for certain what their major source of income is," Giuliani admitted, his voice dry and soft as flour, "but I could take an educated guess." He glanced at Felipe and very nearly laughed. "And in any case, the Mafia is Sicilian. In Naples, it's the Camorra. Amounts to the same thing, I suppose," he mused. "Funny, isn't it. My grandfather and Emilio Sandoz's grandfather were in the same line of work. Sandoz reminds me a little of my grandfather, now that I think of it. He was also a charming man in his own element but very stiff and wary with people he didn't trust or was uncomfortable with. And I felt privileged to be a member of his inner circle. I'd have walked across hot coals for my grandfather. Coming about."

Felipe was too dumbfounded to move and Giuliani had to yank him out of the way of the boom. He let Reyes absorb it for a while and then spoke again, reminiscing. "My father was relatively clean but the family money was as dirty as it comes. I found out when I was about seventeen. Very idealistic age, seventeen." The Father General glanced at Reyes. "I never cease to marvel at the variety of motives men have for the priesthood. I suppose originally, for me, the vow of poverty was a way of compensating."

He began lowering the jib and took over the tiller, to bring the boat into dock. "The first cutter I ever sailed was a gift from my grandfather, and dirty money bought it. Probably bought this boat as well, come to think of it. And it's buying Emilio Sandoz the privacy and protection he needs, even as we speak. That's why we're in Naples, Reyes. Because my family owns this town."

"WHERE DID YOU learn to make gloves like this?" Emilio asked John.

They were sitting outdoors, on opposite sides of a wooden table in the green shade of a grape arbor. Servos whirring spasmodically, Emilio was doggedly picking up pebbles one by one from the table, dropping them into a cup, and then tipping them out again to start the exercise over with the other hand, while John Candotti stitched the latest pair of gloves.

John had been almost glad to see that an earlier design was flawed, a seam running too close to the scar tissue between two of the fingers, rubbing it raw. It was an opening, a way to reestablish some kind of peace between them. Sandoz had barely spoken to him since that first awful day of the hearings, except to accuse John of allowing him to be blindsided.

"I thought you were supposed to help me prepare for this shit," he'd snarled when John approached him the next day. "You let me walk in there *cold,* you sonofabitch. You could have warned me, John. You could have given me some idea of what they said."

John was at a loss. "I tried! I did, dammit! And anyway, you knew what happened——" He thought Sandoz was going to hit him then, as ludicrous as that might have been, a small sick angry man with wrecked hands attacking him. Instead Sandoz had turned and walked away, and refused even to look at John for over a week.

Finally the fury had burned down and today, Sandoz seemed simply tired and depressed. The morning had been difficult. They were going over the death of Alan Pace. Edward Behr speculated that the man's heart might have fibrillated. There'd have been no evidence of that in an autopsy. Emilio seemed indifferent. Who knew? When John offered to redesign the gloves and make a new pair this afternoon, Sandoz shrugged listlessly and seemed willing to sit at the same table at least while Candotti worked on the new pattern.

"I used to make gloves and shoes for a living," John told him.

Emilio looked up. "Everything was mass-produced when I left."

"Yeah, well, it mostly still is but for a while, there were a bunch of us who were going to bring dignity back to human labor," John said cynically, embarrassed to admit this. "Everyone was going to have a trade, and we'd all buy only handmade things, to make a market for it all. We weren't exactly Luddites or hippies, but it was that kind of thing. Make a shoe, save the world, right?"

Sandoz held up his hands, the braces dull in the shade. "That's a movement that's going to pass me by. Unless someone wants to make a market for putting pebbles into cups."

"Well, it's long gone anyhow. You're doing better with those," John told him, motioning at the braces with his thimble. Only a few months ago, Sandoz had almost sweat blood just to close his hand around a stone the size of his fist.

"I hate these things," Emilio said flatly.

"You do? Why?"

"At last. A simple question with an easy answer. I hate the braces because they hurt. And I am tired of pain." Emilio looked away, watching bees service daylilies and roses in the bright sunlight beyond the arbor shade. "My hands hurt and my head is pounding and the braces bruise my arms. I feel like hell all the time. I'm sick to death of it, John."

It was the first time John Candotti had ever heard the man complain. "Look. Let me take them off for you, okay?" He stood and reached across the table, ready to unfasten the harnesses. "You've done enough for today. Come on."

Emilio hesitated. He hated also that he could neither put on nor take off the braces himself and was dependent on Brother Edward to do this for him. He was used to that and to worse, with Edward, but had rarely allowed anyone else to touch him since leaving the hospital. It was a struggle to permit it. Finally, he held out his hands, one after the other.

There was always more pain when the pressure was released, the blood moving back into cramped, exhausted muscles. He closed his eyes and waited, stiff-faced, for the sensation to ease and was startled when Candotti picked up one of his arms and began to massage some feeling back into it. He pulled away, dreading that someone might see them and make some insufferable remark. The same thought occurred to Candotti perhaps, for he didn't protest.

"Can I ask you something, Emilio?"

"John, please. I already answered a thousand questions today."

"It's just—why did they do this to you? Was it torture? I mean, it looks like such a neat job."

Sandoz let out an explosive breath. "I am not entirely sure I understand it myself. The procedure was called *hasta'akala*." Draping his hands on the rough wood of the table like a merchant displaying a length of cloth for a buyer, he stared at them without evident emotion. "It wasn't supposed to be torture. I was told that the Jana'ata sometimes do this to their own friends. Supaari was surprised by how bad it was for us. I don't think Jana'ata hands are innervated as extensively as ours. They don't do much fine motor work. The Runa do all that."

John said nothing, chilled, but stopped stitching and listened.

"It might have been an exercise in aesthetics. Maybe long fingers are more beautiful. Or a way of controlling us. We didn't have to work but then again, we couldn't have. There were servants to take care of us. After. Marc Robichaux and I were the only ones left by then. It was supposed to be an honorable estate, I think." His voice changed, harder now, the bitterness coming back. "I'm not sure to whom the honor accrued. Supaari, I suppose. It was a way of showing that he could afford to have useless dependents in his household, I think."

"Like binding the feet of aristocratic Chinese women."

"Perhaps. Yes, maybe it was something like that. It killed Marc. He never stopped bleeding. He— I tried to explain to them about putting pressure on the wounds. But he never stopped bleeding." He stared at his hands a while longer but then looked away, blinking rapidly.

"You were hurt, too, Emilio."

"Yes. I was hurt, too. I watched him die."

Somewhere in the distance, a dog started barking and was soon joined by another. They heard a woman shouting at the animals and then a man shouting at the woman. Sandoz turned away, bringing his feet onto the bench, and lay his forehead on his drawn-up knees. Oh, no, John thought. Not another one. "Emilio? You okay?"

"Yeah," Sandoz said, lifting his head. "Just an ordinary headache. I think if I could just get some unbroken sleep . . ."

"The dreams are bad again?"

"Dante's *Inferno,* without all the laughs."

It was an attempt at humor but neither of them smiled. They sat for a while, lost in their own thoughts. "Emilio," John said, after a time, "you told us that Marc began eating the native foods at the beginning, while you and Anne Edwards were still acting as controls, right?"

"Shit, John. Give me a break." He stood to leave. "I'm going down to the beach, okay?"

"No. Wait! I'm sorry, but this might be important. Was there anything you ate that Marc didn't?" Sandoz stared at him, his face unreadable. "What if Marc Robichaux was developing scurvy? Maybe that's why he died. Maybe because he'd been eating their food longer than you, or maybe you were getting vitamin C from some food he didn't eat. Maybe that's why he didn't stop bleeding."

"It's possible," Sandoz said finally. He turned away again and had walked a few steps into the sunlight when he jerked to a halt with an involuntary cry and then stood still as a pillar.

John got up instantly and moved around the table, squinting in the dazzle as he went to Sandoz. "What? What's wrong?" Sandoz was bent over, breathing hard. Heart attack, John thought, frightened now. Or one of the spontaneous bone fractures they'd been warned about. A rib or a vertebra simply shattering without warning. "Talk to me, Emilio. Are you in pain? What's wrong?"

When Sandoz spoke, it was with the precision and clarity of a linguistics professor explaining something to a student. "The word *hasta'akala* is a K'San compound probably based on the stem *sta'aka.* The suffix *ala* indicates a similarity or a parallel. Or an approximation. The prefix *ha* makes the stem take on an active aspect, like a verb. *Sta'aka* was a kind of ivy," Emilio said, his voice regulated and even, his eyes wide and sightless. "It was very pretty. It would climb on larger, stronger plants, like our ivies, but it had branches with a weeping growth habit, like a willow." He held up his hands, the fingers falling gracefully from the wrists, like the branches of a weeping willow, or *sta'aka* ivy. "It was symbolic of something. I knew that, from context. Supaari tried to explain, I think, but it was too abstract. I trusted him, so I gave my consent. Oh, my God."

John watched him labor to bring this new understanding to light. It was a bitter birth.

"I gave consent for Marc, as well. And he died. I blamed Supaari, but it was my fault." Bleached and shaking, he looked at John for confirmation of what he took to be an inescapable conclusion. John resolutely refused to follow Emilio's logic, unwilling to assent to anything that would add to the burden of guilt the man carried. But Sandoz was relentless. "You can see it, can't you. *Hasta'akala:* to be made like *sta'aka.* To be made visibly and physically dependent on someone stronger. He offered us *hasta'akala.* He took me to the garden and showed me the ivy and I didn't make the connection. I thought he was offering Marc and me his protection and hospitality. I thought I could trust him. He asked my consent and I gave it. And I *thanked* him."

"It was a misunderstanding. Emilio, you couldn't have known—"

"I could have! I knew everything then that I have just told you now. I just didn't think!" John started to protest, but Sandoz wouldn't listen. "And Marc died. Christ, John. Oh, Jesus."

"Emilio, it wasn't your fault. Even if you'd understood about the ivy, you couldn't have known that they'd do this to your hands," John said, gripping the man's shoulders, helping him control the fall, dropping to his own knees as Sandoz went down. "Robichaux was probably already sick. You didn't cut up his hands, Emilio. You didn't make him bleed to death."

"I am responsible."

"There is a difference between being responsible and being culpable," John insisted.

It was a fine distinction and one which was not very comforting but on short notice, with a man crumpled on the ground in front of him, his face bruised with sleeplessness and now with fresh grief, it was the best John Candotti could do.

IT MUST HAVE been past one in the morning several nights later when Vincenzo Giuliani heard the first signs of the nightmare. He had dozed off reading in the room next to that of Sandoz, having given Edward Behr the night off. "Old men don't need much sleep," he'd told Behr. "You're no good to him if you're as worn out as he is."

There was an unobtrusive monitor near Emilio's bed that carried the sounds of his night into the Father General's room. Like a new parent, alert to the slightest disturbance of an infant's sleep, Giuliani came fully awake the moment the breathing became harsh and irregular. "Don't wake him," Behr had instructed, his own eyes shadowed with the effects of broken sleep and the emotional toll of the aftermath of the nightmares, which were coming now three and four to a week. "It's not always the same dream, and sometimes he gets through it on his own. Just be ready with a basin."

On this night, Giuliani moved out into the hallway, pulling on a robe, and listened for a time before stepping into Emilio's room. There was a full moon and his eyes had little trouble adjusting to the light. Emilio had quieted and Giuliani, relieved, was about to turn away when suddenly Sandoz sat up, gasping. He struggled to get out of the bed, the loose and nerveless fingers tangling in the sheets, and seemed unaware that anyone else was in the room with him. Giuliani went to the bedside, helped him clear the linens, and held the basin until the sickness passed.

Brother Edward had not exaggerated the violence of the vomiting. Vincenzo Giuliani was a sailor who'd experienced a great deal of seasickness but never anything like the gut-wrenching reaction to this dream. When it was over, he took the basin away, rinsed it and brought it back with a plastic tumbler of water. Sandoz accepted the glass, pressing it between his wrists awkwardly and bringing it to his lips. He spat into the basin several times and then let Giuliani take the glass from him.

Giuliani left the room again and brought back a wet cloth to wipe the sweat from Emilio's face. "Ah," Sandoz said ironically, "Veronica."

When Giuliani returned a third time, he went to the wooden chair in the corner of the room to wait for whatever would come next. For a while, Sandoz simply stared at him through lank black hair dampened by exertion, mute and trembling, hunched over on the edge of the bed.

"So," Sandoz said at last, "you have come as a tourist perhaps? To see how the whore sleeps. As you see: the whore sleeps badly."

"Emilio, don't talk like that—"

"The choice of word disturbs you? It did me, at first. But I have reconsidered. What is a whore but someone whose body is ruined for the pleasure of others? I am God's whore, and ruined." He was still now. The physical effects were passing. "What was it you bastards used to call me?"

"God's best beloved," Giuliani said, almost inaudibly, ashamed sixty years too late.

"Yes. I wondered if you'd remember. God's favorite! Isn't that what they used to call a king's mistress? Or his catamite. His favorite?" There was an ugly laugh. "My life has a certain amusing symmetry, if viewed with sufficient detachment."

Giuliani blinked. Sandoz saw the reaction and smiled mirthlessly. He turned away then and used his wrists to pull a pillow up so he could rest his back against the headboard of his bed. His quiet, lightly accented voice was cool and musical when he spoke again.

" 'The moon has set, and the Pleiades; it is the middle of the night.' Are you not concerned to be in the bedroom of someone so notorious?" Sandoz asked with theatrical insolence. He stretched the thin bruised arms out negligently, resting them on the top of the headboard, and raised one knee.

The pose would have been lascivious but for the sheets, Giuliani thought, and at the same time it might have been a deliberately provocative imitation of the figure on the crucifix just above the man's head. Vince Giuliani had been taken in by this kind of double-edged mockery once, but no longer, and he refused to be baited. Given a label, he realized now, Sandoz was apt to show his contempt with burlesque.

"Are you not concerned," Sandoz pressed, with great sincerity, "that, alone and unsupported, you will make a decision that gives scandal?"

It was devastatingly accurate. Giuliani heard his own voice, saw his own pious self-assurance mirrored, and found it difficult not to look away. "What can I do to help you, Emilio?" he asked.

"Does one dream in coma? I have often wondered if a well-placed bullet to the brain would be helpful."

Giuliani stiffened, angry in spite of himself. The man did not make anything easy.

"Failing that," Sandoz continued, "you might provide enough liquor for me to drink myself insensible every night. I have headaches all the time anyway. A hangover would hardly register."

Giuliani rose and moved to the door.

"Don't go," Emilio said.

It might have been a dare. Or a plea.

Giuliani paused and then returned to the corner chair. It was a difficult night but old men do not need much sleep.

21

RAKHAT:
MONTH TWO, CONTACT

SEVEN NOW, SOBERED by the death of Alan Pace, the Jesuit party pulled itself together and began preparations to leave the Eden they'd occupied for almost a month.

Taking stock on the afternoon of the funeral, with the last notes of the Jesuit hymn "Take and Receive" still echoing in his mind, D. W. Yarbrough had carefully weighed the pros and cons of making a trip back to the *Stella Maris* before they set out to find themselves some Singers. The fuel for the lander was limited. Based on the amount burned during their first landing, he estimated that the lander tanks held 103 to 105 percent of what was needed to make a single round-trip from mothership to ground and back, which was pretty damn lucky when he considered it, glancing at the sky. There was enough fuel in storage on-board the asteroid to allow five round trips. Maybe six, but that would be cutting it too fine. Call it five, then, he thought. Reserving fuel for their departure, he figured on four trips over a period of four years to transport supplies and trade goods, with a thin margin for emergencies.

At this point, they had no idea what would be useful for trade, but they did have a notion of how quickly they were going through food. In-creasingly supplemented by native foods and water, their supplies had held out longer than they'd originally estimated. Only Anne and Emilio were still on the control diet brought from Earth, and neither was a big eater. And now there was one less mouth to feed. They had, easily, enough for another week, but D.W. decided that he'd feel better if they established a full-scale food depot, with supplies for at least twelve months. So he had put everyone to work, drawing up lists of things that hadn't been included in the cargo initially.

D.W.'s own list included a rifle, which he intended to bring down without mentioning because he didn't want any big damn discussion about it. And more rope. And he'd just about die before he admitted it, but he wanted to bring down more coffee. The climate had proved reasonably benign, although the thunderstorms could be literally hair-raising and it got too hot to move when the three suns were up simultaneously. They could use lighter clothing and more sunblock.

Most of all, though, he wanted the Ultra-Light. Like all the equipment they'd brought, it was solar-powered—a tiny two-person airplane with wings sheathed in a photovoltaic polymer film capable of running a fifteen-horsepower electric motor. Cute as a bug's ear and a lot of fun to fly. There hadn't been room for it the first time down, not with a full passenger complement. Now they could really use the little plane to scout the territory. Marc's maps were good, but D.W. wanted to fly out ahead and see with his own eyes what they were up against before the party moved out overland.

He tucked his tablet under his arm and walked across the clearing toward Anne Edwards, who noticed him on his way. She was going over her own records, sitting with her back against a "tree" trunk, knees up to support her notebook, which was on-line to the *Stella Maris* library.

"Could have been endocarditis," she said quietly when he was close enough to hear. "Bacterial infection of the heart valves. There was a new form of it I heard about just before we left. It could kill a healthy person pretty quickly, and it was a bitch to find in an autopsy, even at home."

He grunted and hunkered down next to her. "Where would he have picked up the bacteria?"

"Beats the shit out of me, D.W.," Anne said, waving her hand in front of her face to clear off a swarm of gnatlike things they called little buggers. "Might have been carrying it all along, until something weakened his immune system to the point that it overwhelmed his body's defenses. Ultraviolet radiation can suppress the immune system, and we are catching a real dose of UV down here."

"But you're not sure it was, whaddyacallit? That endo shit." He picked up a stick and toyed with it, passing it through his hands, bending it little by little into a hoop.

"No. It's just the best guess I've come up with so far." She closed her notebook. "It's hard to believe that he died just yesterday. I'm sorry about last night."

"Same here," D.W. said, glancing at her with one eye and then looking away, staring out at the forest. He tossed the stick aside. "Warn't good judgment, raggin' at a lady's had a real bad day."

She stuck out her hand. "Peace?"

"Peace," he affirmed, taking her hand and holding it a few moments. Then he let it go and stood up, groaning at the protest his knees made. "You may not want to be friends after I tell you what I've decided we're gonna do next." Anne looked up at him, with narrowed eyes. "I'm goin' back up to the *Stella Maris* and I want George to copilot."

"Oh, my," she said. A blue-green Fast Eddie skittered by her feet and dashed into the leaf litter nearby, and they could hear the Dominicans howling in the forest.

"He was the best of the bunch on the simulator, Anne, and I want him trained on the real thing. And he can check on the life-support systems while I'm loadin' supplies. He ain't had hardly any trouble with space sickness, so there's a good chance he won't get sick this time neither. I knew you'd be pissed, but that's how it parses."

"He'll probably love it, too," Anne said ruefully. "Oh, boy, do I ever hate this idea."

"I ain't askin' permission, Miz Edwards," he said, but his voice was very gentle. He grinned crookedly. "I just thought I'd tell you so's you could cuss me out in private."

"Consider yourself cussed," she said, but she laughed even as she shuddered. "Oh, well. It won't be the first time I've stood around waiting for George to get blown up. Or torn limb from limb. Or smeared across the pavement. Or squashed like a bug. The shit that man does for fun!" She shook her head, remembering the whitewater and the rock climbing and the dirt bikes.

"You ever hear that old joke about the guy who jumped off the Empire State Building?" D.W. asked her.

"Yeah. All the way down, you could hear him say, 'So far, so good. So far, so good. So far, so good.' That is George's life story in a nutshell."

"He'll do okay, Anne. It's a good plane and he's got a talent for the job. I'll put him on the simulator again 'fore we go." D.W. scratched his cheek and smiled down at her. "Ain't in no big damn hurry to crash and burn, my own self. I don't get counted as a holy martyr if we just screw up a landing and pancake into the ground. We'll be careful."

"Speak for yourself, D.W. You don't know George Edwards as well as I do," Anne warned.

IN THE EVENT, the flight went almost without a hitch and George made a beautiful landing, which Anne, hiding behind Emilio and Jimmy with her hands over her eyes, was too scared to watch. When she finally peeked out from behind the two men and between her fingers, George had already climbed out of the lander, yelling and whooping, and was running toward her, sweeping her up to swing her around, talking a mile a minute about how great it had been.

Sofia, smiling at George as they passed, went to help D.W. with the postflight inspection. "You look a little pale," she remarked quietly, moving along the port-side wing.

"He did jes' fine," D.W. muttered, "for a stupid damn sumbitch with more guts than sense."

"A rather more exciting flight than you anticipated," Sofia ventured dryly and smiled with her eyes alone when D.W. grunted and ducked under the fuselage, where he occupied himself with the starboard systems until his heart rate returned to normal.

Anne, still shaking, came over and made a point of congratulating Sofia on the obvious effectiveness of the flight simulator. "I am tempted to say, Thank God!" she said quietly, hugging the younger woman. "But thank you, Sofia."

Sofia was gratified by the acknowledgment. "I must admit I am also relieved to have them back in one piece."

"It is also nice to have the plane back, *mes amis*," Marc said unsentimentally as he and Jimmy wrestled a packing crate out of the cargo bay. And everyone who'd waited on the ground silently seconded that. There was only one way off this planet, and everyone knew it.

GEORGE, WHOLLY SMITTEN with flying, now wanted to try piloting the Ultra-Light as well but had to be content with simply putting the diaphanous miniature plane together the next day. D.W. had already decided that Marc would go up with him on the first flight so the naturalist could get a feel for how the space images corresponded to the actual terrain and vegetation.

While George and D.W. were off-planet, the ground crew had passed the time preparing a runway for the Ultra-Light, which required a forty-meter strip. There were still two stumps to finish pulling, and then they had to wait for the right amount of rain to pack the loose soil down without turning it into a swamp, so it was nearly a week before D.W. and Marc were able to start their flight down a river gorge that passed through a minor mountain range northeast of their position in the clearing.

There had been no indication yet that anyone knew they were there, despite two noisy trips in and one out of the clearing, and that was to the good. Their flight paths had been chosen to minimize the likelihood of passing over inhabited regions, and evidently no air transportation had been developed locally. While still on the *Stella Maris,* George had worked out the AM radio frequencies used by the Singers and recommended that the Jesuit party use UHF and virtually undetectable spread-band encryption for radio communication with the shipboard systems and with each other when separated, to avoid attracting attention prematurely. Even so, D.W. and Marc were forced to maintain radio silence during the last part of their first reconnaissance flight. They did not have full coverage from the satellites they used to relay signals and a period of blackout coincided with the time when the runway was usable.

After fifteen hours, the last five of which were incommunicado, Jimmy broke the silence with a shout. Then they all heard the Ultra-Light's motor and everyone stood to scan the sky for the little plane. "There!" Sofia cried and they watched D.W. circle and then drop down for the bumpy landing.

Marc was smiling broadly as he climbed out of his seat. "We found a village! Perhaps six, or seven days' walk from here, if we move along the river valley," he told them. "Set into the side of some cliffs, about thirty meters up from the river. We almost missed it. Very interesting architecture. Almost like Anasazi cliff dwellings but not at all geometric."

"Oh, Marc!" Anne moaned. "Who gives a shit about the architecture?"

"Did you find any Singers? What do they look like?" George asked.

"We didn't see anyone," D.W. told them, climbing out and stretching. "Damnedest thing. The place didn't look to be abandoned. Not like a ghost town. But we didn't see a soul stirrin'."

"It was very bizarre," Marc admitted. "We landed across the river and watched for a long time, but there was no one to be seen."

"So what do we do now?" Jimmy asked. "Look for another village with some people in it?"

"No," said Emilio. "We should go to the village Marc and D.W. found today."

They all turned to look at him blankly, and Emilio realized that no one had expected him to have an opinion about this. He couldn't stop himself from running his hands through his hair but he straightened and spoke again, with more confidence than usual and in his own voice. "We have been here for some time, in seclusion. To become used to the planet, as we hoped, yes? And now, we have the possibility of investigating this village, also in some privacy. It appears to me that things are proceeding step by step. And next perhaps, we will meet whom we are meant to meet."

"Do you suppose," Marc Robichaux asked, breaking the silence and turning to D.W. with shining eyes, "that this village constitutes a turtle on a fencepost?"

D.W. snorted and laughed shortly and rubbed the back of his neck and stared at the ground for a while, heartily sorry that he had ever mentioned turtles. Then he looked around at the civilians. George and Jimmy were clearly ready to hoist backpacks and go. He shook his head and appealed wordlessly to Anne and Sofia, hoping that one of the women had something logical or practical to contribute. But Anne only shrugged, palms up, and Sofia simply asked, "Why walk when we can fly? I think we should use the Ultra-Light for transport. No fuel problems. We can ferry in personnel and equipment in several trips."

At that, D.W. threw his arms up and looked at the sky in resignation and walked in a circle with his hands on his hips muttering to himself that the whole damn thing beat the livin' shit out of him. But finally he came to rest and gazed at Emilio Sandoz, whom he had known, boy to man, for almost thirty years now. Whose astonishing, diffident, whispered confessions he now heard while fighting back his own tears. For a moment, D.W. was overwhelmed by the sense that he had seen this soul take root and grow and blossom in a way he never would have predicted and could hardly have hoped for and barely understood. A mystic! he thought, astounded. I got a Porter Rican mystic on my hands.

The others were all waiting for his decision. "Sure," D.W. said at last. "Okay. Fine by me. Why not? There's a flat patch where I can land,

outta sight, a few miles south of the village on the same side of the river.
We'll ferry the heaviest equipment in with Mendes, here, 'cause she don't
weigh nothing. Quinn can carry the damn toothbrushes on his trip."

There were cheers then and high fives and a general sense of being
ready to roll and they began talking all at once. In the midst of the commotion, Emilio Sandoz stood silently, as though listening, but he heard
none of the discussion of plans and procedures that went on around
him. When he came back from wherever he had been, it was Sofia
Mendes he saw, a little distance away, as apart from the others as he
was, watching him with intelligent, searching eyes. He met her gaze
without embarrassment. And then the moment passed.

ONE BY ONE, they were carried over forest, along the river
course, and into a drier mountain-lee land, to the staging area D.W. had
identified. They took with them the camping and communications gear
and a two-month supply of food, leaving the bulk of their cargo stored
in the lander, which D.W. locked down and camouflaged. The last thing
each of them looked at as they rose skyward from the runway was the
grave of Alan Pace. No one commented on or admitted to leaving the
flowers.

Everything east of the mountains seemed a little dwarfed and less
colorful than in the forest. The blues and greens and lavenders were
more muted and dusty, the animal species more dependent on stealth
and concealment for safety. There were treelike plants, widely spaced,
but with multiple stems and a tangle of branches in place of the graceful
canopies of the forest. That evening, between the second and third sun-
sets, George found a place in the rocks to conceal the disassembled
Ultra-Light, while the others secured the new food depot. They were
constantly startled as they worked by small gray-blue animals, almost
invisible until they stepped near one, which Anne named coronaries for
the heartstopping habit the little animals had of exploding upward,
grouselike, in brief flights from the ground. Their voices sounded loud
even when they spoke quietly. Without any discussion, they pitched the
tents very close together that night. For the first time since landfall, they
all felt alien and misplaced, and a little scared as they crawled into sleeping bags and tried to get some rest.

The next morning, Marc led them cautiously down the river valley
to a sheltered place where they could see the village, although at first

none of them could make out what he was pointing at. It was a wonder, not to say a miracle, he had noticed it at all, soaring past it in the Ultra-Light. Intended to blend into their surroundings, the masonry and terraces fit seamlessly into the layered, river-cut stone of the cliffside. Roof lines showed sudden displacements, changing height and materials to mimic subsidences and shifts in the rock. Openings were not squared or uniform but varied in concert with the shadowed overhangs where the natural rock had spalled off and fallen toward the river.

Even at this distance, they could see many rooms that opened directly onto terraces overlooking the river. There were large open-weave river-reed parasols, nearly invisible in the surrounding vines and foliage, providing midday shade. These relatively flimsy structures supported D.W.'s impression that the village had been inhabited not long ago; they would not have withstood many storms without upkeep.

"Plague?" Jimmy asked Anne softly. There was still no sign of the villagers, and seeing their emptied dwellings was distinctly eerie.

"No, I wouldn't think so," she said quietly. "There'd be bodies lying around, or mourners, or something. Maybe there's a war going on and they were all evacuated?"

They watched for a while, speculating and studying the village, trying to estimate population and drawing grim whispered conclusions about the missing inhabitants.

"Awright, awright, let's go take a closer look," D.W. said finally.

D.W. posted George and Jimmy as lookouts, armed with radio transceivers, in positions high above the village, where they could see the river and the plain that sloped away eastward from the clifftops. Then he let Marc lead the rest of them up the cliffside, where they began a furtive tour of the dwellings they could enter through the terraces without disturbing anything.

"I feel like Goldilocks," Anne whispered, as they peeked into rooms and moved through passageways and picked their way along exterior rock walkways.

"I was hoping for some artwork that would show us what they look like," Marc admitted. The walls were bare, the stone neither plastered nor painted. There were no sculptures. No representational art at all. There was, in general, a sparseness of furnishings, but evidence of craftsmanship was everywhere. Large cushions with beautifully woven, brilliantly colored covers filled some spaces; other rooms had low platforms, of grained material like wood, that might have been tables. Or benches, perhaps. The joinery was superb.

The inhabitants' departure did not appear to have been rushed. There were rooms or regions of rooms that were apparently used for food preparation, but no food was left out. They found closed containers that probably contained staples but did not open anything, not wanting to tamper with the seals. Pots, bowls, platters, ceramic containers of all kinds were stored on high rock shelves and cutlery was suspended from racks in rafters, high overhead.

"Well, they've got hands," Anne said, looking at the knife handles. "I can't quite work out how I'd hold one of those things, but some kind of fingers are involved."

"They'll be closer to Jimmy's height than ours," Sofia said to Anne. Almost all the storage was far above her reach. That was true at home as well, but it was more extreme here. She found it odd that everything was either very low or very high.

There was no pattern to the rooms that they could figure out on their first pass. Spaces varied in size and shape, often following natural hollows in the rock but with subtle enlargements in volume. In one very large room, they found a vast collection of huge baskets. In a smaller one, beautiful friction-stoppered glassware, filled with liquids. They moved along in the spooky silence for a while longer, expecting at any moment to come face to face with who knew what. Just as they were about to leave, George's voice, tinny in the tiny radio speaker, sounded in the quiet.

"D.W.?"

Anne almost jumped out of her skin at the sound of her own husband's words, and there was a burst of nervous laughter all round, which D.W. silenced with a scattershot glare.

"Right here."

"Guess who's coming for dinner."

"How far off? And how many of 'em?"

"I can just see the first of them coming around a hill about five miles northeast of here." There was a short silence. "Wow. It's a gang of 'em. Walking. Bigs and littles. Looks like families. Carrying stuff. Baskets, I think." There was another brief silence. "What do you want us to do?"

D.W. sorted through their options quickly and was about to say something when Emilio headed out through the nearest terrace, pausing momentarily, and inexplicably, to pick small blossoms from the vines he passed before setting off toward George's outpost. D.W. watched Emilio leave, open-mouthed, and looked at Anne and Marc and Sofia. Then he spoke into the radio. "We're on our way. Meet us where you see us."

They caught up with Emilio as he emerged from the village level onto the plain above the river gorge, and there they were joined by Jimmy and George. From this vantage, they could see an unpaved path that led to a group of several hundred individuals coming their way. Following some inner direction, Emilio had already started down the path with an even stride, covering the ground without haste or hesitation.

"I don't think I'm givin' the orders anymore," D.W. said quietly, to no one in particular. It was Marc who said, "Ah, *mon ami,* I think we are now on the fencepost and we didn't get here on our own. *Deus qui incepit, ipse perficiet.*"

God who has begun this will bring it to perfection, Anne thought, and shivered in the warmth.

The six of them followed in Emilio's footsteps and watched him stoop to pick up small bright pebbles, leaves, anything that came to hand. As if realizing that his actions must seem mad, he turned back to them once and smiled briefly, eyes alight. But before they could say anything, he turned again and continued along the path until he closed the distance to the villagers by half. There he stopped, breathing a little quickly, partly from the walk and partly from the pregnancy of the moment. The others drew close but conceding primacy to him in this, they left Emilio standing a few steps ahead, his black and silver hair lifted and blown by the breeze.

They could hear the voices now, high and melodic, fragments of speech carried toward them on the prankish wind. There was no recognizable order to the march at first, but then D.W. realized that the small ones were bunched toward the center of a mixed crowd and there were large powerful-looking individuals at point and flank, not armed, as far as he could see, but alert and staring directly at the Jesuit party.

"No surprises, no quick movements," D.W. counseled quietly, pitching his voice carefully so it could reach all his people, including Emilio, who remained motionless, a slender flat-backed figure in black. "Stay spread out a little, so you're in full view. Keep your hands where they can see 'em."

There was no panic in either group. The villagers stopped a few hundred paces down the path from Emilio and unburdened themselves of the big well-made baskets, which were filled with something that was not heavy, judging from the ease with which the containers were handled, even by the smaller individuals. They were unclothed, but around their limbs and necks many wore bright ribbons, which fluttered and floated sinuously in the wind. The breeze shifted more decisively then and suddenly D.W. was aware of an exquisite scent, floral, he thought, coming from the crowd. He focused again on the openwork basketry and realized the containers were filled with white blossoms.

For a short while the two groups simply stood and looked at one another, the piping voices of juveniles hushed by adults, murmurs and commentary falling off to silence. As the crowd quieted, D.W. took note of who spoke and who stood silent in the discussion that followed. The flankers and point men remained on guard and aloof from the deliberations.

As D.W. took in the command structure of the group, so Anne Edwards studied the anatomy. The two species were not grotesque to one another. They shared a general body plan: bipedal, with forelimbs specialized for grasping and manipulation. Their faces also held a similarity in general, and the differences were not shocking or hideous to Anne; she found them beautiful, as she found many other species beautiful, here and at home. Large mobile ears, erect and carried high on the sides of the head. Gorgeous eyes, large and densely lashed, calm as camels'. The nose was convex, broad at the tip, curving smoothly off to meet the muzzle, which projected rather more noticeably than was ever the case among humans. The mouth, lipless and broad.

There were many differences, of course. On the gross level, the most striking was that the humans were tailless, an anomaly on their home planet as well; the vast majority of vertebrates on Earth had tails, and Anne had never understood why apes and guinea pigs had lost them. And another human oddity stood out, here as at home: relative hairlessness. The villagers were covered with smooth dense coats of hair, lying flat to muscular bodies. They were as sleek as Siamese cats: buff-colored with lovely dark brown markings around the eyes, like Cleopatra's kohl, and a darker shading that ran down the spine.

"They are so beautiful," Anne breathed and she wondered, distressed, if such uniformly handsome people would find humans repulsive—flat-faced and ugly, with ridiculous patches of white and red and brown and black hair, tall and medium and short, bearded and barefaced and sexually dimorphic to boot. We are outlandish, she thought, in the truest sense of the word . . .

From out of the center of the crowd an individual of middle height and indeterminate sex came forward. Anne watched, scarcely breathing, as this person separated from the group to approach them. She realized then that Marc had been making a similar biological assessment, for as this person stepped nearer, he cried very softly, "The eyes, Anne!" Each orbit contained a doubled iris, arranged horizontally in a figure-eight around two pupils of variable size, like the bizarre eye of the cuttlefish. This much they had seen before. It was the color that transfixed her: a dark blue, almost violet, as luminous as the stained glass at Chartres.

Emilio continued to stand still, letting the person who stood before him decide what to do. At last, this individual spoke.

It was a lilting, swooping language, full of vowels and soft buzzing consonants, fluid and melting, without any of the staccato glottal stops and rhythmic choppiness of the language of the songs. It was, Anne decided, more beautiful, but her heart sank. It was as unlike the Singers' language as Italian was unlike Chinese. All that work, she thought, for nothing. George, who like all of them had been trained by Emilio to recognize the Singers' language, must have been thinking the same thing. He leaned over to Anne and whispered, "Shit. On *Star Trek,* everybody spoke English!" She elbowed him but smiled to herself and took his hand, listening to the speech and tightening her grip as the person stopped speaking and she waited for Emilio's response.

"I don't understand," said Emilio Sandoz in a soft clear voice, "but I can learn if you will teach me."

What happened next was a puzzle to all those in the Jesuit party but Sandoz. The spokesperson called a number of individuals out of the crowd, including several half-grown children, one by one. Each spoke briefly to Emilio, who met their eyes with his own calm gaze and repeated to each of them, "I don't understand." He was almost certain that each had spoken a different language or dialect to him, one of which was indeed that of the Singers, and he realized that they were interpreters and that the leader was attempting to find some language they had in common. Failing in that, the adult returned to the crowd. There was a discussion that lasted a good while. Then a juvenile, much smaller than anyone who'd spoken earlier, came forward with another adult, who spoke reassuringly before gently urging the little one to approach Emilio alone.

She was a weedy child, spindly and unpromising. Seeing her advance, scared but determined, Emilio slowly dropped to his knees, so he would not loom over her, as the adult had loomed over him. They were, for the moment, all alone together, the others of their kinds forgotten, their whole attention absorbed. As the little one came closer, Emilio held out one hand, palm up, and said, "Hello." She faltered only an instant before putting her hand, long-fingered and warm, in his. She repeated, "Hello." Then she said, in a voice as clear and soft as Emilio's, *"Challalla khaeri."* And leaned forward to put her head next to his neck. He could hear the slight intake of breath as she did this.

"Challalla khaeri," Emilio repeated and gravely reproduced her physical greeting with exactitude.

There was a burst of talk among the villagers. It was startling, and the humans stepped back a bit, but Emilio kept his eyes on the child and saw that she was not frightened and did not draw away. He had kept her hand in his and now pulled it gently toward his chest and said, "Emilio." Once again, the child repeated the word, but this time the vowels defeated her and it came out, "Meelo."

Smiling, he did not correct her, thinking, Close enough, *chiquitita*, close enough. He had come somehow to the conclusion that she was a little girl and he was already deeply in love, his whole soul open to her. He simply waited, knowing that she would pull his own hand toward her. This she did, although she drew his hand to her forehead instead of her chest. "Askama," she told him, and he repeated it, accent on the first syllable, the second and third given little emphasis, slurred quickly together, the pitch falling slightly.

Emilio shifted then from his knees, and sat cross-legged in the fine ocher dust of the path. Askama moved slightly as well, to face him, and he knew they could be seen from the side by both groups, native and alien. Before his next move, he turned his head and established eye contact with the adult who'd brought the child forward and who was standing nearby at the edge of the group of villagers, watching Askama steadily. Hello, Mama, he thought. Then he returned his attention to Askama. Rearing back in gentle surprise, he pulled in a little gasp and asked, wide-eyed, "Askama, what's this?" Reaching behind her ear, Emilio's hand suddenly revealed a flower.

"Si zhao!" Askama exclaimed, startled out of the pattern of repetition.

"Si zhao," Emilio repeated. "A flower." He glanced back at the adult, whose mouth was open and ovalled. There was no move, so he went on, producing then two flowers from nowhere.

"*Sa zhay!*" Askama cried, giving him what might be an indication of plural formation.

"*Sa zhay,* indeed, *chiquitita,*" he murmured, smiling.

Soon other children came forward, and their parents moved closer as well, until the two groups, alien and native, merged, enthralled, surrounding Emilio and Askama as he made pebbles and leaves and flowers multiply and vanish and reappear, gathering possible numbers and nouns and, more important, expressions of surprise and puzzlement and delight, watching Askama's face as he worked, glancing at the adults and other children to check responses, already absorbing the body language and mirroring it in a dance of discovery.

Smiling and in love with God and all His works, Emilio at last held out his arms and Askama settled happily into his lap, thick-muscled tapering tail curling comfortably around her as she nestled down and watched him greet the other children and begin to learn their names in the tripled sunshine that broke through the clouds. He felt as though he were a prism, gathering up God's love like white light and scattering it in all directions, and the sensation was nearly physical, as he caught and repeated as much of what everyone said to him as he could, soaking up the music and cadence, the pattern of phonemes on the fly, gravely accepting and repeating Askama's quiet corrections when he got things wrong.

When the talk became more chaotic, he took a chance and began to reply to the children in nonsense, mimicking the melody and general sound of the phrases with great seriousness but no longer trying for accuracy. This tactic had worked well with the Gikuyu, but the Chuuk Islanders had been offended. To his relief, the adults here seemed amused; certainly there were no shouts or threatening gestures as the children shrieked and vied for the chance to have him "talk" to them in this hilarious and silly way.

He had no idea how much time passed in this manner but, eventually, Emilio became aware that his back was cramped and his legs were paralyzed from Askama's weight. Easing the child out of his lap, he staggered to his feet but kept her hand in his as he looked around as though seeing it all for the first time. He spotted Jimmy and Sofia, who called to him, "Magic! You held out on me, Sandoz!"—for this was not in her AI program at all. He found Marc Robichaux next, engulfed in the crowd with a little one sitting on his shoulders so the child could see over the adults. And there was D.W., whose eyes, astonishingly, were brimming. He searched for George and Anne Edwards, finally picking them out, arm in arm, and Anne was crying too, but George beamed at him and called out, voice raised to carry above the ruckus the kids were making, "If anybody asks, I'm a hundred and sixteen!"

Emilio Sandoz threw back his head and laughed. "God!" he shouted into the sunshine and leaned down to kiss the top of Askama's head and pull her up into his arms for an embrace that included the whole of creation. "God," he whispered again, eyes closed, with the child settling onto his hip. "I was born for this!"

It was the simple truth. Nothing else explained his life.

22

NAPLES:
JUNE 2060

"SO THIS CHILD was assigned to learn your language and to teach you hers, is that correct?" Johannes Voelker asked.

"Essentially. The Runa are a trading people who require many languages to do business. As among us, their children learn languages quickly and easily, so they take advantage of that, yes? Whenever a new trading partnership is formed, a child is raised jointly by its family and the foreign delegation, which also includes a child. It takes only a couple of years to establish fairly sophisticated communication. The language is then passed along within Runa lineages. There are stable relationships developed over generations with established trading partners."

It was a gray windless day. They'd left the windows open to the June warmth and the steady sound of the rain, which matched the soft and steady narrative of Emilio Sandoz. Vincenzo Giuliani had changed the schedule so that the hearings took place in the afternoon, allowing Sandoz to sleep through the mornings if the nights had been difficult. It seemed to help.

"And they imagined you to be a child with this function?" Johannes Voelker asked.

"Yes."

"Presumably because you were somewhat smaller than others in the party," Felipe Reyes supposed.

"Yes. And because I carried on all the earliest attempts at communication, as such an interpreter would have. Actually, for a long time, only Mr. Quinn was accepted as an adult. He was about average height for a Runao."

"And they were not frightened at the beginning? Surely they'd never seen anything like you before," Giuliani said. "I find that remarkable."

"The Runa are very tolerant of novelty. And we were obviously not a threat to them physically. They assumed, evidently, that whatever we were, we had come to trade. They fit us into their worldview on that basis."

"How old was the child Askama at the time of contact, would you estimate?" Voelker asked, coming back to the child. Sandoz did not stiffen, Giuliani noted. His voice remained, as it had throughout the session, unstressed and even.

"Dr. Edwards thought at first that Askama was the equivalent of a human child at seven or eight years of age. Later on we decided that she was only about five. It is difficult to compare the species but it was our impression that Runa maturation rates are relatively accelerated."

Voelker made a note of this response as Giuliani commented, "I was under the impression that intelligence was inversely correlated with rate of maturation."

"Yes. Father Robichaux and Dr. Edwards discussed that. I think they decided that it was not a tight correlation, either between or within species. I may be remembering that wrong. In any case, the generalization may not hold in other biological systems."

"What was your impression of the Runa's intelligence in general?" Felipe asked. "Did you find the Runa to be our equals or of greater or lesser capacity?"

There was a hesitation, for the first time that morning. "They are different," Sandoz said at last, moving his arms from the table to his lap. "It's hard to say." He fell silent, clearly trying to settle this in his own mind. "No, I'm sorry. I can't answer that question with any confidence. There is a wide range of variation in intelligence. As among us."

"Dr. Sandoz," Johannes Voelker said, "what precisely was your relationship with Askama?"

"Exasperating," Sandoz said promptly. That got a laugh, and Felipe Reyes realized it was the first sign of Emilio's normal sense of humor he'd seen since arriving in Naples.

Smiling thinly in spite of himself, Voelker said, "I don't suppose you could expand upon that somewhat?"

"She was my teacher and my pupil and a reluctant collaborator in my research. She was spunky and bright. Insistent, relentless and a huge pain in the neck. She drove me crazy. I loved her without reservation."

"And did this child love you?" Voelker asked in the silence that fell at Sandoz's last statement. The man had, after all, admitted to killing Askama. John Candotti held his breath.

"This is another difficult question, like 'How intelligent are the Runa?'" Sandoz said neutrally. "Did she love me? Not maturely. At least not in the beginning. She was a child, yes? She liked the magic tricks. I was the best toy she could imagine. She was pleased by the attention I showed her and liked the status of being a foreigner's friend and she enjoyed ordering me around and correcting me and teaching me manners. Marc Robichaux believed that there was an element of imprinting—a biological factor in her craving to be with me all the time, but it was also her conscious choice. She could get angry with me and resentful when I refused to acquiesce to her demands, and that would upset everyone. But yes, I believe that she loved me."

"'A reluctant collaborator' in your research. How do you mean that?" Voelker asked. "Did you coerce her?"

"No. I mean she was bored by it and became impatient with me when I persisted. I drove her crazy too," Sandoz admitted. "Do you understand the difference between being multilingual and being a linguist?"

There was a murmur. They all recognized the words but no one had ever been called upon to define the distinction.

"The ability to speak a language perfectly does not necessarily confer any linguistic understanding of it," Sandoz said, "just as one may play billiards well without any formal understanding of Newtonian physics, yes? My advanced training is in anthropological linguistics, so my purpose in working with Askama was not merely to be able to ask someone to pass the salt, so to speak, but to gain insight into her people's underlying cultural assumptions and cognitive makeup."

He shifted in his chair and moved his hands again, never able to find a comfortable position for his arms when the braces were on. "An example. One day, Askama showed me a very pretty glass flask and used the word *azhawasi*. My first guess was that the word *azhawasi* was more or less equivalent to *jar* or *container* or *bottle*. But one can never be certain, so one tests. I pointed to the sides of the flask and asked if this was *azhawasi*. No. That had no name. So I pointed to the rim and again, that was not *azhawasi* and had no name. So I pointed to the bottom and asked again. Wrong again. And Askama became annoyed because I kept asking stupid questions. I was also irritated, yes? I didn't know if she was teasing me or if I was confused and *azhawasi* was perhaps the shape of the flask or its style or even the price of the flask. It turned out that *azhawasi* refers to the space enclosed. The capacity for containment was the important element, not the physical object."

"Fascinating," Giuliani commented, and not simply in reference to the linguistic concept. On his own ground at last, Sandoz was an unexpectedly fluent, even expansive speaker. And he had neatly turned the conversation away from Askama, as Voelker had said he would. Interesting that Voelker, of all of them, seemed to have a knack for predicting Emilio's reactions.

There was a pause as Sandoz carefully and slowly closed his braced hands around his coffee cup and brought it to his lips. He set the cup down a little abruptly, almost losing control of the fingers, the ceramic clink loud in the quiet office. These small precise movements were still difficult for him. No one stared.

"Similarly, there is a word for the space we would call a room but no words for wall or for ceiling or floor, as such," he continued, resting his arms on the table, careful not to scratch its polished surface with the wires. "It's the function of an object that is named. You can refer to a ceiling, for example, by noting that the rain is prevented from taking place in this space because of it. Furthermore, they have no concept of borders, such as separate our nations. They speak in terms of what a geographic region contains—a flower for making this distillation, or an herb which is good for that dye. Eventually, I came to understand that the Runa do not have vocabulary for the edges that we perceive separating one element from another. This reflects their social structure and their perceptions of the physical world and even their political status."

His voice was starting to shake. He stopped talking for a moment and glanced at Ed Behr, who nodded and moved to a corner of the office where only the Father General could see him draw a finger across his throat.

"So that, in essence, is what this kind of linguistic analysis involves," Emilio continued, returning his arms to his lap. "Finding the pattern of thought underlying the grammar and vocabulary and relating it to the culture of the speakers."

"And Askama would not have understood why you had difficulty with such simple concepts," Felipe Reyes speculated dryly.

"Exactly. Just as I was frustrated by her inability to understand that I required privacy at certain times of the day and night. The Runa are intensely social. Father Robichaux and Dr. Edwards believed that their social structure was closer to that of a herd than a primate society's looser kinship and social alliances. The Runa found it difficult to accept that we ever wanted to be alone. It was exhausting."

He wanted to go. His hands felt scalded, and it was getting harder to push the morning's news out of his mind. It had helped to have something impersonal to talk about, to give a lecture, but they'd been at this now for three hours, and he was finding it difficult to concentrate . . .

The trouble with illusions, he thought, is that you aren't aware you have any until they are taken from you. There had been a new doctor, several hours of tests. The hands, he was told, could be improved cosmetically but not functionally; the nerves had been severed too long ago to be repaired, the destruction of muscle was too extensive and complete. The burning sensation, which he was experiencing now and which came and went unpredictably, was probably similar to that endured by amputees, a sort of phantom-limb phenomenon. He could straighten the digits almost normally and he had some useful hook grip in two fingers of each hand. That was it. That was how it was going to be—

He realized then that Johannes Voelker had spoken and a denser silence had fallen on the room. How long have I been sitting like this? he wondered. Emilio reached for the coffee cup again, stalling for time. "I'm sorry," he apologized, looking at Voelker after a few moments. "Did you say something?"

"Yes. I said it was interesting how often you change the subject from the child you killed. And I wondered if you were developing another convenient headache."

The cup shattered in Emilio's hand. There was a small fuss as Edward Behr brought a cloth to soak up the spilled coffee and John Candotti collected the broken china. Voelker simply sat and stared at Sandoz, who might have been carved from rock.

They are so different, Vincenzo Giuliani thought, looking at the two

men seated across the table from one another: the one, obsidian and silver; the other, butter and sand. He wondered if Emilio had any idea how
much Voelker envied him. He wondered if Voelker knew.

"... power surge," Felipe Reyes was saying, explaining Emilio's
lapse to them, covering the embarrassment. "You can get erratic electric
potentials when your muscles are tired. This kind of thing used to happen to me all the time—"

"If I keep my feet, Felipe," Sandoz said with soft venom, "who are
you to crawl for me?"

"Emilio, I just—"

There was a brief ugly exchange in gutter Spanish. "I think that will
be enough for today, gentlemen," the Father General broke in lightly.
"Emilio, a word with you, please. The rest of you may go."

Sandoz remained in his seat and waited impassively as Voelker,
Candotti and a white-faced Felipe Reyes left. Edward Behr hesitated by
the door and gave the Father General a small warning look, which went
unacknowledged.

When they were alone, Giuliani spoke again. "You appear to be in
pain. Is it a headache?"

"No. Sir." The black eyes turned to him, cold as stone.

"Would you tell me if it were?" A pointless question. Giuliani knew
before it was out of his mouth that Sandoz would never admit it, not after what Voelker had just implied.

"Your carpets are in no danger," Emilio assured him with undis-
guised insolence.

"I'm glad to hear it," Giuliani said pleasantly. "The table suffered.
You are hard on decor. And you were hard on Reyes."

"He had no right to speak for me," Sandoz snapped, the anger visibly flooding back.

"He's trying to help you, Emilio."

"When I want help, I'll ask for it."

"Will you? Or will you simply go on night after night, eating yourself alive?" Sandoz blinked. "I spoke to Dr. Kaufmann this morning. It
must have been upsetting to hear her prognosis. She doesn't understand
why you have tolerated these braces for so long. They are too heavy, and
poorly designed, she tells me. Why haven't you asked for improvements?
A tender concern for Father Singh's feelings," Giuliani suggested, "or
some kind of misbegotten Latino pride?"

It was subtle, but you could tell sometimes when you hit home. The breathing changed. The effort at control became slightly more visible. Suddenly, Giuliani found he had simply run out of patience with Sandoz's damnable machismo and demanded, "Are you in pain? Yes or no."

"Am I required to say, sir?" The mockery was plain; its target was less clear.

"Yes, dammit, you are required. Say it."

"My hands hurt." There was a pause. "And the braces hurt my arms."

Giuliani saw the quick shallow movement of the chest and thought, My God, what it costs this man to admit he's suffering!

Abruptly, the Father General stood and walked away from the table, to give himself time to think. Emilio's sweat and vomit were familiar now, his body's fragility mercilessly exposed. Giuliani had nursed him through night terrors and had watched, appalled, as Sandoz pulled himself back together, holding the pieces in place with who knew what emotional baling wire. One could not forget all that, even when Sandoz was at his most aggravating, when one felt as though the man perceived the simplest effort to help him as insult and abuse.

For the first time it occurred to him to wonder what it was like to be so frail in what should have been the prime of life. Vince Giuliani had never known illness more debilitating than a cold, injury more damaging than a broken finger. Perhaps, he thought, if I were Sandoz, I too would hide my pain and snarl at solicitude . . .

"Look," he said, relenting, returning to the table. "Emilio. You are, bar none, the toughest sonofabitch I ever met. I admire your fortitude." Sandoz glared at him, furious. "I am not being sarcastic!" Giuliani cried. "I personally have been known to request general anesthesia after a paper cut." A laugh. A genuine laugh. And buoyed by that small triumph, Giuliani tried a direct appeal. "You've been through hell and you have made it abundantly clear that you are not a whiner. But, Emilio, how can we help you if you won't tell anyone what's wrong?"

When Sandoz spoke again, the words were barely audible. "I told John. About my hands."

Giuliani sighed. "Well. You may take that as evidence that Candotti can keep a confidence." The idiot! It was not the sort of revelation that came under the seal of confession. Although it might have felt like that to Sandoz, he realized.

Giuliani got up and went to the private lavatory adjacent to his office. He came back with a glass of water and a couple of tablets, which he placed on the table in front of Sandoz. "I am obviously not among those who believe it is noble to suffer needlessly," Giuliani told Emilio quietly. "From now on, when your hands hurt, take something." He watched as Emilio struggled to pick up the pills, one by one, and wash them down with water. "If this doesn't work, you *tell* me, understand? We'll get you something stronger. I've already sent for Singh. I expect you to let him know exactly what is wrong with these braces. And if he can't make them right, we'll bring in someone else."

He picked up the glass and carried it back to the lavatory, where he remained for a few minutes. Sandoz was still sitting at the table, withdrawn and pale, when Giuliani returned. Taking a chance, the Father General went to his desk and brought back a notebook, tapping out a code that opened a file only he and two other men, now dead, had been privy to.

"Emilio, I have been reviewing the transcripts of Father Yarbrough's reports. I read them last year when we first got word of you from Ohbayashi but now, of course, I am studying them rather more carefully," Vincenzo Giuliani told him. "Father Yarbrough described the initial interaction between you and the child Askama and the Runa villagers much as you have, in outline. I must say that his narrative was far more poetic than your own. He was, in fact, deeply moved by the experience. As I was, while reading of it." Sandoz did not react, and Giuliani wondered if the man was listening. "Emilio?" Sandoz looked at him, so Giuliani pressed ahead. "At the end of his description of the first contact, in a locked file, Father Yarbrough added a commentary meant only for the current Father General. He wrote of you, 'I believe that he was inspired by the Holy Spirit. Today I may have looked upon the face of a saint.' "

"Stop it."

"Excuse me?" Giuliani looked up from the tablet he was reading, blinking, unaccustomed to being addressed in this manner, even in private, even by a man whose nights were now a part of his own, whose dreams interrupted his own sleep.

"Stop it. Leave me something." Sandoz was trembling. "Don't pick over my bones, Vince."

There was a long silence, as Giuliani looked into the terrible eyes and absorbed the implications. "I'm sorry, Emilio," he said. "Forgive me."

Sandoz sat looking at him a while longer, his head turned away slightly, still shaking. "You can't know what it's like. There's no way for you to understand."

It was, in its own way, a sort of apology, Giuliani realized. "Perhaps if you tried to explain it to me," the Father General suggested gently.

"How can I explain what I don't understand myself?" Emilio cried. He stood abruptly and walked a few steps away and then turned back. It was always startling when Sandoz broke down. His face would hardly move. "From where I was then to where I am now—I don't know what to do with what happened to me, Vince!" He lifted his hands and let them fall, defeated. Vincenzo Giuliani, who had heard many confessions in his years, remained silent, and waited. "Do you know what the worst of it is? I loved God," Emilio said in a voice frayed by incomprehension. The crying stopped as suddenly as it had begun. He stood for a long while, staring at nothing Giuliani could see, and then went to the window to look out at the rain. "It's all ashes now. All ashes."

And then, incredibly, he started to laugh. It could be as shocking as the sudden tears.

"I think," the Father General said, "that I could be of more help to you if I knew whether you see all this as comedy or tragedy."

Emilio did not answer right away. So much, he was thinking, for keeping silent about what can't be changed. So much for Latino pride. He felt sometimes like the seedhead of a dandelion, flying apart, blown to pieces in a puff of air. The humiliation was almost beyond bearing. He thought, and hoped sometimes, that it would kill him, that his heart would actually stop. Maybe this is part of the joke, he thought bleakly. He turned away from the windows to gaze across the room at the elderly man watching him quietly from the far end of the beautiful old table.

"If I knew that," Emilio Sandoz said, coming as close as he could to the center of his soul and to an admission that shamed him, "I don't suppose I'd need the help."

IN A WAY, Vincenzo Giuliani considered it a great and terrible privilege to try to understand Emilio, now, at this stage of their bizarrely disjointed lives. Dealing with Sandoz was as fascinating as sailing in dirty weather. One had to make constant adjustments to endless changes in force and direction and there was always the danger of foundering and going under. It was the challenge of a lifetime.

In the beginning, he had dismissed Yarbrough's assessment of Emilio's spiritual state. Discounted it as inaccurate or overwrought. He distrusted mysticism, despite the fact that his order was founded upon it.

And yet, he was willing to take as a working hypothesis the notion that Emilio Sandoz saw himself as a genuinely religious man, a soul looking for God, as Ed Behr had put it. And Sandoz must have felt, at some point, he had found God and betrayed Him. The worst of it, Sandoz said, was that he had loved God. Given that, Giuliani could see the tragedy: to fall so far from such a state of grace, to be on fire with God and let it go to ashes. To have received such a blessing and to repay it with a descent into whoredom and murder.

Surely, Giuliani thought, there must have been some other way! Why had Sandoz turned to prostitution? Even without his hands, there must have been some other way. Beg, steal food, anything.

Pieces of the puzzle were clear to him. Emilio felt himself to be unfairly condemned by men who had never been tested in such inhuman conditions of isolation and loneliness. Giuliani recognized that even to fail such a test bestowed a certain moral authority upon the man. And for that reason, he found it easy to beg Emilio's forgiveness and give him some measure of respect. The tactic seemed to work. There were moments of genuine contact now and then, times when Sandoz was willing to risk some small disclosure in hope of being understood or of understanding something himself. But Giuliani knew that he was being kept at more than arm's length, as though there were something that Sandoz himself couldn't look at, let alone display. Something that could be dreamt of but not spoken, even in the dark of night. Something that would have to be brought into the light.

It was necessary to consider the possibility that Ed Behr was wrong and Johannes Voelker was right. Perhaps, in isolation, Sandoz had turned to prostitution because he enjoyed it. He had loved God but found rough sex . . . gratifying. Such a truth, at the core of his identity, held up for public scrutiny, might haunt his dreams and sicken him. Sometimes, as John Candotti was fond of saying, the simplest solution is the best. No less an observer of the human condition than Jesus once said, "Wide is the gate and broad is the path that leads to destruction, and many go that way."

Patience, Giuliani thought. An old sailor's virtue. First one tack and then another.

His staff in Rome, carefully nurtured and trained these past ten years, was competent. Time, and past time, for him to delegate more of the decisions, to let younger men strengthen as he kept a light hand on the tiller. Time for this particular old priest, for Vince Giuliani, to bring the experience and knowledge of a lifetime to bear on one human problem, to call upon any wisdom he had garnered in his years to help one human soul, one man who called himself, with bitterness, God's whore. Patience. It will take as long as it takes.

Vincenzo Giuliani rose at last and moved toward the windows, where Sandoz had remained all this time, gray as the weather, staring out at the rain. Giuliani stepped in front of him and stood in plain sight, waiting until Sandoz noticed him, for he had learned never to startle the man by coming up behind him.

"Come on, Emilio," Vince Giuliani said softly. "I'll buy you a beer."

23

CITY OF GAYJUR:
SECOND NA'ALPA

VILLAGE OF KASHAN:
SEVEN WEEKS AFTER CONTACT

SUPAARI VAGAYJUR PROFITED from the presence of the Jesuit party on Rakhat before he knew of its existence. This was both
characteristic of him and unusual. Characteristic, in that he had recognized a potential Runa fad before anyone else and took steps to capture
the market just before the trend took off in Gayjur. Unusual, in that he
was not in command of the facts underlying the market before he
moved. It was unlike him to risk so much without investigating first. The
gamble paid off handsomely but even as the profits were totaled, it left
him feeling uneasy, as though he had just missed being killed in a *ha'aran*
duel undertaken while drunk.

Moving through the warehouse with Awijan, his Runa secretary,
who took down his orders and noted his inquiries, Supaari had spotted
one of the Kashan villagers, a woman named Chaypas, standing at a
doorway, waiting for permission to speak to him. She was wearing a cascade of ribbons worked into the circlet worn around her head: a waterfall of color, arrayed gracefully down her back. Lovely, Supaari thought,
and it would quintuple the number of double-length ribbons desired by
anyone who took the fashion up. He turned to Awijan. "Call the run-

ners. Buy ribbon and take possession. Get contracts for all the deliveries available—" Supaari hesitated. How long would it last?

"Someone suggests that the contracts go no further out than Eighth Na'alpa."

Supaari VaGayjur knew better than to second-guess Awijan on a decision like that. "Yes. When you get back, have Sapalla clear out some merchandise to make room for the shipments, even if we have to take a loss on the *berinje*. Delivery after redlight, understood?" One of the many advantages of working with Runa, Supaari had found over the years, was that Jana'ata couldn't see well in redlight but Runa could. It imposed a secrecy that his competitors, sleeping away the red and black hours, didn't even suspect.

He watched as Awijan entered the courtyard, gathering the runners. Having set the transaction in motion, Supaari himself moved smoothly toward the VaKashani woman Chaypas and greeted her in her own language, holding out both hands to her. "*Challalla khaeri*, Chaypas." He leaned forward and breathed in her scent, mingled with that of the fragrant ribbons.

An unusual villager, willing to travel alone and to deal directly with Supaari VaGayjur in his own compound, Chaypas VaKashan returned the greeting without fear. Apart from their attire, they were alike enough to be sisters or near cousins, seen with a casual eye, from a distance. Supaari was more heavily muscled, slightly larger overall, facts enhanced by the padded gown, quilted and stiffened with embroidery; the pattens, which gave him a hand's width of extra height; the headpiece, which provided another measure of stature and identified him as a merchant and, by implication, a third-born child. His clothing today emphasized the differences in their lives, but, when he wished, Supaari could pass for Runa, wearing the trailing oversleeves and boots of an urban Runao. It was not illegal. It simply wasn't done. Most Jana'ata, even most thirds, would rather have died than be taken for Runa. Most Jana'ata, even most thirds, were not nearly so wealthy as Supaari VaGayjur. It was his stigma and his comfort, that wealth.   •

Supaari coaxed Chaypas indoors, away from the foot traffic, so that her ribbons would not be noticed by others of her kind before he had a chance to jump the market. Chatting, he walked ahead of her through the warehouse, showing her the way to his office as though she were not already familiar with it, allowing her to rearrange the cushions to her comfort as he prepared a *yasapa* tea he knew she liked. He served her himself, even pouring it, to show respect: Supaari VaGayjur went his own profitable way.

Taking a place across from Chaypas, he reclined comfortably on the cushions, careful to mimic her own posture as closely as possible. They talked amiably about the outlook for the *sinonja* harvest, the health of her husband, Manuzhai, and the prospects for resolution of a potential dispute between Kashan and Lanjeri over a new *k'jip* field. Supaari offered to mediate if the elders couldn't agree. He had no wish to impose himself on them and he did not relish the long tedious trip out to Kashan, but it would be worth the trouble to keep his scent fresh in everyone's nostrils.

"*Sipaj*, Supaari," Chaypas said, coming to the point of her visit at last. "Someone has a curiosity for you." She reached into a woven pouch and pulled out a small packet made of intricately folded leaves. She held it out to him but he lowered his ears regretfully: his hands were incapable of unwrapping the object carefully. Her own ears flattened abruptly in embarrassment, but Supaari took her gesture as a compliment. The VaKashani villagers sometimes forgot he was Jana'ata. In its own way, in context, it was high praise, Supaari thought, although his eldest brother would have killed her for it and his middle brother would have had her jailed.

He watched as Chaypas picked the strands of wrapping apart gracefully, with a Runao's lovely long-fingered dexterity. She held out to him seven of what he took at first to be beetles or unusually small *kintai*. Then, leaning forward, Supaari inhaled.

It was the most extraordinary thing he'd ever encountered. He knew he was getting esters and aldehydes, and the smell of burnt sugars certainly, but the scent was staggeringly complex. All this from a few small brown objects, oval, incised with a longitudinal line. Supaari covered his excitement with the ease of a man who has made a living of concealment. Even so, it came to him with a jolt that here, at last, was something that might interest Hlavin Kitheri, the Reshtar of Galatna.

"Someone's heart is glad," he told Chaypas, raising his tail with mild pleasure, not wanting to alarm her. "A remarkable scent, full of curiosity, as you say."

"*Sipaj*, Supaari! These *kafay* were given to someone by foreigners." She used a Ruanja word meaning "people from the next river valley," but her eyes were open very wide and her tail was twitching. There was some delicious joke here, Supaari realized, but he let her enjoy the amusement at his expense. "Askama is interpreting!" she told him.

"Askama!" he cried, throwing his hands up in delight, elegant claws clicking. "A good child, quick to learn." And ugly as white water in a narrow gorge, but no matter. If Chaypas's household was interpreting for the Kashan corporation, Supaari would have an exclusive trading relationship with the new delegation, by Runa custom if not by Jana'ata law and, in cases like this, Runa custom was all that counted. He'd based his life on that understanding and if it brought him no honor, it nonetheless provided much of what he savored: risk to stalk, intellectual challenge and a certain grudging deference among his own.

They chatted a while longer. He established that these small *kafay* were only a sample of a much larger store of unusual goods brought by the foreigners, who were staying in Kashan in Chaypas's own household. And Supaari heard with growing interest that they seemed to have no notion of profit, giving their goods away for the food and shelter that was theirs by right, as sojourners. Cunning, he wondered, or some nomadic remnant group, still bartering in the old, clean ways?

Supaari laid the little packet aside and, disciplined, did not allow himself to trail and capture the idea that he had scented in the distance: posterity and a way out of the living death he was born to. He rose instead and refilled Chaypas's cup, asking after her plans. She told him she would be visiting trade partners in the Ezao district. She was in no hurry to return home. All the other VaKashani would be leaving the village soon to harvest *pik* root.

"And the foreigners?" he asked. He was already planning the trip in his mind, maybe in mid-Partan, after the rains. But Kitheri came first. It all hinged on Hlavin Kitheri.

"Sometimes they come with us, sometimes they stay in Kashan. They are like children," Chaypas told him. She seemed a little puzzled by this herself. "Too small to travel like adults but only one to carry them. And that one lets them walk!"

If Supaari was curious before, he was baffled now, but Chaypas was showing signs of nervousness, swaying from side to side, as she often did when she spent too much time in ghost houses.

"*Sipaj*, Chaypas," he said, rising smoothly from his cushions, calculating that enough time had passed for Awijan to have concluded terms with the ribbon suppliers. "Such a long journey you've made! Someone's heart would be glad to send you to Ezao in a chair."

Her tail came up with pleasure and she even trembled a little, her eyes sliding away and closing. This bordered on flirtation and it passed his mind that she was remarkably attractive. He smothered the spark before it caught fire. Third-born, he still had his standards, which were considerably higher than those of his social betters. Urbane and sophisticated in many ways, Supaari VaGayjur was thoroughly bourgeois in others.

He sent a runner for a chair and, stifling yawns, waited with Chaypas in the courtyard until it arrived shortly after second sundown. He could hardly see her as she climbed into the chair but the fragrance of her ribbons was very fine; she had wonderful taste in perfumes, a natural elegance that Supaari admired. "*Sipaj,* Chaypas," he called quietly, "safe journey to Ezao and thence home." She returned his farewell, laughing breathily as the bearers lifted the chair supports, rocking the seat.

It was a luxury few Runa ever experienced, to be carried through the narrow city streets like a lord. Supaari was genuinely pleased to provide her with an evening she would remember, borne through the crowds of urban Runa, safe to go about their personal business in the blushing light of evening, while the Jana'ata slept. The breeze off the bay would carry her new ribbons like cirrus clouds behind her, their fragrance rising like mist from a cataract. By tomorrow, merchants from all over the city of Gayjur would be looking for ribbon at any price, and Supaari VaGayjur would own every scrap of it.

IT WAS SOFIA Mendes's fate to enrich investors who were unknown to her. The heavy black hair, which had inspired Chaypas to invent a new fashion, was at this moment pushed carelessly back, the ribbons Askama had braided into it slipping into disarray. Irritable as Sofia Mendes was, she'd have cut it all off without a thought, had scissors been handy. She'd brewed a cup of coffee out of habit, but it was too hot today to drink it and it cooled at her elbow; soon, such profligacy would be shocking. At the moment, however, beauty, adornment and wealth were further from her mind than usual, which was very far indeed. Her intellect was wholly occupied with the task of finding some sufficiently uncivil response to Emilio Sandoz's suggestion that she was being stupid.

"I can explain it to you again, but I can't understand it for you."

"You are insufferable," she whispered.

"I am not insufferable. I am correct," he whispered back. "If you prefer to memorize each declension separately, please do so. But the pattern is perfectly apparent."

"It's a false generalization. It doesn't make any sense."

"Oh, and I suppose that assigning gender to tables and chairs and hats and declining nouns on that basis *does* make sense? Language is arbitrary by nature," he informed her. "If you want sense, study calculus."

"Sarcasm is not argument, Sandoz."

Emilio took a deep breath and began again with unconcealed impatience. "All right. Once more. It is not abstract versus concrete. If you try to force that rule on Ruanja, you'll make consistent errors. It is spatial versus unseen or nonvisual." He reached out toward the tablet that lay on the table between them and stabbed a finger down at a section of the display, careful not to jar Askama, who had just fallen asleep in his arms. "Consider this group. Animal, vegetable or mineral: these words all denote something that takes up space in some manner and they are all declined with this pattern. You follow?" He pointed to another section of the screen. "In contrast, these nouns are nonspatial: thought, hope, affection, learning. This group takes the second pattern of declension. Clear so far?"

Concrete and abstract, dammit, she thought stubbornly. "Yes, fine. What I don't understand is—"

"I know what you don't understand! Stop arguing with me and listen!" He ignored her glare. "The overall rule is, anything that can be seen is always classified as occupying space, because seeing things is how you know they are spatial, so you use the first declension. The trick is that anything unseen, including but not limited to things that are inherently nonvisual, takes this second declension." He sat back abruptly and then glanced down at Askama, relieved to see she was still sleeping. "Now. I invite you to disprove. Please. Just try."

She had him. Face bright as ivory in the sun, she leaned forward and prepared to deliver the coup de grâce. "Not ten minutes ago, Askama said, '*Chaypas-ru zhari i washan,*' and she used what you call the nonvisual declension. But Chaypas is very large. Chaypas most certainly takes up a good deal of space—"

"Yes. Brava! Perfect. Now, think!"

He was being patronizing. She stared at him, open-mouthed, ready to detonate, when it suddenly came clear. Letting her head fall abruptly into her hands, she muttered, "But Chaypas is gone. So you can't see him. So you don't use the spatial declension. You use the nonvisual, even though Chaypas is concrete and not abstract." She looked up. He was grinning. "I *hate* it when you're smug."

The dark, merry eyes were triumphant. Emilio Sandoz had taken no vow of false modesty. It was a nice piece of analysis and he was immensely pleased with himself, and it had not escaped his own notice that he'd won Sofia's bet with Alan Pace. They'd made contact with the Runa only seven weeks ago, but he already had the basic grammar nailed. Damn, I'm good, he thought to himself, and his grin widened as Sofia stared at him through narrowed eyes, trying to think of some case that wouldn't fit the model.

"All right, all right," she said ungraciously, picking up her tablet, "I concede. Give me a few minutes to get it all down."

They were a good team. Sandoz was a master of this discipline but she was a far better writer, fast and clear. Already three papers bearing the authorship "E. J. Sandoz and S. R. Mendes" had been radioed back for submission to scholarly journals.

Finished with her notes, Sofia looked up and smiled. She had met before, in yeshiva students whom her parents often invited to dinner when she was a girl, this mixture of incisive intelligence and dreaminess, the joyful combative intellectual style and the tendency to fall into an inner world, absorbed and remote. Barelegged and barefoot, Sandoz was tanned to the color of cinnamon, wearing the loose khaki shorts and oversized black T-shirt that had replaced the soutane, impossibly hot in this climate. Sofia herself was equally browned, similarly dark and slender, dressed as simply, and she could understand why Manuzhai had assumed at first that she and Emilio were "littermates." The notion had been funny and embarrassing, as Manuzhai's pantomimed explanation of the word had been, but she could see how a Runao might come to that conclusion.

Askama sighed, stretching out a little. Emilio came to life and looked at Sofia with round-eyed alarm. Askama was dear, but she chattered incessantly; naps like this one were a welcome relief. "I wonder," said Sofia very softly, when it was clear that Askama would not awaken, "if a blind Runao would always use the nonvisual declension."

"Now *that* is an interesting question," Emilio said, inclining his head with respect, and she was tartly pleased to have reestablished claim to an adequate intelligence. He thought a while, rocking the hammock chair gently, one fine-boned foot braced against a *hampiy* stem, fingers stroking the soft fur behind Askama's ears. The sunrise smile reappeared. "If you could feel a thing, you would also know it took up space! Look for something that has contour or form or texture. Wager?"

"*Lejano,* maybe, or *tinguen,*" she suggested. "No bets."

"No guts! I could be wrong," he said cheerfully, "but I doubt it. Try *lejano* first." He smiled down at the top of Askama's head before returning his eyes to the small herd of *piyanot* grazing on the plain beyond the stems of the *hampiy* shelter.

"THEY MAKE A handsome couple, don't they," Anne said as she and D.W. strolled along the edge of the gorge, above the village.

"Yes, ma'am," D.W. agreed. "They do indeed." Everyone else was occupied or asleep, and they had found themselves restless together. Anne proposed a walk, and D.W. was happy to accompany her. Manuzhai had warned them all, repeatedly, against walking alone. A "*djanada,*" whatever that was, might get them; so they traveled in pairs, more to mollify Manuzhai and the other Runa than because of any serious fear of predators or bogeymen.

"Jealous?" Anne asked. "They're both yours in a way, aren't they."

"Oh, hell, I'm not sure jealous is the right word," said D.W., who stopped for a moment to gaze crookedly at Sofia and Emilio, playing house with Askama out in the *hampiy*. He turned back to Anne and grinned lopsidedly and briefly before he squinted off into the west, across the river. "It's kinda like watchin' Notre Dame go up against the University of Texas in the Cotton Bowl. I don't hardly know what to hope for."

Anne laughed appreciatively and leaned her head against his shoulder. "Oh, D.W., I love you. I truly do. Of course, I've always had a weakness for a guy in a uniform."

It was an opening, and he walked through it, smiling. "You, too?"

"The Marines are looking for a few good men," Anne intoned, quoting the old recruitment slogan as they strolled south.

"Yeah, well. So was I." His eyes remained, more or less, straight ahead as he sang quietly, "But that was long ago and very far away."

"Exactly," Anne smiled. "My darling: the nearest closet is four and a third light years from here. Sofia knows. I know. Marc—"

"Is my confessor."

"Jimmy and George don't have a clue, but it wouldn't make a damn bit of difference to either of them," said Anne. "Which leaves Emilio."

D.W. sank slowly to his knees and motioned Anne to stay back. Moving cautiously, he brought his hand out over a little tuft of dusty lavender foliage and remained in position for several seconds. Then his hand shot out, carefully covering and then lifting a small two-legged snakeneck, which had been virtually undetectable pushing its way slowly into something else's burrow, hoping to find lunch. He stood and handed it to Anne.

"Isn't it pretty! Look, you can see a couple of vestigial front legs on this one," she cried, holding it out for him to see. "I never find stuff like that. You are amazing."

"You grow up like I did, ma'am, you learn a fair bit about camouflage."

"I'll bet you do, at that," she said. She put the snakeneck back down by the burrow and they continued their walk. "Emilio thinks the world of you, D.W. Okay, sure. He's probably carrying around some unexamined macho crapola he'd have to reconsider, but he's capable of adjusting an attitude."

"Hell, I know that," D.W. said. "And I'm not ashamed of what I am. But if he'd known when he was a kid, he wouldn't have come within a mile of me. And after all these years of him not knowin', what's the point of sayin' anything?"

"To put down a load. To be accepted, entirely, as you are." He smiled at that without looking at her and draped an arm over her shoulders. "Surely you don't imagine that he'd think less of you."

"Well, now, see. There's exactly the problem, Anne. I'm afraid he'd think more of me. Which is to say, I'm afraid the whole issue would occupy his mind to some extent and I don't want to distract him with trivia right now. Course, he'd work it all through and he'd realize that I'd played straight with him all along—"

"So to speak."

He laughed. "Poor choice of words." He stopped and scuffed a rock out of the ground with his foot. "It's not like I ever lied to him. Subject just never came up. I never asked him if he was straight and he never asked me if I wasn't. Closest we ever came to it was when he asked me about another guy, years ago. I just told him, hell, we ain't all abstainin' from the same thing."

"And what did he make of that?" Anne asked, smiling.

"Took it at face value." D.W. looked at the mountains south of them. Somewhere on the other side of the range was Alan Pace's grave.

"Look, Anne. The way things are is fine. I don't need anything from Emilio. What went on inside my head years ago is my business. And it's history."

She couldn't argue with that. She might have said the same thing herself, had their positions been reversed. "Okay, okay. Message received."

"I 'preciate the thought, Anne, I surely do, and under other circumstances, you might be right. But, here, now—" D.W. leaned over to pick up the rock he'd unearthed and whipped it off across the gorge, loose-shouldered and accurate. It fell just short of the other side and rattled down the cliff to the river below them. "What concerns me is the big picture. You know as well as I do, everything about this mission has been damn near to miraculous. And Emilio is the key to it. I don't want to muddy the waters! I don't want him thinkin' about *me*. Or Mendes either, far as that goes. I ain't gonna make an issue of them workin' together because they're handlin' it okay. And they're doin' some fine research. But, frankly, I'm holdin' my breath."

There was a silence, and Anne sat down, legs dangling over the ledge. D.W. stood for a while, less confident about the stability of the rock formation, but joined her at last and occupied his hands by flipping stones out into the void.

"D.W., I'm not arguing with you. I'm just asking, okay?" He nodded, so she went on, "Let's say the Age of Miracles hasn't closed down altogether yet, okay? Just for argument's sake. And we agree that Emilio is very special. But so is Sofia, right?"

"No kick so far."

"Well, it just seems to me that there is some pretty powerful theology on the side of love and sex and families. It seems to me that a fairly authoritative Personage once commented that it is not good for man to be alone. Rome, along with all closets," Anne pointed out archly, "is very far away. We have been gone almost two decades. Maybe priests can marry now! And in any case, I fail to see how Emilio would be cheating God out of anything by loving Sofia."

"Annie, you are troddin' a path that's worn to bedrock." D.W. reached behind himself and scooped up another handful of pebbles. A spasm of pain crossed his face, but Anne put it down to the topic. "Oh, hell, I don't know. Maybe it wouldn't make a dime's worth of difference. Maybe they'd just be happy and have a fine bunch of kids an' God would love 'em all . . ."

They sat for a time listening to the sounds of the river and staring at the western sky, blazing now with the colors of first sundown. D.W. seemed to be working something out, so Anne just waited until he spoke again.

"Bear with me here, 'cause I'm just stirrin' this around some with a stick. But, Anne," he said softly, "it seems to me that sainthood, like genius, is rooted in a sort of inspired persistence. It's a consistent willing of one thing. It's that kind of consistency and focus I see at work in Emilio."

"D.W., are you serious?" Anne sat still, eyes wide open. "You think Emilio is a s—"

"I didn't say that! I'm talkin' in the abstract here. But Marc and me, we been hashin' it out and, yes, I see the potential for it, and it's my job to protect that, Anne." He hesitated a moment before confessing, "Maybe I shouldn't have but I did in fact use the S-word in one report back to Rome. I tole 'em I think we got us a gen-u-wine big-time mystic on our hands. 'Wedded to God and at certain moments, in full communion with divine love,' is how I put it." He dumped the last few rocks, brushed the dirt off his hands and leaned over to watch the pebbles clatter downward, elbows on his knees, the big-knuckled hands loose between his legs. "Hell of a management problem," he said after a time. "They don't cover this one back home at the Famous Father Superiors School."

Anne found there was nothing she could say. She stared at the clouds in the western sky, piled like whipping cream tinted by strawberries and raspberries, blueberries and mangos. She never got tired of the colors here.

"And, Anne," D.W. continued thoughtfully, "I'm real concerned about Mendes in all this, too. I am awful fond of that girl and I don't want to see her hurt. She's all guts and brains on the outside, God love her, but there's broken glass inside that child. If he's gotta choose, Milio's gonna choose God, and I hate to think how Sofia would take that. So don't you go encouragin' her to take the initiative, unnerstan'?" D.W. got to his feet. Anne noticed that he seemed a little pale, but his next remark startled her out of any inquiry. "Too bad Sofia didn't take a shine to the Quinn boy or Robichaux."

Anne stood up as well and frowned, confused. "Well, Jimmy, of course! But Marc? I thought he was—well, you know. I thought—"

"You thought Robichaux was *gay*?" D.W. roared, and half a dozen coronaries rocketed into the air. He put a bony arm around Anne's shoulders, obviously tickled by the notion. "Oh, my. No-o-o. Not by a wondrous long shot. Marc Robichaux," he informed her as they strolled along, "is in love with capital-N Nature and women are nature at its finest for ole Marc! He loves the ladies. Marc, in his own way, is a kind of mystic, too. God's reality is everywhere for him. It's almost an Islamic theology. Robichaux don't separate the natural and the supernatural. It's all one thing for him, and he adores it all. Specially if it's female." He looked down at Anne, still gawping at him, and laughed at her. "Now, you talk about a management problem! Province had to put ole Marc to work in a boys' school to keep him out of trouble. He never hit on anybody but he is a good-lookin' sumbitch and one thing leads to another. Couldn't say no if a woman came to him. And come they surely did. Best therapeutic lay in Quebec, is what I heard."

"I'll keep it in mind," Anne said, breathless now herself with laughter, but she couldn't help saying, "So celibacy is optional."

"Well, in some sense, it mighta been for Marc, early on. Came a time when he mended his ways. But, now, look here! This illustrates my point about Emilio," D.W. said emphatically. "For Emilio, the separation between natural and supernatural is basic. God is not everywhere. God is not immanent. God is out there somewhere, to be reached for and yearned after. And you're gonna have to trust me on this, but celibacy is part of the deal for Emilio. It's a way of concentrating, of focusing a life on one thing. And I happen to think it's worked for him. I don't know whether it's he found God, or God come and got him . . ."

They could see the *hampiy* shelter again now, sunlight like molten copper streaming in from the west. Askama was still in Emilio's lap, asleep apparently. Sofia's head was bent over her computer tablet. Emilio noticed them and raised a hand. They waved back. "Okay. Okay, I see your point," Anne said. "I'll keep out of it. Maybe it will all work out."

"I hope so. Lots at stake here, for both of 'em. For all of us." He pressed a hand into his belly and made a face. "Damn."

"You okay?"

"Oh, sure. Nerves. I react to everything with my belly. I knew you knew but sayin' something's different."

"What's your theology like, D.W.?" Anne asked, pausing at the top of the path that led down the cliff.

"Oh, hell. On my best days? I try to keep my mind stretched around both experiences of God: the transcendent, the intimate. And then," he said, grinning briefly, "there are the days when I think that underneath it all, God has got to be a cosmic comedian." Anne looked at him, brows up. "Anne, the Good Lord decided to make D. W. Yarbrough a Catholic, a liberal, ugly and gay and a fair poet, and then had him born in Waco, Texas. Now I ask you, is that the work of a serious Deity?" And, laughing, they turned down the steps toward the cut-stone apartment they now called home.

THE OBJECT OF this conversation was unaware of the extent to which the exalted state of his soul was drawing notice. Emilio Sandoz was sweating buckets with Askama curled up on his lap, radiating heat like a fourth sun in the late afternoon. If, instead of assuming that he was meditating on the glory of God or synthesizing some new and closely reasoned model of Ruanja grammar, anyone had asked him directly what he was thinking about, he would have said, without hesitation, "I was thinking that I could really use a beer."

A beer and a ball game on the radio to listen to with half an ear as he worked, that would have been perfection. But even lacking those two elements of bliss, he was and knew himself to be completely happy.

The past weeks had been suffused with revelation. At home and in the Sudan and the Arctic, he had seen acts of great generosity, of selflessness and abundance of soul, and felt close to knowing God at those moments. Why, he had once wondered, would a perfect God create the universe? To be generous with it, he believed now. For the pleasure of seeing pure gifts appreciated. Maybe that's what it meant to find God: to see what you have been given, to know divine generosity, to appreciate the large things and the small . . .

The sense of being engulfed—saturated and entranced—had inevitably passed. No one exists like that for long. He was still staggered by the memory of it, could feel sometimes the tidal pull in some deep stratum of his soul. There had been times when he could not finish any prayer—could hardly begin, the words too much for him. But the days had passed and become more ordinary, and even that he felt to be a gift. He had everything here. Work, friends, real joy. He was swept sometimes with an awareness of it, and the intensity of his gratitude tightened his chest.

There was great contentment in the simplest moments. Like now:

sitting inside a *hampiy* tree with Sofia and Askama, out here on the plain, where they could work in the afternoons while the others slept, without so many interruptions and so much kibitzing. Chaypas had shown them how to make a wonderful breezy shelter simply by pruning out a corridor to the natural clearing inside the trees. The older plants were fifteen to twenty feet in diameter with thirty or forty straight stems, growing bushlike, leading to an umbrella of leaves. The leaf canopy was so dense that it prevented all but the heaviest rainfall from reaching the central region of the tree, and the internal stems died off naturally, leaving a ring of live ones around the outside. All you had to do was clean up the center a little and bring in cushions or hammocks to hang from the branches overhead.

Lulled by the afternoon heat, the dull discussions and the peculiar foreign monotone, Askama would relax and he would feel her breathing slow and the sweet weight of her settling against him. Sofia would smile and nod at the child and their voices would drop even lower. Sometimes they would simply sit and watch Askama sleep, enjoying the rare silence.

The others complained about the constant talk and the physical closeness the Runa liked, the way they crowded around one another and around the foreigners, back leaning against back, heads in laps, arms draped around shoulders, tails curled around legs in a muddle of warmth and softness in the cool cavelike rooms of the cliff. Emilio found it beautiful. He had not realized how starved he was for touch, how isolated he had been for a quarter of a century, wrapped in an invisible barrier, surrounded by a layer of air. The Runa were unselfconsciously physical and affectionate. Like Anne, he thought, but more so.

Emilio pushed the hair off his forehead one-handedly and looked down at Askama, shifting in the hammock chair George had designed for him. Manuzhai made it, working from George's sketch, going beyond the plans he provided, her astonishing hands weaving complicated patterns into the rush basketry. Manuzhai often joined him and Sofia and Askama out in the *hampiy,* and he loved the Runao's low husky voice. Similar to Sofia's, now that he thought of it, but unusual among Manuzhai's people. And he loved the melody of Ruanja. Its rhythm and sound reminded him of Portuguese, soft and lyrical. It was a rewarding language to work on, full of structural surprises and conceptual delights . . .

Sofia snorted and he knew he was right when she fell back against her chair and stared balefully at him. *"Lejano'nta banalja,"* she read. *"Tinguen'ta sinoa da.* Both spatial."

"Note, if you will," Emilio Sandoz said, face grave, eyes alight, "the awe-inspiring lack of smugness with which I greet your news."

Sofia Mendes smiled prettily at a man she was very nearly content to call colleague and friend. "Eat shit," she said, "and die."

"Dr. Edwards has had a lamentable influence on your vocabulary," Emilio said with starchy disapproval, and then continued without missing a beat. "Now that you mention it, shit would, of course, fit the general rules for spatial versus nonvisual declension, but what about a fart? Would a fart be declined as a nonvisual, or would a Runao consider such odors to be in a category that implies the existence of something solid? Your levity is uncalled for, Mendes. This is serious linguistic inquiry. We can get another paper out of this, I promise you."

Sofia was wiping tears away. "And where shall we publish it? *The Interplanetary Journal of Intestinal Gas and Rude Noises?*"

"Wait! There's another category. Noise. Easy. Nonvisual. Has to be. Well, maybe not. Try *enroa.*"

"That's it! I'm quitting. I have had enough," Sofia declared. "It's too hot, and this has become entirely too silly."

"At least it isn't smug," he pointed out.

Askama, roused by the laughter, yawned and craned her neck to look at Emilio. "*Sipaj,* Meelo. What is smug?"

"Let's look it up," Sofia suggested airily, playing at using the tablet dictionary and deliberately talking over Askama's head. "Here it is! Smug. It says, Sandoz comma Emilio; see also: insufferable."

Ignoring Sofia, Emilio looked down at Askama and assured her with perfect aplomb, "It is a term of endearment."

THEY GATHERED UP Askama's toys and the computer tablets and Sofia's coffee cup, which she emptied with a toss, and started back toward the cliff dwellings in the slanting light, one sun down, another dropping fast, and only the third and much dimmer red sun relatively high in the sky. For all the heat of these days, Jimmy Quinn was of the opinion that the weather might well turn soon. The rainfall was decreasing from torrential to merely soaking, and the heat lately had been drier, less enervating. The Runa were uninformative. The weather was just there, not much commented upon, except during thunderstorms, which scared them and seemed to provoke a lot of talk.

Sofia arrived at the apartment long before Emilio and Askama, undelayed by the swarm of children that coalesced around Sandoz, wheedling and teasing, hoping for some new delight or astonishment to appear in his hands. Most of the VaKashani napped during the heat, and the village was just waking up for the second round of daily activities. Emilio stopped to talk to people along the narrow walkways, lingering in terraces, admiring a toddler's new skill or flattering a youngster with a question that allowed the child to show off some new competence, accepting small bits of food or a sip of something sweet as he made his way home. It was dusk by the time he got there and Anne had already lit the camplights, a source of muted interest among the Runa, who might have been dismayed by the tiny eyes of their single-irised guests, but who merely observed the technical compensation for this handicap with sly, shy glances.

"Aycha's little one is walking already," Emilio announced as he ducked in from the terrace, accompanied by Askama and three of her friends, attached to various of his limbs, all talking.

Anne looked up. "So is Suway's. Isn't it darling? Just when a human child would plump down on its behind, these kids shoot those little tails out and catch themselves. There are few things quite as charming as the inept functioning of an immature nervous system."

"Has anyone seen an infant?" Marc asked from his corner of the large irregular room. He'd completed an approximate census that morning; to be honest, he had trouble telling individuals apart. "The population structure here is quite odd, unless there is a distinct breeding season—there are age cohorts with long gaps between them. And seems to me that there should be many more children, given the number of mature adults."

"It seems to me that there are a multitude of children," said Emilio wearily, talking a little loudly above the amazing clamor that four small kids could produce. "Legions. Hordes. Armies."

Anne and Marc launched into a discussion of infant mortality, which Emilio tried to follow but couldn't because Askama was pulling on his arm and Kinsa was trying to climb onto his back. "But they all seem so healthy," Anne was saying.

"Healthy and loud," Emilio said. "*Sipaj, Askama! Asukar hawas Djordj. Kinsa, tupa sinchiz k'jna, je?* George, please, ten minutes? Jimmy?"

George scooped Askama up and Jimmy distracted the other kids long enough for Emilio to go down to the river and wash up in some privacy before dinner. When he got back to the apartment, he found that the household numbers were somewhat reduced that evening. Askama had left to play with her friends, as she often did if Emilio was out of sight for a while. Manuzhai had gone visiting. She might not come back at all; equally likely, she might return with five or six guests who'd spend the night. Chaypas was away on some errand, for some unspecified length of time. People often disappeared like that, for hours or days or weeks. Time seemed unimportant to the Runa. There were no calendars or clocks. The nearest Emilio had come to finding vocabulary for the idea was a series of words having to do with ripening.

"Miz Mendes here says you spent the day bein' brilliant," D.W. drawled as Emilio sat down to eat.

"I said nothing of the kind," Sofia shot back. "I said he had spent the afternoon raising smugness to an art form. It was the analysis that was brilliant."

"A very fine distinction," Anne pointed out. She plunked a bowl onto the wooden table and sank onto a cushion next to George before adding, "Isn't he *awful* when he's right?"

"I am a simple man, just trying to do my job," Emilio said in injured tones, persevering despite the moans, "and for this, scorn and sarcasm are heaped on my head."

"So, what is this brilliant analysis?" D.W. asked grumpily. "I got reports to write, son." He'd put his plate aside almost immediately and Emilio now did the same, having filled up on the snacks pressed on him as he walked through the village. Like Jimmy Quinn, D.W. once observed, the Runa ate damn near anything pretty much continuously, and there was no way to visit anyone without being fed and there was no such thing as "not hungry." It meant that the food supply brought from Earth would last a lot longer than expected. That didn't make the Runa stuff any more palatable, although it did seem to be reasonably nutritious for them.

Emilio spent the next ten minutes explaining the rules for declension he'd worked out that morning. To Sofia's intense satisfaction, everyone else initially confused the ideas with abstract and concrete nouns, as she had. Once they'd all seen the underlying logic of it, it seemed perfectly reasonable, and Anne declared that Emilio was entitled to feel superior for precisely one half hour, which she offered to time for him. He refused the honor, admitting cheerfully that he'd already indulged in a sufficiency of self-congratulation.

"I couldn't have gotten this far this fast without Askama. And, in any case," he said seriously, "there are whole areas of this language that are still closed to me. For example, I am completely confused about gender."

Jimmy cracked up and D.W. muttered, "I wouldn't touch that line with a ten-foot pole," which made Anne choke on her food and everyone else laugh. Emilio blushed and told them all to grow up.

"I wonder what they'd do about an AV display. Or VR stuff," George said, pounding on Anne's back as she coughed and giggled helplessly. They'd been very careful about what they used in front of the Runa. Everyone was engaged in research that required computers but as much as possible, they lived as the Runa lived.

"Marc, what declension do they use for your drawings?" Emilio asked. "You create the illusion of space. They'd use spatial for the paper itself, I think, but what about the images?"

"I can't remember. I'll pay attention next time it comes up," Marc promised. "Has anyone seen what Kanchay is doing? He watched me while I was working on a portrait a few weeks ago and asked for materials. I believe he had never seen two-dimensional representation of volumes before but he's already produced some beautiful work."

"So that's where it started!" George exclaimed. It had seemed like spontaneous combustion. All of a sudden, paper and inks and pigments started showing up in the trade boats and everyone was drawing. Fads like that would flash through the village. It could be unnerving. You would hesitate to blow your nose, afraid the whole village would take up the practice en masse, as a hobby.

"You know, I'm beginning to think God really likes these guys best," Anne said, deliberately sounding like a jealous child. "First off, they've got a much nicer planet than we do. Lovely plants, prettier colors. And they're better looking than we are. And they have better hands." The Runa had five digits, but the innermost and outer fingers were fully opposable to the central three; it was almost as though they could work with four human hands simultaneously. Anne was fascinated by the way Askama would sit in Emilio's lap, fingers busy with her ribbons, plaiting them into one pattern after another. The ribbons were each scented differently and the combination of colors, fragrance and braiding pattern constituted much of Runa fashion. The rest consisted mostly of what you tied them around, as far as Anne could tell. "I mean, we thought thumbs were pretty slick, but we must seem almost crippled to the Runa."

"No, I don't think so," Sofia said. "I asked Warsoa once if our hands looked strange to him and he said, 'If you can pick up food, your hands are good enough.' Very practical outlook."

"The craftsmanship is superb," Marc acknowledged.

"Granted," George said dismissively, "they are great with their hands, but these folks are not the ones who invented radio. Or anything else much more advanced than a chisel."

"They've got glass and metal and pottery," Marc pointed out.

"Trade goods," said George dismissively. "They're not making that stuff in this village. I hate to say it, boys and girls, but I don't think they're all that bright, on the whole."

Emilio was about to protest that Askama was very quick but there was, he thought, something to George's observation. The Runa could be perceptive, but he did occasionally find some of them—not dense, really, but limited somehow.

"The technological basis for this society is gathering," George was saying, disgusted. "They collect food. And flowers, for crying out loud. Damned if I know what they do with them."

"For the perfume trade," Sofia said. "I have the impression that there's a lot of manufacturing in the city. Sandoz, did I tell you I found out the name of the city? It's Gaiger or Gaidjur, something like that. In any case, each village specializes in trading something." She was allowed to sit in on what seemed to be village council discussions and picked up a lot of information that way. "In Kashan, it's blossoms for the fragrance industry. I think the Runa are much more interested in scent than we are. That's why the coffee is so valuable."

Anne cleared her throat and made a small movement with her head in D.W.'s direction, grinning.

Yarbrough grunted, refusing to be bullyragged. To his everlasting irritation, coffee was their choicest trade item. Worse yet, it wasn't even coffee per se, but the aroma of coffee. Sofia would brew some of her awful damn Turkish mud and Manuzhai would hold the cup in her hands, breathe the fragrance in and then pass it around to other guests. When the coffee cooled off, they'd hand it back to Sofia, who'd drink the wretched stuff. The Jesuit party could pay for almost anything by sharing a cup of coffee with someone.

"But George is right," said Jimmy who, like George, was perilously close to being bored by the Runa. The two men were working mainly on downloaded astronomical and meteorological data these days, but the city with the transmitters beckoned. "There's almost no advanced technology here. I haven't seen any sign that they even listen to radio. They can't be the Singers. They don't even like music!"

D.W. grunted an assent. There had been no sung Masses since the first one witnessed by the Runa, who had become agitated and distressed. At first he thought it was the ritual aspects of the behavior that bothered them; the Runa didn't seem to have any religious specialists or ceremonies themselves. But it turned out that if the Liturgy was merely said, the Runa were fine. And they liked the incense. So it wasn't the rites; it was evidently the singing itself.

"Someone is making the boats and the glass and the rest of it," Marc said. "Consider things at home. If you go to the highlands of Bolivia, it is like stepping into the Middle Ages. Travel to La Paz and they're designing satellite components and synthesizing pharmaceuticals. This village is simply at the edge of the more advanced culture."

"And, to be fair, there's very little need for industry here," Anne said. "Daylight almost all the time—who needs electric lights? Rivers all over the place—who needs paved roads or land transport? They eat such a variety of things, they just wait for something to ripen. Why plow when you can just pick?"

"If people like you were in charge of life," George said, "we'd still be living in caves."

"Q.E.D.," Jimmy pointed out, waving an arm at the stone walls around them, and there was a round of applause from everyone but Anne.

Emilio laughed but lost the thread of the discussion at that point, as he often did when too many people had strong opinions and expressed them well; he'd always hated seminars. Where's Askama? he wondered, missing her already. She was with him so continually that he felt as though he had taken over as her parent in some ways, and there were aspects of this strange cross-species pseudofatherhood that were deeply satisfying. But while the VaKashani generally addressed him by name, they also used a kinship term that seemed to make him Askama's older sibling. And Manuzhai sometimes corrected him rather sharply for inadvertent infractions, as though he were also her child. At the same time, there was a commercial aspect to their relationship having to do with trade goods, and he was not at all clear about what was expected of him.

His status among his human friends was sometimes equally confusing. The first time he'd fallen apart during Mass had been frightening, but neither Marc nor D.W. seemed surprised or upset; they were instead oddly careful with him, as though he were pregnant—that was the only parallel that came to mind. It was Sofia who put words to what he felt. "You are drunk on God, Sandoz," she told him flatly one afternoon, and he realized then that what he had believed to be entirely interior had been more apparent than he could have imagined. He wished he had time to think it all through but there was just too much going on, and even when things slowed up for a while, he tended to meditate on beer and baseball.

A pebble landed on his chest. "Sandoz," said Sofia, "pay attention!"

He rose onto his elbows. "What?"

"The question was, is Ruanja related to the language of the songs?"

"I doubt it. My guess is that they aren't even close."

"There! You see?" George cried. "I say we try for the city—"

Drawn back into the argument that ensued, Emilio found himself uneasy about going to the city. Things felt so right here. It might simply be an emotional attachment to Askama and her people, but the notion of starting another language so soon was daunting. He'd taken on two and sometimes three languages simultaneously before, but there had always been someone who spoke Latin or English. Without Askama or someone like her, he'd be badly handicapped when he tried the Singers' language. He waited for a break in the conversation and said, "I think it's too soon. To go to the city."

It was D.W. who asked, "Why do you say that, son?"

"It's been seven weeks! I just don't feel ready for another language and another culture yet. I could do it if I had to, but I'd like to be more solid in Ruanja first. I'm sorry," he apologized suddenly. "I'm holding other people up. It's okay. I'll manage. If everyone else wants to move on, we should go."

Marc's eyes slowly left Emilio's face and he turned to D.W. "Emilio's instincts have been reliable so far. We've taken one step at a time, and this has worked well. There is still a great deal to be learned here. Rather than rush him," Marc said, pausing to clear his throat, "into another language, we should perhaps settle for a time."

"We came because of the songs," Jimmy insisted stubbornly. "We came to find out about the Singers."

"This is true," Emilio said to Marc, shrugging. He was willing to go or stay.

"Okay, okay." D.W. held up a hand. "We ain't gonna make the decision tonight, but it's time to start thinkin' about what comes next."

"George, I admit that there is a sort of simplicity to Runa thinking, but we barely speak their language and we hardly know them," Emilio pointed out. "What seems like simplemindedness may be our ignorance of their subtlety. And it's very difficult, sometimes, to tell ignorance from lack of intelligence. We may seem a little dim to the Runa." He flopped back on the cushion.

"Right," Anne confirmed. "Eat that, techno pigs!"

"I'd rather eat that than eat this," George said, pointing at a bowl still half-filled with what he could only think of as fodder, thoughtfully left for them by Manuzhai, who would be offended if any were left. "This is not eating. It's just chewing."

"It helps if you think of it as salad," Emilio advised, speaking at the ceiling. "But not much."

"It could use some Roquefort," Marc grumbled. He held up a leaf and examined it critically. Feeling ungrateful, he searched for something nice to say. "Runa cuisine has, perhaps, a certain *je ne sais quoi.*"

"Entirely too much *quoi,* for my taste," D.W. said sourly.

Emilio smiled at that and was about to comment when he realized that D.W.'s eyes were closed, which was odd. "Emilio," Marc said, interrupting his thoughts, "have you asked anyone yet about us planting an experimental garden? I would like to get a start on that work."

"If we could grow our own food, they might stop thinking they have to feed us this stuff," George said. He knew if they started a garden, they'd be stuck here for a while, but George Edwards had been a serious gardener back in Cleveland and the idea of trying to grow things here had a certain compensatory appeal. Jimmy would be restless, but that was his problem. "Maybe they're only being polite."

Anne nodded. "I am not a picky eater but I'm not Bambi either. There are just too damned many twigs in it."

"The twigs are the best part!" Jimmy exclaimed. Anne stared at him, aghast. "No. Really! They taste like chow mein noodles."

"Well, I like the food," Sofia declared. There were howls, but Jimmy looked blandly vindicated. "Seriously. I do. It reminds me of the food in Kyoto. Or Osaka."

"*De gustibus non est disputandum,*" D.W. growled, adding darkly, "but some folks got a taste for shit. That stuff is purely dreadful."

Emilio sat up and looked at Yarbrough directly now, but said he'd feel Manuzhai out about the garden idea. The talk moved on and after a while, Jimmy began clearing dishes, his job now that astronomers had been replaced on the active-duty roster by linguists. Emilio waited until the room emptied a little, everyone moving off to their own after-dinner activities, and went to D.W., hunched over and silent, his meal untouched. "*¿Padre?*" he said, dropping down next to Yarbrough so he could look up at the creased and crooked face, hidden now behind bony fingers. "*¿Estás enfermo?*"

Anne heard the question and came over. D.W.'s breathing was shallow, but when Emilio reached up to put a hand on his shoulder, he jumped like he'd been hit with a cattle prod and cried, "Don't!" Anne moved between the two men and spoke quietly to D.W., who answered her questions in monosyllables and remained immobile until he suddenly doubled up and groaned, gripping Emilio's arm in spite of himself.

24

VILLAGE OF KASHAN AND CITY OF GAYJUR: THIRD–FIFTH NA'ALPA

WITHIN AN HOUR, it became obvious that D. W. Yarbrough was very sick. Emilio, hoping that Manuzhai might be of some help, went looking for her and found her in one of the biggest rooms, surrounded by people deep in a discussion of *"pik"* somethings. Everyone's ears cocked toward him expectantly as he entered the room, so he tried to explain what seemed to be wrong with D.W. and asked if anyone recognized this illness, knew what caused it or what might help.

"It is like all sickness," Manuzhai told him. "His heart desires something he cannot have."

"There is no animal whose bite does this?" Emilio persisted. "His belly—his gut gives pain: so." He made a gripping motion with his hands. "Is there a food sometimes that does this?"

That set off an interminable discussion of what for all the world sounded like the arcane rules for keeping kosher, with everyone offering stories of how so-and-so got sick once from mixing long foods with round foods, which triggered skeptical commentary along the lines of whether or not that was true or just an excuse someone had used to get out of doing work, and then several people said they mixed round and long all the time and never got sick. Finally, he began to sway from side to side, to indicate to them that he was getting anxious. This was getting him nowhere.

Manuzhai seemed to understand his need to return to the apartment, so she stood up and took her leave of the rest to escort him home, afraid he'd fall from the narrow walkways connecting the apartments and terraces; no matter what they told her, she remained convinced that the foreigners couldn't see in the dim red light of Rakhat's smallest sun. Askama came with them, clinging to her mother for a change, but she looked up at Emilio and asked with a child's bluntness, "*Sipaj,* Meelo, will Dee be gone in the morning?"

Emilio was speechless. It was his unvarying policy to tell the truth and in truth, after Alan Pace's death, it seemed all too possible that Yarbrough would not live through the night, but he couldn't find the words to speak the thought aloud.

"Perhaps," Manuzhai answered for him, raising her tail and letting it drop in what he had come to believe was the equivalent of a shrug. "Unless he gets what his heart wants."

Finding his voice, Emilio said, "Someone thinks it was something Dee ate or drank that makes him sick."

"Sometimes food makes you sick but many have eaten the same food as Dee and only Dee is sick," Manuzhai said, with unassailable logic. "You should find out what he wants and give it to him."

THERE WAS NO real privacy in Runa life. The apartments had, at most, alcoves or irregularities that could serve to separate some habitual divisions of use. No one seemed to own any apartment, other than by occupying it. Families sometimes left to visit other villages and rooms might be left empty for a little while, but if another family liked the apartment, they moved in; when the travelers returned, they simply chose someplace else in the village to stay. Anne and George Edwards found the lack of a bedroom door embarrassing and they'd appropriated the most recessed region of Manuzhai and Chaypas's apartment, going so far as to set up a tent inside the dwelling. The rest had put up their camp beds in a different place every night or, if the apartment was filled with guests, simply dossed down on Runa cushions wherever there was space.

D.W.'s bed was toward the back of the apartment ordinarily, but Anne had it moved to the entrance so he could get out fast. He'd already had several bouts of intestinal distress and was now lying still, curled around a heated rock wrapped in cloth, eyes closed, face rigid. Sitting on the floor next to him, Anne put a hand on his head, pulling the damp hair off his forehead, and said, "Call if you need me, okay?" He made no sign that he'd heard, but she rose anyway and went to Emilio, who'd just returned with Manuzhai and Askama. "Did you find anything out?" she asked, motioning him away from D.W.'s bed and out to the terrace, where they could talk.

"Nothing useful medically." But he told her what Manuzhai had said.

"Thwarted desires, eh? How Freudian," Anne said softly. It was a Runa notion she had come up against before and she thought it might be a fundamental paradigm of Runa social life. It bore thinking about later, when she had the wits to consider it as an anthropologist.

Sofia joined Anne and Emilio outside. "Okay," Anne said unemotionally, "he went down fast, the diarrhea is very bad, and I am concerned. It's almost like Bengali cholera. If there's vomiting too and he gets seriously dehydrated, it could be big trouble."

"Anne, everyone's had diarrhea and gut pain off and on," said Emilio. "Perhaps he'll just have a bad night and be fine in the morning."

"But." Anne looked at him, her eyes serious.

"Yes," Emilio agreed finally. "But."

"So. What do we do now?" Sofia asked.

"Boil some water and whistle in the dark," said Anne. She stepped to the edge of the terrace and looked out across the gorge. It was a rare night on Rakhat, cloudless and starry, with a single, nearly full moon. The river splashed and foamed around the rocks below her, and she could hear the metallic squeal of a rusted iron gate blowing in the wind—the bizarre call of a redlight *moranor*. "At home, I'd put him on an IV drip and pump him full of drugs. I can approximate a rehydration fluid but the stuff he really needs is in the lander." Shit, Anne thought, and turned around to look at Sofia. "If George put the Ultra-Light together, could you—"

"No one goes back to the lander!" D.W. called out. He was in misery but he was neither comatose nor deaf, and he had heard at least some of what they'd said. "We ain't been back for weeks and the runway is prolly all overgrown. I don't want anybody killed just 'cause I got a damn bellyache."

Sofia went back inside and knelt by his bed. "I can land in the rough. We have to go back sometime. The longer we wait, the worse the runway will get. If you need saline and antibiotics, I'm going tonight."

It was public now, and everyone had an opinion. D.W. struggled to sit up and prove to Sofia he wasn't that sick. Jimmy and George got involved in the argument, with Marc wading in as well. They should have thought of this before, but the time had gone by quickly and besides, they had hesitated to introduce the notion of manned flight to the Runa. They were making things up as they went along; there were no guidelines except the negative example of their predecessors' disastrous interactions with technologically simple cultures on Earth. They had no wish to be taken for gods or to begin a cargo cult here. Even so, they had to go back for supplies eventually and they needed to reestablish the runway soon, so why not tonight?

Manuzhai, distressed by the dispute and swaying, took Askama by the hand and left the apartment to sit on the terrace. Emilio quietly apologized to her as she passed him, and then he went inside.

"Enough," he said softly, and silence fell. "D.W., lie down and be quiet. The rest of you, stop arguing. You are offending our hosts and the discussion is pointless. The Ultra-Light won't fly in darkness anyway, will it?" There was a burst of chagrined laughter. In the press of crisis, no one else had thought of that. Emilio ran his hands through his hair. "All right. Tomorrow is soon enough for a reconnaissance flight, which we will undertake even if D.W. is fine. I can explain the plane somehow. Anne, I'll take the night shift. The rest of you, get some sleep."

Nobody moved at first. Direct orders, issued from the mouth of Emilio Sandoz, Sofia Mendes was thinking, astonished. Evidently, the same observation had occurred to D. W. Yarbrough, who fell back laughing weakly and said, "And I thought you weren't management material." Emilio said something rude in Spanish, and the small knot of anxious people arrayed around Yarbrough's bed dispersed, leaving Emilio and D.W. alone finally, with Anne's repeated instructions—to force liquids and call her if there was any vomiting in addition to the diarrhea—ringing in their ears.

THAT NIGHT, THEY all were awakened over and over by the unavoidable disturbance caused when D.W. was forced to get up suddenly, and he became sicker by the hour. Then just before dawn, they woke again, this time to an unmistakable smell and D.W.'s groan of "Oh, my

God," and lay awake, pretending to be unaware, listening to Emilio's soft Spanish reassurances and Yarbrough's humiliated weeping.

Askama slept on but Manuzhai abruptly rose and left the apartment. Anne lay rigid next to George, listening carefully and weighing the choices as Emilio cleaned up the mess, efficient as a night nurse and as unflappable. D.W. was already mortified. A thirty-year taboo against touch had already been broken. A woman's involvement would only make it worse, she decided. Anne heard Emilio insist that Yarbrough drink some more water, boiled and spiked with sugar and salt. The stuff tasted awful and D.W. gagged on it, but Emilio reminded him that dehydration could kill, and so with a practiced ease born of internship, Anne went back to sleep, trusting Emilio's judgment, if not God's will.

Moments later, Manuzhai returned with a stack of simple woven mats used for infants' beds. Emilio helped D.W. raise his hips and slipped one under him, before covering him again. Manuzhai, who had risen repeatedly to escort the two foreigners down the dark rocky pathway to the river and who had seen the tenderness of care one gave the other, now patted Yarbrough's arm in a gesture of reassurance that was startlingly human and left to spend the balance of the night elsewhere.

LONG AGO, MARC Robichaux had observed that a natural tendency to awaken early in the morning is a necessary though insufficient condition if a man is to survive formation and pass onward to ordination. He had known several men who might have become priests if waking at dawn had not done such violence to their normal sleep patterns.

Among the Jesuit party on Rakhat, Marc Robichaux was ordinarily the alpha to Jimmy Quinn's omega, so the apartment was silent as usual when Marc sat up and looked around. In the brief morning witlessness that afflicts even early risers, the night's events were forgotten; then Marc saw Sandoz in a sleeping bag next to the Father Superior's bed and it all came back to him. His eyes went to Yarbrough, who, Marc saw with relief, was also sleeping.

Marc pulled on khaki shorts and, barefoot, padded noiselessly out to the terrace, where Anne sat with Askama, who was trying to teach her the incredibly complicated version of cat's cradle the Runa played. He looked at Anne inquiringly and she smiled and rolled her eyes heavenward, shaking her head at her own fears.

"And sometimes they just get better," Marc said quietly.

"*Deus vult,*" she replied ironically.

He smiled in return, and made his way down to the river.

THE PRECARIOUSNESS OF their existence on this planet was once again in the forefront of their minds and D.W.'s probable recovery did not remove the sense of dancing on a high wire. By the time Emilio came out to the terrace, rubbing his face muzzily in the midmorning light, George and Sofia were trying to decide if they could rig some kind of rope ladder so somebody could jump off the Ultra-Light as she flew over the clearing at the slowest possible air speed, and then could clear the brush before she attempted to land. Anne was providing graphic descriptions of the sort of really interesting compound fractures that were likely to result from this plan while Marc argued that he might be able to tell from the air whether the growth that had undoubtedly begun to fill in the runway was woody or soft. Emilio, stupefied, stared at them for a few moments before turning away and going back to bed after an interlude at the river.

He slept another couple of hours and when he came back out to the terrace, even D.W. was up, pale and rumpled but feeling a little better and making jokes about Runa's Revenge. Jimmy was back from wherever he'd been, and it appeared that at least one problem was about to resolve itself. That morning, Jimmy had learned that the villagers were about to leave for some kind of harvest.

"*Pik* root," Emilio said, yawning. "I heard about that last night."

"They want to know if we're coming," Jimmy told them.

"Do they want us to?" George asked.

"I don't think so. One of them said it was a long walk and asked me if I was going to carry all of you," Jimmy said. "It was obviously a big joke. Lots of tail twitching and huffing. I don't think they'd mind if we stay home." In fact, it was his impression that the Runa would be just as happy to find out that the foreigners weren't coming. The troop moved at the pace of the slowest member, which had often been Anne or Sofia. No one complained, but it was obvious when they got where they were going that some of the flowers had passed their peak.

"If they all leave, we won't have to explain about the plane," Emilio said, sitting down. The sky was hazy and it felt like it was going to be very hot. Sofia handed him a cup of coffee. Askama spotted him from two terraces away and scampered over, full of questions about D.W., whom she was too shy to address directly, and why had Meelo slept so late and was everyone coming to dig *pik* root?

"*Sipaj*, Askama," Emilio said. "Dee was very sick. Someone thinks we will stay here with him while he rests." The child looked crestfallen, ears at half-mast and tail drooping, but undaunted, she devoted the next half hour to cajolery, trying to talk them into coming. When it became plain that this wouldn't work, she declared herself *"porai"* and threatened to get sick like Dee because her heart was sad. Anne saw an opportunity to start working out what all this "heart sickness" and *"porai"* stuff was about and took Askama off to another terrace.

"Okay. Listen up," D.W. said when Askama and Anne were out of earshot. He was still pretty shaky, but it was important to reestablish command. "Plan A: As soon as the coast is clear, George puts the Ultra-Light back together and Mendes here takes Robichaux in for a look-see. We rely on Marc's fear of untimely death to balance Mendes's overconfidence as a pilot. If he thinks they can land okay, she gives it a shot. Their reward for not crashin' is they get to clean up the runway. If Marc decides it's crazy to land, you turn back, Mendes. No arguments."

"And then what?" Sofia asked.

"Then we'll try Plan B."

"Which is?"

"I ain't thought that one up yet. Shee-it," said Dalton Wesley Yarbrough, Father Superior of the Jesuit mission to the village of Kashan on Rakhat, amid cries of derision. "Get off my back! Hell, I'm a sick man."

RUNA DISCUSSIONS TENDED to drag on for days but once a decision was made, the village mobilized with impressive efficiency. George and Sofia hardly waited until the last tail had disappeared before setting out in the opposite direction for the Ultra-Light cache. The little plane was reassembled within the hour, and Sofia took it up for a quick test run. Jimmy, linked to systems aboard the *Stella Maris*, established that the weather was okay on both sides of the mountain range. There was about seven hours of useful light left.

With unsettling dispatch, Marc and Sofia climbed aboard, strapped in and made ready to leave, the others watching as Yarbrough leaned into the little cockpit, hands moving through the air, miming emergency maneuvers. When Sofia started the motor, D.W. stepped back and hollered with specious sternness, "Don't crash, y'hear? That's an order. We only got one damn Ultra-Light. Come back safe!"

Sofia laughed and shouted, "Be here safe when we get back!" And then they were gone, the little plane rising quickly into the sky, wings tipping twice in farewell.

"I hate this," Anne said, when they couldn't hear the motor any longer.

"You are a worrywart," George said, but he put his arms around Anne from behind and kissed the top of her head.

Jimmy said nothing but he wished now that he'd had George take a look at the weather front coming in from the southwest before he okayed the flight.

"I think they will be fine," Emilio said. And D.W. added, "She's a damn good pilot."

"All the same," Anne said stubbornly. "I hate it all the same."

SEVEN DAYS' JOURNEY north of them, in his wharfside compound overlooking the high seawall that bordered his property, Supaari VaGayjur began that day with a similar sense of the precariousness of his existence. He was about to risk not life and limb but status and dignity. If he failed, it would put an end to dreams he hardly dared acknowledge. The stakes were very high, in that sense.

He broke his fast with a handsome meal, gorging carefully: enough so that he would not need to consider meat again that day but not so much as to slow his thoughts. He spent the morning attending to business with the single-minded intensity of a first-born military man and the plodding thoroughness of a second-born bureaucrat. The only time his concentration broke was when he passed through the courtyard on his way to a storage building. He could not keep himself from glancing upward toward Galatna Palace, set apart like its inhabitant: splendid and useless.

Around him, the city rang and vibrated and rumbled with the noise of manufacture and trade, the treble clang and shriek of metalworking momentarily dimmed by the bass of wooden wheels thundering over cobbles just outside his warehouse; the clamor of craft and commerce merging with the noise of the docks, where six hundred vessels, laden with cargo from all over the southern coast of Rakhat's largest continent, shouldered in toward the wharves of Gayjur, their largest market.

Driven early from his natal compound, Supaari had been drawn to Gayjur as a two-moon tide is drawn to shore. He took passage down-river on a Runa freighter bringing huge baskets of carmine and violet *datinsa* to market. Pride was an expense he could not afford: he helped the Runa cook prepare the sailors' meals to work off his fare. He expected humiliation and rejection; it was all he'd known. But in the four days he spent on that boat moving past the sea-carved filigree of the Masna'a Tafa'i coast, Supaari experienced more kindness and friendship than in all his childhood. The Runa were despised but so was he; by the time he tasted the harsh metallic vapors and oily scents of Gayjur as they hove into Radina Bay, the cook had called him brother and Supaari felt less a youth condemned to exile than a man about to find a treasure, if only he has the wit to recognize it.

Within a season, exhilarated by the challenges and risks of trade in the world's largest commercial city, Supaari knew he had found his place and had formally taken his landname, VaGayjur. He began as a runner, working for another third who had come to Gayjur only five years earlier and who was already prospering beyond Supaari's youthful ability to imagine wealth. He learned the universal laws of trade: buy low and sell high; cut losses and let profits run; smell the emotion of the market but don't give way to it. And he discovered his own niche: a willingness, an eagerness to learn from the Runa, to speak their language and respect their ways and deal with them directly.

His fortune was founded on a chance remark by a Runao from the midlands, visiting Gayjur to find a better market for her village's weaving. There had been unusual rain in the high plateau of Sintaron, she said and commented, "*Rakari* should be good this year." Later that day, Supaari checked with several shippers who worked the Pon riverway. They were making the trip in under five days. The river was high, they told him, with a good, fast current. Using everything he'd saved and pledging two years of his labor against default, Supaari contracted to deliver *rakari* for three *bhali* per bale at the end of the season. He quit as a runner, traveled inland to the *rakar* fields, where the bumper crop was being harvested, and arranged to buy every bale at half a *bhal*. The pickers were pleased to get so much, the *rakar* processors were forced to pay the contract price, and Supaari VaGayjur bought his first yard on the profit.

He developed a reputation for knowing what was happening among the Runa, and while his knowledge was profitable and his wealth envied, its source was disdained and he remained an outsider among the respectable Jana'ata of Gayjur. His world consisted of other thirds, who were his competitors, and the Runa, who were, for all that he enjoyed their company, his prey.

His exclusion from society galled him, but there was a more fundamental source of discontent—something which sucked the savor from Supaari's life, which made him wonder what the point of all his effort was. His brothers, whose inheritance tied them to the small and backward town of their birth, seemed less enviable to him now as he looked around his large and well-managed compound, with its servants and warehouse workers, its runners and office staff, its bustling purposefulness. And yet his brothers had what every third was barred from: descendants, heirs, posterity.

There were ways out of this trap. The death without issue of an older sibling would open the way for a third child, providing it could be proved that the heir had not assassinated the first- or second-born. Sterility, if the older was willing to declare the condition's permanence publicly and yield status to the younger, could also make a family possible. And, in exceedingly rare cases, a third could be rendered Founder and establish a new lineage.

On this last possibility—and on seven small brown kernels of extraordinary scent and the exquisite boredom of Hlavin Kithcri—Supaari VaGayjur now pinned his hopes.

By midday, his ordinary business concluded, Supaari was ready to hire a skimmer to pole across the bay to Fatzna Island, the glassmakers' quarter. As the shallow-drafted boat slid onto fine white sand, the thought occurred to him belatedly that he might have done well to bring Chaypas with him, to advise him on the selection of a vacuum flask. Too late, he thought as he paid off the poler and asked the woman to return for him after first sundown. Then he began a systematic hunt through the shops. In the end, he bought not one but three small presentation flasks, each the finest of its type in his judgment, ranging from the classically ornate to a pure crystal simplicity.

When the poler returned, he asked to be let off near Ezao. Noting with satisfaction the large number of people already wearing the waterfall of ribbons, Supaari tracked Chaypas to one of the cook shops and, explaining briefly, asked her opinion of the flasks.

Chaypas stood. Leaving her meal and Supaari behind, she walked outside and then a short way uphill to a vantage point that gave her a view of Galatna Palace, with its twisted marble columns, its finely wrought and silvered gates, its silken awnings, its glazed tile walls gilded and sparkling in the reflections from the paired three-sided fountains sending droplets of precious scented oils like fire sparks into the sunlight.

"In flood, the heart longs for drought," Chaypas said when she returned, and set the simplest of the flasks before him. Then she held out both her hands to him and said, with a warmth that touched him to his soul, "*Sipaj*, Supaari. May you have children!"

HLAVIN KITHERI WAS a poet, and it had always seemed especially outrageous to him that his title, Reshtar, had such a grand significant sound to it.

Reshtar. When spoken, it emerged in two pieces, slowly, with dignity. It could not be said quickly or dismissively. It had a kind of majesty that the position itself had never matched. It meant, simply, spare or extra. For like the merchant Supaari VaGayjur, Hlavin Kitheri was a thirdborn son.

The two men had other things in common. They had been born in the same season, some thirty years earlier. As thirds, they existed in a state of statutory sterility—neither was allowed to marry or have children, legally. Both of them had made more of their lives than anyone could have expected, given their birth positions. And yet, since their honor derived not from inheritance but from accomplishment, they both existed largely outside the bounds of their society.

There the similarities ended. In contrast to Supaari's decidedly middling ancestry, Hlavin Kitheri was the scion of Rakhat's oldest and most noble lineage, and he had once been third in line to succeed as the paramount of Inbrokar. In a reshtar's case, being a third was not a family scandal but the unfortunate consequence of a poorly timed aristocratic birth. Traditionally, noblewomen were bred frequently because their sons died in high numbers. Supaari's parents had no such justification for their lapse. And while men like Supaari often wondered why they'd been born at all, a reshtar's purpose was explicit: it was to exist, as a spare, ready to step into an elder brother's place if he were killed or incapacitated before an heir was born. Reshtari were trained therefore to versatility, prepared equally for war or for governance; either or neither could be their fate.

In the old days, the probability of succession by a reshtar was high. Now, in the enduring peace of the Triple Alliance, most aristocratic thirds simply lived out their lives in pointlessness: softened by servants, dulled by ease, blunted by sterile pleasure.

There was, however, another path open to reshtari, called, appropriately, the Third Way: the way of scholarship. History and literature, chemistry and physics and genetics, both pure and applied, formal architecture and design, poetry and music, all these were the products of aristocratic thirds. Barred—or liberated—from dynasty, the reshtari of Rakhat were freed—or driven—to make sense of their lives in other ways. If a reshtar was careful not to attract a dangerous faction while in exile and did not arouse a routinely paranoid brother's suspicions, he could sometimes produce a sort of intellectual posterity by making some lasting and significant contribution to science or the arts.

Thus, the princely thirds of Rakhat were the volatile elements, the free radicals of Jana'ata high culture, just as bourgeois thirds like Supaari VaGayjur formed the striving, bustling commercial element of Jana'ata society. The crushing restriction of their lives was like the pressure that turns coal to diamond. Most were lost to it, ground to powder; some emerged, brilliant and of great value.

The Reshtar of Galatna Palace, Hlavin Kitheri, was among those for whom constraint had been transforming. He had redeemed his life and given meaning to it in an unprecedented way. Lacking a future, he became a connoisseur of the ephemeral. A singularity, he devoted himself to an appreciation of the unique. He made himself alive to the moment, embracing its transience and, paradoxically, immortalizing it in song. His days were a form of artistry, arising from an aesthetic of evanescence. He brought beauty to vapidity, weight to hollowness, eloquence to emptiness. Hlavin Kitheri's life was a triumph of art over fate.

His earliest poetry was stunning in its originality. In a culture wreathed by perfumes and incense since ancient times, Hlavin Kitheri turned his attention in the beginning to the most reviled of odors. Faced with the ugly, reeking, clamorous city of his exile, he composed songs that captured and exalted the metallic vapors of the marble quarries, the stinking alkaline bite of the red swamps, the smoky sulfurs and strange fermentations and mephitic phantasms emanating from the mines and factories, the seething mixtures of oily and saline compounds transpiring from the dockyards of Gayjur. Scent: capricious and enduring, vanguard of taste, instrument of vigilance, essence of intimacy and recollection—

scent was the spirit of the world, Hlavin Kitheri sang. His finest work was a haunting poetry of storms, songs that spoke of the slackening and rarefication and elasticity of such scents, transformed by lightning and rain as the wind danced. These songs were so compelling that his concerts began to be broadcast, the first nonmilitary use of radio in his culture's history.

The acclaim did not dilute the cogence of his poetry. He accepted it as validation and, strengthened, turned his mind and his art to a fearless examination of a reshtar's living death. He survived his own unblinking scrutiny. The poetry that resulted, written when Kitheri was only twenty-six, had what many thought would be his greatest influence on his culture.

Robbed of any possibility of reproduction, empty of any future, sex for a reshtar was reduced to its most irremediable physicality, no more satisfying to the soul than a sneeze or the voiding of a bladder. In youth, Hlavin Kitheri had fallen into the trap that snared so many others of his kind, compensating for utter vacuity with numerically staggering indulgence, hoping to make up in sheer repetition of experience what was missing in depth and meaning. In maturity, he came to despise the harem of sterile courtesans and cross-species partners his brothers provided; Hlavin saw it for what it was: a sop thrown to him to dissipate envy of his elders' fecundity.

And so he turned his aesthetic sensibilities to the experience of orgasm and found the courage to sing of that evanescent moment which, for the fertile, brings the weight of the past to bear on the future, which holds all moments in its embrace, which links ancestry and posterity in the chain of being from which he was barred and exiled. With his poetry, he severed that moment from the stream of genetic history, carried it beyond the body's drive to reproduce and the lineal need for continuity and, focusing the mind and soul on it, discovered in climax a reservoir of piercing erotic beauty no one else in the history of his kind had suspected.

In a culture walled in by tradition and heavy with stability, Hlavin Kitheri had created a new subtlety, a delicacy, a new appreciation of raw experience. What had once been merely obnoxious or ignored was now theater and song: scent's veiled and hidden opera. What had once been dynastic duty or meaningless carnality was resolved and purified, raised to an aesthetic voluptuousness that had never before existed on Rakhat. And, scandalously, the Reshtar of Galatna lured even those who could have bred productively to artistic lives of momentary and sterile but ravishing brilliance, for he had changed the world of those who heard his songs for all time. There arose a generation of poets, the children of his soul, and their songs—sometimes choral, sometimes singular, often the call-and-response of the oldest chants—propagated through space on unseen waves and reached a world they could not imagine, and changed lives there as well.

It was to this man, Hlavin Kitheri, the Reshtar of Galatna Palace, that Supaari VaGayjur now sent, in a strikingly simple crystal flask, seven small kernels of extraordinary fragrance.

Opening the flask, breaking its vacuum, Kitheri was met by a plume of sweetly camphoric enzyme by-products giving off notes of basil and tarragon, by chocolate aromatics, sugar carbonyl and pyrazine compounds carrying the suggestion of vanilla, by hints of nutmeg and celery seed and cumin in the products of dry distillation created during roasting. And, overlaying all, the tenuous odor of volatile short-chain carbons, the saline memorial of an alien ocean: sweat from the fingers of Emilio Sandoz.

A poet with no words to describe organic beauties whose origin he could not possibly suspect, Hlavin Kitheri knew only that he must know more. And, because of this, lives were changed again.

25

NAPLES:
JULY 2060

STANDING IN THE hallway, John Candotti and Edward Behr could hear half of the conversation taking place inside the Father General's office quite clearly. It was not necessary to eavesdrop. It was only necessary not to be deaf.

"None of it was published? You are telling me that not one article we sent back was submitted—"

"Maybe I shouldn't have told him," John whispered, rubbing the bump on his broken nose.

"He was bound to find out eventually," said Brother Edward placidly. Anger, he believed, was healthier than depression. "You did the right thing. He's handling it fairly well, in my opinion."

Why, Sandoz had asked John at lunch, why was he being asked about things that were in the records that were sent back? Why didn't they just read the daily reports and scientific papers? John told him that only the Father General had access to the reports. "So, what about all the published papers?" Sandoz asked and when he got the answer, he left the table, stone-faced and seething, and headed directly for the Father General's office.

Candotti and Behr turned at the sound of Johannes Voelker's steps.

He joined them at the door and listened with frank interest as Sandoz said sarcastically, "Oh, fine! So the astronomy and the botany got through the sieve. I'm pleased to hear it, but that leaves ninety percent of what we did—" Another pause. "Vince, people died for the data!"

Voelker, hearing this, raised an eyebrow. Probably pisses him off to hear Sandoz call Giuliani by his first name, John thought. Voelker insisted on imbuing the office of the Father General with as much imperial glory as he could, the better to play Grand Vizier, in John's admittedly biased opinion.

"For the data?" Voelker asked with dry surprise. "Not for Christ?"

"What possible justification is there—" There was a pause and they could hear the Father General's quiet voice but couldn't make out the words without actually laying an ear against the door, an extremity no one was willing to go to, with witnesses.

Felipe Reyes arrived, brows up inquiringly, and came to a sudden halt as Sandoz shouted furiously, "No way. There is no way you can make me responsible for this. Of all the twisted logic and half-baked— No, you let me finish! I don't give a damn what you think of me. There is no justification for suppressing the scientific work we did. That was absolutely first-rate!"

"Your man sounds upset, Candotti," Voelker said quietly, smiling.

"He's a scientist and his work was buried, Voelker. He's got a right to be upset," John said just as softly with as gentle a smile. "How's the secretary biz these days? Scheduled any first-rate appointments lately?"

It would have gotten nastier had Felipe Reyes not stopped them with a look. It is almost hormonal with these two, Reyes thought. Put Voelker and Candotti in a room together and you could practically see the metaphysical antlers growing out of their heads.

They realized then that the shouting had stopped and for a long while there was no indication of what was going on inside the office. Finally, Voelker glanced at the time on his notebook and reached passed John to rap on the door.

To John's vast satisfaction, it was the Father General who yelled, "Not now, dammit."

INSIDE THE OFFICE, Emilio Sandoz was staring at Vincenzo Giuliani in utter disbelief.

"So you see, it was, in retrospect, a wise decision," Giuliani was saying, hands spread placatingly. "If we had published everything as the data arrived, it would have been even worse when it came out later."

Sandoz stood there, rigid, almost unable to take it in. He wanted to believe that it made no difference, but it did. It made everything different, and he tried to remember every conversation they'd had, almost faint with the fear that he'd remember saying something, unknowing, that might have wounded her.

Giuliani pulled out a chair for him. "Sit down, Emilio. Obviously, this is a shock." A scholar himself, Giuliani was not at all happy about the suppression of scientific work, but there were larger issues here, things Sandoz could not be told. He was not proud of himself for bringing Mendes into this, but it was a useful diversion and might unearth some relevant insight if he could get Sandoz to open up. "You didn't know?"

Emilio shook his head, still dazed. "She said something once. Just that she preferred bond-work for a broker to prostitution. I thought she was speaking hypothetically. I had no idea . . . She must have been a *child*," he whispered, horrified. How did she survive being used like that? With all the resources of an adult, it had destroyed him.

She had saved his life, her AI navigation system piloting the *Stella Maris* back to the solar system nearly a year after her own death on Rakhat. He was a broken man, alone, incapable even when whole of coping with the navigational tasks. Sofia's programs had done it all: efficient, logical and competent as their creator. Sometimes he would call up the initial screen that put the AI program in motion and stare at the message she had left in Hebrew. "Live," it said, "and remember." It was more than he could stand to think of, and he forced himself away from it, fighting the descent into migraine. She's dead and I may as well be, he thought. The work doesn't deserve to be entombed as well.

"It makes no difference," he insisted then, and Giuliani realized the diversion hadn't worked. "I want our work published. Moral indignation over the authors' sex lives is irrelevant. And Anne's stuff and D.W.'s! I want all of it published. We sent back something like two hundred papers in three years. It's all that's left of what we were, Vince—"

"All right, all right. Calm down. We can address that issue later. There is more at stake here than you realize. No, just be quiet," Giuliani said peremptorily when Sandoz opened his mouth. "We are talking about solid science, not ripe peaches. The data will not deteriorate. We've already delayed publication for over twenty years for reasons that

have seemed good and sufficient to three successive generals, Emilio."
He was not above applying leverage. "The sooner these hearings are
over and we are clear about what happened on Rakhat and why, the
sooner the Society will be able to make a decision about the wisdom of
publication. And I promise you will be consulted."

"Consulted!" Sandoz cried. "Look: I want that work published
and if—"

"Father Sandoz," the Father General of the Society of Jesus reminded him, hands folded on the table, "you do not own that data."

There was a moment of stunned silence before Sandoz slumped in
his seat and turned away, eyes closed, mouth hard, effectively check-
mated. A minute or so later, one gloved hand went involuntarily to the
side of his head, pressing against the temple. Giuliani got up and went to
the lavatory for a glass of water and the bottle of Prograine he now kept
handy. "One or two?" he asked when he got back. One tablet didn't
quite do the job; two flattened Sandoz for hours.

"One, damn you."

Giuliani placed the tablet in the palm of the glove Sandoz held out
abruptly and watched as the man tossed the pill into his mouth and took
the glass between his wrists. He could manage some things quite well
with Candotti's fingerless gloves on. The gloves reminded Giuliani of
those once worn by cyclists; the athletic allusion made Sandoz seem less
impaired without the braces, if you didn't watch carefully. New braces
were being fabricated.

Giuliani took the glass back to the lavatory and when he returned,
Sandoz was resting his head on the heels of his hands, elbows on the
table. Hearing Giuliani's steps, he said almost soundlessly, "Turn off the
lights."

Giuliani did so and then went to the windows to pull the heavy
outer curtains closed as well. It was another gray day, but even dull light
seemed to bother Emilio when he had a headache. "Would you like to lie
down?" he asked.

"No. Shit. Give me some time."

Giuliani walked to his desk. Rather than open the door and tell the
others himself, he routed a message to the front door, asking the porter
to relay it to the men waiting outside his office: the afternoon's meeting
was canceled. Brother Edward was to wait in the hall for Father Sandoz.

To pass the time, Giuliani did some of what he still thought of as pa-
perwork, reviewing several letters before signing off on transmission. In

the quiet that now settled over the office, he could hear the elderly gardener, Father Crosby, whistling tunelessly outside the windows as he
deadheaded the annuals and pinched back chrysanthemums. It was perhaps twenty minutes later when Emilio's head came up and he sat back
gingerly in his chair, the heel of one hand still pressing hard against the
side of his forehead. Giuliani closed the file he was working on and went
back to the table, sitting in the chair across from Emilio.

Sandoz's eyes remained closed but, hearing the chair move, he said
almost inaudibly, "I don't have to stay here."

"No. You don't," Giuliani agreed neutrally.

"I want that stuff published. I could write the papers again."

"Yes. You could do that."

"There must be someone who'd pay me for them. John says people
will pay to interview me. I could make a living outside."

"I'm sure you could."

Sandoz, squinting into what seemed to him painfully bright light,
looked directly at Giuliani. "So give me one good reason why I should
put up with this crap, Vince. Why should I stay?"

"Why did you go?" Giuliani asked simply.

Sandoz looked blank, not understanding.

"Why did you go to Rakhat, Emilio?" Giuliani asked again gently.
"Was it just a scientific expedition? Did you go just because you were a
linguist and it sounded like an interesting project? Were you just another
academic grubbing for publications? Did your friends really die for the
data?"

The eyes closed and there was a long silence before his lips formed
the word, "No."

"No. I didn't think so." Giuliani took a deep breath and let it out.
"Emilio, everything I have learned about the mission leads me to believe
that you went for the greater glory of God. You believed that you and
your companions were brought together by the will of God and that you
arrived at your destination by the grace of God. In the beginning, everything you did was for the love of God. I have the testimony of two of
your superiors who believed sincerely that something far out of the ordinary happened to you on Rakhat, that you—" He hesitated, not
knowing how far to go. "Emilio, they both believed that you had, in
some sense, seen the face of God—"

Sandoz stood and turned to leave. Giuliani reached out and locked
a hand over the man's arm to keep him from running away but released

it instantly, startled by the strangled scream as Sandoz pulled away violently. "Emilio, please don't leave. I'm so sorry. Don't go." He had seen
before this look of sheer panic, the terror that sometimes swamped the
man when you least expected it. This *has* to be part of it somehow, he
thought. "Emilio, what happened to you out there? What changed
everything?"

"Don't ask me, Vince," Sandoz said bitterly. "Ask God."

HE KNEW IT was Edward Behr who'd come after him. The
wheezing was unmistakable. He'd felt his way down the stone stairs,
blinded by the tears and the lingering pain, and when he realized he'd
been followed, he swore viciously and told Ed to leave him the hell
alone.

"Do you miss the asteroid?" Brother Edward asked curiously. "You
were alone there."

Emilio laughed in spite of it all. "No. I do not miss the asteroid," he
said as dryly as a crying man could. He sat down where he stood, feeling boneless and bereft, and put his head in what was left of his hands.
"There's no bottom to this."

"You're better, you know," Edward said, sitting down. Emilio
looked out at the Mediterranean, gunmetal blue and oily under a flat
pewter sky. "Of course, there are good days and bad days, but you're a
lot stronger than you were a few months ago. You couldn't have sustained an argument like that before. Physically or mentally."

Wiping his eyes on the backs of his gloves, Emilio said angrily, "I
don't feel stronger. I feel that this will never be over. I feel that I will
never be over it."

"Well, I can only speak to the grief. You lost so much and so many
out there." Edward saw rather than heard the sobbing and resisted the
impulse to put a hand out; Sandoz hated being touched. "In the normal
way of things, it takes about a year, when you lose someone you really
care for. Before the worst of it lets go of you, I mean. I found anniversaries the hardest. Not just formal things like wedding anniversaries,
you understand. I'd be going along, functioning fairly well really, and
then I'd realize, today would have been ten years since we met, or six
years since we moved to London, or two years since that trip to France.
Used to lay me away properly, little anniversaries like that."

"How did your wife die, Ed?" Sandoz asked. He'd gotten a grip again. Brother Edward wished he'd let himself go, but there was some overriding need to keep control, something that couldn't be wept away. "You don't have to tell me," Sandoz said then. "I'm sorry. I didn't mean to pry."

"Oh, I don't mind. It helps actually, to talk about her. Keeps her alive to me in some ways." Edward leaned forward, pudgy elbows on his knees, head close to Emilio's now. "It was a stupid thing, really. I was rooting around in the glove box, looking for a tissue to blow my nose with. Can you imagine? I had a cold! Dumb luck. Kind of thing you do a hundred times and it makes no difference and then one bright winter morning, it makes all the difference in the world. Wheel hit a hole in the tarmac and I lost control of the car. She was killed and I was barely scratched."

"I'm sorry." There was a long silence. "Was it a good marriage?"

"Oh, it had its ups and downs. We were actually in a rough patch when the accident happened but I think we'd have sorted things out. We weren't either of us quitters. We'd have done all right, I think."

"Did you blame yourself, Ed? Or did you blame God?"

"Funny about that," Brother Edward said, musing. "There was plenty of blame to go around, but it never occurred to me to blame God. I blamed myself, of course. And the council for not keeping the roadways in good repair. And the wretched little boy in the flat upstairs who gave me the cold. And Laura, for letting me drive when I was sick."

They listened for a while to the mournful screams of the gulls wheeling overhead. The water was too far away to hear the waves, but watching the rhythmic ebb and flow was nearly as soothing and Emilio's headache began to ebb as well. "How did you come to this life, Ed?" he asked.

"Well, I was fairly religious as a child. Then I was an atheist for a while. I think they call that period of spiritual development 'adolescence,'" Edward said dryly. "Then about two years after Laura was killed, a friend talked me into going to a Jesuit retreat. And when we got to the part about following the standard of Christ, I thought, well, why not? I'll have a go. I was at loose ends, you see. Wasn't exactly a Pauline conversion. No voices. And you, sir?"

"No voices," Sandoz said, his voice normal again and a little hard. "I never heard voices and the migraines do not feel like metal bands around my head. I'm not psychotic, Ed."

"I don't believe anyone has suggested that you were, sir," Brother Edward said quietly. "I meant, how did you come to the priesthood?"

It was some time before Sandoz answered, flat-voiced and unexpansive, "Seemed like a good idea at the time."

Brother Edward thought that might be the end of the conversation, but after a few minutes Sandoz said, "You've been on both sides. Which is the better life?"

"I'd never give up the years I had with Laura, but this is the right place for me now." Edward hesitated, then thought it might be as good a time as any to broach the subject. "Tell me about Miss Mendes. I've seen pictures. She was beautiful."

"Beautiful and bright and very brave," Sandoz said, the sound leached from his voice. He cleared his throat and ran an arm over his eyes.

"A man would have to be a fool not to love someone like that," Edward Behr said gently. Some priests were so hard on themselves.

"Yes, a fool," Sandoz agreed and added, "but I didn't think so then." It was a puzzling thing to say and Sandoz followed it with something just as unexpected. "Have you ever wondered about the story of Cain, Ed? He made his sacrifice in good faith. Why did God refuse it?"

Sandoz stood and, without looking back, made his way down the long stairway to the sea. He was small and foreshortened, halfway across the beach to the huge stone outcropping he often retreated to, before Edward Behr realized what he had just been told.

26

VILLAGE OF KASHAN AND GREAT SOUTHERN FOREST: EIGHT WEEKS AFTER CONTACT

ANNE AWOKE THAT night without knowing what had disturbed her. Her first thought, accompanied by a spurt of adrenaline that snapped her eyes open in the dark, was that D.W. was sick again or that someone else had fallen prey to Runa's Revenge. She listened, alert for any telltale sound, but heard only George snoring softly in heavy, dreamless sleep. Knowing that she wouldn't relax until she'd checked on everyone, Anne sighed and thought, I have turned into a semi-mom with a very odd bunch of children. So she pulled on one of Jimmy's giant T-shirts and worked her way out of the tent.

She went first to D.W. and, reassured, moved on to Jimmy's sleeping shape in another corner. She looked, with a pang, at the empty beds of Marc and Sofia and wished she were a praying person so their absence would not fill her with such helpless anxiety. Then she saw a third bed empty but before her heart could lurch, she began to hear the faint clicking of a keyboard. Picking her way along a stone path only a goat could appreciate, she ducked into Aycha's place next door and saw her favorite semi-son kneeling like a scholarly geisha at a low table, typing rapidly.

"Emilio!" she cried softly. "What the hell are you—"

He shook his head without looking up and continued to type. She sank onto a cushion next to him and listened to the night noises. It smelled like rain to her but the stones were still dry. Well, she thought, noticing the radio monitor propped next to Emilio, I'm not the only one sweating it out.

Marc and Sofia had reported that they were going to try a landing. There had been a sickening silence ever since. Jimmy thought this might be due to the severity of the storm on the other side of the mountains, but George said that would only have disrupted signals, not silenced them altogether. No one said anything aloud about a crash.

Emilio typed a while longer and then closed out the file, satisfied that he'd written enough to be able to reconstruct the logic the next morning. "I'm sorry, Anne. I had four languages going in my head at once and if we had added one more—" His fingers flew apart and he made a sound like an explosion.

"How do you keep them all straight?" she asked.

He yawned and rubbed his face. "I don't always. It's funny. If I understand an entire conversation perfectly in Arabic or Amharic or Ruanja or whatever, with no missing words or confusing ideas, I sometimes remember it taking place in Spanish. And I'm losing Polish and Inupiaq."

"Those were the ones in Alaska, between Chuuk and the Sudan, right?"

He nodded and flopped back on a cushion, digging fingers into his eyes. "I may not have done well with them because I was so resentful about having to learn those two. I never got used to the cold and the dark, and I felt that my education was being squandered. Nothing made sense to me." He took his hands away from his face and looked at her sideways. "It's not easy to be obedient if you suspect your superiors are asses."

Anne snorted. Not a very saintly remark, she thought. "At least the Sudan was warm."

"Not warm. Hot. Even for me, hot. And by the time I got to Africa, I was getting better at learning languages in the field. And then—well, professional irritation seemed pretty trivial." He sat up and stared out into the darkness. "It was awful, Anne. No time for anything except feeding people. Trying to keep the babies alive." He shook it off. "I am still amazed that I picked up three languages that year. It just happened. I stopped thinking of myself as a linguist."

"What did you think of yourself as?"

"A priest," he said simply. "That was when I really started to believe what was said at ordination: *Tu es sacerdos in aeternum.*"

A priest in perpetuity, Anne thought. Always and forever. She studied the protean face: Spaniard, Taino, linguist, priest, son, beloved,
friend, saint. "And now?" she asked softly. "What are you now,
Emilio?"

"Sleepy." He grabbed her neck affectionately and pulled her close
to pass his lips over her hair, loosened in sleep, silver-gilt in the camplight.

Anne motioned at the monitor. "Heard anything?"

"I'd have mentioned it, Anne. In a loud and ringing voice."

"D.W. will never forgive himself if anything's happened to those
two."

"They'll be back."

"What makes you so certain, hotshot?"

He spoke from his heart and from Deuteronomy. " 'You have seen
with your own eyes what the Lord your God has done.' "

"I've seen what human beings can do—"

"You've seen *what*," Emilio conceded, "but not why! That's where
God is, Anne. In the *why* of it—in the meaning." He looked at Anne and
understood the skepticism and the doubt. There had been so much joy,
such a flowering within him . . . "All right," he said, "try this: the *poetry*
is in the why."

"And if Sofia and Marc are lying in a heap of wreckage right now?"
Anne demanded. "Where would God's poetry be then? Where was the
poetry in Alan's death, Emilio?"

"God knows," he said, and there was in his tone both an admission
of defeat and a statement of faith.

"See, that's where it falls apart for me!" Anne cried. "What sticks in
my throat is that God gets the credit but never the blame. I just can't
swallow that kind of theological candy. Either God's in charge or He's
not. What did you do when the babies died, Emilio?"

"I cried," he admitted. "I think sometimes that God needs us to cry
His tears." There was a long silence. "And I tried to understand."

"And now? Do you understand?" There was, almost, a note of
pleading in her voice. If he told her he did, she'd have believed him.
Anne wished that someone could explain this to her and if anyone she
knew could understand such things, it might be Emilio Sandoz. "Can
you find *any* poetry in babies dying now?"

"No," he said at last. Then he added, "Not yet. Some poetry is tragic. It is perhaps harder to appreciate."

Anne stood then, tired, for it was the middle of the night, and was about to go back to bed when she glanced back and saw a familiar look on his face. "What?" she demanded. "What!"

"Nothing." He shrugged, knowing his singular congregation very well. "Only: if this is all that is holding you back from faith, perhaps you should just go ahead and blame God whenever you think it's appropriate."

A slow smile started across Anne's face and she sat back down on the cushion next to him, looking speculative.

"What?" it was his turn to ask. She was grinning wickedly now. "What are you thinking, Anne?"

"Oh, I'm just considering a few sentiments I might express to God," she said sweetly, and then clamped both hands over her mouth to keep from laughing out loud. "Oh, Emilio, my darling child," she said behind her fingers in a fey and crafty voice. "I do believe you've hit upon a theology I can live with! I have your permission for this, do I, Father? You are willing to be implicated as an accessory?"

"How rude do you plan to get?" Emilio started to laugh warily but his face was now wholly alive. "I'm only a priest! Maybe we should check with a bishop or something—"

"Chicken shit!" she cried. "Don't back down on me now!" And getting up on her knees, poking him in the chest repeatedly, she began to deliver herself of a series of increasingly impolite, entirely profane and very vigorously expressed opinions on the suffering and untimely death of innocents, on the fate of Cleveland in the World Series of 2018, and on the persistence of evil and of Republicans from Texas in a universe ruled by a deity who had the nerve to claim omnipotence and justice, all of which Emilio earnestly translated, with wondrously pompous and Latinate phrases, into standard groveling platitudes. Pretty soon they were clinging to each other and laughing like loons, and the whole thing got louder and rowdier until George Edwards, roused by the noise, was jolted fully awake by Anne screaming, "Emilio, stop it! Old women have weak bladders!"

"Sandoz," George yelled, "what the hell are you doing with my wife?"

"We're discussing theology, dear," Anne sang breathlessly, snorting in great gulps of air.

"Oh, for Christ's sake!"

"We're still working on theodicy!" Emilio yelled. "We haven't gotten to divine incarnation yet." Which laid them both out again.

"Kill 'em, George," D.W. suggested loudly. "Justifiable homicide."

"Will all of you please shut the fuck up?" Jimmy hollered, which for some reason made Anne and Emilio laugh even harder.

"A New York echo!" Anne cried. "Helloo-o-o!"

"Shut the fuck u-u-u-u-p!" Emilio supplied, doubling over.

"Oh, well, what the hell. Maybe I'll give religion another try," Anne said softly, wiping her eyes as the cleansing laughter faded and they caught their breath. "You think God can handle the kind of crap that I'm likely to dish out?"

Emilio lay back on a cushion, exhausted and happy. "Anne," he said, putting his hands behind his head, "I think God will be glad to have you back."

THE LAST THING Marc Robichaux thought before the crash was, *Merde,* the Father Superior will be furious.

It had looked reasonable to him. The runway was still quite distinct and the vegetation looked soft and leafy. He believed that the root systems might actually be helpful in stabilizing the soil so that the wheels of the plane would not sink. Sofia had landed on many forms of terrain during her training and seemed confident that she could manage this. So they decided to go down.

Neither Marc nor Sofia had counted on vines. They must have been woody, like grapevines, or the plants would have pulled apart when the wheels touched down. Instead they grabbed viciously at the fragile little plane's undercarriage and the sudden stop had thrown him and Sofia brutally into their harnesses. Sitting in the front seat, Marc had a terrifying view of the ground coming up to meet him, but he blacked out before the Ultra-Light tore apart, the safety belts ripping the suddenly stationary framework to pieces as their bodies hurtled forward.

He had no idea how long he'd lain unconscious. It was daylight when they crashed. Both moons were up now. For a while, he kept still, concentrating on each limb and on the pain in his chest, trying to judge the seriousness of his injuries. His legs were numb and, heart drumming, he was horrified, thinking he'd broken his back. But when he moved his head cautiously, he saw that Sofia had been thrown onto him in the wreck and that the numbness was simply due to impeded circulation.

There was blood all over her face but she was still breathing. Marc slowly slid out from under her, trying not to jar her body, all Anne's apocalyptic descriptions of compound fractures coming back to him. He was able to turn and cradle her head as he pulled his legs clear and, in his concern for her, he forgot to be worried about his own body. By the time he got to his knees, he realized that he couldn't be badly hurt himself or the pain would have been worse.

He pulled his shirt up to see why his chest felt so awful and saw in the moonlight the exact outline of the safety harness, drawn in burst skin and ugly bruises; he almost passed out again, but put his head down for a few minutes and was better. Then he looked to Sofia and began to clear away hollow poles and guy wires and polymer film, all that was recognizable from the Ultra-Light. When she was free of the wreckage, Marc got up and made his way to the lander, unlocking the cargo bay door and flicking on the battery-powered lamp inside. When his eyes adjusted, he found the first-aid kit, a portable camplight and a set of insulated emergency blankets, which he carried back to Sofia.

In all their months together, Marc had kept his distance from Sofia Mendes. He found her rather cold, disturbingly self-sufficient, almost unfeminine, but her physical beauty sometimes took his breath away, and he had never permitted himself to draw her, to feel the shape of her with his hands, even on paper at a chaste distance.

Now he knelt at her side. I beg your pardon, mademoiselle, he thought, and with as much detachment as he could muster, still badly shaken himself, searched along her arms and legs for breaks and cuts. Her torso was undoubtedly as bruised as his own but, for many reasons, he simply could not bring himself to determine if she had ribs broken or abdominal injuries. There wasn't anything he could do for such hurts anyway. So he laid out one blanket, moved her onto it and then wrapped her securely in the other before finding his way to the creek for a container of water.

He returned and dampened a clean cloth from the first-aid kit to wipe the dried and fresh blood from her face. He found the oozing source: her scalp was gashed. Fighting nausea at the sight of all the blood, Marc forced himself to feel along the edges of the cut. He couldn't be sure but it seemed that there was no depression in the skull itself. Concentrating manfully on the task, he didn't realize her eyes had opened until he heard her say, "If you've baptized me, you're in a lot of trouble, Robichaux."

"*Mon Dieu!*" he shouted, falling back from her, tipping over the bucket of water, so shocked that the cloth flew out of his hand.

For several minutes, Sofia was treated to an impressive display of agitated Gallic emotion. Her French was academic and Robichaux's dialect was almost incomprehensible to her even when he had not been scared senseless. Nevertheless, she understood quite clearly that he was veering wildly between relief and anger. "I'm sorry I frightened you," she said when he started to slow down.

He held up a hand, swallowing, and shook his head, still breathing double time. "*De rien.*" It was a moment more before he could produce English. "I beg you, mademoiselle. Do not *ever* do that to me again."

"I'll try not to, but I doubt that the situation is likely to recur," she said dryly. "Am I damaged? Are you?"

"As far as I have been able to determine, we are bruised and cut but not anywhere broken. How do you feel, mademoiselle?" Marc pulled up his shirt briefly to let her see the imprint of the belts. "We were thrown forward with a great deal of force. Is it possible that your ribs are broken?"

She moved under the blanket and he saw her face take on an unusual self-absorbed look. "I'm certainly very sore," she admitted. "And I have quite a headache. But I think that's all."

Marc waved a hand limply at the wreckage. "We are both either beloved of God or very lucky."

She rose a little and looked at what was left of the Ultra-Light. "God evidently doesn't love small airplanes. On the other hand, D. W. Yarbrough does. He is going to be very angry about this." Marc rolled his eyes in agreement. Sofia stared at the mess and realized that the destruction of the plane had saved their lives; its framework was designed to go to pieces and absorb the momentum of a crash. She lay back, a little dizzy, and began to calculate the minimum number of hours since they'd gone down. "Marc, does the radio still work? The others must be worried."

He put a palm to his forehead and, muttering in French, went to the remains of their plane, where he began rummaging inefficiently through the ruins. The wind was picking up now, and shreds of polymer film flapped and snapped in the stiffening breeze.

"Robichaux, forget it!" Sofia called. "There's a transceiver in the lander." She sat up with great care, listening to her body. Everything moaned but nothing screamed. Moving the blanket off herself, she pulled the neck of her shirt forward and peered downward. "Very colorful," she remarked and added brightly, "We have matching chests."

"The topography differs considerably," the priest said with a ghost of humor. He came back and sat a little abruptly next to her on the ground, putting his head down again. After a few moments, Marc looked up. "I speak, of course, from inference, not direct observation."

"Marc," she said wryly, "if we are ever in another plane crash together, please feel free to make sure my rib cage is not crushed. Modesty is hardly of paramount importance during medical emergencies." He might have blushed. It was hard to tell in the orange glow of the camplight. There was a roll of thunder and Sofia looked around at the trees flexing in the wind. "We should get inside the lander."

They picked up the blankets and first-aid kit and, using the camplight to find their way, climbed achingly through the portside cargo door. The wind was coming from starboard, so they left the door open and watched the lightning play. The storm was, at the beginning, very violent but soon settled into a steady downpour, loud against the skin of the lander but somehow comforting.

"So," Sofia said, when the noise abated somewhat, "did you?"

"Pardon?" He seemed taken aback by the question.

"Did you *baptize* me?"

"Oh," he said, and then, rather indignantly, "no, of course not."

"I'm glad to hear it," Sofia said, but she was puzzled. If it had been Sandoz, she'd have been willing to joke with him. Some missionary you are, she'd have said, trusting his sense of irony. She was less sure of how to treat Marc, who in any case seemed quite unnerved by the accident. She herself felt remarkably cheerful, on the whole. "Shouldn't you have?"

"Absolutely not. It would have been completely unethical."

He seemed better, more focused, when talking, so she decided to keep the conversation going. "But if I had been dying, would it not have been your duty to save my soul?"

"This is not the seventeenth century, mademoiselle. We do not go about snatching the souls of dying heathens from perdition," he said huffily, but he continued more equably. "If you had earlier indicated that you sincerely desired to be baptized but had not yet taken instruction in the Faith, I would have baptized you, yes, out of respect for your intention. Or if you had regained consciousness and requested it, I would have complied with your wish. But without your permission? Without a prior statement of intent? Never."

He was still a little upset but felt steadier now and pulled himself to his feet slowly, making small noises. Standing at a console, he called up a photographic map of the region between the forest camp and the village of Kashan. "It's going to be a long walk home."

He turned at the sound of her husky laugh. Tinted by half-washed blood and its bruises growing more colorful hourly, the beautiful Sephardic face remained cool and composed, but the eyes smiled as Sofia Mendes looked around her. "Why walk," she asked, arched brows high, "when we can fly?"

THEY SLEPT THEN and awoke late, tight-muscled and sore, but heartened by the poststorm sunlight and by their survival. They made a simple breakfast from the stock in the lander and Sofia reacquainted herself with the plane, going through the exercise of takeoff and landing on the simulator. Marc occupied himself with a brief survey of the forest life-forms he'd studied during their first weeks on Rakhat, taking notes on what might be seasonal changes. And he went to the grave of Alan Pace, neatened it, and prayed for a while.

At midmorning, Sofia climbed stiffly out of the lander and walked over. "We should be ready to go in about two hours."

Marc suddenly straightened. It was a mistake and he groaned, but then he asked, "Have you contacted the others yet?"

"Oh, my God! They've probably given us up for dead by now," Sofia cried, appalled. "I meant to raise them last night. It slipped my mind entirely. Oh, Marc, they must be frantic!"

Marc had never before seen her in the least flustered. It humanized her and, for the first time, he decided that he liked her very much. "Sofia," he said, mimicking her own wry tone of the previous night, "next time we are in a plane crash together, I'm sure you will remember to radio in news of our survival. We are, after all, amateurs at this sort of thing. A few mistakes are to be expected."

"I may have been more shaken than I realized." She shook her head. "Come on. Better late than never."

They went to the lander and tried to contact Kashan but got only dead air. "Blackout," Sofia said disgustedly. It was one of those irritating hiatuses in satellite relay coverage. "Four hours before we get a carrier signal back."

"Ah, well, we shall be home soon, like ones arisen from the dead!" Marc said gaily. Then he added conspiratorially, "Perhaps in his surprise, the Father Superior won't notice that we've smashed his little airplane to bits."

Sending Marc back to his plants, Sofia began a rigorous preflight inspection. There were a hundred potential hazards: little green guy nests in the engines, Richard Nixons roosting in the undercarriage, bugger swarms in the electronics boxes. When at last she was as certain as she could be that the lander was safe to fly, she went aft to the cargo bay and called Robichaux over. "I'll be doing a test startup and then I'll take off for a few practice maneuvers. Would you like to come for the ride or have you had enough excitement for the week?"

"I believe I should prefer to spend the time collecting samples."

If it had been Sandoz, she'd have said, No guts. She smiled at Marc. "I'll be back in half an hour."

He helped her fasten down the bay door and then moved well back to the edge of the forest, out of range of the engine blast. When he turned, he could see her through the cockpit window, wincing as she tightened the straps over a body as sore as his own. She looked at him then, and he put his hands together and raised them over his head in a painful good luck gesture. She nodded, and started the ignition countdown.

To an ex-combat pilot like D. W. Yarbrough, the words "missing in action" always brought a hollow-bellied horror. Planes went down and you didn't know where or why. You knew the odds, but you didn't know the truth. And your next move was always awful with finely calculated risk. Did you send others into danger in hope of an unlikely rescue or did you accept the reality of casualties? There was a price, either way.

D.W. was not one to flagellate himself with knotted cords of regret and hindsight. Nevertheless, he wished with all his heart that he had not yielded to the pressure to let Sofia and Marc go. He should have waited and made the flight himself when he felt better.

As the hours dragged by with no word from them, D.W. had only that coldest of comforts: it had seemed like a good idea at the time. His best guess was that they'd crashed at the lander site. They might have survived, might be too hurt to move. It would take more than a week's march through unknown terrain to reach them, dead or alive. There was no good solution to this problem. He knew he wasn't well enough to make the trek on foot himself. Anne would probably be needed, but he hesitated about sending her overland. Emilio was a good medic and tough enough but small. Better to send Jimmy, who was almost as well trained in first aid as Emilio. If Marc or Sofia survived the seven or eight days it would take to reach them, they'd probably live for one more without expert treatment. So, it would have to be Jimmy, who was big, and George, who was tough and had flown the lander successfully on their last trip to the asteroid. He'd have George pilot the survivors straight to the *Stella Maris,* leave Jimmy with them, and refuel. Then George could come back down at Kashan to ferry Anne up. It would eat into their freedom of movement. They'd be down to three flights by then, but there wasn't any other way.

Shit, he thought. If the survivors were badly hurt, they might be worse off in zero G, if either of them took ill with space sickness. D.W. sighed and was about to consult Anne on the vagaries of the business when he heard a surprising roll of thunder. Usually at this point in the storms, all they heard was the steady drumming of rain on the flagstones of the terraces and the muted roar of the river below them, rising and roiling with runoff.

"That's the lander," Emilio said.

Wishful thinking, was D.W.'s first response. Then his heart lurched as he realized Emilio might be right. He stood and went outside, cold to the bone. "My God," he prayed, searching the sky, "not the lander. Please: not the lander." He listened closely and, in an agony of ambivalence, recognized the engine note.

The others surrounded D.W. now, yelling with excitement and joy. He followed them up the slick stone walkways, Jimmy taking the cliff at a lope, George running behind Jim. D.W. listened, dying a little, to a jubilant Emilio shouting, "I told you so" and "Oh, ye of little faith!" at a laughing, relieved Anne, who was saying, "Okay, okay, *Deus vult* already!" as they climbed the stairs ahead of him. Squinting into the downpour, he lagged behind the saturated exuberant parade, not really over his illness and needing time to come to grips with the disaster before he broke the news to the others.

By the time D.W. could see the plane, Jimmy had thrown back the cargo bay door and was lifting Sofia down. Marc climbed out under his own power. Even at this distance, D.W. could see the black eyes and swollen faces and the painful stiffness with which Sofia and Marc moved. Why hadn't they waited? Why hadn't they radioed home for instructions? He could have warned them! Then, hating to blame others, D.W. asked himself why he hadn't anticipated this. He'd reckoned they'd either come straight back if the landing strip was too dangerous, or land safely. Still befuddled and sick, he hadn't considered that Sofia might simply fly back in the lander if the Ultra-Light got wrecked.

Sofia saw him and, leaving the others behind, walked toward him, face shining and wet and discolored with injury she had risen above, after what must have been an awful crash. She is so beautiful, D.W. thought. And it had taken a lot of nerve to do what she had done. Logical girl, Sofia, brave girl: all brains and guts. And George, too. He'd taken such fearless pleasure in the barrel rolls and loops, not realizing how fine they were cutting things. It's not our weaknesses but our strengths that have endangered us, D.W. thought, and he searched for some way to soften the impact for Sofia, for George, for all of them.

"So," said Sofia, smiling widely as she approached, "we have returned like Elijah, in a chariot of fire!"

He held out his arms and she came to him for an embrace but, grimacing at the pressure against her battered body, moved away and began to describe the crash, one pilot to another, talking with the rushing manic emotion of someone who has cheated death. The others gathered around them and listened to the tale as well. Finally, as the rain began to abate and her need to tell him about the adventure subsided, D.W. saw her realize that something was wrong. "What is it?" she asked. "What's the matter?"

He looked at George and then at the daughter he'd never imagined having. There was the barest chance. If she'd held her speed down. If she'd flown straight to Kashan. If the tail wind was strong enough. If God was on their side. "Sofia, it's my fault! It is my responsibility entirely. I should have warned you—"

"What?" she asked, alarmed now. "Warned me about what?"

"Sofia, darlin'," he said gently, when there was no longer any way to put it off, "how much fuel is left?"

It took a moment. Then her hands went to her mouth and she went white beneath the bruises. He held her while she sobbed, loving her as much as any human being he'd ever known. They all understood then. There was no longer any way off Rakhat.

Jimmy recovered first. "Sofia," he said quietly, his voice close to her ear. "Sofia, look at me." She responded to the calmness and lifted her eyes, swollen now with more than bruises. Shuddering and gulping, still huddled in D.W.'s arms, she looked up into clear blue eyes set deep in a face that knew itself homely at best, framed now by comic spirals of wet red hair. "Sofia," Jimmy said, his voice sure and his eyes steady, "we have everything we need, right here. We have everyone we care about, right here. Welcome home, Sofia."

D.W. ceded her to Jimmy then, and sat wearily down in the mud as Sofia, crying now for a different reason, was enfolded by long arms. Around them, the others were coming out of their shock, George reminding Sofia of his part in it, Anne and Emilio already making jokes about being resident aliens and wondering where to apply for green cards, Marc assuring her this must be the way God wanted it.

Lord, D. W. Yarbrough prayed, this is as fine a bunch of tailless primates as Your universe has to offer. I hope You're proud of 'em. I sure as hell am.

Surrounded by plants of dusty blues and purples, listening to his people come to grips and come together, D.W. put his hands out into the mud behind him and leaned back to offer his face to the rain. Maybe Marc's right, he thought. Maybe this is how it's supposed to be.

27

VILLAGE OF KASHAN:
SEVENTH NA'ALPA—FIFTH PARTAN

WHEN THEY GOT inside, out of the rain, Anne swung into action, examining Marc and Sofia and confirming Marc's inexpert assessment of their physical condition, informing D.W. that he looked terrible. George, Emilio and Jimmy helped her get the three semi-invalids dry and warm, fed and put to bed as the light faded. When it was clear that he could be of no more use to Anne, George Edwards took his tablet next door to Aycha's empty apartment. Anne saw him go. When everyone else was taken care of, she went to her husband and knelt on the cushion behind him, reaching out to massage the back of his neck and then to put her arms around his shoulders. George smiled at her as she moved to his side and leaned over to kiss her but went back to his work without comment.

Four and a half decades together had given them a core of certainty about each other, if not about life itself. Theirs was a companionable marriage of competent and self-reliant equals, and they rarely called on each other for aid or ministration. Anne was used to George's response to crisis: don't panic; take it piece by piece; make the best of it. But she also knew that he'd had a favorite Dilbert cartoon pinned over his desk for years: "The goal of every engineer is to retire without getting blamed for a major catastrophe." There was no way around it. What had happened was in large measure his fault.

George's initial concern was that D.W. and Sofia not take the blame for the fact that the lander fuel had been drawn down past the point of return. Sofia's use of fuel had been sensible. George's had been pure stupid self-indulgence: fooling around, showing off to D.W., trying out maneuvers he'd practiced on the simulator and wanted to do in real life, using up a slim margin for error that he hadn't thought about. So George made sure everyone understood that it was he, George, who'd put them in this position, not Sofia. As for D.W. not anticipating what happened and not warning Sofia against it, George pointed out that nobody had thought of it. "We've got a collective IQ here that goes into quadruple digits," he'd told Yarbrough as they walked back down to the apartment, "and none of us, singly or together, anticipated this. Quit beating yourself up."

Engineers don't go to confession when they screw up; they find a fix. So Anne watched George deal with his own fear and guilt by starting an engineer's rosary: a series of calculations involving the lander's weight, drag, lift, thrust, the prevailing winds, their altitude above sea level, the rotational boost they'd get from their latitude on Rakhat, the distance to the *Stella Maris* at its closest approach to their present position. She knew this was his way of apologizing to the others, of begging pardon for his sin.

Jimmy stayed with Sofia until he was certain she was asleep but joined Anne and George a few minutes later. Emilio brought them all coffee and sat quietly at a small remove, opaque and withdrawn, while Jimmy and George considered the variables. How much weight could they save if they stripped every nonessential piece of equipment out of the lander? Used a single pilot? Which one? D.W. was far more experienced but weighed almost twice as much as Sofia. What if they moved the *Stella Maris* into a more favorable orbit? How hard would that be using remote ground control? Could the lander engine be reprogrammed to squeeze more power out of the remaining fuel?

Several hours later, the outcome was as plain as it was predictable: Murphy's Law held on Rakhat. Their best estimates fell into a zone of ambiguity. If the winds were right, if one of the lower estimates of the lander's stripped weight was correct, if Sofia piloted the plane, they'd still have to maneuver the *Stella Maris* into a lower orbit.

"We can talk to D.W. about that when he wakes up, but I don't

think it's a good idea." Jimmy sat back, leaning his head against the wall
and stretching his long legs in front of him. "The asteroid was a pig to
drive. It wouldn't take much error to sink it into the gravity well."

"And then Rakhat gets to play the dinosaur game?" Anne crossed
her arms over her drawn-up knees, where she rested her chin. "No good.
Not worth the risk."

"Dinosaur game?" Emilio asked, breaking his silence for the first
time.

"One of the best guesses about the reason for the extinction of the
dinosaurs was that a good-sized asteroid smashed into Earth," Anne
told him. "Changed the climate, wiped out big hunks of the food chain."

Emilio held up a hand. "Of course. I knew that. I'm sorry, I wasn't
listening closely enough. So if the *Stella Maris* were to hit Rakhat, it
would wreck the planet."

"No. It's not as bad as that," George said. "We scrubbed off a lot of
speed getting into orbit. If the ship came down in the ocean, it wouldn't
do that much damage. Tidal wave maybe, but it wouldn't destroy the
whole ecosystem."

"I don't think it would be ethical to risk even a tidal wave," Emilio
said softly. "Seven of us. Whole populations on the coast."

"I'm not sure we can find a new orbit that would do us much good
anyhow, if we need an ocean splashdown," said Jimmy. "Might be possible, but it would restrict us to a really narrow orbital band."

"Well, boys and girls, I am really sorry but it's about eight to one
odds we're stuck." George wiped his hands over his face and shrugged
as he filed his calculations to show D.W. later. "We can radio home, but
it will take better than four years for them to get the news, another two
or three years to configure a ship, and then seventeen more to get here."
The younger people might see home again. That was something.

"Still, there's some room to maneuver, and things could be a lot
worse," Jimmy said matter-of-factly. He pulled up the supply lists they'd
assembled for George and D.W. to use on the last trip from the asteroid.
"We figured on a year's worth of stuff for the food depot and brought
down all the equipment we thought would be of most use. Marc had
seeds on his list. We can survive on the native foods, but if we can start
a garden that doesn't get washed away in this endless rain, we'll have
our own plants as well. I think we'll do okay."

George suddenly sat up straight. "You know, there's a chance we
could manufacture more fuel for the lander. We're pretty sure the Singers

know chemistry, right?" he said, looking around. "Maybe after we make contact with them, we can work something out."

It was the first notion that offered any real hope. Jimmy and Anne stared at each other and then at George, who looked like a man who'd just gotten a reprieve. He was already back at work, looking for files on the fuel components.

"How long will the Wolverton tube operate without maintenance?" Anne asked George.

He looked up. "It's set up to be self-sustaining, but we'll lose maybe twenty percent of the plants a year, rough estimate. Marc will know better. There's only seven of us now, so there'll be a smaller oxygen demand. If we can make enough fuel to get back up there even once, then Marc or I could go up and optimize things before the rest of you come aboard. And we might be able to use Rakhati plants as replacements, now that I think of it." He felt better at that. They weren't necessarily doomed.

"And in the meantime," Jimmy said, with modest cheer, "we can still use the *Stella Maris* as a resource. We've got the onboard computer systems and radio relays." He looked at Sandoz, who'd said virtually nothing during the discussion.

Emilio was preoccupied, but he'd followed most of the talk if not the calculations it was based on. He shivered suddenly but then seemed to come fully into focus. "It seems to me that the mission is intact. We came here to learn and we can still send back data." The equivocal face smiled but the eyes, for once, did not. "As you say, everything we need and everyone we care for is right here."

"The twigs aren't that bad," Anne said resolutely. "I could get to like the twigs."

"And," George said, "I just might pull a rabbit out of this hat after all."

SOFIA MENDES AWOKE some twelve hours later, thoroughly disoriented. She had been dreaming, for some reason, of Puerto Rico, which she recognized more from the feel of the soft air than from any geographic clue. There was music in the dream and she asked, "Won't someone get in trouble for singing?" But Alan Pace replied, "Not if you bring flowers," which made no sense to her, even inside the dream.

When she opened her eyes, it took several moments to figure out where she was, and then the misery from every joint and muscle reprised for her the story of the two days just past. She lay still, aching worse than she had the morning before in the forest, and began to work out why she'd dreamt of Puerto Rico. Someone was simmering a *sofrito* and she could detect the earthy smell of beans. The music was real, too, on remote from the *Stella Maris* library. The Runa were gone, she remembered, so they could play music again with impunity. She sat up with infinite care and was startled when Jimmy Quinn, sitting nearby, announced: "Sleeping Beauty has awakened!"

D.W. was the first to duck into the apartment and stare at her, open-mouthed. "I never thought I'd see the day but, Mendes, you look like fifteen miles of bad road. How do you feel?"

"Worse," she said. "How's Marc?"

"Bloodied but unbowed," Marc called from the terrace. "And too stiff to come inside and say good morning to you, mademoiselle."

"God, child, I admire your bladder control." Anne came in. "Allow me to escort you to the nearest riverside. Can you walk or would you like me to call the Quinn taxi service to give you a lift?"

Sofia tentatively swung her legs over the side of her low camp bed and waited a few moments for her head to stop spinning. Jimmy stood and leaned down to offer an arm, which she used to pry herself partially out of her sitting position. "I feel like I've been in a plane wreck," she said, astonished by how entirely pulverized it was possible to feel without actually having broken anything. She took a few bent-over steps and moaned and laughed, but regretted it because her chest hurt so much. "This is awful."

George came in. A veteran of many spectacular lost arguments with steadfastly immovable objects like planets, he watched her hobble knowingly and informed her, "The third day is always the worst."

She stopped moving, bent as a crone, and regarded him narrowly. "Does today count as the second or the third day?"

He laughed sympathetically. "You'll find out tomorrow."

She rolled her eyes, the only body part that wasn't sore, and moved slowly out to the terrace using Jimmy's arm as a crutch. Marc's eyes met hers, but he was otherwise completely immobile, his face too bruised even to smile comfortably. "Robichaux, you look dreadful," she said, truly horrified.

"Thank you. So do you."

"George has a new business scheme," Emilio said, straight-faced. "We're going to build cathedrals. We've been able to obtain employment for you and Marc as gargoyles." He held up the coffee pot. "Look, Mendes: reason to live."

"I'm not certain that's sufficient motivation." She looked doubtfully at the long trail down to the river.

Jimmy, whose blue gaze had rested on her unwaveringly all this time, saw the glance. To have held her in his arms once in twenty-four hours was enough for him. Friendship, he told himself, was all he hoped for. "I carried Marc down," he said casually.

"This is true, Mendes," Emilio assured her, his face smiling but his eyes unreadable.

She'd have shrugged but, in view of how she felt standing still, shrugging seemed rash. "All right. You've got a customer, Mr. Quinn." And he lifted her up with no more effort than if she were a child.

OVER THE NEXT few days, they simply rested, each privately engaged in adjusting to the situation, learning to moderate the swings of hope and despond, trying to balance habitual optimism with sensible resignation. Beyond this, they needed to gather themselves for the next phase of their lives on Rakhat. The immensely difficult work they'd done during the past few years and relentless change had taken a toll; they were all closer to the edge of mental and emotional exhaustion than anyone except Emilio had realized. The others had all left their native lands and their native tongues at one time or another and had all coped with cultures other than their own, but they'd worked within the worldwide international culture of science and technology. Only Emilio had been dropped repeatedly into completely unfamiliar ways of life almost without resources beyond his own resilience and intelligence, and he knew how draining it was.

So he was glad of the respite and felt it a gift and thanked God for it. Marc and Sofia slept a great deal. D.W. did as well. Anne was concerned that Yarbrough had picked up some kind of gut parasite. There were cyclic bouts of diarrhea, a general weakness and a troubling lack of appetite. She now had access to broad-spectrum parasitotropics from the lander pharmacy and had begun dosing him, hoping something that killed worms at home would kill whatever was sapping his strength here. She watched the others for symptoms, but so far only D.W. seemed affected.

George was subdued. His anodyne was to work on representing the lander fuel formula graphically, in anticipation of finding someone who might be willing and able to help them once they made contact with the city people. He was feeling worse than he let on, but George had Anne, whose eyes were often on him although she did not fuss over him. George, Emilio thought, would be all right.

Jimmy, of all of them, seemed the most serene, and it was plain why this should be so. He was unobtrusively attentive, alert to Sofia's needs as she recovered but to Marc's as well, Emilio noted. There was an appealing off-handedness and good humor to his courtship, for that was clearly what it was becoming. What Jimmy had said and done since Sofia's return was so well controlled, so generous and full of respect, that Emilio was sure it would be recognized and valued. And the love that underpinned it all, he thought, might one day be returned.

It came to him then that there might be a child, human children on Rakhat. And that, Emilio thought, would be good. For Sofia and Jimmy. For all of them.

And so, in the quiet days that followed the crash, Emilio Sandoz turned inward for a time and probed the sense of mourning that had come over him, tried to understand why he felt so strongly that something inside him was dying.

Like all of them, he'd been badly rocked by the notion that they might never see Earth again. But as the shock wore off, so did the numbing sense of loss. Jimmy was right. Things could have been much worse; they had what they needed. They might yet get back to the *Stella Maris*, and if they didn't, there was still the real possibility of long-term survival here. Not just survival but a good life, full of learning, full of love, Emilio thought, and took a step closer to the death he felt inside himself.

He had, in the months since arriving on Rakhat, experienced a vast ocean of love and had been content to drift on it, not distinguishing degrees of intensity or relative depths of feeling. That he took pleasure in Sofia's company was undeniable, but it was hardly new. He had been, always, scrupulous in his behavior and even in his thoughts. He had concealed his own feelings and mastered them, and mastered them once more when he recognized that she'd fallen in love with him. They had shared work and humor and comradeship, and they had also shared self-restraint. And this increased his regard for Sofia, made it that much harder not to love her as George loved Anne.

Unbidden, the thought came. Rabbis marry. Ministers marry. And he told himself that, yes, if he were a rabbi or a minister, he would love her as a whole man and thank God for her every day. And if he were an Aztec, he thought ruthlessly, he'd cut the hearts from the living breasts of his enemies and offer blood to the sun. And if he were Tibetan, he'd spin prayer wheels. But he was none of those things. He was a Jesuit, and his path was different.

What was dying, he recognized in those quiet hours, was the possibility of himself as a husband and a father. More: as Sofia's husband and the father of her children. He had not truly understood that he'd kept part of his soul open to that possibility until he'd seen Sofia in Jimmy Quinn's arms in the rain and had felt a cold wash of violent jealousy.

This was, he thought, the first time that celibacy would truly rob him of something. Before, he was aware of the clarity, the singleness of purpose, the concentration of energy, the gifts bestowed by the discipline. Now, he was aware in some much deeper way, not of sexual famine, which was familiar, but of the loss of human intimacy, the sacrifice of human closeness. He felt with an almost physical pain what it would mean to renounce his last opportunity to love Sofia, what it would mean to free her to love Jimmy, who would surely cherish her as dearly as Emilio might have himself. For he was honest with himself: before Sofia turned to another, she would look to him for some sign. If he made any move to encourage her love of him, he had to be prepared to meet it wholly. He knew D.W. and Marc would accept it, that George and Anne would rejoice in it. Even Jimmy, he thought, might take it with good grace . . .

So here it was. A time to ratify or to repudiate a vow made in youth and ignorance, to be lived out in maturity and in full understanding. A time to weigh the extraordinary and spiritual and fathomless beauty that God had shown him against the ordinary and worldly and incalculable sweetness of human love and family. A moment to consider if he would trade everything he had hoped for and had been given as a priest for everything he yearned for and desired as a man.

He did not flinch from the knife. He cut the thread cleanly, a priest in perpetuity. God had been generous with him. He could not stint in return. It did not occur to him to wonder then if Sofia Mendes had been as much a gift from God as all the rest of the love he'd been offered, or if he had been God's gift to her. Two thousand years of theology spoke, five hundred years of Jesuit tradition spoke, his own life to that moment spoke.

God was silent on the matter.

Later that day, Sofia met his eyes as he watched her accept a cup of coffee and a sandwich from Jimmy, who made a comic display of his knightly service. Emilio saw Sofia read him and then look to Jim: already a dear friend, steady and good and strong and patient. He saw her pause and consider, and he felt at that moment like a woman giving a child to adoptive parents—certain it was the right thing, best for the beloved child, good for all. But the grief was real.

HAVING MADE HIS decision, he bided his time, waiting for the right moment for his next move. It came during the quiet of midmorning a week or so later when Marc and Sofia, bruises fading to yellow and green, were moving with notably less lamentation, D.W.'s color was better and George had pulled out of his gloom. Everyone seemed rested.

"I have been considering my present situation," Emilio Sandoz announced. They all looked at him curiously, surprised that he should make such a personal statement. Only Anne caught the tone, and she was already half-smiling, waiting for the punchline. "I have decided that I am happier than I have ever been in my life. And yet," he assured them with great and solemn sincerity, "I would crawl over your dead, burnt bodies if it meant getting to absolutely anything deep-fried."

"*Bacalaitos fritos,*" Jimmy said. Emilio moaned in agreement.

"Beignets with powdered sugar," Marc said wistfully.

"French fries," George sighed.

"Cheese puffs," Anne said with conviction. "I really miss orange food coloring."

"Chicken-fried steak," D.W. said. And added, "Hell. Steak, period."

Sofia stood, creaking a little, and started toward the terrace.

"Mendes, where you goin'?" D.W. called.

"To the grocery store."

D.W. looked at Sofia as though she'd just revealed a second head. But Anne joined her. "To the world's most astoundingly high-tech pantry," Anne explained inexplicably before spelling it out. "To the *lander,* D.W.! To get ready for the party."

Sandoz clapped once, delighted to be understood, and at that the men jumped up to join Anne and Sofia, all except Marc, who simply got up, but with enthusiasm. It was, in fact, exactly what the doctor would have ordered, except Emilio thought of it first. What he needed, what they all needed, he decided, was a feeling of expansiveness, a jolt of freedom to counter the sense of being boxed in, of having options closed down.

They trooped up the cliffside and paraded to the lander, which was filled with food from home, arguing spiritedly about menus until they finally agreed along the way that everyone should just dig in and find some soul food. And as they chattered, it became obvious that meat was on everyone's mind, not just D.W.'s. With the Runa away, they could crank up the music and dance and eat meat, by God, and everyone was ready for that. The Runa were vegetarians, and there was a great outcry the first and only time the humans opened a vacuumpak containing beef; the apartment they'd used was declared off-limits in a way they did not understand and abandoned, whether permanently or temporarily they did not know. So the Jesuit party had been vegetarian as well all these weeks, and they'd eaten mostly fish on the *Stella Maris.*

Striding toward the lander, pleased to see that D.W. was also moving with some of his old energy, Emilio remembered seeing the rifle and suggested suddenly that D.W. take a shot at a *piyanot,* an idea that met with cries of approbation, except from Sofia, who surprised them all by mentioning that Jews don't eat game, but that she could find something in the lander stores. They came to a halt and looked at her.

"Hunting isn't kosher," she told them. No one had heard of this before. She waved off her initial objection. "I don't keep kosher, as you know," she told them, a little embarrassed. "I still found it impossible to eat pork or shellfish, and I've never eaten game. But if you can kill the animal cleanly, I suppose it doesn't matter."

"Darlin', if a clean kill is all you need, I shall be happy to oblige," D.W. said as they reached the lander. He flung open the cargo-bay door, feeling his oats, and fetched out the rifle, a sweet old Winchester his grandfather had taught him to use and which he had brought along partly from sentiment. D.W. checked it over thoroughly, loaded it, and then walked a little way out toward one of the *piyanot* herds that grazed on the plain above the river. Sitting down, he used his own knobby knee as a tripod. Anne watched him sight down the gun, still curious as to how he managed not to be confused by the skewed images his eyes must be taking in, but he dropped a young *piyanot* like a stone at three hundred yards, the report of the gunshot echoing off the hills to the north.

"Wow," George said.

"That's clean enough for me," Sofia said, impressed.

D.W., who was made to endure the title Mighty Hunter for some hours, sauntered off to butcher the carcass with Anne, who later declared the activity to have been an interesting exercise in field anatomy, while the others set up for a barbecue. By early afternoon, they were as happy and relaxed as a prehistoric band of Olduwan hunters, full of unaccustomed and highly desirable protein and fat, feeling well and truly fed for the first time in months. They were savannah creatures, deep in their genes, and the flat grassland with widespread trees felt right in some vague way. The plants of this plain were now familiar, and they knew a number of them that could sustain life. The coronaries only made them laugh, the snakenecks' bites were known to be simply painful and not poisonous to them, although there was unquestionably a venom that killed the little animals' prey. The land around them was beginning to feel like home, in emotion as well as in hard fact, and they were no longer unnerved by their exposure.

Rakhat, therefore, seemed a known quantity to them and when, one by one, they noticed a stranger striding toward them intently, they were only a little surprised, thinking that a barge trader had stopped for blossoms and did not know that the VaKashani were all out digging *pik* root somewhere. And they were not concerned, of course, because the Runa were as harmless as deer.

Later, D. W. Yarbrough would recall how Alan Pace had given such a great deal of thought to the music he would first present to the Singers to represent human culture. The subtle mathematical joys of a Bach cantata, the thrilling harmonies of the sextet from *Lucia di Lammermoor,* the quiet evocative beauties of Saint-Saens, the majesty of a Beethoven symphony, the inspired perfection of a Mozart quartet—all these had been considered. There was an unintentional remembrance of Alan Pace, in the event. George, who'd shared much of Alan's eclectic taste, had picked out the music that was playing over the lander's sound system as Supaari VaGayjur approached them. And while Alan would not have selected this particular piece to introduce human music to Rakhat, what Supaari heard was in fact something Alan Pace had reveled in: the rhythmic power, soaring vocals and instrumental virtuosity, not of Beethoven's *Ninth,* but of Van Halen's arena rock masterpiece, *5150.* The cut, Anne would remember afterward, was appropriate. The song playing was "Best of Both Worlds."

Emilio had his back to the newcomer and, absorbed in shouting along with the chorus, he was the last to realize, from the trajectory of the others' now frightened gazes, that something large and threatening was just above him. He half-rose and turned just in time to see the attack coming.

The blow, had it been aimed at any of the others, would have been either disfiguring or lethal, but Emilio Sandoz had known from earliest childhood the look of someone who wanted to obliterate him, to make him simply cease to be. Without thinking, he dropped under the sweep of the heavy arm, which passed harmlessly over his head, and using all the power in his legs, drove his shoulder upward into the belly, knowing from the explosive grunt above him that he'd emptied the lungs of air. He followed the body as it came crashing down, pinning the arms with his knees, and took up a position with his forearm like an iron bar over the newcomer's throat. Emilio's eyes made the threat plain even to someone who had never before seen such eyes: he could, if he shifted his position a fraction, use his weight to crush the fragile windpipe, and make the present airlessness permanent.

There was a sudden silence—Anne had made a dash for the lander and turned the music off, to decrease the noise and craziness of the situation—and then Emilio heard the metallic click of the Winchester being cocked but he kept his eyes on the person he was choking. "I stopped taking crap like that when I was fourteen," he said quietly in Spanish, for his own satisfaction. He continued in the soft lilt of Ruanja, "Someone regrets your discomfort. Even so, harm is not permitted. If someone lets you up, will your heart be quiet?"

There was a slight movement upward of the chin, body language indicating assent or agreement. Slowly, Emilio eased back, watching for any sign that the stranger would take advantage of size and strength and attack again. Once somebody this size had a grip on him, Emilio knew from painful experience, he would have his own ass handed to him unceremoniously, and so his strategy from earliest adolescence had been to fight quick and fight dirty, to take the other guy out before he knew what hit him. He hadn't had much practice lately, but the skills were still there.

For his part, Supaari VaGayjur, speechless with shock, eyes watering and breath coming back raggedly, simply stared at the . . . *thing* crouching over him. Finally, when he collected enough breath and nerve to speak, Supaari asked, "What *are* you?"

"Foreigners," the monster said peaceably, moving off Supaari's chest.

"That," Supaari said, rubbing his throat judiciously, "must be the understatement of all time." To his utter astonishment, the monster laughed.

"This is true," it said, lips pulling back from white and strangely even teeth. "May someone offer you coffee?"

"*Kafay!* The very thing one came to inquire after," Supaari said with almost equal amiability, recovering a shard of his urbanity from the shambles surprise and horror had made of it.

The impossible being stood and offered him a bizarre hand, evidently meaning to help him up. Supaari extended his own hand. There was a momentary pause and the foreigner's half-bare face changed color abruptly in a way Supaari had no words to describe but before he could analyze that, his attention was swept away by the realization that the monster had no tail. He was so startled by the alarming precariousness of an unassisted two-legged stance that Supaari was hardly aware of it when the being grasped his wrist with a fairly strong two-handed grip and helped him to his feet. And then he was freshly amazed, this time by the monster's size, which made its demonstrated ability to render a fully grown male Jana'ata helpless all the more confounding.

He had no way of knowing that the monster, neck craned upward, was at that moment equally dumbfounded by the same occurrence. In fact, Emilio Sandoz had almost passed out cold for the second time in his life, having just gotten a look at the three-inch-long claws that would have sliced through his neck like butter if he'd hesitated even a moment before ducking.

Supaari, meantime, was trying desperately to adjust to a far deeper shock than Emilio Sandoz was dealing with. Sandoz, at least, had traveled to Rakhat expecting to meet aliens. Supaari VaGayjur had traveled to Kashan simply to meet a new trade delegation and he'd assumed that the foreigners and their *kafay* were from some unexplored region of the forest far south of Kashan.

Disembarking at the Kashan dock, Supaari had not been surprised to see the village deserted, having been told by Chaypas of the *pik* harvest. He instantly detected the odor of roasting meat mixed with a confusing welter of dimming burnt hydrocarbons and stronger short-chain carbons and amines; the meat told him that the traders were Jana'ata, but the other scents were very peculiar.

He was not a man to tolerate poaching, although he was prepared to be reconciled if the traders offered compensation. Then, hitting the top of the gorge at a run, he stumbled at the sight of a huge piece of entirely inexplicable machinery squatting on the plain, half a *cha'ar* inland from the gorge and, tasting the wind more clearly, realized that this was the source of the hydrocarbon stink. The unfamiliar sweat was issuing from a circle of individuals sitting near the equipment. At that point, striding toward them, many emotions were working on him: lingering anger over the idea of poaching, disgust at the ugly odors and the abominable noise of the machinery, fatigue from the long unaccompanied trip, jumpiness at the strangeness of the scene in front of him, a desire to control himself because of the immense potential gain if he established himself as purveyor to the Reshtar of Galatna, and finally a stunned fascination as he drew close enough to see that these were not Jana'ata or Runa or anything else he could identify.

Supaari's overpowering urge to attack was fundamental. As a human being might react to the sudden appearance in a campsite of a scorpion or a rattlesnake, he wanted not just to kill the threat but to destroy it, to reduce it to molecules. And, in this state of mind, Supaari had tried unsuccessfully to decapitate Emilio Sandoz.

Sofia Mendes broke the impasse. Taking Emilio's stunned immobility for an inspiring calm, she brought their visitor the cup of coffee Emilio had offered. "Most Runa prefer only to inhale," she said, holding the cup up to him almost at her arms' length. "Perhaps you will try drinking some, as we do," she suggested, in deference to his undoubted differences from the Runa.

Supaari looked down at this new sprite, this speck that could not possibly be real and that had just spoken to him in very decent Ruanja. Its face and neck were bare, but it had a mane of black hair. The ribbons! he thought, remembering Chaypas's new style. "Someone thanks you," he said at last. He brushed the dust and ground litter from his gown and then accepted the cup, holding it at its rim and bottom between his first and third claw, the central claw counterbalancing it gracefully, and tried to ignore the fact that he was being invited to ingest an infusion of something like forty thousand *bahli* worth of *kafay*.

"It's hot," the tiny particle warned him. "And bitter."

Supaari took a sip. His nose wrinkled, but he said, "The scent is very agreeable."

Tactful, Anne thought, taking in the carnassial teeth and claws. Jesus H. Christ, she thought, a tactful carnivore! But Sofia's gesture pulled her out of her own shock. "Please, our hearts will be glad if you will

share our meal," Anne said, using the Ruanja formula they were all familiar with. I can't believe this is happening, she thought. I'm doing Miss
Manners with a tactful alien carnivore who just tried to cut Emilio in
half.

Supaari turned to this next apparition and saw another barefaced
wonder, its white mane plaited with ribbons. Not responding to Anne's
invitation, he looked around him for the first time and, finding Jimmy
Quinn, he asked incredulously, "Are all these your children?"

"No," Jimmy said. "This one is the youngest."

The Runa had consistently taken this truth as evidence of Jimmy's
wonderful sense of humor. Supaari accepted it. This, as much as his terrifying claws and dentition, told them all that they were dealing with an
entirely different species.

Supaari looked to the others. "Who then is the Elder?"

Emilio cleared his throat, as much to reassure himself that he could
make a sound as to draw Supaari's attention. He turned and indicated
D. W. Yarbrough.

D.W., heart hammering, had not moved or spoken since he'd made
a dive for the Winchester and, priest or not, prepared to blow the alien
bastard in front of him straight to hell. He had thought that he would
see Emilio's severed head fall at his feet and he doubted that he'd ever
forget that moment or the flood of blind rage that would have ended Supaari's life if Emilio hadn't taken care of the situation himself with such
dispatch. "This one is the Elder," D.W. heard Emilio say, "though not
the oldest. His decisions are for all of us."

Supaari saw only a middle-sized monster holding a rod that smelled
of carbon steel, sulfur and lead. With no intermediary to speak his
names, Supaari took the initiative and briefly moved his hands to his
forehead. "This one is called Supaari, third-born, of the Gaha'ana lineage, whose landname is VaGayjur." He waited, ears cocked expectantly
toward Sandoz.

Emilio realized that, as the interpreter, he was supposed to introduce Yarbrough. Winging it, he said, "The Elder is called Dee, first-born,
of the Yarbrough lineage, whose landname is VaWaco."

A warrior, Supaari assumed, quite rightly but for the wrong reasons. Since their common language was Ruanja, he held out both hands,
not knowing what else to do. "*Challalla khaeri,* Dee."

Yarbrough handed his rifle to George with a look that said, Use it if
necessary. Then he stepped forward and laid his fingers in the cupped

hollows of Supaari's long upturned claws. "*Challalla khaeri,* Supaari,"
he said, squinty-eyed, with a pronounced Texas accent and an attitude
that clearly implied the unsaid, You goddamned sonofabitch.

Anne was tempted to laugh out loud but she didn't; forty-five years
of dinner parties will out. Instead she stepped up to their guest and
greeted him in the Runa manner without another thought. When their
hands parted, she said, "*Sipaj,* Supaari! Surely you are hungry from your
journey. Will you not eat with us now?"

He did. All in all, it was quite a day.

28

NAPLES:
AUGUST 2060

Relying on vague directions from the porter and dead reckoning, John Candotti worked his way into the bowels of the retreat house to a dimly lit cellar that had been converted to a modern laundry facility in the 1930s, updated almost a hundred years later and never again since. The Society of Jesus, John noted, was willing to commit to interstellar travel on less than two weeks' notice, but it did not rush into things like new laundry equipment. The ultrasonic washers were antiques now but still functional. In sunny weather, the wet wash was still line-dried. The whole setup reminded John of his grandmother's basement except, of course, she'd used a microwave dryer, rain or shine.

He had almost walked past the room when, listening more closely, he realized that he'd just heard Emilio Sandoz humming. Actually, he hadn't been sure it was Sandoz, since John had never before heard Emilio make any sound remotely like humming. But there he was, unshaven and comfortable-looking in somebody else's old clothes, pulling damp bed linen out of one of the washers and piling it into a rattan basket that was probably older than the Vatican.

John cleared his throat. Emilio turned at the sound and looked stern. "I hope you don't expect to walk into my office and see me without an appointment, young man."

John grinned and looked around. "Brother Edward said they'd put you to work down here. Very nice. Kind of Bauhaus."

"Form follows function. Dirty laundry requires this sort of ambience." Emilio held up a wet pillowcase. "Prepare to be dazzled." He managed to fold it remarkably well before tossing it onto the pile in the basket.

"So those are the new braces!" John cried. The hearings had been canceled for a few weeks while Sandoz worked with Paola Marino, the Milanese bioengineer whom the Father General had brought in when Father Singh couldn't correct the defects in the original braces. Sandoz was reluctant to be seen by anyone new, but Giuliani insisted. Things had evidently gone well. "I am dazzled. That's wonderful."

"Yes. I am very flashy with towels as well, but there are limits." Emilio turned back to the machines. "Socks, for example. You guys send them down inside out, they go back upstairs clean but in the same condition."

"Hey, my dad had the same rule at home." John watched Sandoz work. His grip wasn't perfect and he still had to pay close attention to the movement, but the improvement was remarkable. "Those are really good, aren't they."

"They're much easier to control. Lighter. Look: the bruises are clearing up." Emilio turned and held out his arms for John's inspection. The new braces were radically different, less a cage than a set of wrist splints with electronic pickups. The fingers were supported from below with flat bands, jointed but lying close to his hands. There were finer bands that crossed over the top of the phalanges and a set of three flat straps that held the splints to his metacarpals, wrists and forearms. John tried not to notice how atrophied the muscles were and concentrated on the machinery as Sandoz explained the mechanisms.

"My hands and arms ache, but I think it's because I'm using them more," Emilio said, straightening. "Here's the best part. Watch this."

Sandoz went to a big table meant for sorting and folding the laundry and bent to lay one forearm flat against it. He rocked the arm a little to the outside to activate a small switch and the brace popped open, hinged on the side opposite the thumb. He pulled his hand out and then managed to get it back into position without assistance, although it took a certain amount of frowning effort before he toggled the switch again and the brace reclosed.

"I can do it all by myself," Emilio said with a three-year-old's lisp. He added in his own voice, "You cannot imagine what a difference that makes."

John beamed, pleased to see how happy the man seemed. Everyone had underestimated how depressing the *hasta'akala* had been, he guessed, probably even Sandoz himself. For the first time since being maimed, Emilio was finding new things he could do, instead of new things that were beyond him. As if reading John's mind, Sandoz turned and, with a cocky grin, bent to lift the basket and stood there waiting for comment.

"Very impressive," John said. Sandoz lugged the basket to the screened door, which he pushed open with his back. John followed him out to the clothesline. "That's got to be what? Seven or eight kilos, huh?"

"Better microgearing," Emilio told him and began hanging out the wash. It was slow going. He did okay, but the clothespins were apt to pop sideways out of his grip. "Miss Marino may need to add some friction pads on the thumb and forefinger," he said a little irritably the fourth time it happened.

This was the same man who'd put up with the old braces for months without complaint! It was nice to hear him ease up. There's nothing wrong with this guy that a little honest bitching wouldn't cure, John thought. It was a cheerful oversimplification, he knew, but it was just such a pleasure to see Sandoz do well. "This is going to sound dumb," John warned him, "but those're actually very good looking."

"Italian design," Emilio said admiringly. He held one hand out in front of himself, like a bride gazing at her new ring, and said in an airy English accent, " 'Next year, everyone will be wearing them.' "

"Princess Bride!" John cried, identifying the quote immediately.

" 'Ah, I see you're using Bonetti's defense against me,' " said Emilio, this time in a bad Spanish accent.

" 'Never go up against a Sicilian when death is on the line!' " John declared, sitting on the low stone wall that bordered the side yard. They traded lines from the movie for a while, until John leaned back, locking his hands around one knee, and said, "This is great, man. I never thought I'd see you doing so well."

Emilio stopped moving, sheet in hand, realizing with some shock

that he was enjoying himself. It brought him up short. He hardly knew
what to do with the sensation. There was an almost automatic response:
an impulse to turn to God in gratitude. He fought it down, clinging stubbornly to the facts: he was doing laundry and riffing on *Princess Bride*
with John Candotti and he was enjoying himself. That was all. Paola
Marino was responsible, not God. And he had helped himself. When he'd
realized what an improvement the new braces were, he'd asked to be assigned to the laundry. He needed to work at something, and this would
be good mild exercise, he argued, natural therapy for his hands. He ate
and slept better for it, got through the nights easier. And he was getting
stronger. Sure, he had to stop every now and then, a little winded by the
repetitive stooping and reaching overhead, but he was gaining on it—

John left his perch on the stones, disturbed as always by these sudden motionless trances. "Here. I'll help you with this," he said genially,
to break the silence, and picked up one of the sheets.

"*No!*"

John dropped the sheet and backed away.

Sandoz stood there a few moments, breathing hard. "Look. I'm
sorry," he said. "I was startled, okay? I didn't expect you to be standing
so close. And I don't want help! People keep trying to help! I'm sorry,
but I *hate* it. If you would just do me the courtesy of letting me
judge—" He turned away, exasperated and close to tears. Finally, he repeated more quietly, "I'm sorry. You put up with a lot of shit from me. I
get confused, John. A lot of things get mixed up in this."

Embarrassed and ashamed of the outburst, Emilio turned and bent
to the laundry basket, going back to work. After a few minutes, he said
over his shoulder, "Don't just stand there gawking. Give me a hand with
this, will you?"

Eyes wide, John shook his head and blew out a breath, but he
picked up a pillowcase and hung it on the line.

They finished that basketful in silence and went back into the basement gloom for another load of wash. Setting the basket down, Emilio
waited until John joined him and then heaved a sigh, looking at the
braces once again. "Yes, these are a great improvement but I still can't
play the violin . . ."

John was halfway through a sympathetic murmur when Emilio's
grin stopped him. "Shit," John laughed, and the tension between them
evaporated. "I can't believe I fell for that. You never played the violin,
right?"

"Baseball, John. All I ever played was baseball." Emilio opened another washer and started dropping towels into the basket, feeling that he was back on top of things again. "Probably too old and beaten up to get around a diamond now anyway. But I had good hands once."

"What position did you play?" John asked.

"Second base, usually. Not enough arm to play outfield. I was pretty consistent at bat, mostly singles and doubles. I wasn't that good but I loved it."

"The Father General claims he's still got a bruise where you took his ankle out sliding in to steal third once. He says you were savage."

"This is slander!" Emilio cried. Indignant, he pushed his way out the door again and carried the basket to the line. "Serious, yes. Barbaric, quite possibly. But savage? Only if the score was close."

They worked their way through the basket together, listening to the late morning sounds, pots and pans banging in the kitchen nearby as Brother Cosimo started on lunch, and now the silence was companionable. "You follow baseball, John?" Emilio asked after a while, his voice coming through the rows of wet fabric.

"Cubs fan," John muttered. The Chicagoan's curse.

Sandoz pushed a towel aside, eyes wide. "How bad?"

"Anybody can have a couple of lousy centuries."

"I guess. Wow." Sandoz let the towel fall back into place. There was a thoughtful silence. "Well, that explains why Giuliani brought *you* over." Suddenly John heard the Father General's voice saying: "Voelker, I need someone to take care of a hopeless wreck coming back from Rakhat. Get me a Cubs fan!"

"You're not hopeless, Emilio."

"John, I could tell you things about hopeless that even a Cubs fan wouldn't understand."

"Try me."

When Sandoz spoke next from the other side of the laundry, it was to change the subject. "So. How's San Juan doing this year?"

"Three games out of first. They took the Series in '58," John said, pleased to be delivering good news. Emilio reappeared, smiling beatifically, nodded a couple of times and returned to his work, a contented man. John paused in his progress down the clothesline and looked at Sandoz through a gap in the sheets. "Do you know that this is the first time you've asked about current events? Listen, this has been driving me crazy! I mean, you've been gone since before I was born! Don't you wonder how things turned out? What wars are over and who won and stuff like that? Technological revolutions, medical advances? Aren't you even *curious*?"

Sandoz stared at him, open-mouthed. Finally, he dropped a towel into the basket and backed up a few steps to the stone wall, where he sat down, suddenly exhausted. He laughed a little and shook his head before looking up at John through the veil of black and silver hair that fell over his eyes. "My dear Father Candotti," he said wearily, "allow me to explain something. In the past fifteen years or so, I must have lived in what? Thirty different places? Four continents, two islands. Two planets! An asteroid! Seven or eight ecosystems, from desert to tundra. Dormitories, huts, caves, tents, shacks, *hampiys* . . . I have been required to function in over a dozen foreign languages, often three at a time. I have contended with thousands of strangers, in cultures involving three sentient species and perhaps twenty nationalities. I am sorry to disappoint you, but my capacity for curiosity is tapped out." Emilio sighed and put his head in his hands, careful not to tangle the joint mechanisms in his hair. "John, if I had my way, nothing new or interesting would happen to me ever again as long as I live. Laundry is just about my speed. No quick movements, no sudden noises, no intellectual demands."

"And no damned questions?" John suggested ruefully, sitting next to Sandoz on the wall.

"No damned questions," Emilio confirmed. He looked up, eyes on the rocky hills to the east. "And very little potential for death, destruction and degradation, my friend. I've had a couple of rough years."

It no longer came as a surprise to John Candotti that people found him easy to confess to. He was tolerant of human failings and it was rarely difficult for him to say, "Well, you screwed up. Everybody screws up. It's okay." His greatest satisfaction as a priest was to grant absolution, to help people forgive themselves for not being perfect, make amends, and get on with life. This might be the opening, he thought. "Want to tell me about it?"

Sandoz stood and went back to his basket of towels. When it was empty he turned and saw that Candotti was still sitting there. "I can finish this myself," he said curtly and disappeared back into the basement.

VINCENZO GIULIANI WAS not idle during this time, nor did the Rakhat inquiry come to a halt. The Father General used the hiatus to rethink his strategies. The situation required a different tack and more sail, he decided, and called a meeting with Candotti, Behr, Reyes and Voelker. They were charged with two tasks during these hearings, he told them. One was institutional: to gather information about the mission itself and about Rakhat and its inhabitants. But the other was pastoral. A fellow priest had been through an extraordinary experience and needed help, whether he was willing to admit that or not.

"Upon much reflection," the Father General told them, "I have decided to release to you transcripts of the mission reports by Yarbrough and Robichaux, as well as certain private communications from them." He gave them the passwords necessary to unlock the files. "I am sure I don't have to tell you that this information is confidential. You will find as you read that Emilio has been entirely forthcoming about the mission facts. I believe he means to cooperate fully with us in our first task. He will tell us what happened on Rakhat as long as it does not touch on his personal state of mind, past or present. Which brings us to our second task."

Giuliani rose. "It has become clear to me that there is some private theological aspect to Emilio's emotional problems. I am, personally, convinced of the sincerity of his spiritual engagement at the beginning of the mission." Giuliani stopped pacing and came to rest directly across the table from Johannes Voelker. "I do not ask you to be credulous as you read the mission reports, but I ask you to accept as a working hypothesis the accuracy of the statements of his superiors on this subject." Voelker nodded noncommittally and Giuliani resumed his circuit of the room, coming to a halt by the windows. He pushed the gauzy curtain back and looked outside. "Something happened to him. It changed everything. Until we know what that was, we are sailing in the dark."

As the days went on, Giuliani observed and responded to the sea change in Sandoz himself. The man's general health began to improve again, due to some lifting of the depression and to a set of newly implanted semipermeable rods that released steady doses of vitamins C and D as well as calcitonin derivatives and osteoclast inhibitors, directly into his bloodstream. The fatigue gradually lessened, although it was unclear if this was because he felt better and got more exercise or because his physiological status was becoming more normal. Certainly, he bruised less easily. The probability of spontaneous bone breakage began to recede.

On Brother Edward's advice, Sandoz was given direct access to the drugs he used regularly: Prograine and dHE compounds for muscle

aches, which were now more often from overuse, as he reclaimed
ground, than from the lingering effects of scurvy. Edward felt Sandoz
would use the medication responsibly and would feel freer to obtain relief if he didn't have to ask anyone's permission.

Then Sandoz asked about sleeping tablets. The Father General had
decided to acquiesce to any reasonable request, but Emilio had mentioned suicide on several occasions and Giuliani could not risk being
wrong on this. So he offered a compromise, which Sandoz refused: that
he'd be allowed to use the drugs if someone witnessed him swallowing
the pills. It was hard to know whether Emilio considered this too humiliating to be borne or only unacceptable because he'd hoped to stockpile
the drugs against a future decision to take his own life.

In any case, Sandoz no longer permitted anyone into his room. He
found and removed the monitor near his bed. The dreams and their se-
quelae were his own to manage in privacy. Maybe the sickness had
stopped or maybe he had schooled himself to control even that, as he
now controlled his hands and face and voice, and vomited in silence,
sweating out the nights alone. The only indication that the dreams continued was the hour at which he rose in the morning. If things had gone
well, he was up at dawn. If not, it might be ten o'clock before he
appeared in the refectory for a small breakfast, which he now insisted
on making himself. Brother Cosimo did not offer help after the first
morning.

Felipe Reyes inquired about phantom limb syndrome and Sandoz
stiffly admitted to this and asked if Reyes dealt with this kind of neural-
gia himself. Felipe was fortunate not to, but he knew other amputees
who did and he was aware of how bad it could be. For some, Felipe told
Sandoz, the pain was unrelenting. This information clearly appalled
Emilio, which gave Felipe a measure of the severity of the intermittent
problem for Sandoz. Reyes suggested that Emilio simply call a halt to the
hearings if he was in distress. A few days later Sandoz asked for and received assurance from the Father General that he could end the sessions
at will, without stating any reason. It was, Emilio had evidently decided,
preferable to continuing while distracted and taking a chance on the
kind of breakdown he'd experienced on the day he broke the cup.

In private, Johannes Voelker was given to understand by the Father
General that Sandoz was never again to be accused of malingering.
Voelker agreed and admitted that it was not a productive attitude. The

others were told as well: when Sandoz balked, no one was to press him.
Even gentle handling like John Candotti's drove the man further away.

WHEN THE HEARINGS reconvened after this hiatus, there was
no mistaking the change. They noticed the outward sign first. Sandoz
was able to control a razor better now. The neatly trimmed beard was
back, still black in the main, but with unfamiliar stripes of gray bracket-
ing the long line of the mouth, just as the dark and now uninformative
eyes had come to be bordered by streaks of silver in his hair.

They now saw, for the most part, whomever Sandoz wished them to
see. Sometimes they were dealing with a Spaniard, invulnerable and aristocratic, a man who had rebuilt the castle walls and found some bastion
from which to defend his integrity, and whose composure could not be
disturbed by pointed questions about beloved children, now dead. Or
Mephistopheles, dry-eyed and contained, to whom the lower depths of
hell were known and familiar and drained of swampy emotion. Most often, it was Dr. Emilio Sandoz, linguist, scholar, a man of wide experience, attending a dreary colloquium that had some bearing on his
specialty, after which his work and that of his colleagues might be published at last.

The sessions under this new regime got started with a question from
Professor Reyes, comparative theologian, regarding the likelihood that
the Runa had some concept of the soul. Dr. Sandoz, linguist, was on
home ground and cited the Runa's grammatical categories for reference
to things unseen and nonvisual. Reyes thought this might indicate at
least the capacity to understand the concept of soul, even if they had not
developed it themselves.

"Quite likely," Sandoz agreed. "In comparison to the Jana'ata or to
our own species, the Runa are not notably creative thinkers. Or perhaps
I should say, not original. Once a basic idea has been provided, they are
often quite creative in elaborating on it."

"It seems to me that this idea of 'heart' that keeps coming up might
be analogous to soul," Felipe said.

"Understand that 'heart' is my translation, yes? It might be close to
the concept of soul within a living person, but I don't know if the Runa
believe the essence of an individual persists beyond death—" He
stopped. His body tensed, as though ready to stand, but then the

Spaniard spoke. "When deaths occurred, I was not in a position to inquire about the Runa belief system." And Dr. Sandoz resumed a moment
later, turning to Giuliani. "Anne Edwards sent back several papers on
the subject of 'heart.' May I summarize her observations, sir? Or does
that constitute a form of premature publication?"

"Nothing said in this room is for publication. Please."

Sandoz turned back to Felipe. "Dr. Edwards believed that the concept of 'heart' and the Runa's theory of illness were closely related and
both served as a rather benign means of social control. The Runa are not
openly aggressive and claim never to become angry. If, for example,
someone was refused a legitimate request or was thwarted or disappointed in some way, the aggrieved person would fall into a state of *porai*. When you are *porai*, your heart is sad and you may grow ill or
become prone to accidents. Making someone sad is very bad form, yes?
If you make someone else *porai*, you feel considerable social pressure to
give in to the request or provide compensation to the supposed victim:
apologize or make some gift that restores the victim's heart to happiness."

"There would be a good deal of room for misuse of a concept like
that," Voelker commented. "What prevents people from claiming they
are *porai* simply to obtain presents?"

"The Runa are almost never alone. Hardly any social interaction is
without witnesses, so it is hard for someone simply to lie about an occurrence. However, there was often disagreement about the seriousness
of the victim's state of *porai* and about the amount or kind of compensation due. If the argument got loud, the participants were told that they
were making a *fierno*—a big noise, yes? If you make a *fierno*, it suppos-
edly attracts thunderstorms, which can be violent and frightening."

He paused for a sip of water, handling the glass with remarkably
improved dexterity, although he had to stop speaking and concentrate
on the task. He lifted the glass toward John, as though toasting him.
"New friction pads," he pointed out. John nodded appreciatively and
Emilio continued. "Parents use thunderstorms as mild threats to teach
children not to argue or make fusses to get their way. 'Make your heart
quiet, or we'll have a thunderstorm soon.' The storms are frequent. It is
easy for children to believe there is some connection between their noise
and bad weather."

"What if there's a storm when no one's been arguing?" John asked.
Emilio shrugged and made a face that said, This is obvious, surely.

"Someone in a nearby village has made a *fierno*." And they smiled at the neatness of the thing.

"Prior to the appearance of Supaari VaGayjur, did you have any idea that there existed a second sentient species on Rakhat?" Johannes Voelker asked.

It seemed like an abrupt change in topic and the Spaniard turned to him, clearly expecting and prepared to meet an attack. "No." But then he admitted, "There were indications that we failed to recognize. The Runa have ten fingers, but the numbering system was based on six, for example. Which made sense to us once we found out that the Jana'ata hand has only three digits. And from the beginning, Mr. Edwards and Mr. Quinn noted a mismatch between the Runa culture we observed in Kashan and the culture that produced the radio signals that led us to Rakhat."

The Austrian was surprisingly conciliatory. "Yes. As I recall, Father Robichaux attributed the anomaly to cultural differences in economic and technical development," Voelker said. "It occurs to me—this peculiarity of the Runa language, by which things unseen at the moment are grammatically the same as those which are nonvisual at all times? This must have contributed to the surprise. Even if the Runa had told you about Jana'ata, you couldn't have known they were real, not mythical."

Sandoz looked at him for a long time, as if deciding how to take this change in tone. "Yes," he agreed finally. "In fact, we were told to beware of *djanada*. Obviously, a related word. We considered *djanada* to be a sort of bogeyman, used to keep children from wandering off. We took it as further evidence that, except for Mr. Quinn, we were not considered adults by the Runa for quite some time."

"Father Yarbrough reported that when you first saw Supaari Va-Gayjur, you assumed he was a Runao. Are the two species so similar as that? Or was it only because you were not expecting a second species?" Voelker asked.

"Initially, it was because we were unprepared to imagine that the Jana'ata existed. There were many subtle differences, once we knew what to look for. However, male Jana'ata do resemble female Runa in overall appearance and in size."

"How odd! Only the males?" Felipe asked.

"Female Jana'ata are sequestered and guarded. I cannot say how closely they resemble the Runa, male or female. The Runa sexes," Sandoz reminded them, "are quite alike, but the males are on average a good deal smaller. For a long time, we were confused about their gender because of that and because their sex roles did not match our expectations. Robichaux's *Madonna and Child,* by the way, should perhaps be renamed *Saint Joseph and Child.* Manuzhai was a male." There was a small burst of laughter and comment as the others admitted how surprised they'd been when they'd read this in the mission reports. "Manuzhai raised Askama and was smaller than his wife," Sandoz continued, "so we believed him female. Chaypas traveled extensively and carried on all the trade, which led us to assume that she was a male. The Runa were equally confused by us."

"If the Runa don't wear much besides ribbons," John said, clearing his throat, "couldn't you, um, see—?"

"Runa sexual organs are inconspicuous unless mating is imminent," Sandoz said and continued blandly, "Along with the dentition and claws, this is one unmistakable difference between male Jana'ata and Runa of either sex. It was not immediately apparent because Jana'ata are generally clothed."

Edward Behr, sitting as usual across the room from Sandoz, suddenly had a coughing fit. It was, the Father General thought, as though Emilio were testing his own strength, seeing how far back into the pit he could go. "We are to infer that male Jana'ata organs are not inconspicuous. Are you trying to shock us, Father Sandoz?" Vincenzo Giuliani asked in a light, bored voice, which he hoped was convincing.

"I wouldn't presume to know what would shock you, sir. I was explaining the limits of the similarity between the species."

"This Supaari VaGayjur," Johannes Voelker said, "he owned the village of Kashan?"

Giuliani looked up. Now who's changing the subject? he thought.

"No. Well, perhaps, in a manner of speaking. He did not actually own the real estate or the Runa villagers." Sandoz shook his head, more certain as he thought it through. "No. My understanding was that he owned the rights to trade with them. If they were dissatisfied, the VaKashani could have solicited another merchant to buy Supaari out, although he would have been given an opportunity to adjust his agreements with the VaKashani to address their concerns. It was in many ways an equitable contractual arrangement."

"How were the Runa paid?" Felipe asked suddenly. "The descriptions of their village seem to indicate that they were not terribly materialistic."

"They obtained manufactured goods in payment for blossom harvesting. Perfumes, boats, ceramics, ribbons and so forth. And there was a system of banking in which profits were accumulated. The income from any given village was pooled. I don't know how they handled things when a family moved from one village to another." Sandoz stopped, apparently struck by the problem for the first time. "I suppose that if a certain village were known to have a large account and if others moved in to benefit from the situation, a lot of hearts would become *porai* and the freeloaders would be made to feel embarrassed."

"Who enforced the contracts between the Runa and merchants like Supaari?" Giuliani asked.

"The Jana'ata government. There is a hereditary bureaucracy run by second-born sons that sees to the legal aspects of trade and there are special courts for interspecies disputes. The judgments are enforced by the military police, who are first-born Jana'ata."

"And the Runa do all the productive work," John guessed, disgusted.

"Yes. Third-born merchants like Supaari VaGayjur broker trade between the species. Merchants, like Runa village corporations, are taxed to support the Jana'ata population."

"Do the Runa obtain justice in Jana'ata courts?" Felipe asked.

"I had limited opportunity to observe such things. I was told that the Jana'ata value honor and justice highly. They believe themselves to be stewards and guardians of the Runa. They take pride in doing their duty toward their inferiors and dependents." He sat quietly for quite a while and then added, "For the most part. In addition, it should be noted that the Jana'ata comprise only three to four percent of the VaRakhati population. If their rule were to become odious, the Runa could conceivably rise against them."

"But the Runa are nonviolent," Felipe Reyes said. He had developed a mental model of the Runa as peaceful innocents living in Eden, at odds with the reports from the Contact Consortium. This, for Felipe, was one of the overriding puzzles of the mission.

"I have seen the Runa defend their children." There was a pause; Giuliani saw the tension, but Sandoz went on. "From what I have read in the Wu and Isley report, there are Runa who have reached their limit of tolerance. Their only weapon would be their numbers. Jana'ata military police are ruthless. They have to be. They are vastly outnumbered."

This was virgin territory, Giuliani realized. "Emilio, you may recall that Supaari VaGayjur reportedly told Wu and Isley that there had never been trouble between the Jana'ata and the Runa before our mission arrived."

"Supaari may have been pleased to think so. The Runa do not write histories." Sandoz stopped to drink again. He looked up, brows raised, eyes dispassionate. "I speak only from analogy, gentlemen. There were no Taino or Arawak or Carib historians, but there was certainly conflict in the Caribbean. Both before and after the arrival of Columbus."

Voelker broke the silence that fell at that, returning to his earlier theme. "Surely it is unusual for two species to resemble each other so closely. Are they related biologically as well as culturally?"

"Dr. Edwards was able to obtain blood samples for genetic analysis. The two species were almost certainly not related, except distantly, as mammals like lions and zebra are related. She and Father Robichaux thought the similarities might be due to convergence: a natural selection in the evolution of sentience that led the two species to similar morphological and behavioral traits. I think not." He stopped and looked to Giuliani, a scholar whom he expected to understand why he was uncomfortable. "You understand that I speculate, yes? And this is not my field, but—"

"Of course."

Sandoz stood and walked to the windows. "The Jana'ata are carnivores, with a dentition and forelimb adapted for killing. Their intelligence and capacity for complex social organization probably evolved in the context of cooperative hunting. The Runa are vegetarians with a broad range of diet. Their fine motor control likely derived from manipulative skill associated with the exploitation of small seeds, picking blossoms and so forth. Their three-dimensional memories are excellent; they carry very precise mental maps of their environment and the changing array of seasonal resources. This may account for the evolution of their intelligence, but only in part." Sandoz stopped and stared out the window for a few moments. Beginning to tire, Edward Behr thought, but doing well. "The paleontology of our own planet has many examples of predators and prey locked in competition, ratcheting upward in intelligence and sophisticated adaptation. A biological arms race, one might say. On Rakhat, in my opinion, this competition resulted in the evolution of two sentient species."

"Are you saying that the Runa were the *prey*?" John asked, horrified.

Sandoz turned, face composed. "Of course. I believe that Jana'ata morphology is a form of mimicry, selected for during predation on Runa herds. Even now, Runa prefer to travel in large groups, with the smaller males and young in the center of the troop and the larger adult females on the outside. A hundred, two hundred thousand years ago, the resemblance between the two species was not nearly so striking, perhaps. But Jana'ata who could best blend in with the female Runa at the edges of the herd were the most successful hunters. The Jana'ata foot is prehensile." Sandoz paused, and again Giuliani saw the effort it took to go on. "I imagine the hunters simply fell in step with a female toward the back of the troop, reached out to snare her ankle, and brought her down. The more closely the hunter resembled the prey in appearance and behavior and scent, the more successfully he could stalk and kill her."

"But they cooperate now," Felipe said. "The Jana'ata rule, but they trade with the Runa, they work together—" He didn't know whether to be dismayed by the prehistory or uplifted by the present state of coexistence.

"Oh, yes," Sandoz agreed. "The relationship would certainly have evolved since those days, as would the species themselves. And all that is speculation, although it is consistent with the facts I observed."

Sandoz walked back to the table and sat down. "Gentlemen, the Runa fulfill many roles in Jana'ata culture. They are skilled in crafts and they are traders and servants, laborers, bookkeepers. Even research assistants. Even concubines." He expected the outcry, was prepared for it, had rehearsed his presentation of this topic, and he continued with emotionless thoroughness. "It is a form of birth control. Supaari VaGayjur explained this to me. As stewards of their world, the Jana'ata impose strict population controls. Jana'ata couples may have more than two children but only the first two may marry and establish families; the rest must remain childless. If later-born individuals do breed, they are neutered by law, as are their offspring."

They were speechless. It had seemed perfectly reasonable to Supaari, of course.

"Jana'ata of proven sterility, often neutered thirds, sometimes serve as prostitutes. But cross-species intercourse is, by definition, sterile," Sandoz told them coolly. "Sex with Runa partners carries no risk of pregnancy or even of disease, as far as I know. For this reason, Runa concubines are commonly used as sexual partners by individuals whose families are complete or who are not permitted to breed."

Felipe, shocked, asked, "Do the Runa consent to this?"

It was Mephistopheles who laughed. "Consent is not an issue. The concubines are bred to it." He looked at each of them in turn as they took in the implications and then hit them again. "The Runa are not unintelligent and some are marvelously talented, but they are essentially domesticated animals. The Jana'ata breed them, as we breed dogs."

29

VILLAGE OF KASHAN:
YEAR TWO

SUPAARI VAGAYJUR, THEY found, was an ideal informant, a man who moved with knowledgeable ease between the Runa and the Jana'ata, able to see both ways of life from a point of view that few in either society shared. Irony and objectivity formed the converging lines of his perspective. Shrewd and humorous, he saw what people did and not simply what they said they did, and he was well suited to the task of interpreting his culture to the foreigners.

Anne, shrewd and humorous herself, dated her affection for him from the moment he managed to tell Sofia that the scent of coffee was "agreeable," even as he was almost certainly thinking that the flavor was revolting. Alien savoir faire, Anne thought admiringly, as she watched him overcome what must have been a staggering shock. Laudable aplomb. What a guy.

It was Anne Edwards's greatest delight that humans and VaRakhati of both species shared basic emotions, for though she was a woman of highly trained intelligence, she passed all experience through her heart. As an anthropologist, she had loved the fossil Neandertals she studied with a ferocity that embarrassed her, considered them maligned and misunderstood because they were ugly. For her, their browridges and heavy bones receded into insignificance in comparison with their care for the infirm among them and their loving burial of the many children who died around the age of four. Anne had almost wept one day, in a Belgian museum, when it came to her that these children had probably died in springtime, replaced at the breast by younger siblings while still too small to withstand the rigors of the leanest season of the year without a mother's milk. What were physical differences, when one knew that such children were buried with flowers on boughs of evergreen?

So Anne looked beyond Supaari's claws and teeth, hardly cared about his tail, and took only anatomical interest in his prehensile feet, revealed when he was comfortable enough to remove his boots after dinner that first afternoon. It was his ability to laugh, to be astounded, to be skeptical and embarrassed, proud and angry and kind that made her love him.

He could not pronounce her name, simple as it was. She became Ha'an, and the two of them spent countless hours together in those first weeks, asking and answering as best they could thousands of questions. It was exhausting and exhilarating, a sort of whirlwind love affair that made George cranky and a little jealous. Sometimes, she and Supaari were overcome by the sheer strangeness of their situation, and they were reassured that they were both moved to laugh when this happened.

Despite this goodwill, they were often at an impasse. Sometimes Ruanja had no words to convey a Jana'ata concept that Supaari was trying to describe or Anne's vocabulary was too limited for her to follow the thought. Emilio sat at their sides, translating when his knowledge of Ruanja bettered Anne's, expanding his grasp of that language, getting a start on Supaari's own K'San language, which Emilio already suspected had a monstrously difficult grammar. Sofia participated as well, for her vocabulary included many trade terms and she already had some understanding of the commercial aspects of the Runa-Jana'ata relationship, although she'd previously assumed that the differences between the groups were simply those of country folk and city folk.

Marc was often called upon to sketch some object or situation in Runa life for which they had no words and which Supaari could elucidate, after he'd gotten over the initial surprise of seeing Marc's drawings. Once that hurdle had been jumped, Jimmy and George pulled up visuals on tablet screens for him. Supaari would sometimes be struck by parallels or would describe differences. "Here it is done in a similar manner," he would tell them, or "We have no such thing as that object," or "When this happens, we do thusly." When Anne judged Supaari ready to handle it, George modified a VR headset for him and began to show him the virtual realities of Earth. This was even more frightening to him than Anne had anticipated, and he tore the headset off more than once but kept going back to it with a horrified fascination.

D.W., his own self, never warmed to Supaari, but the Winchester eventually went back into storage. Yarbrough said little during the sessions with the Jana'ata but often suggested lines of inquiry for the following day after Supaari, yawning hugely, retired at second sundown. There were seven of them and only one of Supaari, so they held back, not wanting to make the encounter feel like interrogation. He, after all, was still coming to grips with the very idea that they could exist, that their planet could exist, that they had traveled an incomprehensible distance by means of propulsion he was wholly unprepared to understand, simply to learn about him and his planet. No such notion had ever entered his head.

That the Jana'ata were the dominant species on Rakhat seemed probable from the beginning of their relationship with Supaari. They were used to carnivores being at the top of food chains and accustomed to killer species being in charge of a planet. And, to be honest, they'd been vaguely disappointed by the Runa. The stateliness and deliberation and placidity of Runa life made the humans feel almost drugged; the constant eating, the constant talk, the constant touching dragged on their energy. "They are very sweet," Anne said one night. "They are very boring," George replied. And Anne admitted in the privacy of their tent that she was often tempted during interminable Runa discussions to shout, "Oh, for chrissakes, who gives a shit? Get on with it!"

So despite their inauspicious introduction to Supaari, they were glad to be dealing with someone who came to a decision on his own, even if that decision was to take somebody's head off at the shoulders. They were happy to find someone on Rakhat who was quick on the uptake, who caught jokes and made them, who saw implications. He moved faster than a Runao, did more things in a given day without making such a damned production out of it. His energy levels came closer to their own. He could, in fact, exhaust them. But then he crashed at second sundown and slept like a gigantic carnivorous baby for fifteen hours.

That the relationship between the Jana'ata and the Runa was asymmetrical became unquestionable when the VaKashani Runa returned to their village, huge baskets filled with *pik,* a few days after Supaari's arrival in the village. Great deference was shown to the Jana'ata. He was, for all the world, like a Mafia don or a medieval baron, receiving Runa families, laying hands on the children. But there was also affection. His rule, if that was the proper word, was benign. He listened carefully and patiently to all comers, settled disputes with solutions that struck everyone as fair, steering participants toward a conclusion that seemed logical. The VaKashani did not fear him.

There was no way for the foreigners to know how misleading all of this was, how unusual Supaari was. A self-made man, Supaari was not reticent about his early life and his present status, and since all the surviving members of the Jesuit party came from cultures on Earth that value such people and disdain hereditary privilege, they were prepared to see him in a somewhat heroic light, a plucky boy who'd made good.

Alan Pace might have been better equipped to handle the class aspects of Rakhati society, since Britain still retained some traits of a culture that takes good breeding seriously. Alan might have understood how truly marginal Supaari was, how little access he had to real sources of power and influence, and how much he might crave such access. But Alan was dead.

WHEN, TOWARD THE end of Partan, it was time to see the Jana'ata off after those first extraordinary weeks, the entire population of Kashan, alien and native, accompanied Supaari to the dock or hung from terraces to call farewells and toss flowers on the water and float long scented ribbons in the wind.

"*Sipaj,* Supaari!" Anne said quietly as he prepared to cast off, the chatter and press of Runa all around them. "May someone show you how our people say farewell to those we feel fond of?"

He was touched that she should wish this. "Without hesitation, Ha'an," he said in the low and slightly rumbling voice she was now familiar with. Anne motioned him to bring his head closer and he stooped low, not knowing what to expect. She rose on her toes and her arms went around his neck and he felt her tighten the pressure slightly before she let him go. When she drew back, he noticed that her blue eyes, almost normal in color, were glistening.

"Someone hopes you will come back here soon and safely, Supaari," she said.

"Someone's heart will be glad to be with you again, Ha'an." He was, Supaari realized with surprise, reluctant to leave her. He climbed down into the powerboat cockpit and looked up at the others of her kind, each one different, each a separate and peculiar puzzle. Suddenly, because Ha'an wished it, Supaari was moved to please the others, and so at last made a decision he'd found troublesome. He looked around and found the Elder. "Someone will make arrangements for you to visit Gayjur," he told D.W. "There are many things to be considered, but someone will think on how this may be done."

"WELL, MY DARLING children," Anne announced gaily, shaking off the sadness of Supaari's departure as his powerboat disappeared around the north bend of the river and the Runa began moving back up to their apartments, "it is time for you and me to have a little talk about sex."

"Memory fails," said Emilio, straight-faced, and Marc laughed.

"What if we had a review session?" Jimmy suggested helpfully. Sofia smiled and shook her head, and Jimmy's heart rose but then went obediently back where it belonged.

"What's this about sex?" George asked, shushing Askama and turning to look at Anne.

"Good grief, woman, is that all you ever think about?" D.W. demanded.

Anne grinned like the Cheshire cat as they started up the cliffside together. "Wait until you guys find out what Supaari told me yesterday!" The path narrowed at that point and they strung out into a line, Askama chattering to George about some long, elaborate story they'd been making up together until she saw Kinsa and Fayer, and the children took off to play.

"It seems, my darlings, that we have been caught in a web of sexism, but so have our hosts," Anne told them when they arrived at the apartment. It was filled with Runa, but endless cross talk was normal to them now and she hardly noticed the other conversations. "Jimmy: the Runa think you are a lady, and the mother of us all. Sofia, you are taken to be an immature male. Emilio: an immature female. They don't know quite what to make of D.W. and Marc and me, but they're pretty sure George is a male. Isn't that nice, dear?"

"I'm not sure," George said suspiciously, sinking onto a cushion. "How do they decide who's what?"

"Well, there is a certain logic to it all. Emilio, you seemed to have guessed correctly that Askama is a little girl. Fifty-fifty chance, and you won the toss. The trick is that Chaypas is Askama's mother, not Manuzhai. Yes, indeed, darlings!" Anne said when they stared at her in shock. "I'll come back to that in a minute. Anyway, Supaari says that the Runa females are the ones who do all the business for the village. Listen to this, Sofia, this is really cool. Their pregnancies are fairly short and they aren't much inconvenienced by them. When the baby is born, mom hands the little dear over to daddy and goes back about her business without missing a beat."

"No *wonder* I couldn't make sense of the gender references!" Emilio said. "So Askama is in training to be a trader, and that's why they think I am also female. Because I'm the formal interpreter for our group, yes?"

"Bingo," said Anne. "And Jimmy, they think, is our mom because he's the only one big enough to seem like a full-grown female. That's why they always ask him to make decisions for us, maybe. They only think he's asking D.W.'s opinion to be polite, I guess." Yarbrough snorted, and Anne grinned. "Okay, now here's the neat part. Manuzhai is Chaypas's husband, right? But he is not Askama's genetic father. Runa ladies marry gentlemen they believe will be good social fathers, as Manuzhai is. But Supaari says their mates are chosen using"—she cleared her throat—"an entirely separate set of criteria."

"They pick out a good stud," D.W. said.

"Don't be crude, dear," Anne said. Chaypas and her guests decided to go to Aycha's to eat and suddenly the apartment emptied out. When they were alone, Anne leaned forward and continued conspiratorially. "But yes, that was certainly the implication. I must say, the custom has a certain rude appeal. Theoretically, of course," she added when George pouted.

"So why are they only 'pretty sure' I'm a male?" George asked petulantly, his manhood under oblique attack from two quarters.

"Well, aside from your virile good looks, my love, they have also noted how wonderful you are with the children," Anne said. "On the other hand, you don't show much interest in collecting blossoms, so they're a little confused by you, actually. Same for Marc and D.W. and me. They think I might be a male because I do most of the cooking. Maybe I'm sort of the daddy? Oh, Jimmy, maybe they think you and I are married! Obviously, they don't have a clue about relative ages."

Emilio had become increasingly thoughtful and D.W., watching him, began to chuckle. Emilio didn't laugh at first, but he came around.

"What?" Anne asked. "What's so funny?"

"I'm not sure funny is the word," D.W. said, right eye on Emilio, one brow up speculatively.

Emilio shrugged. "Nothing. Only: this notion of separating the roles of genetic father and social father would have been useful in my family."

"Might have saved some wear and tear on your sorry young ass," D.W. agreed.

Emilio laughed ruefully and ran his hands through his hair. Everyone was looking at him now, curiosity plain on their faces. He hesitated, probing old wounds, and found them scabbed over. "My mother was a woman of great warmth and a lively nature," he told them, choosing his words carefully. "Her husband was a handsome man, tall, strong. Brunette but very light-skinned, yes? My mother was also very fair." He paused to let them absorb this; it didn't take a geneticist to work out the implications. "My mother's husband was out of town for a few years—"

"Doing time for possession and sale," D.W. supplied.

"—and when he returned, he found he had a second son, almost a year old. And very dark." Emilio sat still then, and the room was quiet. "They did not divorce. He must have loved my mother very much." This had never occurred to him before and he had no idea how he should feel about it. "She was charming, yes? Easy to love, Anne might say."

"So you took the blame for her," Anne said astutely, hating the woman for letting it happen and silently berating God for giving this son to the wrong mother.

"Of course. Very poor taste, being born like that." Emilio looked briefly at Anne, but his eyes slid away. A mistake, he realized, to speak of this. He had tried so hard to understand, but how could a child have known? He shrugged again and steered the talk away from Elena Sandoz. "My mother's husband and I used to play a game called Beat the Crap out of the Bastard. I was about eleven when I worked out the name, yes?" He sat up and threw the hair out of his eyes with a jerk of his head. "I changed the rules for this game when I was fourteen," he told them, savoring it, even after all the years.

D.W., who knew what was coming, grinned in spite of himself. He'd deplored the random violence of La Perla and worked hard to find ways for kids like Emilio to settle things without knifing somebody. It was an uphill battle in a place where fathers told sons, "Anybody give you shit, cut his face." And this was advice given to eight-year-olds on the first day of third grade.

"Our esteemed Father Superior," he heard Emilio tell the others with vast enjoyment, "was in those days a parish priest in La Perla. Of course, he did not condone unpleasantries among family members, however tenuously related. Nevertheless, Father Yarbrough did impart a certain wisdom to young acolytes. This included the precept that when there is a substantial difference in size between adversaries, the larger man is fighting dirty simply by intending to take on a much smaller opponent—"

"So nail the sumbitch 'fore he lays a hand on you," D.W. finished, in tones that suggested the sagacity of this was self-evident. He had, in fact, taught the kid a few little things in the gym. Emilio being small, surprise was necessarily a prerequisite to some maneuvers. The subtlety came in making the boy understand it was okay to fight in self-defense when Miguel came home mean-drunk, but it was not necessary to take on a whole neighborhood of taunting kids.

"—and while there is a certain primitive satisfaction in decking an asshole," Emilio was telling them with serene respect for his mentor, "this should not be indulged in without temperance and forbearance."

"I sort of wondered where you learned to do what you did with Supaari," Jimmy said. "That was pretty amazing."

The conversation drifted off into stories of a priest Jimmy had known in South Boston who'd boxed in the Olympics and then D.W. started in on a few sergeants he'd known in the Marines. Anne and Sofia started lunch and listened, heads shaking, to tales of certain illegal but remarkably effective hockey moves available to alert goalies in the Quebec league. But the talk came back to the Jana'ata Handshake, as Supaari's attack on Sandoz was known among them, and when it veered toward Emilio's childhood once more, he stood.

"You never know when an old skill will come in handy," he said with a certain edgy finality, moving toward the terrace. But then he stopped and laughed and added piously, "The Lord works in mysterious ways."

And it was impossible to tell whether he was serious or joking.

THE CRUISE DOWNRIVER from Kashan seemed to Supaari to go more quickly than the trip out from Gayjur. The first day, he simply let his mind go blank, his attention absorbed by the eddies and drift-wood, the sandbars and rocks. But the second day on the river was a thoughtful one, full of wonder.

He had been deluged by new facts, new ideas, new possibilities, but he had always been quick to grasp opportunities and willing to take friendships where he found them. The foreigners, like the Runa, were sometimes startlingly different from his people and often incomprehensible, but he liked Ha'an very much—found her mind lively and full of challenge. The rest of them were less clear to him, only adjuncts to the sessions with Ha'an, translating, illustrating, providing food and drink at bizarre and irritating intervals. And to be honest, they nearly all smelled alike.

He would buy the rented powerboat outright when he got back, Supaari decided, watching a good-sized river *kivnest* breach and roll nearby. The purchase price had been rendered trivial; he had examined the foreign goods, knew now the dimensions of the trade he could broker. Wealth beyond counting was guaranteed. This trip alone had yielded a fortune in exotica. He had explained his business to the foreigners and they were happy to provide him with many small packets of aromatics, their names as marvelous as their scents. Clove, vanilla, yeast, sage, thyme, cumin, incense. Sticks of brown cinnamon, white cylinders called beeswax candles which could be set afire to give off a fragrant light that Supaari found enchanting. And they'd given him several "landscapes" that one foreigner made on paper. Beautiful things; remarkable, truly. Supaari almost hoped the Reshtar would turn them down; Supaari rather liked these landscapes himself.

It was obvious that the foreigners had no understanding of the value of their goods, but Supaari VaGayjur was an honorable man and offered the interpreter a fair price, which was one in twelve of what he'd get from Kitheri and, at that, a substantial amount. A great deal of embarrassing confusion ensued. Ha'an had tried to insist the goods were

gifts: a disastrous notion that would have prevented resale. The small,
dark interpreter and his sister with the mane sorted that out but then—
what was his name? Suhn? Suhndos? He'd tried to hand the packets directly to Supaari! What kind of parents did these people have? If
Askama hadn't guided her counterpart's hands to Chaypas's for the
transfer, the VaKashani would have been cut out of the deal entirely.
Shocking manners, although the interpreter had abased himself prettily
enough when he recognized the mistake.

Because the VaKashani were hosts to the foreign delegation and
thus entitled to a percentage of Supaari's profit, the village would move
nearly a year ahead of schedule closer to breeding rights. Supaari was
pleased for them, and slightly envious. If life were as simple and straightforward for a Jana'ata third as for a Runa corporation, his own problem
would have been solved. He could simply buy breeding rights and get on
with it, having proven his fiscal responsibility and obedience to the government. But Jana'ata life was never simple and rarely straightforward.
Deep in the Jana'ata soul there was an almost unshakable conviction
that things must be controlled, thought out, done correctly, that there
was very little margin for error in life. Tradition was safety; change was
danger. Even Supaari felt this, although he defied the instinct often and
to his profit.

The storytellers claimed that the first five Jana'ata hunters and the
first five Runa herds were created by Ingwy on an island, where balance
could be easily lost and annihilation was the price of poor stewardship.
Five times the hunters and their mates erred: leaving things to chance,
killing without thought, letting their own numbers grow uncontrolled,
and all was lost. On the sixth attempt, Tikat Father of Us All learned to
breed the Runa and Sa'arhi Our Mother was made his consort and they
were brought to the mainland and given dominion. There were other
stories about Pa'au and Tiha'ai and the first brothers, and on and on.
Who knew? Maybe there was some truth in it all, but Supaari was a
skeptic. The Ingwy Cycle was too pat an explanation for duogeniture,
too convenient for the firsts and seconds justifying their grip on the
world.

It didn't matter. Whether the legends grew from ancient seeds of
truth or sprang fully formed from the self-interest of the rulers, Supaari
thought, things are as they are. He was a third; how, then, to convince
the Reshtar of Galatna that Supaari VaGayjur was worthy of being created Founder? It was a delicate business and required subtlety and cun-

ning, for reshtari were rarely generous in granting to others the very prerogative denied themselves. Somehow, Hlavin Kitheri must come to believe it was in his interest to bestow this privilege. A pretty puzzle for Supaari VaGayjur.

He let the problem go, for pursuit can drive the quarry away. Better to stroll along, alert for opportunity, wasting no effort on mad dashes and undignified chases. If one is patient, he knew, something always comes within reach.

AFTER SUPAARI'S FIRST visit, the Jesuit party settled into a routine that made their second full year on Rakhat as productive and satisfying as they could have hoped for.

They were given their own apartments, two of them, thanks to Supaari, who had arranged it when Anne admitted that they found it wearying to be with the Runa all the time. She also told him, privately, that D.W. was not well and sometimes found the distance to the river difficult. Supaari had no guess as to the cause or cure for the Elder's illness but thoughtfully specified living space further down the cliffside than Manuzhai's home.

Sofia lived with Anne and George. The apartment next door became a dormitory for the unmarried men and an office for everyone. Anne's side was home. This orderly division of use was, they found, a great improvement over the endless ad hoc arrangements made day by day when they were living with Manuzhai and Chaypas.

They now knew from Supaari that they were not just tolerated by the VaKashani but welcome. They had fit into the economic structure of the community by providing Supaari with goods that benefited the village and, in their own minds, this allowed them to be more assertive about requesting small accommodations, like limits to overnight visits and periods of privacy during the day. They still did a lot of visiting and often had guests who stayed overnight, especially Manuzhai and the ubiquitous Askama, but there was now some privacy on a regular basis. The relief was startling.

That year Anne, Sofia and D.W. devoted most of their time to writing up the interviews with Supaari, with an emphasis on Runa biology, social structure and economy, and on Runa-Jana'ata cooperation. Every paragraph written generated a hundred new questions, but they took it one step at a time and a stream of papers went back to Rome, week after week, month after month. In recognition of the partnership she felt with Supaari, Anne suggested listing him as the second author on all their papers. Sofia, instructed by Emilio's generosity in this, did so immediately. Eventually D.W. took up the practice as well.

Emilio Sandoz, a contented spider in the center of an intellectual web, collected lexemes, semantic fields, prosody and idiom, semantics and deep structure. He answered questions, translated and aided research for all of them, while collaborating with Sofia on an instructional program for Ruanja and with Askama and Manuzhai on a Ruanja dictionary. Marc had begun sketching and painting the Runa and their lives within days of arriving, and this continued as the seasonal round was played out. To Emilio's delight, the Runa referred to Marc's images using the spatial declension. And now when the women left on trading expeditions, they commissioned a portrait from Marc or his apprentices, so they could be with their families even as they traveled, Chaypas explained. Absent mothers were gone but not invisible.

George and Jimmy installed improvised plumbing and a pulley system for hauling things up and down the cliffside. The Runa soon added similar arrangements to the other apartments. And then there was George's ever-elaborating waterslide complex down by the river's edge, which the kids adored and which they all, native and alien, worked on sporadically.

The Runa took everything in stride. Nothing ever seemed to surprise them, and it had begun to seem that they were incapable of astonishment. But toward the end of Supaari's first visit, Marc had asked if the merchant knew of any objection to the foreigners starting a garden. Ruanja, Emilio found, had no word for plants grown in an artificial ecosystem, so Supaari was shown images of gardens. Familiar with the notion, Supaari brought the subject up with the Kashan elders and obtained permission for Marc to plant.

And so, for no good reason that the VaKashani could conceive, Marc Robichaux and George Edwards and Jimmy Quinn set about digging in ground where no useful roots grew. They used giant spoons to lift up big bites of dirt and then simply put the dirt back where it had been, but upside down. The Runa were absolutely flabbergasted.

That this mysterious activity was hard physical labor for the foreigners made the whole business funnier. George would pause to wipe his brow, and the Runa would quake with laughter. Marc would sit a while to catch his breath, and the Runa would gasp with merriment.

Jimmy worked doggedly on, beads of sweat sparkling on the ends of his coiling red hair, and Runa observers would comment helpfully, "Ah, the dirt is much better that way. Big improvement!" and wheeze in a transport of amusement. The Runa were capable of sarcasm.

Soon, Runa from other villages came to watch the gardeners while their children played on the waterslide, and George began to feel a retroactive sympathy for the Amish farmers of Ohio, unwilling tourist attractions subjected to stares and pointing fingers. But the initial hilarity tapered off as the garden took shape and the Runa began to perceive the geometric plan underlying the foreigners' inexplicable work. The garden was a serious scientific experiment and careful records of germination and yield would be kept, but everything Marc Robichaux did was beautiful and he laid the garden out as a succession of interlocking diamond-shaped and circular beds, edged in herbs. George and Jimmy constructed trellises and adapted the Runa terrace parasols to shade the lettuces and peas and to control the downpours of rain. Manuzhai, intrigued now, joined them in this, and the resulting structures were lovely.

The "dry" season on Rakhat turned out to be reasonably well suited to the husbandry of Earth plants. As the season progressed, it could be seen that the rows and hills of vegetables were thoughtfully planned. Scarlet-stalked Swiss chard rose over beds of emerald spinach. Zucchini and corn and potatoes, tomatoes and cabbages and radishes, cucumbers and feathery carrots, red beets and purple turnips—all were incorporated into overflowing parterres, interplanted with edible flowers: pansies and sunflowers, calendula and Empress of India nasturtiums. It was glorious.

Supaari came back to Kashan periodically and dutifully admired the flourishing potager on his third visit. "We Jana'ata also have such gardens. The scents are different from yours," he said tactfully, for he was greatly offended by some of the foreign odors, "but this is more beautiful to the eye." He took no interest in it thereafter, considering it a harmless eccentricity.

Supaari, they noticed, brought his own food from the city with him and ate in privacy, in the cabin of his powerboat. Sometimes he also brought Runa with him from the city, memory specialists who were apparently like living textbooks, who could answer some of the more technical questions the foreigners asked. And there were written materials as well, in the K'San language and therefore completely incomprehensible except for the engineering drawings. George and Jimmy were particu-

larly interested in radio, and they wanted to know about power generation, signal production, receiving equipment and so forth. Supaari found
this understandable, since he knew in a somewhat foggy way that the
foreigners had come to Rakhat because they'd overheard the Galatna
concerts somehow, but he was unable to give them much information.
He knew of radio only as a listener. This ignorance was frustrating to the
technophiles.

"He's a merchant, not an engineer," Anne said in Supaari's defense.
"Besides, the last human with a clear grasp of all the technology he used
was probably Leonardo da Vinci." And she invited a disgruntled George
to tell Supaari how aspirin works.

Supaari was, at least, able to explain why the Runa disliked music.
"We Jana'ata use songs to organize activities," he told Anne and Emilio,
as they sat outside in a *hampiy* equipped with cushions, unconcerned
about the light drizzle falling. He seemed to have trouble finding the correct Ruanja phrasing for this. "It is something we do only among ourselves. The Runa find this frightening."

"The songs or the activities the songs organize?" Anne asked.

"Someone thinks: both. And we also have—there is nothing in Ruanja—*ba'ardali basnu charpi*. There are two groups, one here and one
here." He motioned to indicate that these groups would stand opposite
each other. "They sing, first one group and then the other. And a judgment is made, for a reward. The Runa don't like such things."

"Singing contests!" Anne exclaimed in English. "What do you
think, Emilio? Does that make sense to you? It sounds like competitive
singing. They used to have contests like that in Wales. Fabulous choirs."

"Yes. I should think the Runa would avoid competitions like that.
Porai is built into the situation. All the contestants would want to win
the prize." Emilio switched to Ruanja. "Someone thinks perhaps the
hearts of the Runa become *porai* if one group is rewarded but not the
other," he ventured and explained his logic to Supaari, to test the model.

"Yes, Ha'an," the Jana'ata said, thinking Emilio was merely translating. He leaned back onto an elbow comfortably and added with a
tone that Anne found wry, "We Jana'ata do not have such hearts."

But Supaari brought no other Jana'ata with him and stalled when
George and Jimmy repeated their request to see the city and meet others
of his people. "Jana'ata speak only K'San," he told them when pressed
for a reason. It was unusual, he let them understand, that he had learned
Ruanja; ordinarily, it was the Runa who were required to learn Jana'ata

languages. It was a lame enough excuse that they accepted it as a polite fiction, and D.W. reckoned ole Supaari was probably keeping their existence secret to preserve his monopoly on the trade. The Jesuit party was familiar with capitalism and didn't begrudge the merchant his corner on the coffee and spice market. So while Yarbrough was getting anxious to make contact with someone in authority, they tried to be patient. *Cunctando regitur mundus,* after all. In the meantime, Emilio stepped up his work on K'San.

At last there came a day, a Rakhati year and a half after their arrival in Kashan, when Supaari told them that he had worked out a way for them to visit Gayjur. It would take some time; there were many arrangements, and the visit would have to wait until after the next rainy season. He would not be able to come upriver to visit them during that time but he would return at the beginning of Partan and take them to the city. His plan hinged somehow on their ability to see in redlight, but he was indirect about why this should be so.

In any case, they were reasonably content with the situation as it stood. They were all productively employed. Supaari had been wonderfully helpful in many ways, and they did not want to impose on his good nature. "Step by step," Emilio would say, and Marc would add, "It is as it should be."

During this time, the health of the Jesuit party remained good, on the whole. They were free of viral illness since there was no disease reservoir here that could affect them. Jimmy broke a finger. Marc was badly bitten by something he'd found while poking around and lifting up rocks; it got away, so they were never sure what the culprit was, but Robichaux recovered. George confirmed Manuzhai's fears by falling off a walkway one night, but he wasn't seriously hurt. There was the usual run of cuts, bruises, blisters and muscle pulls. For a while Sofia had a lot of headaches, trying to cut back on coffee because the VaKashani now swayed with dismay whenever the foreigners actually drank the stuff instead of selling it. After a month of doling out analgesics, Anne suggested that Sofia should just do her drinking in private. Sofia adopted this solution with relief.

In general, it was a tidy little practice for Anne Edwards, M.D., flawed only by despair for one of her patients. His spirit and mind remained strong, but D. W. Yarbrough's body was failing him and there was, as far as she could determine, nothing in this world Anne could do about it.

IT WAS PREDICTABLE, when they thought about it later, that the Runa would begin to garden. Once the Runa understood what all the ludicrous labor had produced, once they had seen how beautiful a garden could be, once they knew that food could be grown close to home, they seized upon gardening with typical enthusiasm and creativity. From Kashan, the practice moved along river courses to other villages and along the coast toward Gayjur. Anne, questioning Runa visitors and using satellite data, tracked the spread, said it was a textbook case of diffusion and wrote it up.

Marc and George accompanied the first Runa gardeners on expeditions to *pik* and *k'jip* fields and helped them bring back transplants. Seeds were collected, slips taken and rooted. Some crops failed but others flourished. New plants were added. The foreigners were glad to provide potatoes, which the Runa loved, and to share beets and even popcorn, which was an enormous hit, both as entertainment and as food. When Sofia wondered if this sharing of seeds and transplants from Earth might trigger some sort of ecological disaster, Marc said, "All the varieties I brought have very low volunteer-germination rates. If they or we stop taking care of the gardens, these plants will die off in a year."

Freed from the endless marching from home to naturally growing food sources, their diet supplemented by garden produce, the VaKashani and their neighbors grew visibly opulent. Fat levels rose. Hormone production kicked in at concentrations that brought on estrus, and life got a good deal more interesting in Kashan and the surrounding villages. Even if Supaari had not tipped Anne off to the general outlines of Runa sexuality, she'd have worked it out by observation alone that year: there was no real privacy in Runa life.

And the Runa, she discovered, were in fact quite curious about where little foreigners came from, so to speak. "Earth" was not the answer they were interested in. So, with sex and pregnancies and new households suddenly of universal interest, Anne explained certain aspects of human behavior, physiology and anatomy. This soon led to a new accuracy in the way Ruanja personal pronouns were applied to the foreigners.

And though single-irised eyes were affectionately averted and human commentary was thoughtfully circumspect in the sexually charged atmosphere of Kashan, there was no way for the courtship of Jimmy

Quinn and Sofia Mendes to go unnoticed. The VaKashani were delighted by the couple. They showed this by being rowdy and lewd, making bawdy remarks that frequently went beyond the suggestive into the
realm of the expository. Jimmy and Sofia took it all in the good-natured
spirit with which it was given. Shyness was not a luxury they were
vouchsafed. And to be honest, as friendship deepened and a love was at
long last permitted to flourish, there was only one person around whom
they felt shy. Nothing was ever spoken among the three of them; to
speak would solidify truths that had been kept, at some cost to them all,
insubstantial. Emilio did not join in the ribaldry or joke with them the
way he might have with another couple. But now and then, when they
returned together from a walk or looked up and saw him across the
room, they would know that his eyes had been on them and they found
in the still face and quiet gaze a benediction.

When at last it came, fully two months after Sofia was ready for it,
Jimmy's proposal was typically comic and her response typically decisive. "Sofia," he said, "I am painfully aware of the fact that I am, for all
practical purposes, the last man on Earth—"

"Yes," she said.

And so on the fifth of Stan'ja, approximately November 26, 2041,
in the village of Kashan, Southern Province of Inbrokar, on the lavender
and blue and green planet of Rakhat, James Connor Quinn and Sofia
Rachel Mendes were married under a *chuppah,* the traditional open-
sided canopy of Jewish weddings, decorated at its corners with streamers of yellow and amethyst, of green and aquamarine, of carnelian and
lilac, scented with something like gardenia and something like lily.

The bride wore a simple dress Anne made from a silken Runa fabric that Supaari provided. Manuzhai made the circlet of ribbons and
flowers Sofia wore around her head, with streamers of many colors woven into the crown, falling to the ground all around her. D.W., not much
heavier now than Sofia and very frail, gave the bride away. George was
the best man. Anne was supposed to be the matron of honor, but decided
to cry instead. Askama was the flower girl, of course, and the VaKashani
loved this element of the ritual, so close to their own aesthetic. Marc Robichaux officiated at the ecumenical ceremony, working some rather
lovely Ruanja poetry into the Nuptial Mass. Anne knew that the husband would stomp on a glass at the end of a Jewish ceremony, but the
closest she could come to that tradition was to suggest that Jimmy break
a Runa perfume flask. Then D.W. said that in view of Sofia's dedication

to the stuff, a coffee mug would be appropriately symbolic, so they used a pottery cup instead. And Marc ended the service with the Shehecheyanu, the Hebrew prayer for first fruits and new beginnings. Sofia stared, wide-eyed, when she recognized the French-accented words and then saw Marc concentrating on the lips of his language coach. When she turned to Emilio Sandoz, standing a little distance away, he smiled, and thus she received his wedding present.

There was a feast, with plenty of twigs and popcorn. And there were games and races, which had winners and losers but did not make anyone *porai* because there were no prizes. It was a good-hearted amalgam of Runa and human customs and cuisine. Afterward, Anne, who had done as much work on these arrangements as any Earthside mother of the bride, made it clear that Jimmy and Sofia were to be left strictly alone on their first night. Entering into the spirit of the thing, the VaKashani constructed a doorway for the apartment given to the new couple: a trellised screen of woven vines, decorated with flowers and ribbons. Escorted home, Jimmy and Sofia thanked everyone, laughing, for their very helpful instructions, and found themselves alone at last, the sounds of communal merriment receding and merging into somewhat more private celebrations as the third sun set.

Truths had been told, long before this night. In the delicious days of waiting that they gave themselves, as wedding plans went on around them, they spent hours in the shadowy filtered light of a *hampiy* shelter paved with cushions. There were many things to share: family legends, funny stories, simple biographical details. One afternoon Jimmy had lain next to Sofia, marveling at her small perfection and his good fortune. He had never assumed that she was coming to him an innocent and so, tracing the pure line of her profile with his finger, he looked down at her, his deep-set smiling eyes filled with erotic speculation, and asked in low tones of intimacy that left no doubt about his meaning, "What pleases you, Sofia?"

She burst into tears and said, "I don't know," for it had never occurred to her that anyone might ask such a thing. Startled, Jimmy kissed away salty tears, saying, "Then we'll just have to find that out together." But, puzzled by the strength of the reaction, he knew there was something behind this and looked at her, searching for it.

She had meant to keep this one region of her past behind its old defensive walls, but the last barrier between them came down. When he heard it all, Jimmy thought his heart would break for her but he only sat and held her, long arms and endless legs enfolding her like a nestling, and waited for her to quiet. Then he smiled into her eyes and asked, in the dry academic tones of an astronomer discussing a theoretical point with a colleague, "How long do you suppose I can go on loving you more every day?" And he devised for her a calculus of love, which approached infinity as a limit, and made her smile again.

So there were no more walls to be scaled, no more fortresses to defend by the fifth of Stan'ja, a month that marks the start of summer on Rakhat, when the nights are very short and full of stars and racing clouds and moons. But that first night was long enough for him to lead her in a private wedding dance, seeking the rhythm of her heart. And the moonlight, filtered through flowers and vines and streamers of color and fragrance, was very good for finding the way together to moments worthy of a Rakhati poet's song.

Later that summer, as rain fell, such a moment shimmered and paused on the brink, and then began the ancient dance of numbers: two, four, eight, sixteen, thirty-two, and a new life took root and began to grow. And thus the generations past were joined to the unknowable future.

30

VILLAGE OF KASHAN AND CITY OF GAYJUR: YEAR THREE

"So, what do you think? Rain's probably done for the day. Feel lively enough for a walk?" Anne asked D.W.

"Well, now, I cain't say as I'm inclined to rush into a decision like that." D.W. took a sip of the meat broth Anne had brought him and then laid his head back against the hammock chair. His gaze traveling down the long meandering ridge of his nasal bones, he fixed her with a look of judicious consideration. "I thought maybe I'd save my strength up so's I can watch some mud dry later on."

She smiled, and it was gratifying that he could still make people smile.

He kept the mug in his hands for a while, to warm them, but then began to worry that it would slip out of his fingers, so he set it aside on the little table that Sofia and Emilio had once used as a desk out in this *hampiy*. The shelter was his now, had become pretty close to a permanent residence for him, barring really bad weather. He liked to be out where he could see the southern mountains or look northeast to find the line where the plains merged into sky. Manuzhai or Jimmy carried him down to the apartment if the weather looked to get ugly and then carried him back up to the *hampiy* when things settled down; he couldn't climb the cliff anymore on his own. Emilio stayed with him nights, so he wouldn't be alone. D.W. had worried about being a pain in the ass for everyone but felt better about it when Sofia told him, "It is your duty to let us help. Even your Jesus knew that: taking care of the sick is a commandment. It's a mitzvah for us."

"Finish that soup," said Anne, breaking into his reverie. "Doctor's orders."

"'Finish that soup!' You're pretty damn brisk," he informed her indignantly, but he picked up the cup with both thin hands and forced himself to continue working on it until he'd drunk it all. He made a face, which was a little redundant given how he looked when he wasn't making a face. "Everything tastes like metal," he told her.

"I know, but the protein does you good." Anne reached out and put a hand on his wrist for a brief squeeze.

She had tried everything she could think of. Half-killed him with parasiticides. Put him on an all-Earth diet from the lander stores. Boiled the rainwater he drank after passing it through all the filters and chemical treatments. Stopped the chemical treatments, thinking maybe they made it worse. Two or three times she thought they'd gotten the damned thing on the run, whatever the hell it was. He'd start to put on some weight, get some color and energy back, and then he'd slip again.

He was the only one affected. So, of course, they both wondered if he'd brought something with him, was carrying something from home. But all the crew members had been put through a fine-meshed medical sieve before they left, and D. W. Yarbrough had once been abundantly healthy, strong as a lean old racehorse. Maybe something had gone subtly wrong with his physiology: he was sequestering something that was usually excreted or some enzymatic process had gone to hell.

"It's not that bad, Annie," he'd told her once. "Most of the time, it's just bein' tired."

"If you really loved me, you'd get well, dammit. I hate patients who refuse to make their doctors appear omnipotent. It's very rude."

He knew bluster when he heard it. "People are mortal," he'd told her. "You and I both know there's lots worse ways to go."

Anne had turned away, blinking rapidly, but snuffled in a breath vigorously and got ahold of herself. When she spoke again, her voice was firm and irate. "It's not the fact or the method, it's the timing that pisses me off."

D.W. came back to the present with a start, wondering if he'd dozed off. "C'mon," he said, working his way forward in the hammock chair and then resting on its edge before standing. "Let's walk. I'll blow off the mud today."

"Right." Anne slapped her hands on her knees and pushed herself up, shaking off the worry. "Go for broke, I say. Live for the moment."

They moved slowly, not saying much, walking along the gorge edge toward the southern mountains, D.W. setting the pace. Anne kept a careful eye on him, knowing that they shouldn't go very far because D.W. would have to walk back. Ordinarily, she could count on having someone to carry him home if he wore himself out, but they were alone in Kashan for the first time since the lander disaster. The Runa were out harvesting a flower called *anukar*. George, Marc and Jimmy had gone off with Supaari to see the city of Gayjur, at last. So there was no one around to help but Sofia, pregnant and nauseated, and Emilio, who was asleep. He'd been up most of the night with D.W., who'd had another bad time of it.

To Anne's surprise, and to his own, D.W. did all right. They got as far as their old place on the ledge, which had a comfortable flat spot and a good view of the ravine and the western sky. "If I set down, you reckon you can haul my raggedy old ass up again?" D.W. asked her.

"Leverage, my darling. If you can dig your heels in, I can get you on your feet." She let him take hold of her arm and leaned back to steady his descent before sitting down next to him. They were quiet a while, as he got his breath back.

"When I am gone—" he started. Anne opened her mouth, but he shut her up with a look. "When I am gone, and I expect that's three, four days off now, Marc Robichaux will be de facto Father Superior. I can't make that appointment, but it'll be almost nine years till we can get a radio order back from Rome." He stopped and, out of habit, scuffed his hand around in the dirt, feeling for pebbles, but he'd long since scoured the spot of rocks, so he gave up and let his hands go loose in his lap. "Now listen up. Marc's a good man but he's not a leader, Anne. And Emilio surprises me sometimes but he's off in his own world a lot. Neither one of 'em is much good in a crisis—"

"Well, they've always had you or some other superior to rely on. Maybe they'd rise to the occasion."

"Yeah. I've thought of that. But I worry about things. George is a good staff man, but I don't see him as a line officer, beggin' your pardon.

If y'all don't get back, Anne, if this fuel idea of George's craps out? If you're here permanently, then you're going to need some kind of structure to keep from going nuts." He paused. "I been workin' it through in my mind. There's got to be one voice givin' the orders. I'm all for advice and consent, but you're too isolated and too vulnerable not to have some clear chain of command. One voice. But it don't have to be a Jesuit's voice, okay? Now, my opinion: you and Sofia are going to be the brains of the outfit. Don't argue with me, I ain't got the time nor the energy. The Quinn boy is bedrock. I want you to work it so Jimmy becomes recognized as the one who decides."

She started to protest but, hearing it, she remembered the hours after Alan's death and the way Jimmy came through when they realized they were marooned. She nodded.

"Now, I've said something along these lines to Marc and Emilio. Not in these terms, but they understand what I'm saying. The real struggle will be gettin' Jim to accept that he's the best person for the job. He'll want you or Sofia to take over." Yarbrough stopped. He lifted his arm and meant to put it around Anne's shoulders but that was more than he could manage, so he just put his hand over hers. "Annie, you feel too much and Sofia thinks too damn quick for her own good. Jim's got a fine strong balance to him. Y'all give him the benefit of your intuition and your intelligence and your knowledge. But let him decide."

"So Jimmy gets to be Elder after all," she said, trying to lighten the moment a little. But it wasn't a light moment, so she told him, "It's a good plan, D.W. I'll midwife it along as best I can."

D.W. smiled and she felt his hand tighten a little around hers, but he only looked at the sky, talked out.

He meant to tell her about his grandmother, who'd lived to be ninety-four and didn't recommend it. He meant to tell her to watch that Supaari character, there was something about him, and Anne shouldn't let herself get blinded by sentiment. He meant to tell her how really happy he'd been, even these last months. He thought he had a few days left. But death has its own agenda and its own logic, and it caught them both unaware, with less warning than they expected.

"MY GOD," GEORGE breathed. "There it is."

"Jesus, Mary and Joseph," Jimmy whispered. "It was worth the wait."

Marc Robichaux pulled himself away from the panorama and looked toward Supaari VaGayjur, serenely piloting the little powerboat through the buoyed channels toward the city. "*Sipaj*, Supaari. We thank you for this," he said quietly.

The Jana'ata merchant's chin lifted slightly in acknowledgment. He had planned their arrival thoughtfully, bringing them around the headland and into Radina Bay a little before second sundown. Ringed by three mountains, white stonework and red clay masonry gleaming in the lush pearlescent light, Gayjur embraced the crescent harbor in a long sweep from southeast to northwest; the deepening darkness hid the tangle of ships and derricks and warehouses and shops nearest the docks and their eyes were drawn upward toward Galatna Palace, set like a jewel in the deep aquamarine vegetation of the central mountain. This was the best time of day to see the city—when the sky took on colors that always reminded Supaari of marble from Gardhan. It was also the safest time to bring the foreigners into port.

Marc smiled at Jimmy and George, transfixed by the sight, and was glad for them. For almost six years of subjective time, these two men had dreamed of seeing the City of the Songs, which they now knew to be Gayjur. Whenever Supaari was in Kashan, they'd hinted, bargained, very nearly demanded and almost begged him to take them there. They wanted to see a real city, they told him. They had trouble explaining why they were so anxious to go. They had no Ruanja words for much of what interested them, which was everything. They wanted to find out what the buildings looked like, see where the food came from, where the sewage went, how the universities and government and hospitals were run, what transportation was like, how electricity was generated and stored and used. They wanted to talk to chemists, physicists, astronomers, mathematicians. See how the principles of the wheel, the lever and the inclined plane played out on this planet. Everything. They wanted to know everything.

Marc himself was less frantic to get out of Kashan, but he too yearned to see the architecture and the art, to hear the music and see the sights. Were there parks? Museums? Zoos! And Supaari said there were gardens. Formal or unplanned, utilitarian or purely decorative? Were there houses of worship? Who went? Were there religious specialists— priests or priestesses, monks, adepts? Did they believe in magic, in God or gods, in fate, in destiny, in the reward of good, the punishment of evil? How were the milestones of life marked? With cadenced ceremony or brief informal acknowledgments? And the food—was it better in the city? What did people wear? Were they polite or pushy, punctilious or casual? What was crime? What was punishment? What was virtue and what was vice? What was fun? Everything. Marc too wanted to know everything.

Finally, after stalling them for a full Rakhati year, Supaari VaGayjur had deemed the considerations to have been fully considered, the arrangements adequately arranged and the time, at long last, ripe for their visit to his adopted city. On the three-day trip downriver from Kashan, moving past slow trade barges and small skiffs, he answered as many of their questions as he could. They were interested in the sulfur-aluminum batteries that powered his craft, the material from which the hull was made, the waterproof coatings, the navigation equipment. When he finally convinced them that he simply used the boat, he did not make it, they went on to questions about the city itself, and when at last he could stand no more and told them finally, "Wait! You shall see it all shortly," they talked among themselves in H'inglish, never resting from their curiosity.

They stopped overnight at two villages along the way, the first one just above the Pon delta and the second on the Masna'a Tafa'i coast about twelve hours out of Gayjur. As in Kashan, the foreigners were accepted by the Runa without fuss. Supaari simply introduced them as traders, from far away. He was counting on this kind of reception by Va-Gayjuri Runa as well and was heartened to see the reality of it in these outlying villages, after so much worried anticipation. He began to hope things would go well. But once again he made the foreigners promise that they would only go out at redlight, and even then accompanied always by his Runa secretary, Awijan. It was important that they not be seen by other Jana'ata.

This restriction was in direct opposition to D. W. Yarbrough's desire to make contact with the Jana'ata government. It was past time, he believed. If the Jesuit party hung around much longer without making itself known, the authorities might think there was something sneaky about them, wonder why they'd kept themselves a secret such a long time. But they owed Supaari a debt of gratitude for all his assistance and in the end, D.W. decided that they should abide by his rule. "Get the lay of the land, this trip," Yarbrough told Marc and George and Jimmy before they left. "When you get back, y'all talk it over and decide what the next move is." He knew he wouldn't be a part of the discussion. He knew that he was dying. They all did.

Now, faced with Gayjur itself, the three humans understood that it would be a real job just to get a superficial impression of the city in the six days allotted to this visit. Marc Robichaux began to feel that this was another of the step-by-step increments they were meant to take.

Coming within line of sight to his compound, Supaari radioed Awijan, announcing their arrival, and steered the little powerboat through the towering mass of shipping. He docked with insouciant skill and a yawn and pointed out his compound's gateway with casual pride, trusting its impressive size and the obvious signs of prosperity to tell his visitors that they were dealing with a man of consequence. "Shall you rest now or go out to see the city?" he asked them, knowing full well what they would say. When they said it, he handed them over to his secretary and told them to trust Awijan to escort them properly and to answer their questions. He, Supaari, was going to sleep now and would see them the next day, in the morning at second sunrise.

AND SO, WITH as much preparation as they could have hoped for, Marc Robichaux, Jimmy Quinn and George Edwards plunged into an alien city for the first time. It was all very well to expect to be surprised and confused, but it was sheer bedlam to experience. The scents and noise of Gayjur assaulted them: warehouses filled with the sweet and spicy and grassy fragrances of perfume components; docks and shipyards smelling of wet sail, rotting sea life, sealants and paint, sailors and loaders shouting; cookshops and street stalls and factories turning the air fragrant and stinking by turns with soups and ammonia and frying vegetables and solvents. There was a vast amount of exchange going on, of buying and selling, of business being done in temporary but well-made booths with handsome fittings leaning against beautifully built masonry walls. Vendors hawked unidentifiable objects from pushcarts, simply designed and nicely balanced. Moving through the cramped side-streets, they caught glimpses through half-open doors of Runa working with their ears clamped shut amid a deafening clamor of hammers and chisels, drills and electric saws.

The pace was much faster than in Kashan, and there was far more variety of physical type, Marc noticed. The dockworkers were stockier, sturdy and drop-eared; there were others, robed as Supaari had been when they met him, but smallish and subtly different in the face, alert and fine-boned, with a direct and disturbing gaze, and Awijan was one of these. And there were differences in coat: the colors and textures varied, some rough and curling, others silkier and longer than normal in Kashan. Regional variations, Marc thought. Immigrant populations, perhaps, natural in a port city.

It was a weird feeling, walking along in plain view, undeniably strange, and yet no crowds gathered, no children screamed or pointed or hid. They were noticed and commented upon quietly as they passed through the streets, but when Awijan offered to buy them kebablike sticks of roasted vegetables, the vendor simply handed them their food with ordinary courtesy. They might have been buying pretzels in Philadelphia.

As night fell, Awijan led them back to Supaari's compound and took them through an open courtyard, past many small storage buildings, along the edge of an impressive warehouse, and then into the living quarters, spare and plain-walled but hung with brilliant tapestries and cushioned with deep carpets. After years of sleeping in the huddled company of Runa, they were astonished to be given small private rooms and found the circular bedding on raised platforms nestlike and very fine to curl up in. They slept soundly until long past first sunrise.

It was midday when Supaari met them for their first and his only meal. As they reclined against the pillows and cushions along the walls, a long low table was carried in and then paved with a stream of plates and bowls and platters emerging from the kitchen. There were roasted meats, soups, extraordinary things that appeared to be seafood stuffed with pastes of something savory and then formed somehow into loaves and sliced, and fruits they had not seen before and many kinds of vegetables, plain and with sauces and carved cunningly and left whole. There were strong flavors, and delicate and bland and spiced. The service was soft-footed and discreet, and the meal took hours. Awijan sat nibbling at a little distance and observed; Marc noted the next day that the dishes that had pleased no one were gone from the array and those that the guests had most enjoyed were prominently offered again, surrounded by other choices not seen earlier.

That second evening, Awijan took the foreigners farther uptown, and it was on this tour that they began to get a feel for the strangely hybrid layout of the city. There was, they now realized, the skeleton of rational gridwork, a rectilinear system of main streets well paved with good heavy cobbles and a system of canals, dividing the city into segments that linked incoming freight from the countryside or ocean to processing and distribution centers in the city.

The city was not crowded in the way that the teeming ports of Earth were. There were no beggars, no limbless cripples, no emaciated loners picking through garbage or potbellied children tugging at weary despairing parents. There was an increasingly noticeable contrast between the rich and the poor as they moved uphill and the congestion thinned and the buildings became more imposing, but it did not disturb the humans as they might have been disturbed in Rio or Calcutta or Lima or New York. Here, one had the impression that prosperity was attainable, that people were competent and confident and either on their way up or content to be where they were. The makeshift markets and bustle seemed due to a desire to get down to business without a lot of extraneous bother over display. And there was a kind of beauty in that.

They saw no schools but many small shops and little factories and minifoundries in which apprentices absorbed skills by patient accretion. For all the movement and hustle in the streets, there were gates to small yards in which families could be seen at rest, eating under wide overhanging eaves, sheltered from the rain but outside in the evening air. There was an eerie quiet sometimes, when the sounds of soft-booted feet and musical Runa voices and the plashing patter of steady rain were all that could be heard as they passed through districts where the trade, like tailoring and embroidery, involved no metal.

On their third evening, Awijan took them across the bay to the glassmakers' quarter to see the manufacture of spectacular serving pieces like those that graced Supaari's table: clear, heavy, polished glass with streamers of sparkling bronze-colored aventurine ribboning through the bodies of the bowls. Marc had the impression that there were two main aesthetic traditions, one encrusted and heavy with decoration, the other rather spare and clean. Made for Jana'ata and Runa, respectively, he guessed, gazing across the bay to Galatna Palace and the surrounding hillside compounds, with their mosaics and fountains, their high walls crenellated and corbeled, their facades barnacled with ornament. More money than taste, Marc thought uncharitably. Galatna had an overevolved look, like that of classical Chinese architecture, as though it had been worked on too long, layered and added to more than was strictly good for it.

He questioned Awijan about this as they toured the next shop. "Most Jana'ata prefer such things as those," Awijan told him, indicating the highly decorated items, and added in a low confiding voice, "Someone's eyes get tired looking at them." Which confirmed Marc's admiration for Runa chic.

And yet on their final day in the city, Marc was forced to modify his dismissal of Jana'ata art. George and Jimmy had finally made it clear that the one thing they must do without fail was talk to a chemist about fuel for the lander. It took a fair bit of explaining, but Supaari finally caught on to what they were trying to say and Awijan dispatched a runner to a local distiller of perfumes who brought back a thin-faced and somewhat nervous-looking chemist. With graphics of the periodic table of elements to establish some common ground and 3-D displays of fuel components to work from, the chemist was quick to catch on to the problem. To the belly-deep relief of the foreigners, the formula did not seem at all daunting.

But Marc's eyes glazed over during the technical discussion that followed and Supaari, equally bored, asked if perhaps Robichaux would like to see something of Jana'ata art. The suggestion was so casual that Marc, who was beginning to know Supaari, suspected immediately that Supaari had planned it in advance. A two-passenger chair was summoned, and Marc was given a hooded robe that was far too large and helped into the curtained conveyance. Supaari declared that he himself would accompany the Foreigner Marc on this excursion, leaving Awijan behind to assist George and Jimmy with the chemist.

It was full daylight and Marc, peeking through the spaces between the curtains as they were carried uptown, caught glimpses of new areas of the city and got an entirely different impression of the place. Here, Jana'ata were everywhere and conspicuous. "In robes," Supaari murmured, a little sarcastically, "as heavy as their responsibilities, headdresses as lofty as their ideals." The faces were very like the Runa faces Marc was familiar with, but there was a hollow-cheeked and wolfish look to them that left him uneasy. Unlike Supaari, they seemed not lively but frighteningly intent, not friendly but coldly courteous, not humorous but keenly observant, and above all: unapproachable. Everywhere,

Runa stepped back, bowed or nodded or turned aside. Marc shrank back into his enclosure, now feeling in his gut some of the reasons behind Supaari's repeated warnings about other Jana'ata, and gave thanks to God that they'd encountered the Runa first.

The commotion of the city receded as they continued uphill and turned toward the mountain south of Gayjur. At length they arrived at a solitary stone building, low-lying and horizontal in plan, galleried and deeply eaved. Supaari told Marc to wait out of sight, and then disappeared for some time. When he returned Supaari leaned in through the curtains and whispered, "You are an elderly Jana'ata lady here to observe the ceremony for your serenity. For this reason, you must be alone. You understand?" Marc lifted his chin and understood very well. Jana'ata were capable of lying, he observed with some amusement. Supaari continued very quietly, "Someone has purchased the exclusive viewing rights. They will clear the courtyard so you may enter the balcony. It is not permitted to speak Ruanja here. Say nothing."

When they were alone except for the Runa chaircarriers, Supaari assisted Marc out of the chair and led him, head down under his hood and dripping oversized Jana'ata draperies like a child playing dress-up, into the building and across a central open area with scented fountains. Holding up his robes, keeping his hands concealed under the long oversleeves, Marc found himself ascending a ramp to a second-level gallery. He was so intent on not tripping over his garment and keeping his alien anatomy under wraps that he hardly glanced at anything around him until they reached a small curtained room, like a box at the opera. Supaari stepped in first and found his position before drawing the front curtains close together. Then he motioned Marc in and closed off the back curtain, leaving the box in semidarkness, indicating with a gesture that it was safe for the foreigner to throw back his hood.

"You shall stand back a little, but watch carefully," Supaari whispered. "It is very beautiful. Like your 'landscapes.' "

Marc was charmed by this compliment but very worried that they were taking some terrible risk. Before he could say anything, the ceremony began, and since they were already in as deep as he imagined they could get, he decided to trust Supaari's judgment and God's plan.

Moving slightly so he could see through the small gap in the curtain, Marc looked down into a little room of quiet perfection, the gray dressed-stone walls nearly mortarless and shining like polished granite, the floor paved with flags of something veined and figured like pink marble. There was a large, low, black stone bowl, filled with some colorless liquid, and around this knelt six plain-robed Jana'ata. At the knees of each was an array of pottery cups, containing pigment, and behind each, a small brazier in which some kind of incense had been set burning. The scent reached Marc just as the chanting began and although he had been told that these were artists, it all recalled for him the mood and awe of worship.

Then, in time with the telling of some epic poem, leaning toward the bowl in a balletic movement of body and arm, the adepts each dipped their styluslike talons into the pigment pots and touched the surface of the black bowl's contents. For an exquisite moment, colors appeared: blending, spreading, dispersing in a radiant mandala. Again and again, the artists, chanting and dipping and swaying in time, touched the liquid surface with magic and color, the shimmering patterns changing with every hypnotic verse, the incense growing more powerful . . .

Later, Marc would have no memory of leaving the box or of climbing into the chair again. The swaying rhythmic movement of the carriers merged in his mind with the poetry he had heard, and the ride back to the harbor compound of Supaari VaGayjur was a mixture of half-dreamt visions and floating moments of reality. Slumped against Supaari and staring with dilated eyes inside his fabric cocoon, Marc noted at one point with vague and distant interest that they were going past a public square of some kind. He saw through a space in the curtains three Runa publicly put to death, their throats slit as they knelt with their backs to the Jana'ata executioners, who stood behind them and drew their heavy claws across their victims' throats as cleanly and humanely as kosher butchers.

This scene registered at some level, but Marc could not be sure if it was real or a doped hallucination. Before he could inquire about it, the image drifted away, lost in pulsating bursts of glowing color and rhythmic chant.

IT WAS NOT, evidently, a day meant for sobriety.

Assured now that the lander fuel could be duplicated, George and Jimmy were alternately limp with relief and jubilantly keyed up. Awijan did not entirely grasp the motive behind the transaction just concluded but saw the foreigners' need for celebration and felt moved to make this possible for them.

For a time, Awijan did not act on this feeling, for she was an unnaturally controlled and unspontaneous Runao, the product of several hundred generations of selective breeding and a thorough education. Supaari's first yard boss, she had quickly moved up to secretary, and he had always treated her as an equal, subordinate in position but not inferior. Indeed, Awijan's bloodlines were more ancient and in some ways superior to those of Supaari himself, a fact that he noted with characteristic amusement at the irony. And though the other Jana'ata merchants disapproved of Supaari's almost egalitarian relationship with the Runa in general and there was ungrounded gossip about him and Awijan, she had enjoyed full use of her own capacities and lived in a good deal of physical comfort. The price Awijan paid for her position in life was solitude. She had no peers, nor anyone to look to for guidance. She rarely ventured beyond Supaari's compound except on business, bearing proper identification and taking care to appear deferential to Jana'ata and Runa alike. She had no wish to arouse either outrage or envy. It made for a tense, compressed life. One had to have an outlet.

"Tomorrow you shall return to Kashan," she told the foreigners, who had treated her with respect and kindness. "Someone would like to invite you to share a meal. Shall this be acceptable?"

It was. It was altogether acceptable. And so, as Marc Robichaux was carried, dozing, through the streets of Gayjur toward Radina Bay, Jimmy Quinn and George Edwards followed Awijan out of Supaari's compound and into a Runa neighborhood a little distance inland from the harbor. Standing with her at a gateway, they found themselves looking into something like a restaurant or perhaps a private club, filled with Runa of many types, exuberant and louder than the humans were accustomed to hearing them.

"Jeez, it's like the wedding," Jimmy said, smiling broadly.

They moved inside and Awijan led them to a corner where people made room for them on the padded floor. Huge platters of food circulated from hand to hand through the crowd, along with beautiful plates of jellied lozenges and these, George and Jimmy found, were delicious. There was no dancing or music but there was a storyteller and all around the room, there were games of strength and gambling going on and cash was definitely changing hands. Nudging Jimmy as they settled onto the cushions, George murmured, "I guess city Runa don't get *porai* as easy as country Runa."

Soon even the reserved and self-contained Awijan opened up and joined in the raucous commentary on the storyteller's tale, and the two foreigners were delighted to find their Ruanja good enough to understand the funny parts. George and Jimmy and Awijan ate and watched and listened and talked, and at some point in the evening, one of the Runa challenged Jimmy to a sort of arm-wrestling competition. Jimmy tried to beg off, saying, "Someone would be sad to make your heart *porai*," which he meant as courtesy but which was in fact exactly the kind of backward insult this crowd loved. So the two unlikely competitors squared off across a low table, Awijan coaching Jimmy with stupendously unhelpful athletic advice and George cheering wildly when Jim took two of the five contests in spite of being handicapped by the lack of a stabilizing tail. And they all three had some more of the jellied stuff, sweet and tart and cool on the tongue, to celebrate.

The crowd's attention shifted then to another pair of happy combatants and Jimmy eventually lay back flat, his legs out straight, and put his hands behind his head, smiling serenely at Awijan and then at George, who sat cross-legged and motionless next to him. He is a wonderful-looking man, Jimmy thought suddenly. White hair sweeping back in silken waves from a tanned and splendid old face, George Edwards was the very embodiment of venerable dignity: Seneca amid a gathering of statesmen reclining on Roman daybeds, if you could overlook all the tails.

As though feeling Jimmy's eyes on him, George turned toward the younger man. There was a pregnant pause. "I can't feel my lips," George announced, and then he giggled.

"Me neither. But I do feel something." Jimmy pondered this feeling. It required the entirety of his concentration to identify it. "I feel meself suddenly overcoom with a startlin' desire to sing 'Danny Boy.'"

George rolled himself into a ball laughing, fists pounding the cushion on either side of his knees with uncoordinated appreciation. Jimmy sat up and snaked out a long arm to snare another jellied thing from a passing tray. He frowned at it with unfocused but mighty scientific interest. "Jaysus, Mary an' Joseph! What d' fook is this stuff?"

"Alien Jell-O shots!" George sang breathlessly. He leaned toward Jimmy to whisper something but misjudged his center of gravity and fell over. "Bill Cosby would be so proud!" he said, sideways.

"And who d' fook would Bill Cosby be?" Jimmy demanded. Not waiting for an answer, he blinked at George with owlish deliberation and confided in his own South Boston accent, "I am hammahd."

George Edwards spoke fair Ruanja, good Spanish and excellent standard English. He considered "hammahd." He compared the sound to many mental templates. He found a match. "Hammered!" George cried triumphantly, still sideways. "Trashed. Destroyed. Totaled. Wiped. Bombed. Smashed. Wrecked."

Jimmy stared down at the small gelatinous timebomb shimmering innocently in his limp hand. "This stuff is great," he declared to no one in particular, since George continued to chant his litany of synonyms, unperturbed by the lack of attentive audience. "You don't even have to take time off from the party to pee."

And Awijan, who had not understood a single word her howling guests were saying, nevertheless gazed upon them with beneficent pleasure. For Awijan was wholly relaxed and utterly unconcerned about her peculiar life and its almost unremitting tensions: quietly and intentionally and magnificently drunk, among friends.

SUPAARI WAS AWARE of his secretary's occasional need to dissipate the uneasiness she fell prey to, and although he was surprised that she had taken the foreigners with her to the club, he was not angry. Truth be told, he enjoyed the almost complete silence that prevailed during their first day's journey back to Kashan.

The second day was a little more animated but now the foreigners were thoughtful. Supaari suspected that they would have a great deal to say to one another when they reached the privacy of their homes and companions in Kashan. He knew from their meals together and their questions and comments that Gayjur had not disappointed them and that his hospitality had been appreciated. This pleased him. He now looked forward to doing the same for Ha'an and the others, more confident that he could control the situation in the city.

Supaari recognized that the silence on their last day of travel was of a different quality, although he could not have known why. In fact, as they came around the last bend of the river and Supaari tied up to the

Kashan dock, Marc Robichaux, George Edwards and Jimmy Quinn were preparing themselves to be met by people in mourning.

Knowing that D.W. was close to the end, they'd offered to postpone the trip to Gayjur but he'd insisted they go on, not trusting Supaari to make the offer a second time after stalling them a whole year. So they had said their good-byes before they left. Now, they could see Sofia spot them from her terrace and watched as she and Sandoz picked their way down the cliffside to the dock. The ravaged faces of Emilio and Sofia told them, they thought, all they needed to know. Climbing out of the boat, Jimmy went to his wife and stooped low to hold her while she cried. Marc Robichaux, taking in the obvious, said quietly, "The Father Superior." Mute, Emilio nodded but continued to look at George, as he had from the moment he'd emerged from the Quinns' apartment and come within sight of the returning travelers.

"And Anne," George said, uncomprehending but certain, the heart in him going dead.

Emilio nodded again.

THE RUNA WERE still out harvesting *anukar,* so they were alone. Supaari came with them to Sofia and Jimmy's apartment, having been told only that Ha'an and the Elder had been killed. He was shocked and could see the distress all around him. They love one another, he thought, hardly knowing whether to envy or pity them.

Fia, the tiny one with the black mane, told the tale. Knowing Supaari had been fond of Ha'an, she repeated parts of it in Ruanja for him. Dee and Ha'an were killed by some kind of animal, she told him. "Manuzhai and the others told us to be careful for *djanada.* Someone thinks a *djanada* attacked them."

"This was not an animal. *Djanada* are Jana'ata, do you understand? But these are dishonorable men. The killer was VaHaptaa," Supaari said, making his contempt obvious. "Do you understand this word? Haptaa? In Ruanja, it is *brai noa.*"

The small, dark interpreter spoke for the first time, in Ruanja first and then in H'inglish for the others. "*Brai noa.* Without a home. VaHaptaa is 'from nowhere.' Landless, perhaps."

Sandoz, Supaari remembered then. He had learned the names of Ha'an's companions slowly but had trouble with the interpreter's. Meelo, the Runa called him. And Ha'an had called him Emilio. And the

Elder had called him Son, and the others called him Sandoz. So many names! They had confused Supaari at first. "VaHaptaa are criminals," Supaari explained. "They have no place. They are outsiders: *n'jorni.*" He searched for some simple parallel. "Do you recall the first day of our meeting? Someone was angry because it is a crime to take meat without permission. This taking is called *khukurik.*"

"Poaching," Sandoz said, lifting his chin to show he understood.

"VaHaptaa take without permission. *Khukurik* is not permitted. You should kill that one if you see him again," Supaari told them. "Someone would thank you for this service. And the VaKashani will also be grateful. VaHaptaa are dangerous to them: *djanada,* do you understand?"

They did now, they thought. Too late, but now they understood.

Supaari bid them farewell after that, feeling it was time to leave the foreigners to their own death rituals. Sandoz accompanied him to the dock, always courteous if he understood how to express respect. Supaari knew the foreigners well enough now to realize that insult was always born of ignorance, not malice. "*Sipaj,* Sandoz. Someone is sorry for your loss," he said, climbing down into the boat.

Sandoz looked at him. The strange brown eyes were less disturbing to Supaari now; he was used to the tiny round iris and knew that Sandoz and the others did not see through some sorcery but in a normal way. "You are kind," Sandoz said at last.

"Someone will return before the end of Partan."

"Our hearts will be glad of it."

Supaari cast off and backed the powerboat around the dock, turning it into the southern channel toward the village of Lanjeri, where he had business to attend to. He looked back once before his boat rounded the bend and saw the foreigner still standing on the dock, a small black silhouette against the Kashan cliffside.

THE LONG EVENING passed with George alternately sitting and pacing, sobbing suddenly and then laughing through the tears, telling Jimmy and Sofia stories of Anne and of their marriage, and then falling silent. It was almost impossible to go home to where Anne wasn't, but George finally moved to leave. Sofia burst into tears again, undone by memories of her widowed father's grief and by her own sadness and by the thought of losing Jimmy as George had lost Anne. Pressing George's hand against her belly, she said with fierce conviction, "You are this baby's grandfather. You will live with us." And held him until the crying stopped and got him into the bed Jimmy made up. The two of them watched over George until at last he slept.

"I'm all right," Sofia whispered to Jimmy then. "See about Emilio. It was bad, Jimmy. You can't imagine. It was terrible."

Jimmy nodded and kissed her and left to check on the priests, neither of whom had been seen for hours. Stooping to peer into their apartment, he saw how things were and motioned Marc outside. "D.W. would tell you to write up the damn report," Jimmy said very softly, stepping back to the far side of the terrace with Marc. "It can probably wait until tomorrow, if you don't feel up to it."

A fitful smile appeared on Marc's face, pale in the moonlight. He understood that he was being offered a good excuse to shirk his real duty, which was to comfort Emilio somehow. He regretted his own lack of pastoral experience. What could one say? Sandoz, he knew, had been prepared for the Father Superior's death, but Anne, too—a staggering blow, to lose them both at once, and horrifically. "Thank you. I shall write the report tonight. It will be good to have something to do."

Marc ducked into the apartment for his tablet, hesitated, and then picked up the Father Superior's, with its preprogrammed transmission codes; Yarbrough had shown him how to use it, knowing this day was coming. He looked to Sandoz, concerned that this practical reminder of D.W.'s passing would distress him, but Emilio seemed not to know Marc was in the room. Returning to the terrace, Marc told Jimmy quietly, "I shall be in Aycha's apartment." He turned back toward Sandoz and then faced Jimmy again, giving a small shrug.

Putting a hand on Marc's shoulder, Jimmy looked past him at Emilio sitting in the gloom. "It's okay. I'll see what I can do."

Jimmy went inside. For a while, he was as helpless as Marc had been, unable to imagine what was keeping Emilio from falling apart. The Irish weep and drink and sing and talk at a wake, so George's reaction had seemed normal and predictable to Jimmy, a kind of grief he understood. But this . . . You poor macho bastard, Jimmy thought suddenly, realizing that Sandoz probably just wanted some privacy so he could finally cry without witnesses and shame. Jimmy got to his feet but then hunkered down on his heels so he could see Emilio's face.

"*¿Quieres compañeros o estar solo?*" he asked gently, to be sure before he left Sandoz alone.

"*Soy solo.*"

Jimmy was almost out of the apartment before he caught the change in the verb and went back. "*Mírame, 'mano.* Look at me!" he said, dropped down to Emilio's level again. He put his hands on Emilio's shoulders and shook him a little. From a great distance, Emilio's eyes came to him. "You are *not* alone, Emilio. Sofia loved them and I loved them, too. Do you hear me? Maybe not for so long, maybe not so deeply, but truly and well. We loved them, too." It was only then, saying it, that the reality of the deaths hit Jimmy, and no burden of stoicism dammed up his tears. Emilio's eyes closed and he turned his head away and then at last, Jimmy understood the rest of it. "Oh, Jesus. You're not *alone,* Emilio. I love you. Sofia loves you. And our kid's gonna need an uncle, man. You're not alone. You've still got us, right? Oh, Jesus," he said again, taking Sandoz in his arms. "That's better. Thank God! That's better . . ."

It was over sooner than Jimmy thought was good for him but at least there'd been some release. Jimmy waited until he thought the time was right and then, wiping his own eyes on his sleeve, lifted Sandoz to his feet. "Come on. No one sleeps alone tonight. You're coming with me." He steered Emilio out of the apartment and, voice roughened by tears, called to Robichaux, "Marc, you come on up to our place, too. No one sleeps alone tonight!"

WHEN JIMMY BROUGHT Emilio and Marc into the apartment, Sofia was still awake, dark eyes huge in her small face, lips and eyelids swollen. She had heard what her husband had called out to Marc and guessed what had given rise to it. Flooded with love, she thought to herself: I have chosen well. She watched, too worn out to help, as Jimmy cobbled together sleeping cushions for the two priests. Marc was subdued but fine. Emilio, she knew, was not fine but he was spent, and slept almost as soon as Jimmy covered him.

When everyone else was taken care of, Jimmy came to her and she took his hand, getting to her feet wearily. They walked out to their terrace and sat close together in the two-person glider George and Manuzhai had built, Sofia nestling under Jimmy's arm, her small hand on his thigh. Jimmy set the chair in motion and for a while, they rocked in companionable quiet. It was clouding up. Moons that had been bright only half an hour earlier were already reduced to hazy glowing disks in the sky. Sofia felt the baby move and drew Jimmy's hand to her belly and watched his face light up, his red-rimmed eyes unfocused as he listened with his fingers to the dance within her.

They spoke then, with the dear and ordinary intimacy of the well-married in the eye of a storm. George was doing okay, considering. Marc was getting his bearings. Emilio seemed stunned but had been able to cry a little.

"And you, Sofia? You look so tired," Jimmy said, worried about her and the child. My God, he thought suddenly. What will we do without Anne? What if the baby is breech? Please, God, let it be a girl, a tiny girl who takes after Sofia and my mom. An easy birth, please, God. And he wondered if they could get back home before the due date if the lander fuel could be manufactured soon enough. But he said, "Do you want to tell me about it tonight or wait until later?"

She had sworn she would never again keep anything from him. Her vow to herself and to him: she would not carry burdens alone. So she began, voice pitched low, to tell him of the past two days.

"SANDOZ? I'M SORRY." She watched him struggle awake, feeling terrible for waking him. "I'm sorry," she repeated as he sat up blinking.

Emilio looked around him, a little confused yet. Then his eyes opened wide and he asked anxiously, "D.W.?"

Sofia shook her head and shrugged. "It's only that I heard something a while ago. I'm probably being an alarmist, but Anne and D.W. have been gone a long time. I think we should go find them."

Still thickheaded, he nodded agreeably: Sure, absolutely, if you say so. And looked around for his clothes, his hand dropping onto his discarded shirt, where he looked at it for a moment, as though he had no idea what to do with it. Finally, he seemed to come fully awake and Sofia said, "I'll wait outside."

As he dressed, she berated herself for timidity. "I should have gone out myself," she called. "I shouldn't have gotten you up." Emilio was showing the effects of broken nights spent nursing D.W. and needed all the sleep he could get during the day. She felt like a caricature of a pregnant woman, scared of noises, apt to burst into tears for no good reason. The early weeks of her pregnancy had been an embarrassing emotional roller coaster.

"No. It's okay. You did the right thing." A minute later, Sandoz appeared on the terrace, reasonably alert. He'd had perhaps four or five hours of sleep.

They went first to the *hampiy* and saw the cup with its dregs of soup. Stepping back outside, Sandoz looked around. "It's quiet out there," he drawled, squinty-eyed, like an old-time cinema cowboy. "Too quiet." He said it to make her laugh, and she smiled but wished she could see Anne and D.W. somewhere.

"They usually walk off that way." He waved vaguely toward the south. "You stay here. I can manage." D.W. was so thin now that Emilio could almost carry him alone. He and Anne could lock hands and make a sort of sling for him.

"No," Sofia said, practical even about her own emotional upheavals. "I'll only sit and worry. I may as well come." He looked at her doubtfully so she added, "It's all right. I feel fine. Really."

They were still north of the lander when they began to know something was wrong. The wind must have shifted because their first indication of what had happened was the odor, the unmistakable smell of blood. Emilio went to the lander and quietly opened the cargo door a few inches, enough to reach in and grab D.W.'s Winchester. "Get inside, lock the door and stay there," he told her. He checked to see that the rifle was loaded, that a round was in the chamber, and walked around the lander without looking back.

She was not sure what made her disobey the order. Maybe she was frightened to be alone and unknowing or simply determined not to shrink from whatever was waiting, but she followed him around the lander and saw then, as he did, the carnage, indistinct in the distance. Even from where they stood, some things were clear. Whatever Sandoz had thought to do with the rifle, it was too late now. Emilio turned, ashen, and saw her. "Stay here," he said, and this time she did as she was told, frozen by memories of her mother's corpse.

She watched Emilio move toward the bodies, saw the rifle fall from his hands, saw his head turn down and away. He looked back toward it all almost immediately, and she saw his hands rise toward his head as he stood, taking in the details. She knew suddenly that it was insupportable for him to be alone with this. I am Mendes, she thought, and she forced herself to go closer but stumbled at the sight of it, and fought nausea. Nimrod, she thought numbly. The hunter of Genesis, whose prey was man.

Emilio turned and saw her moving toward him again. She meant to pull him away from it or hold him, but before she could get closer, he said in a quiet level voice, "There are tarps and a shovel in the lander." He looked at her, eyes steady and dry, until finally she realized why he wanted her to leave. Craven, she walked back to the plane. When she returned, he was streaked and smeared and soaked with blood, and had laid the two bodies out, putting limbs in position. He wiped his gory hand on his shirt and then reached out to close the eyes, smooth the hair.

She was almost blind with tears now but as silent as Emilio. She wanted to help him unfold the tarps, but her arms wouldn't seem to move and so, alone, he covered the butchered bodies of the father of his soul and the mother of his heart. Sick with reaction, Sofia moved to the edge of the cliff and vomited over the side. All she could think of was what a meager meal they must have made.

The graves took a long time, the ground stony and grudging. Emilio dug close by; it was unthinkable to move the bodies in pieces. He had been too busy with the language research to help with the garden, so his hands were not hardened to the shovel. After a while, Sofia realized that he needed gloves and went for them, glad to be able to help somehow. She decided next to collect rocks in a pile, to put over the graves when the time came. That accomplished, she sat and watched, but left again an hour later to fill a canteen for him. As the long Rakhati evening wore on, he would now and then stop digging and stare hollow-eyed and at those times, Emilio would accept water from her wordlessly. Then he would lean to the task again, the relentless sound of the shovel filling the world. At dusk, Sofia got a camplight from the lander and stayed with him until he was done, sometime after midnight.

Emilio climbed out of the second grave and sat for a time, hunched on the ground with his head in his hands. Then he stirred and pushed himself to his feet. Sofia had by that time come to some sticking point. Together, they laid the remains of D. W. Yarbrough and Anne Edwards to rest, and the shoveling began again.

When the mounds were covered with stones, the brief, endless night was over and they simply stood staring at the graves, too exhausted to think or speak. Sofia leaned over and turned off the camplight, its orange glow lost in the light of morning. When she straightened, she found herself looking directly into the eyes of Emilio Sandoz and was appalled by what she saw.

How long had they known each other? she wondered. Was it ten years? In all that time, she had never even called him by his given name . . . She tried to find words for him, some way to let him know that she had the measure of this loss, knew the weight and depth and breadth of it, and shared it.

"Emilio," she said finally, "I am your sister and we are orphaned."

He was, she thought, too tired to weep, too shocked, but he looked at her and nodded, accepting it; let her come to him then and hold him. And when at last they embraced, she was a married woman, pregnant with his friend's child, and he was a priest in perpetuity, gutted by grief, and they clung to each other in dumb, bewildered misery.

She led him by the hand down the cliffside, stopping for clean clothes, which she carried to the river. They washed away the blood and dirt and sweat, and dressed, and she brought him to her home, as eerily silent as the first day they'd entered this strange and beautiful village. She fixed them both something to eat; he refused at first, but she insisted. "It's a Jewish law," she told him. "You have to eat. Life goes on." Once he took the first bite, he was ravenous and finished everything she put in front of him.

She knew as clearly as her husband would the next evening that no one should sleep alone, not now, not after all that, so she put him to bed, in Jimmy's place, and cleaned things up a little before lying down next to him. It was then that she felt the baby move for the first time. She was motionless for a moment, astonished and absorbed. Then she reached toward him and took his hand and held it against her belly. There was a breathless pause and then again the turning, the quickening. Life goes on, she meant for him to understand. Death is balanced.

"I did not mean to be cruel," she would tell Jimmy the next night, despairingly, her small hands fisted. "I only wanted him to feel a part of life again."

Emilio sat up suddenly and twisted away from her, shattering at last. She realized then how it must have seemed to him and begged him to forgive her, trying to explain. He understood, but it was so vivid and his isolation now seemed total, and he could not speak. She rose on her knees behind him and held him as tightly as she could, as though to keep his body from going to pieces. He was so worn out, but the sobbing lasted a long time. Finally he lay down again, his back to her, hands over his face. "God," she heard him whisper over and over, "God."

She lay down behind him and pulled her knees up close, cradling the shaking body until she felt the spasmodic shuddering diminish and heard his breathing slow and grow even. And so they slept: bereaved and exhausted, with mourning as their chaperone.

31

NAPLES:
AUGUST 2060

IT WAS A desiccated version of Sofia's story that the Father General and his colleagues heard from Emilio, but they had Marc Robichaux's report from that night and from the days that followed.

"The VaKashani were kind," Sandoz told them. "When they returned and found out what had happened, they made certain no one was left alone. It was, I believe, in part a desire to comfort us but I think they were concerned that the VaHaptaa hunter who had taken Anne and D.W. was still in the region, looking for more easy prey. They were afraid for their children, naturally, but also for us because we obviously did not know how to take care of ourselves. And we had attracted trouble."

The headaches were very bad, clusters of them coming only hours apart, crushing thought and prayer, pressing even grief out of his mind. The Runa expected emotional distress to cause illness, but they were concerned that they could find no way to compensate him. Askama would lie down next to him in the dark, waiting it out with him, and he would awaken to find her eyes on him, searching for signs that he was better. She was older, more mature by then. "Meelo," she said in English one morning, "can you not be glad again? I am very worried you might die." It was a turning point, a lifeline he was able to grasp, and he thanked God for it. He didn't want to frighten her.

"Father Robichaux reported that there were a lot of babies at that time," John said. It seemed to him, reading the reports, that these births might have provided some sense of renewal. Indeed, Robichaux had felt this, marveling that he had forgotten "what a joy a new child can be, what a simple pleasure it is to have a baby's damp head on one's shoulder." In the last report Robichaux filed, about two weeks after the deaths of Anne Edwards and D. W. Yarbrough, Marc wrote that George Edwards had been greatly heartened by the infants placed in his arms, the press of new life around him. The Quinns, too, were awaiting a birth.

But at John's words, Emilio's face took on the careful neutral look that now told them all he was working hard. "Yes. There were a lot of babies." He sat very still but looked steadily at Johannes Voelker. "It was the gardens."

Knowing that he was being addressed directly for some reason but unable to see why, Voelker shook his head. "I'm sorry. I don't follow."

"The mistake. What you've been waiting for. The fatal error."

Voelker flushed and glanced at the Father General, who remained impassive, and then looked back at Sandoz. "I deserved that, I suppose." Sandoz waited. "I deserved that," Voelker repeated, without qualification.

"We had all the information, really," Emilio said. "It was all there. We just didn't understand. I think perhaps that even if we had been told directly, we would not have understood."

They listened to the clock ticking and watched him, not sure if he'd go on or leave. Then Sandoz came back to the room from where he had been and began to speak again.

THEY HEARD THE singing first. Martial and strongly measured. Snatches of it, from a distance, carried on the wind. The VaKashani stirred and gathered themselves, and moved up onto the plain to watch the patrol approach. Why hadn't they stayed in the apartments? Why hadn't they run? They might have hidden the babies, he thought later. But then again, they'd have laid down a trail that any half-competent predator could have followed. What would have been the point? So they circled—the infants, the children, the fathers in the center—and waited on the plain for the patrol to arrive.

Later on, when he'd lived in Gayjur for a while, he understood better the limitations of village Runa; it was incomprehensible at the time. They gave the babies up. They must have known at some level that they would not be allowed to keep them, but the juices of life had risen in them and they'd chosen their own mates and nature, unnaturally aided by the foreigners' gardening with its richer food close by for the eating, had taken its course.

"They breed to their feed, you see," Sandoz told the others. "I realized this later, and Supaari confirmed it. The system is balanced so that the Runa are ordinarily untroubled by sexual desire. They have a family life, but they don't breed unless the Jana'ata want them to. Normally, their fat levels stay low. They travel out to naturally growing resources. It costs energy to do this, yes? The gardens upset the balance." He looked from face to face, to see if they understood. "It's difficult to take it in, isn't it. You see, the Jana'ata don't keep Runa in stockyards or enslave them. The Runa work within the Jana'ata culture because they want to. They are bred to it, and it is normal for them. When a village corporate account reaches a certain level, they are provided with extra food, extra calories, and this brings the females into estrus."

Suddenly, a phrase from a report came back to Giuliani. "Passive voice," he said. "I wondered about it when I read it. Dr. Edwards said their mates were chosen using criteria other than those used for choosing spouses."

"Yes. Subtle, isn't it. Their mates were chosen *for* them: by Jana'ata geneticists. The Runa select anyone they like to marry but they are bred according to the standards of the Jana'ata." He laughed, but it was not a good sound. "It is, when you think about it, quite a humane system, compared to the way *we* breed meat animals."

Felipe Reyes blanched and breathed, "Oh, my God."

"Yes. You see it now, don't you?" Sandoz looked at Voelker, who had not yet realized. Then Voelker's eyes closed. "You see it now," Sandoz repeated, watching Voelker react. "The standards in the city, for specialists, are very high. But nothing is wasted. If the result of a mating is not up to standard, the offspring is removed as soon as possible, before an attachment can be formed. A sort of veal, one might say." Johannes Voelker looked as though he might be sick. "The village Runa are in some ways the most fortunate. They gather food and fibers and other plant products, very much as they might have without Jana'ata interference in their lives. Their breeding is strictly controlled, but they are not preyed on as they were in prehistory, except for the occasional Va-Haptaa poacher, who still exploits the Runa in the old way, as free-range food. Supaari told us that. When was it? About two days after Anne and D.W. were killed. I myself used the word, *poacher*. I simply didn't realize that it implied the existence of legal use of the meat."

"It wouldn't have made any difference, Emilio," John said.

Sandoz stood suddenly and began to pace. "No. It wouldn't have. I understand that, John. It was already too late. The gardens had been planted. The babies had been conceived. Everywhere. All over Inbrokar. Even if I had understood the day Supaari told us, it wouldn't have made any difference." He came to rest in front of Voelker. "We asked permission. We considered the ecological impact. We simply wanted to feed ourselves, not to be a burden on the village." He stopped and then, rigorously honest, added, "And we wanted something familiar to eat. No one saw any harm in it. Not even Supaari. But he was a carnivore! He thought the garden was ornamental. It never occurred to him that we would grow food."

The Father General sat back in his chair. "Tell us what happened."

Emilio stood still and looked at Giuliani for a long time, as though confused. Then he told them.

THE JANA'ATA OFFICER was evidently aware of the unauthorized breeding and ordered the Runa to bring the babies forward. This was done with near silence, only some of the older children like Askama keening. The humans had been concealed in the center of the crowd. They might have escaped detection if Sofia had not gone forward, Sandoz thought. Or perhaps not. Their scent might well have been picked up within moments even if they hadn't called attention to themselves.

"We had no idea what was going to happen. We just went up to the plain because everyone else did," Sandoz said. "Marc was the only one of us who'd seen any Jana'ata besides Supaari, and he was very uneasy about this patrol. The VaKashani asked us to stay in the center and keep quiet, and Marc thought this was correct. He was very agitated, yes? He told me he'd seen something in the city but he couldn't be sure he'd understood it. Manuzhai told us to be quiet, so I never found out what he meant. All I knew was that Marc was frightened, but the Runa seemed to be taking the situation fairly calmly. Then the patrol began to kill the babies."

Emilio sat down and put his head in his hands. Brother Edward went to the lavatory for the Prograine, but Sandoz was talking again when Behr came back into the office, and he ignored the bottle of pills Ed put next to him. "There is a phrase in Hebrew," he was telling them. "*Eshet chayil*: woman of valor. Sofia realized what was happening before the rest of us."

"And she resisted," Giuliani said, realizing now how violence had become linked with the Jesuit party.

"Yes. I heard her say it first, but then it was picked up by the VaKashani and became a sort of chant: 'We are many. They are few.' She said this and then she walked forward." He saw her at night, in the dreams: head up, a princely posture. "She lifted one of the babies from the ground. I think the Jana'ata commander was so astonished by her existence that he simply couldn't move at first. But then the whole village surged forward to retrieve the children, and when the Runa moved, the patrol began to react very quickly." He sat, breathing deeply, eyes wide, staring at the table. "It was a bloodbath," he said finally.

Voelker leaned forward. "Perhaps you would like to stop now?"

"No. No. I need to finish this." Emilio's head lifted and he looked at the bottle of Prograine but did not touch it. "The patrol, I think, was out of control for a time. I believe it was the combination of shock over our presence and outrage that the Runa had moved against them. And what Sofia said was terrifying to them, yes? You must understand that the Jana'ata also strictly limit their numbers to those that can be sustained by this system of breeding. Their population structure is almost exactly that of a predator species in the wild, about four percent of the prey population. Supaari explained this to me. So to hear the Runa chanting, 'We are many. They are few'—this must have been nightmarish for them."

"I can't believe you're defending them," Felipe said, aghast. There was a burst of talk, argument about the Stockholm syndrome. Emilio put his hands over his head while it went on. Suddenly he brought his fists down to the table with soft control, careful not to damage the braces, and said with quiet precision, "If you keep up this noise, I will have to quit."

They fell silent then, and he pulled in a careful breath. "I am not defending them. I am trying to explain to you what happened and why. But it is their society, and they pay their own price for their way of life." He looked, hard-eyed, at Reyes and demanded, "What is the population of Earth now, Felipe? Fourteen, fifteen billion?"

"Almost sixteen," Felipe said quietly.

"There are no beggars on Rakhat. There is no unemployment. There is no overcrowding. No starvation. No environmental degradation. There is no genetic disease. The elderly do not suffer decline. Those with terminal illness do not linger. They pay a terrible price for this system, but we too pay, Felipe, and the coin we use is the suffering of children. How many kids starved to death this afternoon, while we sat here? Just because their corpses aren't eaten doesn't make our species any more moral!"

Giuliani let this outburst burn itself out. When Sandoz got ahold of himself again, the Father General repeated, "Tell us what happened."

Emilio looked at him, as though lost, but finally realized that he had gone off track. "I believe the patrol meant only to kill the infants, originally. Supaari told me later that if the villagers bred a second time without permission, it would have been a capital offense for the females who'd given birth. But because the Runa resisted, the patrol overreacted. They clearly meant to crush the riot."

"How many were killed?" Giuliani asked levelly.

"I don't know. Perhaps a third of the VaKashani. Maybe more." He looked away. "And Sofia. And Jimmy. And George." Emilio finally gave in and reached for the Prograine. Too late, most likely, for it to do any good. They watched him as he washed down two of the tablets and drained the glass of water.

"And where were you?" Giuliani asked.

"Toward the center of the crowd. Askama was very frightened. When the killing started, Manuzhai and I were trying to shield her with our bodies. Chaypas was killed, defending us."

"And Father Robichaux?"

"He ran." Sandoz looked at Felipe and said softly, "I'm not defending him either, but there wasn't anything he could have done. We were the size of half-grown children and it was utter chaos. There was no chivalry. Anyone who came within reach was cut down." He was almost pleading with them to understand. "We were completely unprepared for this! Supaari was so different. Try to imagine what it was like!"

"The Jana'ata military is the martial arm of a sentient predatory species," Voelker said quietly. "And they were defending civilization as they know it. It must have been terrifying."

"Yes." It was getting harder. "I've got to have the lights out." Voelker got up to take care of it for him. Then he heard the Father General's voice again.

"Tell us."

"I was taken prisoner immediately." He could hear Askama, screaming his name. "Marc was hunted down without difficulty. We were taken with the Jana'ata patrol. From village to village. I don't think they necessarily understood that we were responsible for the gardens. They didn't know what to make of us. They had a job to do, and they took us along. I believe they meant eventually to bring us to the city of Inbrokar, to the capital. In every village along the route, the gardens were burned and there was a slaughter of innocents. I've got to finish this." He stopped, concentrated on keeping his breathing steady. "Marc—you understand that the gardens were Marc's, yes? To witness this slaughter—" A few more minutes. "The Jana'ata eat only once a day. We were offered food each morning and then force-marched for many hours. Marc refused to eat. I tried to persuade him, but he would only say something in French. A few words."

He took his hands away from his head and tried to look at them. "I am illiterate in many languages," he told them. "I have learned to speak Arabic and Amharic and K'San, but not to read them. French is the only language I read but do not speak. It is very different in its spoken form, yes?" The light was too much. He closed his eyes again. "When I tried to make Marc eat, he would say, *'Ill son, less and sawn.'* Something like that. I should have recognized it . . ."

"Ils sont les innocents." It was Giuliani's voice. "It is hard to think the unthinkable. They were offering you the meat of the innocents."

Emilio was trembling badly now. "Yes. Later, I myself saw what— Nothing was wasted. Ed?" He managed to hold on until Brother Edward got him to the lavatory, and when the sickness passed, Ed replaced the vomited Prograine with an injected dose. He had no idea who took him to his room but before he fell asleep, he said, "I dream of it sometimes."

Johannes Voelker, the beads of a rosary passing through his fingers, was with him when he awoke. "I am sorry," he said.

IT WAS TWO days before Sandoz was able to continue. "You told us that you believed you were being brought by the military to the capital city," Giuliani began. "I take it you did not reach—" He consulted his notes. "Inbrokar."

"No. Supaari told me later that he arrived at Kashan about two days after the massacre. He attended to matters there and then came after Marc and me. He had to guess at the route, I suppose. I think we were on the march for perhaps two weeks before he caught up with us. This period of time was very confused. And we were not functioning well. I tried to get Marc to eat. I— He was not able to do this. After a while I gave up."

"But you ate the meat," John said. "After you knew."

"Yes." Emilio stopped, searching for some way to explain. "There was a time in the British military when it was possible to punish a man with as many as eight hundred lashes. Have you read of such things? Some men actually survived this, and they reported that after a time, they no longer felt any pain. They felt only a sort of hammering. It was like that, in my soul. Do you understand? To watch the children killed, to eat the meat. After a time, it felt only like hammering." He shrugged. They were trying, but he knew they couldn't imagine it. "Anyway, Supaari caught up to the patrol. By the time he found us, Marc was very weak. I think the commander would have killed him soon. He was slowing them up." There had been no emotion when he saw Supaari. He and Marc simply sat on the ground, too tired to think or hope or pray. Even with the meat, he was exhausted. He knew he couldn't keep Marc on his feet much longer, that he was close to collapse himself. "I think Supaari bribed the commander. There was a long discussion. It was in a language I didn't know."

"So Supaari took you back to Kashan?" John prompted, when the silence went on too long.

Sandoz roused himself. "No. I don't know that we'd have been welcome there. He took us to Gayjur. To his own compound. I never saw Kashan again."

"Based on Father Robichaux's descriptions of his time in that city, you would have been relatively safe there, as long as you kept out of sight," the Father General said. "Or perhaps I am wrong?"

"I believe Supaari originally meant it to be safe for us. He may not have been clear about his own motives. He felt some duty toward us, perhaps. He was fond of Anne, genuinely, I believe. And we had made him a very wealthy man. He was quite empathetic for a Jana'ata. I think he could imagine to some extent what it might be like, to be alone and unsupported."

Vincenzo Giuliani became very still, but Sandoz did not notice. I deserved that, Giuliani thought, echoing Johannes Voelker's remark, even if it wasn't intentional.

"In any case," Sandoz was saying, "he evidently decided to ransom us and brought us to his home and took responsibility for us. He made us part of his household."

"That was when he took you to see the ivy, the *sta'aka*?" John asked.

"Yes." For once, he did not have to explain. Sitting impassively, his mind drifted as John Candotti told the others about the *hasta'akala*. About the way the hands were made to look like the trailing branches of ivy, which grows on stronger plants, to symbolize and enforce dependence. John now realized why Marc died. "What if Marc was developing scurvy?" he'd asked Sandoz. "Was there something you ate that Marc didn't?" It wasn't scurvy that killed Marc Robichaux, it was starvation and anemia. And, quite possibly, despair.

HE REALIZED LATER that he'd gone into clinical shock about halfway through the destruction of his left hand. Over the next few days, he would come to himself at intervals, damp and cold and suffering from a thirst unlike anything he'd experienced previously. It seemed impossible to draw enough breath and when he slept, there were dreams of suffocation or drowning. Sometimes, dreaming, he would reach for something, trying to pull himself to air, and his hands would spasm as a dog's legs will twitch during dreams of running, and he would awaken screaming as the involuntary motion sent thin bolts of phosphorescent pain up the long nerves of his arms.

For a time, the heavy immobility of bloodlessness kept him from looking at what had been done. His hands felt clubbed, swollen and throbbing, but he could not lift his head to see them. Periodically, someone would come and exercise his fingers, stretching them flat. He had no idea why this was done. He knew only that the stretching was agony and, sobbing, begged for it to stop. His pleas were in Spanish and therefore unintelligible, but it wouldn't have mattered if he had spoken a pure

and perfect High K'San. They believed it was necessary to prevent con-
tractures from spoiling the line of his fingers' fall from the wrist. So they
let him scream.

As his body slowly replaced the blood he'd lost, he was able to
move, but there was no profit in it. The scabs were forming then and the
itching that heralded healing maddened him. They tied him down to
keep him from tearing at the bandages with his teeth, frantic and weeping with misery. His struggles against the binding may well have prevented blood clots from forming in his legs and breaking loose to kill
him with stroke or heart attack. And, God help him, he had eaten the
meat on the long march from Kashan and so had undergone the *hasta'akala* when decently nourished. These things, for good or ill, probably saved his life.

His first sentence in Ruanja was a request to know Marc's status.
"That one is not strong," he was told, but he was too exhausted from
the effort of asking to hear the answer and slept dreamlessly for once.

When next he woke, his head was clear and he was alone, unbound,
in a sunlit room. With great effort, he got himself to a sitting position
and looked at his hands for the first time. He had nothing left to react
with, too weak even to wonder why it had been done.

He was still sitting, hunched and pallid and staring at nothing,
when one of the Runa servants came in. "Someone's heart will sicken if
he does not see Marc," he said as firmly as he could.

Like twin infants put in different rooms to keep them from waking
each other up, the two foreigners had been separated. The Runa knew
that the sheer physical stamina evidenced by screaming meant that the
smaller of the two would likely survive. They had hope of the quiet one
but not much, and took him away to keep his strength from being
sapped by the other's constant waking. "That one is sleeping," Awijan
told Sandoz. "Someone will bring you to him when he wakes."

Two days later, he sat again in wait for her, determined now to go
to Marc no matter what. "Someone's heart will stop if he does not see
Marc," he insisted, and stood, moving toward the door on thin legs
empty of bone. The Runao caught him as he fell and, muttering, carried
him through the compound to the room where Marc was sleeping.

The stink of blood was everywhere and Marc was the color of rain.
Emilio sat on the edge of the sleeping nest, his own ruined hands in his
lap, and called Robichaux's name. Marc's eyes opened, and there was a
glimmer of recognition.

He had no clue to what Marc said during those last hours. In Latin, he asked Marc if he wished to confess. There was more whispered French. When it stopped, Emilio said the absolution. Marc slept then and he did as well, sitting on the floor next to the bed, his head resting next to Marc's right hand, still seeping blood. Sometime that night, he felt something brush his hair and heard someone say, *"Deus vult."* It might have been a dream.

In the morning, when the sunlight hit his eyes, he awoke, stiff and wretched. Rousing himself, he left the room and tried to get a Runao to call a healer or to put pressure on the oozing wounds between Marc's fingers. Awijan only looked at him blankly. Later, he wondered if he'd remembered to speak Ruanja. Maybe he'd used Spanish again. He would never be sure.

Marc Robichaux died about two hours later without regaining consciousness.

"FATHER ROBICHAUX WAS in poor physical condition when this procedure took place," John was saying, "and did not survive it."

Emilio looked up and saw that everyone was staring at his hands. He put them in his lap.

"It must have been very difficult," the Father General said.

"Yes."

"And then you were alone."

"Oh, no," Emilio said softly. "Oh, no. I believed that God was with me." He said this with great sincerity and because of that, it was impossible to know if he was serious or if this was mockery. He sat and looked into Vincenzo Giuliani's eyes. "Do you believe that? Was God with me?" He looked around at each of them: John Candotti, Felipe Reyes, Johannes Voelker, Edward Behr, his eyes coming to rest again on Giuliani, who found it impossible to speak.

Sandoz rose and went to the door, opening it. Then he paused, struck by a thought. "Not comedy. Not tragedy." Then he laughed, a feral sound, devoid of humor. "Perhaps farce?" he suggested. And then he left.

32

NAPLES:
AUGUST 2060

"I THINK PERHAPS that I was a disappointment to Supaari,"
Sandoz told them the next day. "Anne was a delight to work with, and
they had enjoyed each other a great deal. I was not nearly so amusing."

"You were grieving and terrified and half-dead," Voelker told him
flatly. And John nodded, in agreement at last with something Johannes
Voelker had said.

"Yes! A poor dinner companion." Sandoz had a bright and brittle
sound to him this afternoon. Giuliani was openly disapproving of this
strange glittery mood; Sandoz ignored him. "I'm not sure Supaari really
thought through the idea of formally accepting me as a dependent. It
might have been a sort of spontaneous gesture of interplanetary goodwill. Maybe he wished he'd let the government have me after all." Sandoz shrugged. "In any case, he seemed primarily interested in the trade
aspects of the situation, and I was not much good to him as an economic
adviser. He asked me if I thought that there might be other parties coming from Earth. I told him that we had radioed news of our situation
back to our home planet and that it was possible others might come. We
had no way of knowing when. He decided to learn English from me be-

cause it is our lingua franca. He had already started to pick it up from Anne."

"So. You had work as a linguist," Giuliani said lightly. "For a time, at least."

"Yes. Supaari was making the best of things, I think. We had many conversations, once I was well enough to sort out which language I was supposed to use. It was good English practice for him, and he explained many things to me. You should be grateful to him. Most of what I understand about what happened came from him. He was very helpful."

"How long were you with him?" Giuliani asked.

"I'm not really sure. Six to eight months, perhaps? I learned K'San during that time. Appalling language. The hardest I've ever learned. Part of the joke, I suppose," he said, inexplicably. He stood up and began to walk around the room, jumpy and distractible.

"Did you hear anything of the violence that Wu and Isley reported?" Giuliani asked, watching him move from place to place.

"No. I was quite isolated, I assure you. I imagine, however, that with characteristic creativity, the Runa were beginning to expand on Sofia's suggestion that they were many and the Jana'ata were few."

"Wu and Isley asked after you as soon as Askama brought them to Supaari's compound," Giuliani said, pausing when he saw Sandoz flinch. "Supaari told them that he had made other arrangements for you. What was the phrase he used? Ah. Here: 'more suited to his nature.' Can you tell us why you were removed from the household?"

There was an ugly laugh. "Do you know what I said to Anne Edwards once? God is in the why." He would not look at anyone now. He stood with his back to them and stared out the window, holding the gauzy curtain aside, careful with the hardware of his brace, so as not to snag the fabric. Finally, they heard him say, "No. I don't know what he meant by that, except that somehow he believed he was justified in what he did."

"In what he did," Giuliani repeated quietly. "You did nothing to cause your removal?"

"Oh, *Christ*!" Sandoz spun to face him. "Even now? After all this?"

He walked to his place at the table and sat down, shaking with anger. When he spoke again, his voice was very soft, but he was obviously fighting rage, braced hands rigid in his lap, eyes on the table. "My position in the household of Supaari VaGayjur was that of a crippled dependent. Supaari was not a flighty person, but I believe he must have tired of me. Or perhaps he simply felt that I had fulfilled my role as a language tutor when he became competent in English and that it was time for me to take up another position, so to speak." He looked directly at Giuliani then. "My residential and occupational preferences were not inquired into at any time. How explicit am I required to be?"

HE WAS ASLEEP when they came for him, just past dawn. Caught in the web of a dream, he was at first unsure if the hands were real or imagined, and by the time he knew, their grip was unbreakable. Later on, when he asked himself if there might have been some way to escape, he knew the question was folly. Where could he have gone? What shelter would he have found? Equally pointless: the struggle, the demands for an explanation. The first blow drove the air from his lungs, the second knocked him nearly senseless. Efficient, they wasted no additional time in beating him. Half-dragged, half-carried, he tried to memorize the streets and had an impression that the route was fairly consistently uphill. By the time they arrived at Galatna Palace, his head was clear and he was able to breathe without pain.

Arms pinioned, he was escorted past the fountains he'd seen from Supaari's compound and taken through a side entrance to the palace, down hallways bright with colored tiles and floored with marble and jasper, past internal courtyards, under vaulted, ribbed ceilings. The simplest aspects of the interior were gilded, walls overlaid by silver-wire trellis, each diagonal defined and sparkling with a jewel: emerald and ruby and amethyst and diamond. He saw, in passing, a formal room of ecclesiastical proportions fitted out with a wide indoor canopy in a yellow silken fabric figured and embroidered in turquoise and carmine and spring green, tasseled and fringed with gold thread, its richness echoed by the piles of cushions, ivory and red and blue, their plush fabric creased and divided by braid and costly welting.

Room after room: there was nothing straight that could be made curved, nothing plain that could be given a pattern, nothing white that could be brilliant. The very air was embellished! Everywhere, there was scent: a hundred fragrances and odors he could not name or recognize.

It was, he thought crazily, the most spectacularly vulgar place he'd ever been in. It looked and smelled like a cheap whorehouse, except the

jewels were real and each dram of perfume probably cost a village corporation's yearly earnings.

He tried both Ruanja and K'San each time they encountered someone new, but no one would respond and he thought at first that all the
servants were mutes. As the day wore on, he was given short orders in a
form of K'San that was unfamiliar to him, as High German might be unfamiliar to someone who spoke Low. Go there. Sit here. Wait. He did his
best to comply; he was cuffed when he got something wrong. It was he
who became mute.

In the days that followed, he was held with an odd mixture of freedom and constraint. There were others kept, as he was, in subtle but effective cages. They were able to move from cage to cage but not inside
the palace proper. A zoo, he thought, trying to make sense of all this. I
am in some kind of private zoo.

The others were a bizarre but beautiful group of Runa and some
Jana'ata, and there were a few individuals whose species he was unsure
of. The Runa who shared his cushioned captivity came to his assistance
when he needed help because of his hands. They were extraordinarily affectionate and friendly and tried to make him feel a part of whatever odd
society existed within the ornate and costly walls of Galatna Palace. In
their way, they were kind, but they seemed almost stupid, as though bred
for looks alone, with coats of unusual color, brindled or pied, one
striped like a zebra. Most had fine-boned and overbred faces, a few had
manes, several even approached taillessness. None spoke the dialect of
Ruanja he'd learned in Kashan.

The captive Jana'ata were kept in a separate enclosure and paid
him no attention, even though he could not detect any difference in
their status within the zoo. They were heavily robed, with headdresses
that covered their faces, smaller than Supaari. Later he found out they
were females, and still later he realized that they must be the kind of
sterile partners Supaari had told him about. He called to them in
K'San, asked them to explain to him what this place was, but they kept
to themselves. He was never able to get them to speak to him in any
language.

He had been fed irregularly but well in Supaari's household, like the
pet of a small child who'd wanted a puppy but then lost interest. Here
the food was provided ad libitum because, he supposed, so many of the
others were Runa, who required more constant meals. It was an improvement in theory, but he had no appetite. The Runa always seemed

touchingly pleased when he accepted food from them. So he ate, to repay their kindness.

It came to him that he was now perfectly useless, probably kept as a curiosity, as unique and odd as the gaudy trinkets he'd seen stuffing the alcoves and jamming the shelves of Galatna that first day. And then he was fitted with a jeweled collar, and his humiliation seemed complete. He was, he thought, the exact counterpart of a capuchin monkey kept on a golden chain by some sixteenth-century European aristocrat.

Supaari, however cool and perplexing, had at least been an intellectual companion. Now he tried to steel himself for the predictable effects of utter loneliness, to be patient with the hollow unreality he felt. He did sums and sang songs in his head and tried to pray but stopped when he realized that he was mixing the languages up. He was no longer certain of the differences between Spanish and Ruanja, and that frightened him as much as anything that had happened to him so far. The worst moment came when he realized that he couldn't remember the name of his neighborhood back in Puerto Rico. I am losing my mind, he thought, one word at a time.

He was confused and vaguely frightened all of the time, but he forced himself to keep some kind of schedule, to exercise. This amused his Runa colleagues, but he did it anyway. There were scented baths, as elaborate and horrible as the rest of the place. As no one gave him orders about this, he chose the water with the least offensive perfume and did his best to keep himself clean.

"TELL US," HE heard the Father General say.

"I thought that I had been sold as a zoological specimen," Emilio Sandoz said, trembling violently now, staring at the table, each soft word a separate act of self-control. "I believed, for a while, that I was in a menagerie owned by the Reshtar of Galatna. An aristocrat. A great poet. The author of many songs, yes? A gentleman of catholic tastes. It was, in fact, a kind of harem. Like Clytemnestra, I was compelled to master submission."

IT WAS PERHAPS three weeks or a month later when one of the guards came to the cageside and spoke to the others, who huffed and twitched and crowded around him. He had no idea what anyone was saying, had made no effort to learn anything beyond the most rudimentary phrases of the language spoken here. It was a form of denial, he supposed. If he didn't learn the language, he wouldn't have to stay. Stupid, of course. For reasons he could not have articulated, he was suddenly afraid, but he calmed himself with thoughts that would, very soon, shatter his soul. He said to himself: I am in God's hands. Whatever happens now to me is God's will.

He was given a robe, obviously made specially for him, cut down to his size. It was staggeringly heavy and hot but preferable to parading around naked. He was taken, arms held firmly, to a plain and empty white room, unscented and unfurnished. It was astonishing. He was so relieved to be out of the welter, the visual and olfactory and auditory confusion, that he very nearly sank to his knees. Then he heard Supaari's voice and, heart racing, felt a rush of hope, thinking that he would surely be released. Supaari will take me home now, he thought. It's all been some mistake, he thought, and forgave Supaari for not coming sooner.

He tried to speak when Supaari entered the room but the guard cuffed him in the back of the head and he stumbled forward and fell, thrown off balance by the unfamiliar weight of the robe. He was long past anger at the abuse and felt only shame at falling. Pushing himself to his feet, he looked again for Supaari and found him, but saw then a Jana'ata of medium stature and vast dignity, with violet eyes of surpassing beauty that met and held his own with a gaze so direct and searching that he had to look away. The Reshtar, he realized. A man of learning and artistry, he knew. Supaari had told him of the Reshtar: a great poet. The author of the sublime songs that had brought Emilio Sandoz and his companions to Rakhat—

And then, suddenly, everything made sense to him, and the joy of that moment took his breath away. He had been brought here, step by step, to meet this man: Hlavin Kitheri, a poet—perhaps even a prophet—who of all his kind might know the God whom Emilio Sandoz served. It was a moment of redemption so profound he almost wept, ashamed that his faith had been so badly eroded by the inchoate fear and the isolation. He tried to pull himself together, wishing he'd been stronger, more durable, a better instrument for his God's design. And yet he felt purified somehow, stripped of all other purpose.

There are times, he would tell the Reshtar, when we are in the midst of life—moments of confrontation with birth or death, or moments of beauty when nature or love is fully revealed, or moments of terrible loneliness—times when a holy and awesome awareness comes upon us. It may come as deep inner stillness or as a rush of overflowing emotion. It may seem to come from beyond us, without any provocation, or from within us, evoked by music or by a sleeping child. If we open our hearts at such moments, creation reveals itself to us in all its unity and fullness. And when we return from such a moment of awareness, our hearts long to find some way to capture it in words forever, so that we can remain faithful to its higher truth.

He would tell the Reshtar: When my people search for a name to give to the truth we feel at those moments, we call it God, and when we capture that understanding in timeless poetry, we call it praying. And when we heard your songs, we knew that you too had found a language to name and preserve such moments of truth. When we heard your songs, we knew they were a call from God, to bring us here, to know you—

He would tell the Reshtar: I am here to learn your poetry and perhaps to teach you ours.

That is why I am alive, he told himself, and he thanked God with all his soul for allowing him to be here at this moment, to understand all this at last . . .

Intent on his own rushing thoughts, and by the certainty and rightness that he felt, he made little effort to follow the conversation that went on around him, although it took place in Supaari's own K'San dialect. He was not shocked when the robe was removed. Nudity was normal to him now. He knew that he was alien, that his body held as much interest for a man of learning as his mind. What educated man would not be curious, seeing a new sentient species for the first time? Who could fail to comment on the oddity of nearly complete hairlessness, the undeveloped nose? The strange dark eyes . . . the astonishing lack of tail . . .

" . . . BUT A PLEASING proportion, an elegant muscularity," the Reshtar was saying. Admiring its neat and graceful compactness, he moved thoughtfully around the exotic body, one hand trailing, his fine claws leaving on the hairless chest thin lines that quickly seeped red beads. He passed his hand around the shoulder and, regarding the curve of the neck, encircled it with his hands, noting its delicacy: why, one could snap the spine with a single gesture. His hands moved again, lightly caressing the hairless back, moved lower, to the bizarre void, the fascinating stillness and vulnerability of taillessness.

Standing back, he saw that the foreigner had begun to tremble. Surprised at the rapidity of response, the Reshtar now moved to test readiness, lifting the foreigner's chin and staring directly into the dark unreadable eyes. His own eyes narrowed at the reaction: the head turned quickly in submission, eyes closed, the whole body quaking. Pathetic, in a way, and untutored, but with great appeal.

"Lord?" It was the merchant. "It is acceptable? You are pleased?"

"Yes," the Reshtar said, distracted. He looked at Supaari and spoke then with impatience. "Yes. My secretary has the legal work in hand. You may contract the binding with my sister on whatever date seems propitious. Brother: may you have children." His gaze returned to the foreigner. "Leave me now," he said, and Supaari VaGayjur, rendered Founder of a new lineage for his service to the Reshtar of Galatna, in company with the guard who had escorted Sandoz from the seraglio, backed out of the room.

Alone, the Reshtar circled once more but came to rest behind the foreigner. He dropped his own robe then and stood, concentrating, eyes closed, on the fresh outpouring of scent, more intense, more complex than before. A powerful, stirring fragrance, unparalleled and irresistible. A musk redolent of unfamiliar amines, of strange butyric and caprylic carbon chains, misted by the simple chaste dioxides of shuddering breath and stirred by waves of iron bloodscent.

Hlavin Kitheri, Reshtar of Galatna Palace, the greatest poet of his age, who had ennobled the despised, exalted the ordinary, immortalized the fleeting, a singularity whose artistry was first concentrated and then released, magnified, by the incomparable and unprecedented, inhaled deeply. We shall sing of this for generations, he thought.

LANGUAGE, HIS LIFE'S work and his delight, which had failed Emilio Sandoz word by word, now deserted him utterly. Shuddering in violent moronic waves, he could smell the nauseating glandular reek of his own terror. Mute, he was unable even to think the word for the unspeakable joyless rite that was coming, not even when his arms were seized from behind. But when the powerful prehensile feet locked over his ankles and the belly settled in behind him and the probing began, he went rigid with panic and fathomless horror, understanding finally what was about to happen. The penetration, when it came, made him scream. Things became very much worse after that.

Perhaps ten minutes later he was pulled to an unfamiliar room, bleeding and sobbing. Left alone, he vomited until he was exhausted. He did not think for a long while but only rested, eyes open in the deepening darkness. Eventually, a servant came to take him to the baths. By that time, his life was irrevocably divided, into before and after.

IN THE QUIET of the Father General's office, only Johannes Voelker spoke. "I don't understand. What did the Reshtar want with you?"

My God, Giuliani was thinking, genius may have its limits but stupidity is not thus handicapped. How could I have believed— Eyes closed, he heard Emilio's voice, soft and musical and empty, saying, "What did he want with me? Why, the same thing a pederast wants with a little boy, I imagine. A nice, tight fit."

In the shocked silence, Giuliani's head came up. *Romanità*, he thought. *Know the act and move ruthlessly when the time is right.* "You are many things, but you are not a coward," the Father General said to Emilio Sandoz. "Face it. Tell us."

"I have told you."

"Make us understand."

"I don't care what you understand. It won't change anything. Believe what you like."

Giuliani tried to remember the name of a painting by El Greco: a study of a Spanish nobleman in death. *Romanità* excludes emotion, doubt. *It has to be now, here.* "For your own soul, say it."

"I did not sell myself," Sandoz said in a fierce whisper, looking at no one. "I was sold."

"Not good enough. Say it!"

Sandoz was still, his eyes unfocused, each breath coming with mechanical regularity as though carefully planned and executed, until the moment came when he leaned away from the table, put a foot on its edge and sent it crashing over, splintering in the volcanic explosion of rage, scattering the other men to the edges of the room. Only the Father General remained where he was, and all the sounds of the world were reduced to the ticking of an ancient clock and the harsh, laboring breath of the man standing alone in the center of the room, whose lips formed words they could hardly hear. "I gave no consent."

"Say it," Giuliani repeated, unrelenting. "Make us hear it."

"I was not a prostitute."

"No. You weren't. What were you then? *Say* it, Emilio."

Each word separate, the threadbare voice breaking on the last: "I was raped."

They could see the cost to him, the price of saying this. He stood swaying slightly, the armature of his face demolished by the work of thin, fine muscles. John Candotti breathed: "My God," and somewhere Emilio Sandoz found, inside himself, the black and brittle iron required to turn his head and endure, unflinching, the compassion in John's eyes.

"Do you think so, John? Was it your God?" he asked with terrifying gentleness. "You see, that is my dilemma. Because if I was led by God to love God, step by step, as it seemed, if I accept that the beauty and the rapture were real and true, then the rest of it was God's will too, and that, gentlemen, is cause for bitterness. But if I am simply a deluded ape who took a lot of old folktales far too seriously, then I brought all this on myself and my companions and the whole business becomes farcical, doesn't it. The problem with atheism, I find, under these circumstances," he continued with academic exactitude, each word etched on the air with acid, "is that I have no one to despise but myself. If, however, I choose to believe that God is *vicious*, then at least I have the solace of hating God."

Looking from face to face, he watched comprehension working its way into their minds. What could any of them say? He almost laughed. "Can you guess what I thought just before I was used the first time?" he asked them as he began to pace. "This is rich. This is very funny! You see, I was scared but I didn't understand what was going on. I never imagined—who could have imagined such a thing? I am in God's hands, I thought. I loved God and I trusted in His love. Amusing, isn't it? I laid down all my defenses. I had nothing between me and what happened but the love of God. And I was raped. I was naked before God and I was raped."

The agitated pacing halted as he heard his own words, his voice almost normal until the end, when it fell away into uncomprehending grief, when he knew at last his own devastation fully. But he did not die, and when he could move again, and breathe once more, he looked at Vincenzo Giuliani, who said nothing, who met his eyes and would not look away.

"Tell us." Two words. It was, Vincenzo Giuliani thought, the hardest thing he had ever done.

"You want *more*?" Sandoz asked, incredulous. Then he was moving again, unable to keep still or silent a moment longer. "I can provide endless detail," he offered, theatrically expansive, merciless now. "It went on for—I don't know how long. Months. It seemed like eternity. He shared me with his friends. I became rather fashionable. A number of exquisite individuals came to use me. It was a form of connoisseurship, I think. Sometimes," he said, stopping and looking at each of them, hating them for their witness, "sometimes, there was an audience."

John Candotti closed his eyes and turned his head away, and Edward Behr wept silently.

"Distressing, isn't it. It gets worse," he assured them with savage cheer, moving blindly. "Extemporaneous poetry was recited. Songs were written, describing the experience. And the concerts were broadcast, of course, just like the songs we heard—is Arecibo still collecting the songs? You must have heard some of the ones about me by now." Not prayer. Christ! Not prayer—pornography. "They were very beautiful," he admitted, scrupulously accurate. "I was required to listen, although I was perhaps inadequately appreciative of the artistry."

He looked at them one by one, each of them pale and speechless. "Have you heard enough? How about this: the smell of my fear and my blood excited them. Do you want more? Would you like to know precisely how dark the night of the soul can get?" he asked, goading them now. "There was a moment when it occurred to me to wonder if bestiality is a sin for the beast, for that was certainly my role in the festivities."

Voelker suddenly moved to the door. "Does it make you want to vomit?" Sandoz asked with thin solicitude, watching as Voelker left the room. "Don't be ashamed," he called. "It happens to me all the time."

Sandoz spun back to face the rest of them. "He wanted it to be my fault somehow," he said informatively, looking at each of them, eyes lingering on Candotti's. "He's not a bad guy, John. It's human nature. He wanted it to be some mistake I made that he wouldn't have made, some flaw in me he didn't share, so he could believe it wouldn't have happened to him. But it wasn't my fault. It was either blind, dumb, stupid luck from start to finish, in which case, we are all in the wrong business, gentlemen, or it was a God I cannot worship."

He waited, shaking, daring them to speak. "No questions? No argument? No comfort for the afflicted?" he asked with acrid gaiety. "I warned you. I told you that you didn't want to know. Now it's in your minds. Now you have to live with knowing. But it was my body. It was my blood," he said, choking with fury. "And it was my love."

He stopped suddenly then and turned away from them at last. No one moved, and they listened to the ragged breathing stop and hold and then go on in defiance. "John stays," he said finally. "Everyone else: get out."

Trembling, he faced John Candotti, waiting for the room to clear, Giuliani gracefully sidestepping the wreckage on the floor, Brother Edward hesitating by the door, waiting for Felipe Reyes, white-lipped, to pass, but leaving finally and pulling the door shut with a quiet click. John wanted more than anything to look away, to leave with the others, but he knew why he was there and so he stayed and tried to be ready for what he had to hear next.

When they were alone, Sandoz began again to pace and talk, the soft awful words pouring out as he moved sightlessly from place to place in the room.

"After a while, the novelty wore off and it was mostly the guards who came. By that time they were keeping me in a little stone-walled room without lights. I was alone and it was very quiet, and all I could hear was my own breathing and the blood ringing in my ears. Then the door would open and I would see a flare of light beyond it." He paused then, seeing it, no longer able to tell how much was real and how much was dream turned nightmare. "I never knew if they were bringing food or if—if . . . They kept me isolated because the screaming disturbed the others. My colleagues. The ones in the drawing you saw, back in Rome, do you remember? Someone from the harem must have drawn it. I found it in with my food one day. You can't imagine what that meant to me. God left me, but someone remembered where I was."

He stopped then and looked directly at John Candotti, who stood paralyzed, a bird caught by the cobra's gaze.

"I decided finally that I would kill the next person to come through the door, the next one who . . . touched me." And then he was pacing again, the hands rising and falling as he tried to explain, to make John understand. "I— There was nowhere to escape to. But I thought, If I'm too dangerous, they'll leave me alone. They'll kill me. I thought, The next time someone comes in here, one of us is going to die, I don't care which. But that was a lie. Because I did care. They used me hard, John. They used me hard. I wanted to die."

He stopped again and looked helplessly at Candotti. "I wanted to die, but God took her instead. *Why,* John?"

John wasn't following this. But it was a question he'd had to answer before, asked so often by survivors, and he was able to say, "Because, I suppose, souls are not interchangeable. You can't tell God: Take me instead."

Sandoz wasn't listening. "I didn't sleep, for a long time. I waited for the door to open and I thought about how I could kill someone without my hands . . ." He was still standing, but he was no longer seeing John Candotti. "So I waited. And sometimes I would fall asleep for a few minutes, I think. But it was so dark. It was hard to tell when my eyes were open. And then I could hear footsteps outside my cell, and I got up and stood in the far corner, so I could use the momentum, and the door opened, and I saw a silhouette, and it was so strange. My eyes already knew but my body was so primed. It was like—the nerves fired without my telling them to. I crashed into her so hard . . . I could hear the bones in her chest snap, John."

HE TRIED DESPERATELY to take the force against his ruined hands, to cushion the shock, but before he could make his arms come up, they'd both cannoned into the stone wall and Askama was crushed by the impact.

He found himself on the floor, supporting his weight on his knees and his forearms, with Askama crumpled beneath him, her face so close to his that he could hear her whisper. She smiled at him, blood bubbling in the corner of her mouth and seeping from a nostril. "You see, Meelo? Your family came for you. I found you for them."

He heard the voices then, human voices, and looked up from Askama's corpse half-blinded by the brilliant light of second dawn pouring through the door. Saw their eyes, single-irised, as frightening to him now as his own eyes must have been to Askama when she first met him. Recognized the look of blank shock and then of revulsion.

"My God, you killed her," the older man said. And then he fell silent, taking in the jeweled necklace, the naked body decorated with scented ribbons, the dried and bloody evidence of the priest's most recent employment. "My God," he repeated.

The younger man was coughing and holding his sleeve over his nose, to filter the stench of blood and sweat and perfumes. "I am Wu Xing-Ren, and this is my colleague, Trevor Isley. United Nations, External Affairs Committee," he said at last. He was almost but not quite able to keep the contempt out of his voice as he added, "You must be Father Sandoz."

There was a sound that began as laughter, as shocking and outrageous as anything they could see or smell, and ended as something more difficult to listen to. The crisis went on for some time. Even after the hysteria was exhausted, they got nothing sensible from the man.

"WHY, JOHN? WHY did it all happen like that, unless God wanted it that way? I thought I understood . . ." His voice trailed off, and Candotti waited, not sure what to say or do. "How long has it been for you, John?"

John, the sudden shift taking him by surprise, frowned at Sandoz and shook his head, wanting to understand, but not able to follow the train of thought.

"I figured it out once. Twenty-nine years. I get confused about the time, but I was fifteen and I'm supposed to be forty-five now, I think." The frayed nerves holding him up snapped abruptly, and he sank to the floor. John went to him and knelt nearby and listened, and Emilio wept as he whispered, the words thin and silvery. "See, I know a lot of men make accommodations. They find someone—someone . . . to help them. But, the thing about this is: I didn't. And I—I thought I understood. It was a path to God, and I thought I understood. There are moments, John, when your soul is like a ball of fire, and it reaches out to everything and everyone equally. I thought I understood."

And then suddenly, Emilio wiped his eyes and pulled in a shuddering breath and when he spoke again, his voice was normal and ordinary and tired and, for that reason, sadder than anything John Candotti had heard before. "So, anyway, I was about forty-four, I guess, when it—when . . . it happened, so it must have been about twenty-nine years."

His lips pulled back into a terrible smile, and he began to laugh, the glistening eyes bleak. "John, if God did this, it is a hell of a trick to pull on a celibate. And if God didn't do it, what does that make me?" He shrugged helplessly. "An unemployed linguist, with a lot of dead friends."

His face hardly moved, but the tears began again. "So many dead, because I believed. John, they're all dead. I've tried so hard to understand," he whispered. "Who can forgive me? So many dead . . ."

John Candotti pulled the smaller man to him and took Sandoz in his arms and held him, rocking, while they both cried. After a time, John whispered, "I forgive you," and began the ancient absolution, "*Absolvo te—absolvo te . . .*" but that had to be enough, because he couldn't say the rest.

"THAT WAS AN abuse of power," Felipe Reyes hissed. "You had no right— My God, how could you *do* that to him?"

"It was necessary." The Father General had left the building, walking swiftly from his office down the long echoing hallway, throwing open the French doors and passing outside to the garden, hoping to pull his thoughts together in sunshine and in quiet. But Reyes had followed him, furious, outraged that Emilio Sandoz had been made to speak with so many witnesses.

"How could you do that to him?" Reyes persisted, implacable. "Did you get some kind of perverse pleasure from listening to—"

Giuliani rounded on him and silenced the other priest with a look that froze the words on his lips. "It was necessary. If he were an artist, I'd have ordered him to paint it. If he were a poet, I'd have ordered him to write it. Because he is who he is, I made him speak of it. It was necessary. And it was necessary for us to hear it."

Felipe Reyes looked at his superior for a moment longer and then sank abruptly onto the cool stone of a garden bench, surrounded by summer blossoms in dazzling sunlight, shaken and sickened and unconvinced that any of it was necessary. There were sunflowers and brilliant yellow daylilies, delphinium and liatris and gladioli, and the scent of roses from somewhere nearby. The swallows were out now, as the evening approached, and the insect noise was changing. The Father General sat down beside him.

"Have you ever been to Florence, Reyes?"

Felipe sat back, open-mouthed with disgusted incomprehension. "No," he said acidly. "I haven't felt much like touring. Sir."

"You should go. There's a series of sculptures there by Michelangelo that you should see. They are called *The Captives*. Out of a great formless mass of stone, the figures of slaves emerge: heads, shoulders, torsos, straining toward freedom but still held fast in the stone. There are souls like that, Reyes. There are souls that try to carve themselves from their own formlessness. Broken and damaged as he is, Emilio Sandoz is still trying to find meaning in what happened to him. He is still trying to find God in it all."

It took Felipe Reyes, blinking, several moments to hear what he'd been told, and if he was too stiff-necked to look at Giuliani for the time being, he was able at least to admit that he understood. "And by listening, we help him."

"Yes. We help him. He will have to tell it again and again, and we will have to hear more and more, until he finds the meaning." In that instant, a lifetime of reason and moderation and common sense and balance left Vincenzo Giuliani feeling as weightless and insubstantial as ash. "He's the genuine article, Reyes. He has been all along. He is still held fast in the formless stone, but he's closer to God right now than I have ever been in my life. And I don't even have the courage to envy him."

THEY SAT THERE for a long while, in the late August afternoon, the light golden and the air soft, the small near sounds of the garden punctuated by a dog's barking in the distance. John Candotti joined them after a time. He sat heavily on the ground across the garden walkway from their bench and put his head in his hands.

"It was hard," the Father General said.

"Yes. It was hard."

"The child?"

"The closest legal term might be involuntary manslaughter." John lay back, flattening some ground cover, unable to stay upright any longer. "No," he amended after a time. "It wasn't an accident. He meant to kill, but in self-defense. That Askama was the one who died—that was an accident."

"Where is he now?"

Candotti, drained, looked up at them. "I carried him up to his

room, sleeping like the dead. That's an awful phrase. Anyway, asleep.
Ed's with him." There was a pause. "I think it did him good. It sure as
hell didn't do me any good to hear it, but I really think he's better now."
John put his hands over his eyes. "To dream of all that. And the children . . . Now we know."

"Now we know," Giuliani agreed. "I'm sitting here trying to understand why it seemed less awful when I thought it was prostitution.
It's the same physical act." He wasn't the Father General. He was just
plain Vince Giuliani, with no answers. Unknowing, he trod the path of
reason that Sofia Mendes had traveled all those years before. "I suppose
a prostitute has at least an illusion of control. It's a transaction. There is
some element of consent."

"There is," Felipe Reyes suggested wanly, "more dignity in prostitution than in gang rape. Even by poets."

Giuliani suddenly put his hands to his mouth. "What a wilderness,
to believe you have been seduced and raped by God." And then to come
home to our tender mercies, he thought bleakly.

John sat up and glared red-eyed at the Father General. "I'll tell you
something. If it's a choice between despising Emilio or hating God—"

Surprisingly, Felipe Reyes broke in, before John could say something he'd regret. "Emilio is not despicable. But God didn't rape him,
even if that's how Emilio understands it now." He sat back in the bench
and stared at the ancient olive trees defining the edge of the garden.
"There's an old Jewish story that says in the beginning God was everywhere and everything, a totality. But to make creation, God had to remove Himself from some part of the universe, so something besides
Himself could exist. So He breathed in, and in the places where God
withdrew, there creation exists."

"So God just leaves?" John asked, angry where Emilio had been
desolate. "Abandons creation? You're on your own, apes. Good luck!"

"No. He watches. He rejoices. He weeps. He observes the moral
drama of human life and gives meaning to it by caring passionately
about us, and remembering."

"Matthew ten, verse twenty-nine," Vincenzo Giuliani said quietly.
" 'Not one sparrow can fall to the ground without your Father knowing
it.' "

"But the sparrow still falls," Felipe said.

They sat for a while, wrapped in their private musings.

"You know, he was always a good priest," Felipe told them, re-

membering, "but it must have been about the time that they were planning the mission, something changed in him. It was like, I don't know,
sometimes he would just—*ignite*." Felipe's hands moved, making a
shape like fireworks. "There was something in his face, so beautiful.
And I thought, if that's what it's like to be a priest . . . It was like he fell
in love with God."

"Offhand," said the Father General wearily, in a voice dry as August grass, "I'd say the honeymoon is over."

THE SUN WAS already fairly high when Edward Behr awoke to
the sound of a coffee cup rattling on a saucer. Blinking, he sat up in the
wooden chair where he'd spent the night and groaned. He saw Emilio
Sandoz standing by the night table, carefully setting the coffee down, the
servos releasing his grip almost as quickly as natural movement might
have.

"What time is it?" Ed asked, rubbing his neck.

"A little after eight," Sandoz told him. Wearing a T-shirt and a pair
of baggy pants, he sat on the edge of his bed and watched Brother Edward stretch and scrub at his eyes with his pudgy hands. "Thank you.
For staying with me."

Brother Edward looked at him, sizing things up. "How do you
feel?"

"Okay," Emilio said simply. "I feel okay."

Emilio stood and stepped over to the window, holding the curtain
aside, but couldn't see much: just the garage and a little bit of hillside. "I
used to be a pretty fair middle-distance runner," he said conversationally. "I did about half a kilometer this morning. Had to walk most of it."
He shrugged. "It's a start."

"It's a start," Edward Behr agreed. "You did well with the coffee,
too."

"Yeah. Didn't crush the cup. Only spilled a little." He let the curtain
fall. "I'm going to go get cleaned up."

"Need any help?"

"No. Thanks. I can manage."

No anger, Brother Edward noticed. He watched Emilio open the
drawer and pull out clean clothes. It took a while, but he did fine. As
Sandoz moved toward the door, Brother Edward spoke again. "It's not

over, you know," he warned. "You don't get over something like that all at once."

Emilio stared at the floor for a while and then looked up. "Yes. I know." He stood still a few moments and then asked, "What were you, before? A nurse? A therapist?"

Edward Behr snorted and reached for the coffee. "Not even close. I was a stockbroker. I specialized in undervalued companies." He didn't expect Sandoz to understand. The generality of priests, vowed to poverty, were hopelessly ignorant of finance. "It involved recognizing the worth of things that other people discounted."

Sandoz didn't see the connection. "Were you good at it?"

"Oh, yes. I was very good at it." Brother Edward held up his cup and said, "Thanks for the coffee."

He watched Sandoz go and then, sitting very still, in silence, Edward Behr began his morning prayers.

AT TEN, THERE was a metallic rap at the Father General's door, and when he called out, "Come in," he was not surprised to see Emilio Sandoz enter the office, managing the lever without any hesitation and shutting the door behind him.

Giuliani started to stand, but Emilio said, "No, please. Sit down. I just wanted—I wanted to thank you. That couldn't have been easy for you to do."

"It was brutal," Vince Giuliani admitted. "And all I had to do was listen."

"No. You did more than that." Sandoz looked around the office, which seemed oddly empty. Unexpectedly, he gave a short laugh and his hands went to his hair, as if to run his fingers through it, an old nervous habit, now likely to tangle the joint mechanisms of the braces. He let his hands fall. "Sorry about the table. Was it valuable?"

"Priceless."

"Figures."

"Forget it." Giuliani sat back in his chair. "So. You seem better."

"Yeah. I slept well. I'll bet poor John Candotti didn't, but I did." Emilio smiled but added, "John was great. Thank you for bringing him here. And Ed. And Felipe. Even Voelker. I couldn't have—" He grimaced and turned away for a moment but came back almost immediately. "It was like—like vomiting poison, I suppose." Giuliani said nothing, and Emilio continued, with only a little irony, "Seems to me I heard somewhere that confession is good for the soul."

The corners of Giuliani's mouth twitched. "That, certainly, was the principle upon which I was operating."

Emilio went to the windows. The view was better from this office than from his room. Rank hath its privileges. "I had a dream last night," he said quietly. "I was on a road and there was no one with me. And in the dream I said, 'I don't understand but I can learn if you will teach me.' Do you suppose anyone was listening?" He didn't turn from the windows.

Without answering, Giuliani got up and went to a bookcase. Selecting a small volume with a cracked leather binding, he paged through it until he found what he wanted and held it out.

Sandoz turned and accepted the book, looking at the spine. "Aeschylus?"

Wordlessly, Giuliani pointed out the passage, and Emilio studied it a while, slowly translating the Greek in his mind. Finally, he said, "'In our sleep, pain which cannot forget falls drop by drop upon the heart, until, in our own despair, against our will, comes wisdom through the awful grace of God.'"

"Show-off."

Sandoz laughed but, turning toward the window again, he read the passage over. Giuliani walked back to his desk and sat down, waiting for Sandoz to speak again.

"I was wondering if I could stay here a while longer," Emilio said. He had no idea he was going to ask this. He'd meant to leave. "You've been very patient. I don't mean to impose."

"Not at all."

Sandoz didn't turn back to look at the Father General, but Giuliani heard his tone change. "I don't know if I'm a priest. I don't know if— I don't know . . . anything at all with certainty. I don't even know if certainty is what I should want."

"Stay as long as you like."

"Thank you. You've been very patient," Emilio repeated. He moved to the door and the braced fingers closed neatly over the lever.

"Emilio," the Father General called out to him, voice pitched low, carrying easily in this quiet room. "I'm sending another group out. To

Rakhat. I thought you ought to know that. We could use your help. With the languages."

Sandoz went motionless. "It's too soon, Vince. I can't think about that. It's too soon."

"Of course. I just thought you should know."

He watched Sandoz leave. Unaware of his own movement, schooled by old habit, Vincenzo Giuliani rose and went to the windows, and stood looking, for how long he had no idea, across a grassy open courtyard to a complex panorama of medieval masonry and jumbled rock, formal garden and gnarled trees: a scene of great and beautiful antiquity.

ACKNOWLEDGMENTS

AS A FORMER academic, I feel uneasy without footnotes and a huge bibliography; even as a novelist, I believe several of the hundreds of sources I used must be named. Richard Rodriguez's *Hunger of Memory* taught me how scholarship boys feel. The gorgeous prose of Alain Corbin in his book *The Foul and the Fragrant* was the inspiration for the Reshtar's early poetry. And *Molly Ivins Can't Say That, Can She?* but D.W. could, so I thank Ms. Ivins for insight into Texans, turtles and armadillos. The notion of predator mimicry comes from Dougal Dixon's *The New Dinosaurs,* as does the snakeneck, which I found too charming an idea not to propagate. Emilio's moment of illumination in the last chapter derives from Arthur Green's theology in *Seek My Face, Speak My Name.* Finally, Dorothy Dunnett may consider *The Sparrow* one long thank you note for her splendid Lymond series.

Thanks also to my mother, Louise Dewing Doria, whose "Just do it" attitude long predates the sneaker commercial, and to my father, Richard Doria, who's always taken me seriously. Maura Kirby believed in this book long before I did. Don Russell dug me out of plot holes, designed the *Stella Maris* and is the source of Emilio's sense of humor. Mary Dewing taught me how to write; our fifteen-year correspondence was my apprenticeship. Mary also read every draft of this book and never failed to find a way to make each one better. Many friends helped me improve the manuscript; I thank Tomasz and Maria Rybak, Vivian Singer and Jennifer Tucker in particular for critical readings at critical times. Charles Nelson and Helene Fiore were crucial links to the world of publishing. Stanley Schmidt gave me encouragement and invaluable advice; Mary Fiore did the same and then opened doors that led to Jen-

nifer McGlashan and to Miriam Goderich and my invincible agent, Jane
Dystel. And I will always be grateful to David Rosenthal of Villard and
Leona Nevler of Ivy-Fawcett for their support and faith in this book.
And I fall to the feet and kiss the collective hem of the staff at Villard,
who worked very hard for this book and graciously tolerated a new author's anxiety. Ray Bucko, S.J., proofed the final draft of *The Sparrow*
and is himself proof that there are real Jesuits as extravagantly funny
and plainly good as the guys I made up. He is not responsible for any remaining misrepresentation of Jesuit life—I am the author and I outrank
him. Thanks also to the ladies of the Noble Branch of the Cleveland
Heights Library, who brought a ton of reference works within easy
reach.

A final note to Don and our son, Daniel, who hardly ever complained about all the time and attention and love I lavished on fictional
characters when my dearest real people were right downstairs: Thanks,
guys. You're the best.

M.D.R.

The
Sparrow

MARY DORIA RUSSELL

A Reader's Guide

A Conversation with Mary Doria Russell

Q: Until *The Sparrow* you had only written serious scientific articles and technical manuals. How did you end up writing a speculative novel?

A: The idea came to me in the summer of 1992 as we were celebrating the 500th anniversary of Columbus's arrival in the New World. There was a great deal of historical revisionism going on as we examined the mistakes made by Europeans when they first encountered foreign cultures in the Americas and elsewhere. It seemed unfair to me for people living at the end of the twentieth century to hold those explorers and missionaries to standards of sophistication and tolerance that we hardly manage even today. I wanted to show how very difficult first contact would be, even with the benefit of hindsight. That's when I decided to write a story that put modern, sophisticated, resourceful, well-educated, and well-meaning people in the same position as those early explorers and missionaries—a position of radical ignorance. Unfortunately, there's no place on Earth today where "first contact" is possible—you can find MTV, CNN, and McDonald's everywhere you go. The only way to create a "first contact" story like this was to go off-planet.

Q: How did religion come to play such a central role in the story?

A: At the time I wrote this I was in the process of bringing religion back into my own life. I was brought up as a Catholic but left the Church in 1965 when I was fifteen. After twenty years of contented atheism I became a mother. Suddenly I was in a position of having to transmit my culture to my son. I needed to decide what things to pass on and what things to weed out. I realized my ethics and morality were rooted in religion and began to reconsider those decisions I had made when I was young. I found myself drawn to Judaism and eventually converted. When you convert to Judaism in a post-Holocaust world, you know two things for sure: one is that being Jewish can get you killed; the other is that God won't rescue you. That was the theology I was dealing with at the time. Writing *The Sparrow* allowed me to look at the place of religion in the lives of many people and to weigh the risks and the beauties of religious belief from the comfort of my own home.

Q: What exactly are the risks and beauties of religion?

A: The beauty of religion is the way in which it enriches your understanding of what your senses tell you. I see no conflict between scientific and religious thought. They are just two very different ways of interpreting what we see all around us. What I gained was a cultural depth, a perspective that reaches back 3,200 years. There's a certain kind of serenity that comes from knowing that the ethics you draw on have been tested and re-tested by one thousand generations in every possible cultural and ethical climate, and that they have been found reliable and useful by so many people for so long under many different circumstances.

The risks have to do with believing that God micromanages the world, and with seeing what may be simply coincidence as significant and indicative of divine providence. It's very easy then to go out on a limb spiritually, expect more from God than you have a right to expect, and set yourself up for bitter disappointment in his silence and lack of action.

Q: Where did the idea come from for the two alien races on Rakhat, the Runa and the Jana'ata?

A: It started with a look at two australopithecine species from Earth's prehistory: herbivores and carnivores/scavengers. I began by thinking, What would it be like if the herbivores were still around? That was the beginning of the idea. Then I asked myself, What would civilization be like if a carnivore had domesticated its prey species? That's where I came up with the idea for the relationship between the Jana'ata and the Runa. The Jana'ata are a carnivorous herding society that breed their prey, the Runa, for intelligence and adaptability as well as meat.

Q: What's the hardest thing about using two narrative lines to tell a story?

A: Pacing. You have to stop and think, Who does the reader want to be with now? Some time ago I realized the books that kept me turning pages were the ones that had two or more story lines. It's a structure I admired as a reader. As a writer, having two story lines proved to be of great value. When I played out my imagination in one story line I could take a break from it and turn to the other with fresh enthusiasm. The tricky part is in introducing two separate sets of characters in the first one hundred pages. There's a lot of setup that goes into it and you have to keep readers interested while developing the new characters.

Q: What sort of writing routine do you have?

A: I sit down in the morning when my husband's at work and my son's at school, and I spend seven hours in front of the computer. My working method is to make yardage every day. I don't expect to throw a long bomb each time I sit down to write. Occasionally a whole chapter does come all at once but that's the exception rather than the rule. The main thing to remember is that writing happens by doing the writing.

Q: Are any of your characters based on real people?

A: Some of them are. Anne and George share a biography with my husband and me, within certain limitations. Anne was willing to go to another planet and I won't even go camping. Nevertheless, she speaks fairly clearly in my voice. I used my brother's voice for John Candotti. There's a kind of "Chicago attitude" in his character that came from my brother. There were also real people who gave me the voice of D.W. One of them is a Texas congressman and the other a real-life New Orleans provincial. Emilio is his own person. I know nobody like him. I'm not sure I could be friends with a person like that. He's too intense in a lot of ways. Sofia is also her own person.

Mary Doria Russell

Q: Why did you use the Jesuits as main characters and how did you gain such insight into their world?

A: The reason for using the Jesuits was simple logic. If we were to receive incontrovertible evidence of an extraterrestrial culture that could be reached in a human lifespan, who would go? I thought of the Jesuits because they have a long history of first contact with cultures other than their own. The problem was I knew no Jesuits at the time I wrote this. And you can't just knock on a Jesuit's door and say "I'm writing a first novel about Jesuits in space. Tell me your intimate thoughts about being a priest." What I did have, however, was access to dozens and dozens of autobiographies written by priests and ex-priests during the last thirty years. Since Vatican II, 100,000 priests have left the active priesthood. Many priests have written autobiographies in which they discuss the motives that brought them to the life, the satisfactions and frustrations of the priesthood, why they decided to leave it behind, or why they remained true to the vocation.

Q: One reviewer calls this "a parable about faith—the search for God, in others as well as Out There." Another says it's about "the problem of evil and how it may stand in the path of a person's deepest need to believe." How do *you* describe the themes in this book?

A: The central theme is an exploration of the risks and beauties of religious faith. If there isn't a God, then Emilio Sandoz is all alone. And yet he's terrified of the God he thinks he has discovered. But the story also revolves around the theme of family. One of the things I noticed after the story was finished was that all the main characters are childless, and yet they create a family for themselves. They relate to one another as son and daughter, brother and sister, uncle and aunt, grandparent and grandchild. It seems to me that this kind of spiritual kinship is tremendously important to all the people in this book. And the fact that they don't have close genetic kin—they have no children to leave on Earth—gives them a kind of wistful freedom. Anne and George would have made terrific parents but they're childless. Emilio, Jimmy, and Sophia become their surrogate kids. Those ties—that spiritual tension—was every bit as strong and resilient as genetic ties—perhaps even stronger.

Q: Why did *The Sparrow* have to end the way it did?

A: Because I needed to ask questions in their starkest terms. What happens to Emilio Sandoz is a holocaust writ small. He survives, but loses everyone. Now he has to live in its aftermath.

Q: What's the moral of this story?

A: Maybe it's "Even if you do the best you can, you still get screwed." We seem to believe that if we act in accordance with our understanding of God's will, we ought to be rewarded. But in doing so we're making a deal that God didn't sign onto. Emilio has kept his end of a bargain that he made with God, and he feels betrayed. He believes he has been seduced and raped by God, that he's been used against his will for God's own purpose. And I guess that's partly what I'm doing with this book. I wanted to look at that aspect of theology. In our world, if people believe at all, they believe that God is love, God is hearts and flowers, and that God will send you theological candy all the time. But if you read Torah, you realize that God has a lot to answer for. God is a complex personality. I wanted to explore that complexity and that moral ambiguity. God gives us rules but those are rules for us, not for God.

Q: What's your next project?

A: I'm working on a sequel to *The Sparrow* titled *Children of God*. Emilio Sandoz goes back to Rakhat, but only because he has no choice. God is not done with him yet.

Q: What has been the toughest thing about writing the sequel?

A: The fact that there are so many people who are passionate about the original characters and care so much about the issues. Writing a sequel has been a real high-wire act. I've got to be able to reproduce those elements of the first book that people responded to strongly but I don't want to repeat myself. I have to break new ground. I hope that I have done that but it has not been an easy trick to pull off. What the second book does is reverse the story's emphasis—two thirds of the action takes place on Rakhat and one third on Earth. *Children of God* explores what happens to the people on Rakhat because Emilio Sandoz was there. There are children born because of him, and children are always revolutionary. Things that we would put up with ourselves can become intolerable when we see our children forced to face the same circumstances.

Q: What do you want readers to get out of this book?

A: That you can't know the answer to questions of faith but that the questions are worth asking and worth thinking about deeply.

Reading Group Questions and Topics for Discussion

1. How do faith, love, and the role of God in the world drive the plot of this story? One reviewer characterized this book as "a parable about faith—the search for God, in others as well as Out There." Do you agree? If so, why?

2. This story takes place from the years 2019 to 2060. The United States is no longer the predominant world power, having lost two trade wars with Japan, which is now supreme in both space and on Earth. Poverty is rampant. Indentured servitude is once more a common practice, and "future brokers" mine ghettos for promising children to educate in return for a large chunk of their lifetime income. What kinds of changes do you think will occur by the twenty-first century—with governments, technology, society, and so on? Do you think America will lose its predominant status in the world?

3. Do you think it likely that we will make contact with extraterrestrials at some time in the future? What will the implications of such an event be? We've always viewed Earth, and human beings, as the center of the universe. Will that still be the case if we discover alien life forms? How will such a discovery change theology? Does God love us best? Will such a discovery confirm the existence of God or cause us to question his existence at all?

4. If, sometime within the next century, we hear radio signals from a solar system less than a dozen light years away from our own, do you think humankind would mount an expedition to visit that place? Who do you think might lead such an expedition? If you had to send a group of people to a newly discovered planet to contact a totally unknown species, whom would you choose? Is the trip to Rakhat a scientific mission or a religious one?

5. *The Sparrow* tells a story by interweaving two time periods—after the mission to Rakhat and before. Do you think this

makes the story more interesting and easier to follow or more difficult to follow? How does this story differ from other stories you have read?

6. Why do you think Sandoz resists telling the story of what happened on Rakhat?

7. A basic premise of this story is an evaluation of the harm that results from the explorer's inability to assess a culture from the threshold of exploration. Do you see any parallels between the voyage of the eight explorers on the Rakhat mission and the voyages of other explorers from past history—Columbus, Magellan, Cortez, and others—who inaccurately assessed the cultures they discovered?

8. Despite currently popular revisionism, many historians view the early discoverers of the fifteenth and sixteenth centuries not as imperialists or colonists but as intellectual idealists burning to know what God's plan had hidden from them. Do you agree? Does this story make you reconsider the motives of those early explorers?

9. One of the mainstays of the *Star Trek* universe is the "prime directive" which mandates the avoidance of interference in alien cultures at all costs. Would the "prime directive" have changed the outcome of events on Rakhat?

10. In an interview, the author said, "I wanted readers to look philosophically at the idea that you can be seduced by the notion that God is leading you and that your actions have his approval." What do you think she means by that? In what way was Emilio Sandoz seduced by this notion?

11. The discoverers of Rakhat seem to be connected by circumstances too odd to be explained by anything but a manifestation of God's will. Do you think it was God's will that led to the discovery of and mission to Rakhat, as Sandoz initially believes? If that's the case, how could God let the terrible aftermath happen?

12. How is Emilio Sandoz's faith tested on Rakhat? One reviewer suggests that in his utter humiliation and in the annihilation of his spirit, Sandoz is reborn in faith. Do you agree? Consider Sandoz's dilemma on page 394. Did God lead the explorers to Rakhat—step by step—or was Sandoz responsible for what happened? If God was responsible for bringing the explorers to Rakhat, does that mean that God is vicious?

13. One reviewer wrote, "It is neither celibacy, faith, exotics goods, nor (as Sandoz bitterly asserts) the introduction of one of humanity's oldest inventions that leads to the crisis between humans and aliens. The humans get into trouble because they fail to understand how Rakhat society controls reproduction. In short, they fail because they fail to put themselves into the aliens' shoes." Do you agree? If so, why? If not, why not?

14. Is confession good for the soul? Do you think Emilio Sandoz will ultimately recover—both as a man and as a priest—from his ordeal?

15. Why do you think it's so important to Emilio to stand by his vow of celibacy when he so obviously loves Sofia Mendez?

16. The Jesuits saw so many of their fellows martyred all over the world throughout history. Why aren't they more sympathetic in dealing with Sandoz—a man victimized by his faith?

17. What is this story about? Is it a story about coming face-to-face with a sentient race that is so alien as to be incomprehensible, or about putting up a mirror to our own inner selves?

Excerpts from reviews of
Mary Doria Russell's
The Sparrow

"It is science fiction brought back to the project with which it began in the hands of a writer like Jules Verne: the necessity of wonder, the hope for moral rectitude, and the possibility of belief."

—*America*

"Russell's debut novel...focuses on her characters, and it is here that the work truly shines. An entertaining infusion of humor keeps the book from becoming too dark, although some of the characters are so clever that they sometimes seem contrived. Readers who dislike an emphasis on moral dilemmas or spiritual quests may be turned off, but those who enjoy science fiction because it can create these things are in for a real treat."

—*Science Fiction Weekly*

"*The Sparrow* tackles a difficult subject with grace and intelligence."

—*San Francisco Chronicle*

"*The Sparrow* is an incredible novel, for one reason. Though it is set in the early twenty-first century, it is not written like most science fiction. Russell's novel is driven by her characters, by their complex relationships and inner conflicts, not by aliens or technology."

—*Milwaukee Journal Sentinel*

"It is rare to find a book about interplanetary exploration that has this much insight into human nature and foresight into a possible future."

—*San Antonio Express News*

A Reader's Guide

"Two narratives—the mission to the planet and its aftermath four decades later—interweave to create a suspenseful tale."
—*The Seattle Times*

"By alternating chapters that dramatize Sandoz's tough-love interrogation with flashbacks to the mission's genesis, flowering, and tragic collapse, *The Sparrow* casts a strange, unsettling emotional spell, bouncing readers from scenes of black despair to ones of wild euphoria, from the bracing simplicity of pure adventure to the complicated tangles of nonhuman culture and politics....The smooth storytelling and gorgeous characterization can't be faulted."
—*Entertainment Weekly*

©Dina Rossi

ABOUT THE AUTHOR

MARY DORIA RUSSELL received her B.A. in Cultural Anthropology from the University of Illinois-Urbana, her M.A. in Social Anthropology from Northeastern University, and her Ph.D. in Biological Anthropology from the University of Michigan—Ann Arbor. In the process of earning her degrees, Russell studied linguistics, genetics, anatomy, archaeology, and geology—all of which have found their way into her critically acclaimed debut novel.

Prior to *The Sparrow*, Russell had only written scientific articles—on subjects ranging from bone biology to cannibalism—and technical manuals for medical equipment as complex as nuclear magnetic resonance scanners. In her own words, she admits, "I had a great time, published a lot of stuff, won a bunch of awards and grants, but eventually got fed up with academia and quit." Making the transition from scientific and technical writing to fiction wasn't easy. Russell estimates, however, that "only about twenty-two anthropologists, worldwide, read my academic publications and *nobody* reads computer manuals, so I figured that if even just my friends read my novel, I'd be way ahead in terms of readership because I have a lot of friends."

A recent convert to Judaism, Russell has nevertheless maintained a strong connection with the Catholic education of her childhood. Asked why she created such a detailed look at faith in a higher power and religion in her debut novel, Russell explains, "I wanted to evaluate, as an adult, issues that had lain dormant for me since adolescence, to study the religion of my youth, to revisit the source of my values and ethics. That's why I chose to write about men who are collectively among the most admirable and best educated of Catholic priests, the Jesuits. Writing *The Sparrow* allowed me to weigh the risks and the benefits of a belief in God, to examine the role of religion in the lives of many people."

Mary Doria Russell lives in Cleveland, Ohio, ("and likes it very much, thank you") with her husband, Don, and their son, Daniel. She is currently working on the sequel to *The Sparrow*, titled *Children of God*.